Meet Me at
St. Margaret's

Meet Me at
St. Margaret's

—

WILLIAM M. O'BRIEN

PALMETTO
PUBLISHING
Charleston, SC
www.PalmettoPublishing.com

Copyright © 2023 by William M. O'Brien

All rights reserved.

No portion of this book may be reproduced, stored in a retrieval system, or transmitted in any form by any means– electronic, mechanical, photocopy, recording, or other– except for brief quotations in printed reviews, without prior permission of the author.

First Edition

Paperback ISBN: 979-8-8229-2614-1

"Ah!" said Mrs. Gamp, walking away from the bed, "he'd make a lovely corpse."

— Charles Dickens

THE STRANGEST THING, *after the uproar subsided, was that I found myself engrossed in a large canvas once again. Everyone kept asking me, 'What were you trying to do, climbing up there like that?' I had no idea, and enough sense to put it out of mind. However, a variant of that insidious question soon infected my mind. What had I been doing, all along?*

A period of sulking at the studio produced some crazy stuff. I made a drawing of Liberty, that wanton girl, in a sexy slip, slumped before a glowing computer screen, wondering who's the fairest of them all. I depicted George Washington in the garb of an Anglo-Saxon chieftain, crossing the Mississippi in a huge jon boat. On the far shore one sees the descendants of the soldiers of Hernando de Soto; shrunken heads are impaled on stakes all along the river's edge. At some point I ran across Lady Butler's solemn Remnants of an Army. *I improvised on that theme by having a larger party of more modern stragglers, just arriving at Jalalabad.*

And then I fell into a long meditation on the city's hapless patron saint. He arose before me, as if to bear witness on his own behalf. I began a serious work to be called, The Apotheosis; *a portrait of one highly reputable man captured in his last station in life. I put all else aside to concentrate on the death of St. Louis, which occurred during his second Crusade. I imagined him alone on the field of battle, his mind reeling, taking his last breaths. He is having an epiphany, losing all the cultural knowledge which has shaped his life's course. His sense of glory is being expunged from his heart, in his final gasps.*

He cannot believe what the fates have done to him. All that architecture of faith has collapsed into dust, unto which he also must return, and this now seems a far, far richer substance. His psyche is stupefied. He has a strange vision. Nothing that has ever been, is ever truly past; all must be sustained forever. All in fact must be right there before him. He imagines a distant future that will be unlike anything he has ever considered before, but it weighs too heavily on his faltering mind. He is about to topple over; his only prop being his sword, which is stuck in the ground. His grisly, empurpled hand clutches the butt end; thus offering an echo of the improvised cross held aloft by the bronze figure on the hill outside our Art Museum.

He feels a palpable longing for the physical world, certain he knows nothing. He lets go of his entire misconstructed life, dimly aware that eternity leers at him with roguish insolence. By that fugitive light in his eye he might be one of the first persons to experience the dawn of consciousness. He is a sort of witness, as if time and history are just now beginning for the human race. He divines the unimaginable prospects that lie ahead of us, and how barren his own past has been. He is standing apart from himself, staring into the pitiless face of time. Yes, to bring that feeling of his pathos to the canvas, for viewing in one's time. The symbolism was not entirely clear, but I could see his noble face, his burning eyes, his lonely, dying passion.

1

In the Loop an elderly man was sitting at a table outside Pliny's café, lost in his own world. He stares at the quiet scenery along Delmar Boulevard; a familiar strip of urban life, now full of ghosts because of the plague.

Isaiah moves his glass of red wine into a ray of sunlight, which passes through the liquid body to become a very compelling cloud of active photons. He twirls the glass to create a dance of crimson veils upon the receptive blank page of his sketchpad. A sudden movement inside causes him to turn his head towards the plate glass window, where he faces his own visage.

His eye sockets are vacant. To himself he appears as a statue. He feels that deathless aspect as he peers into the dark glass. He turns away out of scorn for something not so very clear to him. He was never considered handsome. His protuberant nose is out of proportion on the long face, the enlarged eyes are too far apart. It were as though his features were molded from disparate patterns. The sensual lips suggest desires of an aesthete, and yet the mouth is twisted harshly by his ascetic nature.

Maybe it's the other way around; at any rate, the gold-splintered brown eyes, ever straining, reveal his sensitivity to being looked at too closely.

A lanky waiter, wearing a mask, came out to see if his only outdoor customer was ready for another drink. Isaiah shook his head. He had barely touched his first drink. The young waiter vanished without a word. Isaiah had his mask stuffed in his shirt pocket. He was dressed in natty attire. He looked at his phone resting on the table; his son had still not responded to his recent text. Theo had lectured him often enough, about the need to answer texts in a timely fashion; and now he was not doing so himself. Theo was helping his father sell his prints on a website he had created for him.

Isaiah pondered how his son's attitude had changed after the unfortunate incident outside the museum. Upon seeing his father pilloried on the web, the son was overcome by anger. However, that filial gallantry dissipated, and the disturbing imagines were put away in the brief he kept on file concerning the father's high crimes and misdemeanors.

The irony of Isaiah's recent plunge into notoriety was that it had worked wonders for his sales figures. That's how things went in the world. He took a sip of his wine, leaning back, thinking, "One must savor the fruits of victory, forget the costs of the campaign. Damn you, King Pyrrhus! To hell with sitting on one's rock, brother Sisyphus!" He knew how quickly matters could change. Why was nothing ever as good as one had hoped it would be?

He strove to remember a time when he had been truly happy; surely there were many times with Edith. When were those, exactly? Nothing came to mind! How strange. Was this a distortion in his memory, caused by grief? She was the only person he knew who had died of the virus, and he felt an inward shudder. Other deaths, from other causes, filed past him in a grisly parade. Several close friends had died years before, and it was said they had died too soon. One could only cringe at the notion.

There were worries enough to go around. A great deal of civil unrest was troubling the land, and he found it increasingly difficult to believe in his own convictions. He felt remorse for his lack of remorse. He had suffered delicate pangs, after losing his mother, and then his father. It was not so long ago that he was overcome by the loss of his uncle Isaac. And then there had been the death of his childhood friend Stephen. That was a ghastly blow. It seemed terribly wrong, and he could not reconcile himself to that loss. Stephen had become a journalist, of considerable note, one burning with quixotic ambition to write only the truth on all matters. In time he had splintered his lance against the armored divisions that guard the fields of power.

Isaiah listened to a chorus of insects raising apocalyptic alarms, and recalled a scene at Edith's townhome. She had chosen a passage to read aloud from a novel by Charles Dickens. It was vexing that he could not remember which novel contained this passage. Was it from *The Old Curiosity Shop*? The passage adroitly limned that religious desire to believe our dearly departed are still out there, still aware of us, still caring about us. Even more so, because, after all, it is *we*, the living, who matter the most! Oh, what if she could speak to him now, what would she have to say?

He was spending an inordinate amount of time simply driving around in his new car. He was once more exploring the rivers that snake about the region. He worried about his friend, Timothy O'Rourke, who might want to use his car. The poor bastard was now retired, and having to make do on foot. He was one of the few people in his profession who had achieved tenure, only to lose it. And his unforgivable crime? Abusing his right to free speech; espousing views that were presently deemed to be anathema. He smiled to think of the firebrand O'Rourke had once been, and how he had been humbled.

"He's a piece of work," he mused. "An original piece, anyway." Isaiah feels the warmth of his condescension.

"No, better yet, we should say Marx is an aboriginal; belonging to a primitive, prophetic school."

They first met in a different era, before the deluge of instantaneous messaging (which had caused Marx so much grief). Now information could be sent from anywhere, at any time, to anyone, who might be anywhere, and able to receive these packets in the same moment, on a personal device carried in one's hand. Isaiah could not understand how this technology had created an insatiable appetite to be constantly in touch with other persons. To him the incessant communication was like the chattering of caged monkeys. You still there? Are the bars still up on your cage? Do you ever think about jumping one of the keepers to get hold of the keys?

He and Marx (as he called O'Rourke) had long been regulars of the Loop cafés. Marx was solely dependent on his Social Security allotments. He was trying to get by without having his own internet connection. He used the library for this purpose, and it was irksome to be sometimes mistaken for one of the vagrants who used that space for warmth and security.

Timothy usually spurned Isaiah's offers of help. It was unfortunate that every man's dignity was sensitive to the imbalance of fortunes. This had never been an issue before. In the past Isaiah was the one who sometimes had to scrape to get by, scratching at odd labors, as a fancy house painter, to sustain his standard of living. Marx had always seemed secure, but apparently the imprudent fellow had not saved enough. Isaiah was always trying to instill this virtue in Theo's mind.

"Where the hell is Gallagher?" He whispered. Raphael had offered to write an article about him, and possibly, if that went well, a biography. He could not remember what he had said; it was pretty nebulous, as is so much of the overly sincere talk conducted over drinks at the end of an evening.

He did not relish the prospect of an amateur writer raking indiscriminately through his past endeavors. How explain that convoluted journey to anyone else, when he could not do so for himself? He also feared losing the chance to exploit the sensation he had caused; such marketable noise wanes rather quickly. He feared being exposed for too long a period to the corrosive effects of derisive humor.

'You've brought this on yourself.' Words from his mother? No, it couldn't be. He shook his head, and sipped his wine. Months ago he had attempted to educate himself on the virus. These organic mites were a conundrum. The tiny devils are not alive, and yet they propagate by invading living hosts to borrow their genetic material. They are perfect barbarians, laying waste, and never dreaming of Valhalla, or any other higher kingdom.

"What if we end up being a sort of virus?" Isaiah had ventured one time. "Maybe our last contribution will be the frozen strands we hurl into space. Other life forms may find the intricacy of our makeup to be rather useful in some way."

"Will they find any of our moral structure there?" The ex-professor O'Rourke intoned quietly.

The waiter came out again, and seeing Isaiah hold up his hand, retreated as if he'd been offended. Isaiah checked the time. He was growing impatient. He wanted to find out exactly what kind of article Raphael intended to write. The easy approach would be to tell the 'human story'; one laden with adroit, comic touches. He feared the waves of more laughter, for such can undermine a reputation. Sure, what was that now?

Isaiah recalled a phrase he had chanced upon recently, from *Nicholas Nickleby*, describing how the mind can "dwell with a pleasant sorrow" in scenes of the past. It had only been a month since Edith was taken to the hospital; her body in revolt against itself. She died of asphyxiation, in a temple of medical science. Isaiah remembered her strength, forbearance, and unshakable complacency. His mind seized on an image of her being alone in her bed just as O'Rourke appeared before him.

"What's the matter?" Timothy asked.

Isaiah looked up with a confused look, shaking his head, to negate further inquiries.

"How long have you been here?"

"This is my first drink. I'm nursing old memories."

"I'd like to have a nurse, who could attend to my needs. Deliver my pot, and then smoke it with me! Maybe stay the night to supervise my cardiovascular exercises."

"I'm sure there's an app for that."

"It would be too expensive."

The waiter came out and took Timothy's order for a draft beer; he retreated without saying anything else.

At the early stages of the pandemic O'Rourke swore he had been infected previously, and his body's defenses had fended off the contagion. Thus, he inferred his constitution was no longer at risk, and he did not need to wear a mask. For some reason Isaiah no longer had any desire to argue with him, or anyone else, on these issues.

"Are you waiting for someone?"

"Yes."

"Who?"

"Raphael—"

"Oh, not that guy again."

"He wants to write an article about me."

Timothy blew out a derisive stream of air, shaking his head.

"He thinks—"

"Time to cash in on the notoriety you've garnered."

"Yeah, I guess so. My paintings are really selling. I'm getting new opportunities for portraits."

"The guy ought to talk to me if he wants to write your story. I'd tell him about the early years."

"I doubt he'd be interested in those years."

"Why not?"

"Too much material. I'm not sure what he has in mind, to be honest."

"Hey, I meant to tell you, I have some of your pieces from long ago. Would you want those back?"

"For what?"

"To sell?"

Isaiah made a noncommittal sound.

"Do you care if I sell them?"

"No. Why should I?"

"It's just that, I could use the money. I wouldn't let go of them, otherwise."

"No problem. Talk to my son. He's helping me to sell them online, and I'm trying to teach him how to deal with the folks at the gallery . . . He might be able to get you the best price."

"It's just that, you know, I'm just a Philistine."

"It makes no difference to me."

"Well, I may do that. I see Theo, now and then, down here in the Loop. Is he able to get pretty good commissions for selling them?"

"No, that's not how I've arranged it, for now. He has to learn the trade before we get into that sort of thing."

"I see." Marx leaned back and stared at his friend. "Are you paying him anything at all?"

"Not yet."

"The art of keeping costs and people down."

"He needs to learn the business first! It's not about the money, right now. I'm teaching him the ropes . . ."

"He's been impressed, called to serve on the gun deck of the HMS Meriwether?"

"How are you making out these days?" Isaiah asked pointedly.

"Well, you know how it is. But there is some news. The ground floor woman is yelling at her new boyfriend, the same way she used to yell at her last one. I can hear her screeching at him when he comes over to see her."

"She kicked him out?"

"Oh yeah. That was a big scene."

"She's consistent in her mating practices."

"I think the guy's in a state of shock. He'll have to take his regular lashings over the phone, like the ex-husband had to, for a while there. I hear the kid of this last one screeching, like he's condemning him, too, for his bad form."

"There's another kid?"

"There's a new baby down there.

"She has two others, right?"

"Yeah, they're wild things; those two. They're starting to roam around the Loop. I think she has a job in the Loop. She's walking . . ."

"She seemed civil enough to me when I saw her last time." Isaiah spoke as if to himself. "You can see why she can't stay out of trouble, though, with that body, and that attitude, and her clothing."

"Oh, she's fit enough, ready for any struggle."

They laughed in a hearty fashion; reviving a dormant bravado.

"There's also a new woman in my building," Timothy's voice changed, as if he spoke of great mysteries.

"Oh yeah?" Isaiah prodded.

"She shields her eyes like a momma cat when she sees me."

"She's afraid you're some kind of revolutionary, on the losing side of things." Isaiah felt guilty as soon as he heard himself fashion this indirect reference to the man's loss of tenure, and far worse, his pension.

"But the thing is, she is not avoiding me, not exactly." Timothy almost whispered. He did not seem to be paying much attention to his friend's rough banter. "I'm trying to ascertain where she's come from. How did she end up in this tenement?"

"Have you talked to her?"

"No, but she talks to Mary."

"Who's Mary?"

"The ground floor woman, Mary Jones."

"Oh yeah? You finally introduced yourself?"

"No, I heard them talking."

"You're eavesdropping on them?"

"I can't help it. I hear them through the window. She's taken a shine to the girl, I believe."

"Quite the little drama you have unfolding there."

In his younger days Isaiah would have approached the ground floor woman to see if he could take photographs of her. He had done a series of portraits, made from such photographs, which he published in various magazines. He had gained a following for these depictions of random people he had encountered in the Loop.

"Maybe I *should* paint her."

"When was the last time you did that kind of street portraiture?"

"Oh man, it's been a long time. Back when I thought I would have enough time to do everything."

"Yeah."

"Now I'm just a lone, lorn creature."

Marx laughed tepidly at this old, worn, signature quote of his old pal.

They sat in silence for a while, each contemplating the curious quietude of the Loop.

"I kind of like this bizarre lack of activity everywhere." Isaiah mused out loud.

"It's like everything is running in the wrong direction." Timothy replied. "Like us, going backwards in time."

"Do you think a man ought to leave something to his son?" Isaiah asked abruptly.

"You've done well, haven't you? You used to tell me, all the time, how you've saved, and saved; and since you don't pay your current labor force, I'm sure you'll be able to leave something for Theo, won't you?"

Isaiah's face pulled taut at the facetious remark, before responding. "I have my savings, but I'm talking about something else. A sense of values, those imperishable strains—"

"You mean, like wisdom?"

Isaiah instantly regretted broaching this subject, which he was not prepared to explicate, even to himself.

"Wait, are you talking about the family name?"

Isaiah breathed out his forced amusement, shaking his head at such a ridiculous suggestion.

"Wait, are you becoming more spiritual?"

"I don't know about that."

"You've always scoffed at religion. Maybe you're like the last Herod, serving under the last Roman governor."

Isaiah had to smile at this riposte, a fair exchange to his forays against the humbled state of the defrocked professor.

"As his father, though, I ought to be able to profess faith in something, of a more lasting nature. A life should be like a body of work. We live by certain verities that ought to be preserved, don't you think?"

"I cannot advise you there. Perhaps you should consult Lord Chesterfield for the edification of your only lineal descendant." He smiled at the sharp frown he had incited. "Although, I am getting strange thoughts myself these days. Sometimes, after smoking a good pipe, I imagine myself addressing the entire species, like a prophet coming out of the desert."

"Oh, there's Raphael" Isaiah exclaimed.

"You watch, he'll bring up the Gang of '73. He'll want us to admit him."

"No, that's not even a thing anymore. You and I are the last of that miserable tribe."

Raphe was standing by their table, nodding affably and with guarded reserve. Both men at the table looked up and had to shield their eyes from the sun to make out the newcomer's shiny head and bony shoulders.

"Good timing. We were about to wander into the desert of philosophy." Marx quipped. "And this one has no sense of the terrain, nor can he stomach wild locusts."

Isaiah assumed a rueful aspect, as he swept a negligent glance over the countenance of his disheveled friend, who leaned back, smiling impishly. Raphe paid little attention, taking a seat at the table. Isaiah laid his hand protectively on his sketchpad, ready to face more serious concerns.

2

Raphael wore a mask handfashioned out of plaid cloth. To be amenable Isaiah put on his mask, and Timothy frowned at this appeasement. He refused to be coerced.

Raphael laid his newspaper on the table.

"Did you see what happened?" Timothy asked, looking down at one of the headlines.

Isaiah murmured his aversion to more talk of politics. Raphael leaned over and quoted an egregious text made by the Bête Noire, who presently inhabited the White House. They deplored his dribblings, and moved on to bemoan the fact there had been another violent episode on the streets. Isaiah imagined berserk pawns rushing forward on a great chess board, attacking all other pieces and each other; wild peasant upheavals taking place under the noses of kings, queens, bishops, and knights, none of whom mattered to the pawns anymore.

He reflected on his own political awakening, under the aegis of one prim, not always proper, Millie Gnamper; his first serious relationship after his rocky divorce. She wore short hair of a rather brutal cut, plain dowdy clothes, and steely, round, cerebral eyewear. She was lithe and wiry; a kinetic bundle of volatile passions. She made his nerves crackle like a string of firecrackers and was scathingly clever in her professional acuity and belligerence. Her mind was superbly equipped to master rough tactics used in partisan warfare. When arroused by his naïveté, ignorance, or indifference, her tongue let loose a dragon's torrent.

In the bedroom she sloughed her armor like a cicada. Her desire quaking in every cell of her being. In no role did she practice mercy as a virtue; at times, Isaiah swore he could see bluish tongues of flame licking out of her mouth, right after their bodies fell apart, to lay in glistening, bewildered satiation. He often wondered what had been sacrificed by this maid in all these burnt offerings that had to be scorchingly done. Sometimes she called out a name unknown to him, and he had learned not to inquire, as it always ended up being one of her political foes.

She worked at City Hall, a strange, baroque building that looked like something built to house the concubines of a French king. She had portioned out to him many sordid secrets. He had made numerous sketches of that remarkable building; the facade appeared to be plastered all over in multiple layers of some weird stucco dredged from the river bottom.

He imagined enormous plumbing fixtures must be needed to keep such a temple cleansed of the venality that washes through its chambers. In his drawings, published in the popular city rag, *Muddy Currents*, there were always crocodiles or wild dogs to be seen loitering on the front lawn. Sometimes vultures squatted on the roof. He liked to show the laundry hanging outside the windows; a touch inspired by Canaletto's work, *The Stonemason's Yard*.

"I'm just one of the orderlies," Millie explained to him. "You have to act as though you see nothing, and have no scruples, just like the rest of them."

"I see." He had answered.

"Oh, shut up. Don't you judge me! I'd like to see you try and make a difference. I've done my share, believe me. You would not have been able to do as much as I have done. Why, when I was younger . . ."

She had been older than him; as ever he had feared to recline upon the Viennese couch. She became very frigid, as he recalled, when faced with expressions of his decayed ideals. At other times she laughed at his unwillingness to take the political world seriously. At times his heresy was strangely soothing to her, until it was intolerable. In parting, she accused him of having no loyalty to anything.

Coming back to the present, Isaiah found the others were arguing about a book published when they were all young enough to be fairly agog over such garish ephemera. It was entitled, *The Culture of Narcissism*.

"Now that idiocy has gotten so common, it's insipid." Marx said.

"What is?" Raphe inquired sharply.

"That inane concept that human nature changes every generation, so that a new crop of grasping intellectuals can write popular tracts deploring the sad state of affairs as they obtain *today*."

"In *War and Peace* Tolstoy derides the intelligence of those who lament fresh depravities unique to the present times. But to some extent such changes do occur; it is a real thing, believe me." Raphe replied heatedly.

"It's always been a real thing, believe *me*! It has to do with the human will to power. What accounts for Louis XIV, the Sun King, his pretty notion of '*L'Etat c'est moi?*' Or Job's petition that God step down and face him? Not to mention that man crying out in the ninth hour, 'My God, my God, why hast thou forsaken *me!*' Are you familiar with the history of Hollywood moguls? The fine liberals who own estates in the Hamptons. The crowd at the Met Gala. The predilection of our kind to breed show dogs, and English royals? The sexual sports of Jack Kennedy?"

"At least they have show trials for the dogs." Raphael quipped dryly.

"Hey, I. Thomas, help me out here!"

"What the Dickens. I haven't heard you go off like that in a while."

"What's that?" Marx swung around, sensing an attack on his flank. In fact, Isaiah was thinking of a fictional character, Mr. Dombey, the businessman who strove to break the spirit of his proud, beautiful wife. He explains one of the main tenets to his chief sycophant, who secretly plots against him; "The idea of opposition to Me is monstrous and absurd."

"I was just thinking, Charles Dickens was a narcissist. He loved nothing more than being on stage playing roles before his adoring fans." Isaiah mused aloud. "All that worshipful attention—he craved it like a drug."

"Dickens wrote sweet mush for the masses," Marx spat out, irritated that his friend would not lend support in his cause of launching strikes against the interloper.

Isaiah lapsed into his reveries as the other two resumed arguing. He was thinking of Edith, and how they started an exclusive book club; it had only two members. The club was devoted to the novels of the inimitable Charles Dickens. He had proposed the idea partially in jest; she had taken it up with surprising aplomb.

Their private club had prospered for a decent spell, and then declined, and was resurrected, several times, until it expired in spastic, shuddering motions. For him, the life of that salubrious force was forever dwindling down, as if his soul were aloft in one last, autumnal torpor, suggestive of some former state of glory, now irrevocably lost.

Isaiah recited from the Book of Dickens: 'A wonderful fact to reflect upon, that every human creature is constituted to be that profound secret and mystery to every other.'

"Who said that?" Raphael asked.

"That's from his Right Reverend, Charles Humpty Dumpty Dickens," Marx answered. "

"That's right." Isaiah said, rather pleased with himself.

"Are you still reading him like you did in the old days, with that damned monomania?"

"I keep going back to his works. The stuff is still fresh to me."

"You're incorrigible, refusing to seek out other reading material. That's your buried spiritualism asserting itself; devoting yourself to one set of sacred texts."

"His works contain an abundance of riches. I guess they are like secular gospels."

"A secular scripture for the agnostic folks." Marx said, shaking his head, emitting a twittering sound, with his mouth held slightly open. "What about the actual gospels, have you ever read those?"

"No, but they were assimilated when I attended St. Margaret's."

Marx emitted a derisive grunt. He had read the Bible numerous times, in his office as an historian, ever interested in the historiography of his species.

"Did any of us have anything like a religious fervor, back in the day?" Isaiah was very serious.

Marx looked at him quizzically, as if a cryptic sign had been brandished. "Define religious."

Isaiah shook his head and laughed.

"I haven't read much of Dickens," Raphe confessed, "I'm not sure why that's so." He was feeling put upon, as an intruder, even though he had been invited to come here.

Isaiah began considering a drawing; a phantasmagoria of historical figures. He thought of a large painting, to be called *The Springs of COVID-19*, in which the overwrought behaviors caused by the pandemic appeared in an actual cauldron, holding a fermenting mash, ever bubbling, ever cooking the whole body politic. It was meant to somehow recall the lurid scenes when heretics were tortured and witches burned for refusing to profess the truths then being prescribed by power.

"Are you listening to this?" Marx's strident voice shattered his quiet, seething reverie.

"No." Isaiah spoke with amusement

"He's saying," nodding at Raphe, "that all this violence in the streets is unprecedented."

"No I'm *not*; that's ridiculous." Raphe retorted, making a pained expression. "I'm only saying something new is happening, in reaction against the unrepentant racism of the country."

"Something is happening," Isaiah agreed. "That cop, kneeling on the neck of George Floyd, that changed things. Everyone could see what that was."

"It was sickening." Raphe said.

"That callous disregard of a defenseless human being, who was in agony, struggling for life." Isaiah grew animated. "The gleeful satisfaction you could see graven on the cop's face. Using physical cruelty to torture, and thus dominate, another person. He acted so smug, as though his behavior were sanctioned by some higher, Nietzschean good, redounding to the betterment of society." Isaiah's voice broke under the strain of his intense emotional state.

"A lot of cops have always been—" Timothy began his own lecture.

"Do you remember that photo of the Nazi soldier?" Isaiah interrupted him. "Sitting on the edge of a ravine, the machine gun laying across his lap, smoking a cigarette, waiting to shoot more people, who would then tumble into the pit of their grave."

"Do you think we're on the verge of something like that now?" Timothy asked.

"I don't know. You're the one always preaching to me that human nature doesn't change that quickly.

That's still a part of us; it's just a matter of circumstances, right?"

"I'm not so sure of these things, at least not as I was in the past." He murmured, causing Isaiah to look closely at his averted face.

"There definitely is change in the air," Raphe asserted.

"Real societal change occurs at a very deep level." Marx retorted.

"Everything happens at a deep level." Raphe replied with an air of annoyance.

The other two began discussing the fact many college students were promoting censorship as a practical means of blotting out erroneous ideas. Isaiah had to wonder if it had been different in their youth; his own son laughed at his uneasy explanations of his youthful idealism.

Isaiah had always voted for Democrats. He thought it was important to support a progressive agenda; but he also knew how phony many of the leaders were, lusting after the material rewards, and the social status, and giving way to powerful, amoral interests, as a matter of course. It seemed to be a new thing the way esteemed politicians now prized the sort of mindless worship afforded rich celebrities.

The debate at the table, like so much else in his life, seemed unreal to Isaiah. He was reminded of the wonderful satire of the party system found in *Bleak House*; wherein the difference between stated beliefs and actual behavior was laid bare in hilarious refrains. The farce of the Coodles and Doodles waging war for the spoils had not changed all that much, not in essence.

"They lie for a living." Isaiah whispered during a lull in the conversation of the other two men. They both looked at him with injured faces, not sure what he was talking about. They were, however, familiar with his casual usage of non sequiturs, and soon resumed the argument they were having.

Isaiah could not understand how so many people came to revere mediocre political figures, as though they were paragons, instead of larcenous employees, who cannot be trusted to work the cash register. There being no proper supervision, by an ignorant electorate, nothing is ever truly reconciled. He thought of David Copperfield's exclamation, regarding his disgust with the sham nature of politics, after his stint reporting on Parliament: "I am quite an Infidel about it, and shall never be converted." That was the author speaking, from his own experience.

"Well, are we going to discuss our project?" Raphael asked, raking Marx with a withering glance.

"Don't let me stop you." Marx growled while standing. He said with a sardonic intonation, "Don't forget to ask him about Deborah Spencer."

"Who's that?" Raphe asked, but Isaiah only shook his head, watching the curious rolling gait of his ursine friend, receding down the sidewalk.

"Tell me about the beginning, the first drawings you remember doing. It began when you were a child?"

"You want to start doing this here?"

"Sure, let's jump in. I need to hear you telling me about yourself."

"Well, now that you mention it, my mother took me to the Art Museum, and I saw some Van Goghs; and it sent me rushing back to my box of crayons." Isaiah was surprised at himself, he had never spoken of this with anyone.

"Those made a big impact?"

"She told me, long afterwards, that I started imitating what I had seen, making sketches in my coloring books. I would add boats and trees, and such, into the designs in the book. She bought me a large Van Gogh book, and I began drawing in the pages of the book; emulating his work." He laughed at himself.

"You've been drawing ever since?"

"I have."

Raphael got him to reveal his earliest artistic habits. In his recollections Isaiah fell into a trance. He was not sure later which incidents he had spoken of and which he had only uncovered for his own perusal.

"Is that enough, for now?" He needed to be alone to sort things out.

"Yeah, that was a good start."

"I'm not sure that was very coherent!"

"That was good, though, you went right back to the genesis. I mean, that's how it sounds. That's been your life, ever since, hasn't it?"

That's been my life? There's supposed to be more to it than that, I suppose . . .

"I'll catch you later, then." Raphael rose and passed out of his vision, as if he were one of those specters he had drawn forth to crowd around him for a moment before vanishing again to remain forever lurking about, getting ready to accost his present contentment.

Isaiah remained at the café, considering how his relations with his mother had gotten so bad that he created a false narrative. He had told himself she had never really encouraged him in his artistic development. The erratic play of memory made him uneasy, and he was forced to get up and stride awkwardly down the street. He wanted to feel he was moving towards something, even though he had no destination in mind. In the next moment he stopped abruptly, to get his bearings, and began retracing his steps to get back to his new car. He relaxed in the leather seat, pleased to take his time inhaling that industrial cologne of clean new things.

3

Later that week Raphael came over to Isaiah's apartment to conduct another 'session'; which term caused uneasy laughter, being rather suggestive of psychoanalysis.

"We'll tread as lightly as you want." Raphe responded wryly, as if such worries were preposterous in this trivial project. "It will be an account of how things were, as seen from your own perspective."

They settled down in the spacious living room. Raphael began to study the place in silence. Isaiah never cared that much about his home décor; he sought utility and comfort, unable to take that notion of 'style' very seriously. His walls were appointed lavishly with pictures that spoke to him.

"My taste has always been rather unfinished," he tried to explain.

"At some point, I would like to hear you say something about each of these pictures." Raphe swept his arm across the crowded walls.

Raphael was sitting on the couch, his writing materials spread on the coffee table in front of him. Isaiah sat in his favorite reading chair, able to peer past Raphael, out his front windows, at the unperturbed oaks trees, whispering among themselves.

"So, do you want to know all that David Copperfield kind of crap?" Isaiah began, facetiously.

"I guess that's up to you, I wasn't—"

"I was spared the evil stepfather business. No escaped convicts, no cemetery scenes, no child labor in a local shoe factory."

"Now, what are you talking about?" His pale blue eyes could be bland and intensely critical at once.

"The impossibility of capturing reality in any written document meant to—"

"This is just an article. It's not an official biography!" He laughed in a shrill burst, and stopped abruptly. "So tell me something about those early river pictures, that brought you some success."

"Ah, I have been thinking about those—"

"But first, I thought we'd explore that episode at the statue."

"Why delve into that, it's not germane to anything—"

"It is kind of why we're here, isn't it? That sparked a renewed interest in your work, and *is* the reason I have a chance at placing this piece with a magazine."

"There was plenty of interest in my work, long before that happened."

"Sure, but look, this makes for a good story. You were in all the papers. Tell me, was there any reason you selected that monument?"

"Selected it?"

"What was on your mind?"

"I don't know." Isaiah stared at the impervious oaks. "I'm not sure."

"Have you ever painted that statue in the past?

"Oh, there were many drawings. You know, I'm not sure I like the idea of even mentioning that incident in this article. What good would that do me?"

"Well, let's put that aside for now. This is supposed to be your chance at explaining your work."

"Okay."

Raphe smiled at the look on his face. "How *do* you see yourself, as an artist."

"How do I see myself?" Isaiah was confused.

"Okay, what was the first big picture that you did. I've read you first came to be known for those huge landscapes of the river. But before that, you did one on the East St. Louis race riots, you called it *U. S. Pogrom*. I was trying to study that online this morning. I mean, what did people say at the time?"

"Well, I wanted to take a stab at historical scenes; those had always fascinated me." He was remembering how he had used his grandmother's youthful face for one of the maniacal white furies present at the massacre. He had stolen one of her photographs to use for this purpose.

"There was a furor caused by the way you depicted the young white women in that scene. You made them look so normal, wholesome, like the neighbor girls—"

"The type used in hair spray commercials."

"I read somewhere that your portrayal was meant to be a criticism of society women."

"That seems so long ago." He fell into a gloomy silence. Many of his models were, in fact, just the sort of women he had always yearned to know intimately, but who were always beyond his social and virile reach.

"There's really not much critical material out there on that piece, not that I could find."

"They wouldn't even write about it in *Muddy Currents*. That surprised me, that he was afraid to address the issue objectively. I saw it as a catalyst. There were so many events in our history. The Red Summer. I mean, it was pervasive."

"Your lack of notice might have been a case of St. Louis being St. Louis?"

"No doubt. It got swept away pretty quickly."

"The shocking details were so stark. And you had the river winding off in the background —"

"People started looking at me differently."

"How so?"

"It was more than a little disturbing, how some people, people I knew really well, changed towards me, overnight." It were as though *he* had no right to broach such subjects, and had been found guilty of desecrating a sacred narrative. They wanted to teach him a lesson; the curating of that story belonged to a higher caste of leading citizens.

"What else do you remember from that time?"

"Some questioned my motivation. Was I just trying to stir things up, or what? It's always the same thing." He glowered. "It's maddening. And there was hardly any talk about the historical event itself, which was bizarre. "They were only concerned about the fracas I had caused."

"Someone called you the enfant terrible. Not such a bad thing, for an artist?"

"Yeah, he called me the enfant terrible of the Loop." Isaiah smiled ruefully. "We were rivals; he was mocking me. He was then prominent in the drip, smear and splatter crowd. A protégé of the Wallpaper School."

"You've never gotten along with that abstract art crowd, have you?"

Isaiah made a weary face. "It's never attracted me that much."

"Tell me about your primary influences."

"Oh my god, that's a long and winding road."

"Just start talking about it. You said Van Gogh—"

"He was the head master, during my apprenticeship. I kept him close at all times. I was scared of merely copying things. But that magical style he created for himself, how he had managed to come up with that, now *that* was marvelous to me. I wanted to learn how to turn that to my own use. And his dedication was inspirational." Isaiah began to share his adoration of the mad colorist of Arles. Raphe was taking notes as his subject expressed his feelings in exceptional language.

After a prolonged session they drank beers and talked of other topics.

"Hey, I meant to ask you; what was O'Rourke talking about? Something about you and Lady Spencer?"

"What?" Isaiah was perplexed.

"Were you into Lady Diane or something?" Raphe spoke delicately, afraid to scare off his subject.

"No." Isaiah was startled; then a harsh burst of laughter came forth; thinking of his *Antidotes for Inequality*. "I did a series of guillotines under construction outside the official residences of kings and queens. I did one at the Windsor castle. That print still sells."

"Was O'Rourke a fan of the English princess, then?"

"What?" Isaiah chuckled, his body shaking all over. "Well, in his own weird way. He collects object lessons from historical figures, which he uses to shame ignorant people."

"Do you want to express your political opinions in the piece?"

"No! That's not... I don't know where you got this idea about English royalty."

"I know O'Rourke said to ask you about Spencer—"

"Oh!" Isaiah slapped his knee. "He was teasing me, about Deborah Spencer."

"Who's she?"

"She was a girl I knew at St. Margaret's, up north—"

"In Ferdinand?"

"Yes."

"Near where Molly lives?"

"Yes."

"She's the one who suggested I consider doing this piece, and maybe, depending on how things go, an actual biography."

"Really? She thought a biography was a good idea?"

"I'm not sure what she's thinking. She knows I'm trying to keep my hand in something, and she prompted me to call you to see about doing the article. She knows an editor who might be interested."

"Do you see her very often?"

"Now and then. She reaches out to me. She's always been good at—"

"I haven't seen her in a long while. Is she still there by the church grounds?"

"There on Elizabeth, yeah."

"She's still with Jacob?"

"Yes, why do you ask?"

"Oh nothing. Who knows anything, anymore."

Raphael looked at him closely. After a moment they talked some more about the project, and it was decided Isaiah should make notes about topics he would like to discuss in the next meeting.

"If you can formulate a set of artistic principles of any kind, jot them down."

"Sure thing." Increasingly Isaiah was dismayed by the prospect of going through with this project. It was too soon; surely it was like inviting a curse upon his future work.

After Raphe left Isaiah had to contend with all that he had roiled up from the past. He was dazed, as if stranded in a debris field of regrets, having to do with so much that had happened in his life. The more he thought about the course of his life, the more urgent became that damning question, what had any of it really meant?

4

It was late morning, long past the sweet, early hours that siphoned some relief from the night's restoring cisterns. A mass of nervous enervation had settled heavily upon all forms of breathing life. The trees stood very still, as if enduring heroic trials, due to prideful heritage, earning the honors handed out sparingly by their demanding mother.

Some hours earlier Isaiah had gone walking, hoping to enjoy the green spaces and trees along Delmar in that early light. He struggled, feeling sharp pains in his legs, barely making his way to the Loop. He arrived at Java Monkey with his brow sopping wet. He bantered with members of the staff, feeling conspicuous as the old-timer who has to exert himself to manufacture good cheer. He enjoyed sitting outside alone in the shade, casting himself back in time. During his walk home he labored, and whispered to himself that he must not try that journey again, not any time soon.

At home he tried to compose notes on his early career, but his mind wandered among senseless details.

Then he was suddenly trying to make sense of what had happened that fateful day outside the Art Museum. He had gone there not paying any attention to the protesters gathered around the statue. Inside he had stared a long time at the disfigured *Head of St. Roch*. When he exited the museum he had been thinking of Edith . . .

The week before he had attended her burial; none of her people acknowledged his presence. He had been so determined to be there, for her, he had said to himself, and then, upon encountering them, it all felt wrong. For most of them it was the first time they had ever seen him. It made him angry, even ashamed, that he had allowed them to see him paying his last respects. After she was laid to rest he went off by himself; taking a seat on the porch of the stately crypt built for the beer baron, Adolphus Busch. On his tiny sketchpad he began drawing the vista before him; trying to memorialize a feeling he could not possibly enunciate.

He removed from his pocket several pages he had torn from a paperback copy of *The Old Curiosity Shop*. He had meant to read these words over her grave, but then he could not do it while under the interdict of her peoples' massed disdain. He had almost stepped forward to throw the pages into her casket out of spite . . .

The anger had lain dormant until that moment outside the museum, where he suddenly felt antagonized by both groups of protesters. He was incensed to see them vying for attention in that way. One faction advocated toppling the equestrian statue. In their eyes this king had been a fanatical religious bigot, and a chauvinistic, proto-fascist harbinger of the the many state-sponsored horrors yet to come.

The other party wanted to defend the legend, the relic, the patron saint of the city. They decried senseless, barbaric iconoclasm. To these presumed Catholics he was truly a venerable personage. His sainthood was real enough; there had been miracles, the paperwork had been registered and filed away. The symbolism of the august horseman, dressed and girded for battle, could only help to keep the natives in good order.

"Tear it down!" He heard voices shouting. The loyalists cried against this sacrilege. Some in the crowd wished to take this opportunity to reason with their opponents. Isaiah remembered shaking his head at this ludicrous spectacle; sensing the formation of those chaotic tempers that activate the feral instincts of a mob.

He could not forget the crazed, desperate anguish, the strident voices, the contorted features, the spray of spittle, the palpable force of uncontrolled anger radiating off their faces. The latency of violence was crackling in his ears as he walked by, giving them a wide berth, shaking the dust, or so he thought. He was beset by his recent allegorical vision of the beast thirsting for blood.

In the parking lot he had paused to look back, as if mesmerized by the wicked dance steps of these tainted salt creatures of the earth. Standing by his truck he must have had some coherent thoughts, which he could no longer reconstruct. And then he took the ladder off his truck, and began dragging it across the face of Art Hill with a grim visage. He was soon engulfed by a crowd, who escorted him to the base of the statue.

"Tear it down!" A louder chant erupted as he placed the ladder against the pedestal. They were jostling below, to keep him steady and to haul him down, as he climbed. He dismounted in a shaky manner, amazed at what he was doing. He stood next to the horse. And he was preparing to say something; what had he to say?

Everyone was shouting at him. He grew dizzy and leaned on the ladder, as though it were a balustrade, and then he was falling over and having to clutch the ladder as he lost his balance. He had pushed himself off, and there was an instantaneous roar from the people on the ground. He swayed out into a dangerous space, his eyes sweeping the horizon, his stomach leapt as he went over like he was on a carnival ride. A host of hardy people below stepped forward, raising their arms, coming together in a press, lowering him safely to the ground.

"Whoa! You got lucky there, buddy!"

"What were you trying to do up there?"

"Watch out. He might be crazy!"

They crouched over him, to see if he was physically okay. By then none supposed he was right in the head. In his disoriented state he could only stare rather stupidly at the blur of insensible faces. They granted him the privileges appertaining to one whose mind wasn't right. He took up his ladder and headed for home, too bewildered to feel ashamed. Some wanted to expropriate his ladder, to finish the work he had clearly botched. Others demanded that he be left alone. His inexplicable behavior only caused each contingent to intensify their rhetorical clashes.

The next day his phone brought awful tidings; videos were circulating online. His creepy descent made it into the papers. The blaring headline in *Muddy Currents* reeked of malice, Drunk Gains Audience With Saint Louis. It was the lead story, no doubt scripted by the son of the owner, his old boss, Herbert Hruuck, who seized the chance to act on ancient grievances. The story spoke of the rise and fall of a cartoonist . . .

That jab of Hruuck, the Younger, still irked, and he had actually been quite sober. The way the news was able to create a false narrative, with such ease, was painful to reflect upon. After the laughter died down, some advised that he ought to take legal action against them. How does one prove he had been sober, after the fact? He declined every chance to explain himself. How address the question of his mental state? Any interview would no doubt turn hostile. Were you seeking publicity? That must be it, right? Lucky for you; I heard the trick worked!

You cannot explain to the world at large that you believe the human psyche is a great Faustus, forever at play, accepting bad favors and bargains. He had learned the perils of taunting those who are capable of installing your persona into virtual stocks. You are never only speaking to the people in front of you; and the beastly public, when it takes a rude shape, demands such exquisite ceremonies of respect, for whatever mindless notions they take up, and will surely take umbrage to prove their loyalty is beyond measure, or question, and their latest cause is absolutely consonant with Truth. That might be one of the reasons great politicians, who claim only selfless motives, while toiling vigorously in an utterly corrupt system, become such extravagant caricatures of what they hold themselves up to be in life.

5

Isaiah was making a routine visit to see how Marx was making out at the Newgate apartment complex, just off the Loop.

After he knocks he hears Timothy respond as if he were a sentry being awoken on duty.

"It's me!" Isaiah yells back. The door opens and Marx is already retreating into his den.

"What's going on?" Isaiah asks, upon entering and shutting the door.

"Not much." He had just been napping. "It's not the British Museum, or anything. I can't burrow in to study like in the old days. I had to free most of my serfs." His books were referred to in this way.

Isaiah stands in the small living room, making a survey of the usual clutter in the cramped living quarters. It might have been the receiving dock of an antiquarian book-dealer.

"The woman across the hall is acting strange."

"Oh yeah?" Isaiah was intrigued. "Maybe she's like a lost lady, banished from her estate. Perhaps a fortune is to be made." Isaiah laughs. Timothy ignores him, staring at his door, as though attempting to see through it. What is she doing, that you find so puzzling?"

"She watches a lot of TV. And plays classical music."

"That's *very* strange. Have you called the police?"

Timothy frowned. They both took seats.

"Say, what have you got there?"

Isaiah was holding a new copy of the *White Album* wrapped in clear plastic, which he extended to his friend.

"I've been wanting to get this one." Timothy placed the gift among his other vinyl records. He had started collecting these just before he lost his position.

"Let's listen to something else." Isaiah said equably. He knew O'Rourke preferred to play each new album the first time when he was alone, while smoking marijuana.

"What about that *Sounds of Silence* album I bought you"

"Yeah, sure." Timothy was not pleased at his friend's flaunting of his largesse.

"On second thought, we should listen to Prine." Isaiah had also bought him several Prine albums; it made him feel good about himself to act in a benevolent fashion.

"Good idea." Timothy repaired to the record crates he used for storage, to recapture a touch of the old days. "I have been listening to him a lot lately."

John Prine had passed over into his great soundtrack that April; the coronavirus was cited as a contributing cause of his departure. Listening to his music had been an integral part of their lives for a very long time. His death struck a knell for those lost times of promise, when sorrows were but the gloomy preludes to the joyous movements certain to come along in the vastness of future prospects.

Isaiah sat near the large picture window looking out at a rather sickly pin oak, choked by galls. He ran his eyes over the scraggly branches. He began to think of Molly Gates, whom he had not seen in such a long time. He remembered that she had once painted the trees in her neighborhood with a rather fine, delicate, and studied verisimilitude.

They listened devotedly to the album, *Diamonds in the Rough*. Timothy sat in his heavy reading chair. He did not own a television, and books were strewn everywhere like blocks scattered around ancient ruins. Isaiah noticed several new posters had been added to the Sixties montage posted on the walls; those of Hendrix, Joplin, and Jim Morrison.

As they listened to the music Isaiah kept glancing at O'Rourke, whose elfin spirit was shining forth from his eyes. His visage bore an uncanny resemblance to an iconic photograph of Karl Marx. Timothy felt pity for the retired college professor, of labor history, who had come to the end of his term in a bitter fashion.

"You cannot go wrong with Prine." Timothy spoke conclusively after "Souvenirs" finished playing.

"No," Isaiah whispered, amazed at how powerful the music was, evoking the moral surety of his youth, despite his present belief that decadence was overwhelming every sector of society.

Having known each other so long, they had come to treat the fear of viral contagion the way family members were doing; braving the potential presence of the invisible Enemy with guarded skepticism. Timothy did not smoke his pipe out of respect for his friend, who did not partake of the venerable weed.

The efforts of Isaiah to patronize his friend had altered their relations, often putting them at odds, for no apparent reason. The animus of inequality had been roused, fostering petty rivalries. Sometimes it seemed as though the finances of one were being pitted against the erudition of the other, as they wrangled over proxy issues to gain precedence on imaginary social scales.

"You sure there's nothing you need from the grocery store? It's okay, you can use my car."

"No. I'm okay. I can walk to the library." He twisted around, looking out his front window. "Did you hear the ground floor woman when you were coming up?"

"No. Why?"

Timothy laid back in his chair and listened to the music very intently. Isaiah got up to inspect a poster of Melanie Safka, taken during her debut at Woodstock.

"I used to really like her song, 'Peace Will Come'; still do, in fact, but I don't believe in it anymore."

"Not something we'll see, not if we live as long as Noah. States using violence, that's not going to end any time soon." Marx asserted in his strange, late manner.

"What do you still believe in?" Isaiah queried, still ranging his eyes over the posters.

"Ha!" Marx appraised his friend's face. "I don't know how to answer such a question."

"What do you make of all this civil unrest out there?" Isaiah asked. "All the violence between random people."

"It's a tinderbox; considering all the issues."

"I get that, but all the random acts of violence. People turning on each other, like animals."

"Smoldering resentments at the injustice of the status quo. The brutal agency of the police, controlling the streets. The idolatrous worship and maldistribution of wealth. The sanctimonious elites preaching to the proles, while enjoying the spoils of the haute bourgeois global village. The average worker's anger at being despised by the rich and their glib minions, the party leaders. Yeah, there are reasons aplenty."

"It's telling, though, that the violent ones are usually the least realistic in their demands. And they want radical, even ludicrous, changes to be made right now."

"Some of these militants, who have no real power, are unconscious of what they're doing; leaping into the breach, anyway they can manage, to push for change, goaded on by personal afflictions. I believe that sometimes a destructive sensibility arises and a small portion of the population, the ones feeling the most disenfranchised, are driven to disrupt the conventional modes. The streets act as proving grounds. The violence tests the stability of the various controlling hierarchies. The normally productive gears become broken, causing heat, sparks, and fire. Repairs have to be made on the fly, as fierce competition never stops, and this keeps the whole mechanical racket clanking forward towards our unknown ends."

"Marx, you're going off the deep end on me again. Doesn't it feel like we're repeating an endless cycle. And everyone is wearing different costumes this time. It's unreal to me."

"A gradual evolution of power is always happening. Now it's being accelerated, but this will not bring a fair and equable arrangement; that's not what people actually want. I've begun to consider that history has finally caught up with America." Timothy was again a pedagogue.

"What do you mean?" Isaiah sat down once more

"In the beginning, it was about land, to quote Conrad, 'taking it away from those who have a different complexion or slightly flatter noses.' And there was great freedom, for some, not all; however, freedom often leads to brutal ends. For two centuries people have known how rare this is, for so many to have a chance at a decent life with so much freedom. Now, our vast plenty forces us to face the question of the great prophets, can we have real justice, for all? It's never existed before. The motto, 'we hold these truths to be self-evident,' engraved on our national pediment, that's being effaced as individuals are allowed to amass enormous fortunes."

"It just seems like, at some point, we became inured to how things really are, and then stopped caring, while keeping up the pretense that the same old structure is good enough."

"What's the line? 'Mithridates, he died old.' That sums up our comfort with hypocrisy. How do you like your new car?"

"The new car smell is really nice."

Marx laughed in his quick chortling way, head bobbing up and down. "What is revealed, and what is kept hidden, in the scared crypt of history; that is another subject. It has been clear to me for some time now, that people do not seek égalité; quite the opposite. We are wired to seek power, and disguise this in cultural terms. We've devised incredible facilities for knowing things, solving problems, compiling useful data, and ingenious ways to cause wealth to flow upwards to a few, as if by the very laws of nature."

"You're becoming more philosophic." Isaiah observed his friend's proud smile with envy. He possessed a sturdy resilience in his agreeable, corpulent frame. His shirts were always in the process of coming untucked, his sleeves always partially rolled up on his arms. By appearance, he was a badly rumpled man, however, he possessed an imperturbable sense of his own dignity.

"Social media shines a harsh light on our species; we look pretty bad there."

"No, it's not a pretty picture." Isaiah agreed.

Timothy began clawing at his heavily salted dark beard while recounting the renewal of a feud he had had online with one of his estranged friends. "I should have known better than to take the bait." He shook his head.

"You sound like maybe you have too much time on your hands." Isaiah tried to lighten the mood.

"I suppose that's a lot of it. Remember the hours we used to spend talking about politics? What does any of it mean now?"

"Back in the glory days, we were so sure of ourselves. Searching for meanings in a mug of beer!"

"Perhaps it is time to put aside the past."

"But still, what a time it was." Isaiah fondly phrased these words, invoking a favorite song. "Remember Emma?" Isaiah asked with awakened vigor.

Timothy laughed from his belly. "She was something." The woman in question was in fact named Naomi; she had been a fellow Ph. D. candidate, along with Marx, at the most prestigious university in town. His friends started calling her Emma, in reference to Emma Goldman, and at first this irritated Timothy, and then it only amused him, after falling headlong into love. Then the opinions of his friends no longer mattered. It was easy to discountenance ignorant fools from the vantage of a superior carnal position. Naomi naturally disregarded his friends, as any queen would the antics of her peasants. She was fiercely independent, and her mantra became, 'I'm not staying in St. Louis.'

"One thing I do find very strange," Marx mused aloud, "is this outlandish return to Puritanism. This insistence on forcing people to behave according to the dictates of self-appointed moral commissars. It strikes me as a dark omen, that certain people are claiming absolute moral authority; professing it is their duty to identify and punish heretics. History is clear on what happens with that zealous type, once they get their hands on real power."

"Yes, you've told me, often enough." Isaiah retorted. "I've seen you wrestling with all that Marxist dogma in your day."

"In my day." Marx assumed his gnomic aspect. "Is my day gone?" The merry twinkle flashed out from his hairy visage.

"All these ahistorical young people are convinced they know what the truth is, in every political argument. It's frightening. They brook no argument."

"Did that happen to us?"

"Yes." He laughed. "But at least we were *reading*!" They exchanged a look.

"Not so much me." Isaiah confessed. "But I listened to those who had; that's what was good about the gang. What did you say to me once, 'My head was aloft in prismatic clouds gathered from the fumes of romantic landscapes.' That was pretty harsh of you, my friend. And maybe a good treatment for my distempers, I suppose."

The chest of Marx began to rumble with pleasure as he bore witness to the staying power of his jibes. "At least we learned it was imperative to distrust all persons holding power." Marx offered in resigned tones.

"That is, until we got a taste of the good life ourselves, then we only wanted to make sure we could keep our places there."

"You were on that trip more than me."

"No. That's what you really think?"

"You were always more ambitious than me."

"What? That's not true. Do you really think that's how it was?"

"I believe so. Is now any different?"

"Well, there's nothing wrong with having ambition. It's a matter of what is actually wanted, and what one is willing to sacrifice to obtain it." He stared out the window, after speaking, as if he had lost his bearings in his own defense.

"Everything looks different now, doesn't it?"

"No doubt of that. Listen, I have some chores to do. You probably want to fire up your pipe. Say, are you sure you don't want to borrow the car for anything?"

"I'll let you know. The larder is full. I've been walking a lot more. It feels like I'm getting ready for spring training again." Isaiah had noticed Marx had put up a picture of his former high school self in his varsity football uniform. He had played defensive tackle, earning some faraway local acclaim.

Isaiah made his way out as Timothy began to gather his paraphernalia to conduct another therapeutic session. He sifted through his albums, finally unwrapping the iconic *White Album*. He got high, and relaxed in Buddhistic style, staring out the window. He listened to the complexity of the music in a meditative trance. His mind soon made its way back to those impossible scenes he had shared with Naomi; the incontestable *one*, who had known him like no other being ever had before, or since.

Seen through the mists of time, the two figures could be imagined again caught up in stormy passions, as though it were a movie scene barely remembered. There was only lurid gleams, wild, primal, garden delights, and ghostly pangs. She had once meant everything to him. Then she made it clear that she was just passing through, and he never believed her. His besotted heart would not allow him to entertain such heresy. For a while she encouraged him to move away with her

Since the first kiss she had been dominant. Her frequent command, 'Let's fuck,' made him her playful slave. She teased him for being an impoverished divinity student, trapped in the pages of a Dostoevsky novel. He began to read those novels because of her. She devoured books in a way that astonished him. He often said afterwards that she had a preternatural instinct for ingesting, digesting, and shitting good books.

"She knew how to dissolve the pith to fortify her own fiber. She takes what has meaning for her, and voids the rest."

She was the only person who ever lectured a passive, attentive Marx on historical topics. Listening to her declaim on feminist issues tamed his animal nature. He could not get past the intelligence, the imperious, willful, unrepentant hauteur. His stolid, pig-iron love was transmuted by her exotic sensuality and personal alchemy. When he affirmed he wanted to complete his studies in St. Louis she left and never looked back.

It was strange to be visiting these shrines, much as the ancients offered sacrifices at their local temples. His poor notions of love had been transfigured into awe as elemental powers changed his being. She was a grandiose historical figure, in his own book of life. He marveled over the fact his own history should have produced an epic of ennobling pity. Such that it might have been the entire human race that had suffered this blow, instead of one man's corruptible romanticism!

He was borne away, and came out of his reverie, after placing *Tea for the Tillerman* (side two) on his turntable. In short order his mind was revolving about the idea of this strange lady who lived just across the landing. She had recently taken the preposterous step of reproaching him, by speaking directly to him through his door.

"How do you feel?" She had asked one time from the landing. Marx held his breath for a moment. At the time he was smoking his medicinal herbs, while listening to the Moody Blues (*In Search of the Lost Chord*), and traveling far off into the rich tonal clouds. Her odd message quavered in his consciousness. How does one know *how* one feels? No one knows the origins of such metaphysical occurrences. Do you think we would act differently if we could order such things to our own liking? The audacity of the woman!

Then again, smelling the pot, did she regard him as a criminal element? Was it a warning? Was she challenging his right to seek a better vantage for looking into his private reality. Who was *she* to propose an unchanging status quo to the likes of him! Then he was sure he heard her door quietly open, and then close again. Her soft footsteps registered in his disturbed mind with infinite subtleties of phantom forces he had thought defunct. Upon reflection he was not sure he had even heard an external voice.

"Is everything alright in there?" The next week she was at it again. He was ensconced in his chair, afloat on a cloud of heady fumes, listening to Jefferson Airplane (*Surrealistic Pillow*); and again he could not utter a single word. *In there?* Was she intimating that his bookish den was a sink of moral disorder? Did she mean that his historical explorations were analogous to a waste site, full of seething gases, that might catch fire in his mind, and spread outwards to engulf her dwelling? She probably believed he ought to be watching TV all the time! *She* was clearly entranced by that soulless necromancer.

Once his mind was pitched to hear and decipher any further signal, she went silent on him. He was appalled that she failed to prosecute her esoteric inquiries. Wait a minute; was she out there now, listening to him? Should he surprise her on the landing? She was truly devilish in her stealth. How did *she* end up in this squalid tenement? Other voices admonished him for having been so reckless as to lose his tenure.

His confusion turned to anger. He began cursing his true enemies; the administrators wed to the donors, like moral eunuchs were to princes. These had cast him out. He was made to beg for silver pieces, wandering afield to feed from popular troughs. And then, the year of the plague was upon them. Several old friends had lost their minds, and had to be taken care of by lowly footmen given to vengeful little cruelties.

He had observed other friends becoming deranged in their hatred of the Bête Noire. They conjured apocalyptic fables to explain his vulgar, and rather trite, ascendancy. What they perceived to be unraveling before them, on the various screens, to which they were inextricably bound for psychic sustenance, was nothing less than a sort of Biblical prophecy, as interpreted by atheists circling around in the usual barren deserts of academia.

They refused to let Marx lecture them on the truth, as an elusive dialectical principle, for the real problem, he was hardly sure himself anymore on these things, and the real problem, in truth, he had to wonder though, the real issue, so perplexing, was why had she stopped speaking to him through his door? There was so much more that needed to be said if she wished to state her premise, before she might attempt to prove her argument. Something was missing. By cabalistic means she had enjoined him to question all he was doing, thus begging many more questions, none of which he could state clearly to himself, even now. What was the true impetus behind this late unearthing of Naomi, the very one who had originally overturned the tables at his temple? Why would he seek to measure now all that he had lost because of that decision to live here no matter what? Should he be asking more of himself in some way? What *was* he still doing here, living like a glorified squatter?

6

One day Isaiah met his son for lunch at Vedi Napoli in the Loop. Theo was working at a job he hated, and forewarned his father that he could not afford to be late getting back to the office. At other periods he had stated vehemently that he did not care if he ever returned to that stupid asylum.

On his own initiative Theo had mastered the intricacies of constructing active spreadsheets, bristling with macros to manipulate the data. This allowed the middle managers to conjure scenarios that titillated their upper managers. By these efforts Theo had risen above his former colleagues, the harried claims adjusters, who lived below decks, tethered to stationary phones banks, at the mercy of demonic voices.

Whenever Theo had to pass by his old comrades they looked upon him as a craven pet of the ruling class. He was in limbo, assisting in the process of insuring people against the hazards of life, while maximizing corporate profit. It is truly a crazy dance of inelegant figures. Once having gained access to data concerning company salaries, he deduced he was getting the royal shaft.

When Isaiah attempted to express an interest in his work, Theo retorted angrily that he didn't want to discuss 'all that crap.' He was taking night classes; 'learning how to code.' It pained him to have to explain these things. His standard demeanor with Isaiah was a weary, aggrieved sulk.

"Did you talk to Mrs. Kinfe?" Isaiah asked as they finished wolfing down their hamburgers and fries.

"Not yet."

Isaiah opened his mouth to remonstrate.

"I said I will, and I will!" Theo stopped him cold, able to gauge exactly when to impede the flow of paternal instructions.

"She shouldn't be kept waiting."

"Oh, of course not." Theo looked up, his palms lifted upwards, as if addressing a judicial gallery. "By no means, must Madame Kinfe be kept waiting."

"What does that mean?"

"Besides, I thought Lady Knobler was your key contact at the gallery, for all the routine business decisions."

"She is. I've told you that, but still, what's considered routine is a matter of circumstances, which can change. She controls what happens there on a day to day basis; all that's already been settled."

His son glared at him, as if rendered speechless by his father's distortion of long established truths. Isaiah frowned as if confused by his son's incomprehensible obstinacy, and proceeded to lecture him.

"You're new to this kind of business. Natalie owns the gallery; she needs to get comfortable with you. You know, she could have me swept out of there in a heartbeat."

Theo's face expressed revulsion at the servile attitude his father affected towards the gallery owner. "So, you're admitting that she'd dismiss you, after all this time, out of caprice?"

Isaiah looked down, shaking his head, exasperated by his son's refusal to understand what has been explained to him numerous times. It was the nature of the business, based as it was on the support of wealthy patrons. The waiter came to remove their plates, leaving the bill. Isaiah placed his credit card on the table. Theo looked at it with a sour face, and then watched as his father quaffed the last drops of his wine, and turned his face away as though injured.

"Nothing is ever certain." Isaiah wished to impart a congenial note to finish the meal. "You can't depend on relations of the past."

"But your things are selling better than ever now."

"Not better than ever, on my actual paintings." Isaiah corrected him. He didn't add that his productivity had slackened rather badly.

"I'm just saying, she's not going to cut off her own nose, just to spite her face, is she?"

"There's no telling what she's liable to do. That's a different world they live in."

"Isn't that your world, too?"

"Not like it is to them. No, I paint houses, remember? Pretty pictures of cartoon characters to grace the bedroom walls of genteel brats."

"You haven't done that in a while, have you?"

"No, but I mean, I'm not in those circles, where one can casually pick out a small drawing by Manet; 'Please deliver this next week. We are planning a little soirée for the senator.' Completely different worlds—"

"Oh yes. You are not from one of those good families, like Madame Kinfe—"

"She's not from old money! It's different for her, too; she has to appeal to her social betters, and so—"

"Social betters." Theo muttered contemptuously. "Can you even hear yourself?"

"I just say it that way to make it clear."

"Why do you always take their side?"

"Whose side?"

Theo shook his head, having decided beforehand to avoid just this kind of exchange, struggling against himself. "I just don't understand all the fuss. If these people are honorable—"

"Honorable?" Isaiah shook his head. What would Marx make of such a statement, especially in this context? The richness of it all made him speechless, for a moment. "Theo, there's no honor in business, not in the selling game. I don't care if it's art, or industrial motors, or anything else. It's about the exchange of money for things and there must be a profit." He slapped the table in his exasperation.

"Oh sure, I don't know anything about that, working at an insurance company. I only pick through their financial entrails every day to ascertain the current price of shedding blood unlawfully."

"You know what I mean."

"Dad, just tell me the truth."

"That's what I'm trying to do, make it all clear to you. I know it sounds crass, but you can't change society."

Theo leaned back, a strange, ominous calm descending upon him. This dramatic change alarmed his father. "I want to know something."

"Okay, fine. Just ask me then, what?"

"Did you ever cheat on Mom?"

Isaiah fell back as though he had been shoved by an inexorable force. His mouth came open but no words came out.

"It's a pretty simple question. Yes or no?"

"Those were different times."

"Yeah." His voice was now strident. "You've told me plenty of times how different those days were, except for when you're lecturing me how things don't really change that much, over time." He folded his arms and stared at his father.

"Theo, that's not any of your business."

"Why isn't it?"

"It just isn't. You should know that."

"I should know a lot of things about not needing to know certain things, according to you, when anything has to do with the family."

"That's not fair. It's just that I—"

"Refuse to tell me anything about those days."

"No I don't. What are you saying?"

"Nothing." He had been thinking lately that his entire childhood was lost to him. His parents had divorced before he began kindergarten. He had only indistinct impressions, and a crazy movie reel, composed of contorted faces and angry speeches. For a long while they had reproached each other through him, the innocent, ignorant arbiter! Now he lived in a netherworld, hearing mournful cries passing across generations. In his worst moments he felt threatened by the baleful fates, whom he had provoked by his own dishonor.

He wanted to hear some fragment of the truth that might let him begin to resolve things and settle the turmoil of his soul. He could not accept this was also to be *his* lot. He could not avoid feeling that much of his anger was really about his own divorce. It made him feel like a failure. His father's presence often disturbed these awful memories; causing him to dredge up wrongs that bore the mark of a shared lineage.

"I guess now I'm thinking like you."

"What?" Isaiah was utterly disconcerted.

"The Meriwether men don't stay married, and they don't talk about it, right?"

Isaiah shook his head. They both fumed in silence a moment, looking about in agitation. Isaiah always grew even more exasperated during these spats when reflecting upon the fact that Theo was handsome, just like his paternal grandfather. And now he was reaching that treacherous milestone, nearing forty, when the existential adjusters of whole life policies examine the books, enforcing liquidation of unworthy investments.

"What?" Isaiah swung around; he had been looking out the window at a young couple traipsing along so blithely on that early, blind path of untested happiness.

"I said, are you ready?" Theo demanded. His face was a glowering, prehistoric head carving. Without looking at one another they exchanged perfunctory salutations, tinged with flecks of weak conciliation. Theo rushed out, cursing the fact he would be late, and blaming his father.

Isaiah sat at the table nonplussed. Why would he talk of his own mother that way? What was the point? He could not even begin to understand what his life had been about in those days.

Upon leaving the restaurant Isaiah paused to glance at a painting of his, hanging beside the door. It depicted a common street scene in ancient Pompeii; in the background a wisp of black smoke is rising from Mount Vesuvius. That had been a flush period of time for him. The sales were ringing a beautiful chime in his ears. The unbidden voices of personal devils asked, "But do you consider yourself a real artist?"

In his old, old crowd, the earliest, it was customary to scorn monetary success. He had learned to keep his corrupt joy to himself. He still regretted that his success came after the wife left and became a banker. She would have known how to celebrate his success — was that fair to say, or just more (now putrid) spite?

He walked to Timothy's apartment building. It had an identical twin across a small courtyard, where black tenants lived. In Timothy's block there were only white folks. Isaiah mused upon this ironic relic of the city's deplorable history of racial separatism. In this instance it was not by decree, but only a residue of detestable cultural norms.

Isaiah encountered Mary, the ground floor woman outside the building's front door. She was smoking with great intensity. Isaiah heard piercing trills coming from her new baby inside. She stared at him for one second, and then looked away, her eyes flashing defiantly. He had meant to address her, but shrank before her hostile manner.

To his eye she was resplendent as a type; the healthy, attractive, uncouth, defiant, sexually adept young woman. She had no social status, except that of her ego's rough projection. Her bleached hair was a wild, tangled, erotic mass, befitting the look of a wicked screen goddess. She was barefoot, wearing cut-off jeans and a tight buttoned blouse. Her tight clothes sculpted sensual forms that captivated his and nearly every other passing eye.

Isaiah blushed as he strode to clamber up the stairs. On the landing he accosted a mature, slender lady dressed in casual, tasteful attire. She was just coming out of her apartment. They were both startled. Isaiah noticed the acrid odor of burning cannabis, and the sounds of the Yes album, *Close to the Edge,* coming from O'Rourke's domicile.

"Medicinal." He found himself explaining. The woman smiled in a sardonic fashion. Her hair was put into a stylish arrangement, and shone with rich brown hues. Her demure features expressed self-assurance, as her lucid brown eyes sparkled with wry amusement.

"Oh, I forgot something." He said to the woman, and retreated down the stairs.

He jogged across Delmar and made his way around to the rear of the building, next to the Tivoli theater, and climbed the iron stairway leading to his studio. Once in his gloomy space, he felt strangely at home. He moped around, scolding himself for being so purposeless. He rummaged through old sketchbooks, dismayed by the accretion of so much damning evidence of all that he'd left undone. While going through boxes buried in one remote corner he was astonished to find an object stolen during one of his teen pranks.

He shook his head, as if in a stupor, while hefting the finely carved figure of an infant. It was still holding up his tiny hands, as if beseeching him to confess his sins! He had completely forgotten he had stolen this famous baby out of a crèche. It was found on the front lawn of a church on Florissant Road. He placed the thing back in the box where it had lain on a nesting of rags for so long. He brushed his hands together vigorously.

He turned to other boxes, unpacking numerous photo albums. It occurred to him he might show these to Raphael. He had once used his Leica camera to document his life. He had enjoyed using a light meter, and framing every shot, and then having to wait for the film to be developed, and inspecting the prints, selecting which ones he would have enlarged, to serve as templates for oil paintings.

Theo had recently advised him to consider finishing some of his past efforts, to sell the prints, or even try selling them as they were, since 'none would be the wiser.' That comment stung; nonetheless, Theo was learning something about selling prints, if nothing else, and these were selling briskly on their website, which he had not visited in some weeks. He thought of doing so now, but decided against it. He had assured Theo that he trusted him to maintain the site. It wasn't entirely true, however, and every time he looked at it he became critical about various aspects.

He toasted his successes with himself after decanting wine from a bottle he took from the rack he kept in his studio. He settled into his one comfortable chair. He stared up through the skylight. He looked about him, surveying this dwelling where he had settled at the bottom of things. His was a mind let loose now, able to swim in a sort of galactic pool of clean and dusty light.

After savoring his glass of wine he rose to position his large sketch of the dying St. Louis in front of his chair. He adjusted one of his numerous lighting fixtures to illuminate the portrait. The piece left him feeling dejected. It had no meaning for him. He could see nothing of value in any part of its design. He put the work back, out of the way, so he could relax once more in his chair, with another sanguinary offering from the ageless vine. He gradually drifted into a state suggesting something like infinite repose.

Deciding to have no more wine, and certain he could not work, he made firm resolutions. He would resurrect his original methods, using photography to discover workable images. He had been unstoppable in those days, making those long treks into remote places, each day becoming a memorable sojourn, bravely bringing away the natural loot he had discovered and folded into the clutches of his own devices.

What was the difference now, merely age? He missed the discipline that film had imposed on his routines. The advantages of digital processing were immense, and yet, the infinite possibilities were also daunting, not to mention sacrilegious to his first principles. Ah, those never last very long, do they? Well, when in Rome, circa Nero. He would purchase a better color printer. The only question, where to start this renaissance? Not with the Loop. Well, no matter, he could always plot his course, and he would do that later; for now, it was good to turn towards action. Yes, that was the very thing, and this newfound resolve called for more wine!

7

One day, while driving to the bank to deposit checks, Isaiah opted to take a detour through a labyrinth of backstreets. He wanted to survey the many riotous gardens sprawling across front lawns. To see all that superfluous abundance blooming; showing what happens when the will exerts itself to achieve some good, and unprofitable end. A sort of blessing for every passing soul . . .

After gawking for a short while, he maneuvered onto a larger thoroughfare, where he noticed a ragged line of wild chicory plants. These had sprouted from the narrow seam between the curb and the sidewalk; sturdy natives unafraid of harsh conditions, ever living in open defiance of public mowers. He had once done a series of these urban stalwarts, thriving in the overgrown abandoned plots seen in the most blighted areas of the city. *What had he ever been trying to say?*

He began observing the people who were going about on foot; taking note of every person's gait, posture, garb, and individual gestures. He drove through Forest Park, listening to music, observing the larger crowds induced by the closing of so many venues. He then proceeded to his studio and for some reason was flooded with memories of being a political cartoonist for *Muddy Currents*.

That first day Mr. Hruuck had welcomed him into his office, taking an immediate interest, having heard 'good things' about his work. They agreed he should use an alias, to avoid diluting his credence as a serious painter. That didn't work; the simplicity of the stripling! Hruuck wisely believed in keeping each persona separate as a means of lowering his costs, thus increasing the surplus value he might pocket.

Isaiah began drawing the Bête Noire as a caricature, even though the outlandish creature transcended this genre altogether. He was more preposterous than norms allowed any publican to be while serving in any official capacity. The persona might have been drafted by the incisive pen of Charles Dickens, had he only known of this later, rank grafting of celebrity populism onto TV capitalism.

Soon Isaiah was thinking of all the presidents he had drawn in a humorous vein. He had taken liberties, having very little actual knowledge of the real persons behind each public mask. He pondered the fact that the citizens hardly ever know anything about these people, nothing close to the complete truth, until long afterwards. Once they are given back to the earth the scholars start digging into the records; unseemly facts are uncovered only after society has moved on, and no one really cares anymore.

He began to sketch Jack Kennedy, sprawled out at the White House swimming pool. Naked women are lolling on the deck. His lackeys wear togas. He decides to draw LBJ seated on the toilet; a trembling subordinate is handing him a secret communique. It spells out the details of an incident that requires his attention, something that occurred at a tiny village known as My Lai. He had done a cartoon once called *Our Lies*.

He now depicts Richard Nixon with eight limbs, entangled in a web, like a demented spider who has lost the use of his spinning faculties. He portrays Gerald Ford as an obsequious footman, holding open the door of 'The Beast.' He could not bring himself to satirize Jimmy Carter. He believed he was the last man to leave the office and live with his dignity intact; unlike the sad lackeys of power, or the bold climbers, who sought gross material gains and high status. More than ever now they seek that meretricious, purifying flame of celebrity, that bestows a delusory chance at the best possible lifestyle to be found anywhere on this earth, if you can stomach the fare.

Isaiah began moving about, stewing in his resentments. He stumbled over the box containing the crèche baby, and shoved it aside in frustration. He sat down to brood more intently. When had he lost his interest in politics? Even when he was making cartoons for *Muddy Currents*, there seemed to be no purpose to any of it. The metabolism of government lives on a stomach lined with the bacteria of secrecy, which breeds pathological deception. Who wants to rake through what comes out of those sickly bodies? Marx had mocked his blasé attitude in those early years.

"History depicted in cartoons. I've never understood that sort of glib rendering. "

"I do it for the money, and the practice. I don't really care."

"That's no way to do anything, is it? Wait, practice, for what?"

He had no idea. In truth, however, it was a sort of noble profession, used by the best talents for telling truths about the powerful. He had never cared to stay abreast of all those dismal affairs. His barbs were often stolen property. To be really good, required an awful lot of topical reading, and he never wanted to spend his time covering the histrionic machinations of all those sordid actors.

He now believed voters act as they do, when making choices in the political arena, because they are essentially, in that role, insensate pack animals. Wolves do not convene grand juries every time they murder one of their own. And now the people were becoming like good Romans, and just turning down one's thumb was not enough to sate their thwarted lusts. They were having their own blood sports out in the streets.

It was curious to reflect that the techniques used in caricature were also relevant in his portraits. One has to flatter, and cajole, *and* be true to life, lest the subject feels deceived, hurt, or scorned. The people must not say, 'That's not him!' It might be okay, if they marvel, 'That looks better than him!'

Later in the day Isaiah was at home reading a book when Raphe arrived at his apartment. He sees the open sketchbook and begins perusing the images.

"What is this?"

"I used to do political cartoons."

"Can I get copies of those to look at?"

"Sure. It's not very interesting."

"It would be good context for the piece."

Isaiah made a grating sound, not wanting to entertain the idea of Raphe talking to Hruuck about him as he was in those days. They settled down in the living room.

Raphe pulled a pad of paper from his satchel. He began interrogating Isaiah, striving to get a chronology fixed in his notes. After several hours of this Isaiah became distressed.

"We're only discussing my progress through time."

"Yeah? I need to get the chronology down first. I could use a break..."

"Let's have a beer."

They listened to music in the afternoon light. Raphe was looking through photo albums.

"Do you still get together on a regular basis, with that Gang of '73 crowd?" Raphe asked.

"Not really. I mean, a little, but not like the old days. And nothing at all since the start of the pandemic."

"Yeah, it's really strange now."

"In effect, it's just me and Marx."

"The Marx Brothers."

"Yeah." Raphe was the only one who had ever called them that, back when he was trying to become a regular member.

"Molly said you were a provincial native of the Loop."

Isaiah looked at him, his eyes narrowing, taking a good look at Raphe's sardonic smile.

"Tell me again, how did you meet Molly?"

"Paul Hereford introduced me to her. She and Jacob used to come out to see him, that year he moved back to Chouteauville—"

"Oh yeah. I forgot." He rose from his seat and asked over his shoulder, "Do you want another one?"

"Sure." Raphe picked up a large art book from a stack of the same lying on a table.

They both resumed drinking and listening to music; both flipping through large glossy biographies of famous dead painters.

"Let me show you something," Isaiah said. He went to his workroom and brought forth several of his photo albums. Many of the pictures were annotated, providing locations, dates, and names. Raphe began perusing the contents of these albums quite avidly.

"Wow. You recorded a lot of information here. It's like I'm scraping through layers of time."

"It seemed like a good idea, for some reason, to record those details."

"These are good scrapbooks. This will help a lot."

Raphe was suddenly bent over the table, staring at something very intently, as if he had been transported to another realm.

"What are you looking at there?"

"What?" He looked up as if coming awake. He was pale. "Oh nothing. Those old scenes, they really bring me back to that time. We're the same age . . ."

"I know. So, you and Paul Hereford were good friends, when you were growing up?"

"Yes, we both grew up in Chouteauville. He was over at my house all the time. We had the Mississippi river right outside. We used to roam up and down that river for days on end."

"I never met him, but he was good friends with my uncle Isaac, back when he was hanging out with Molly. And, how do you know Dilsey?"

"Her mom moved next door to Paul, right after he moved back to Chouteauville, and built his river home. She was just a girl at the time. You could not help being drawn to her open curiosity about everything. She thought we were quite interesting. Ha! She was keen to learn about the world, and I guess we helped her a little, there. Who knows?"

"She's become a very interesting woman."

"I should have done a better job of presenting her in *The Vampires of Eden*; that book we put together about Paul's last year. Have you ever seen that book?"

"No."

"I can get you a copy, if you want."

"Sure, do that."

Isaiah excused himself to go to the bathroom; upon returning he found Raphael was standing, glancing at the clock on the wall.

"I have to go. I just remembered something I have to do. So, this was pretty helpful." Raphael seemed somewhat agitated. Isaiah noticed that he had arranged all the photo albums in a neat stack on the table. He had hoped he might ask to borrow these for his research.

"We can talk later." Isaiah said, sensing that Raphe was bolting for some reason.

"Yeah, sure." Raphael paused at the door, as if to say something more, but then proceeded to make a hasty exit.

"We'll talk later, then." Isaiah called after him.

"Okay." He did not look back.

Isaiah was puzzled by this abrupt departure, fearing it betrayed the fact Raphael was losing interest in writing the article.

It was peculiar how they danced around the topic of Molly; as if both were chary of saying too much about her. It occurred to him that Raphael might well be offering his services only because she had petitioned him, out of some desire to help him, or maybe both of them? This would explain his strange behavior just now. In a spiteful reaction Isaiah said to himself, I don't need any favors. He should tell him he was no longer interested in this dumb magazine article. It would probably attract more ridicule. He mopped his face with one hand as if trying in vain to rub away his embarrassment.

8

A golden afternoon, greatly enriched by the heraldry of autumn's stirring, even blazing, unsettled dust. In this timeless frame of mind, accompanied by choral strains of remembrance, the world is nicely smoothed out in pastels. One feels a reverence for a sublime purpose that promises rewards are surely yet to come.

Isaiah leans over his drafting table, staring out at the white oaks, observing the wonderful delicacy of shading on the branches. He considers how useless a camera can be in capturing these subtleties. Only the naked eye senses the infinite dynamism inherent in natural light.

"My old friend," he whispers to himself; "the deathless photon . . ."

He had moments ago read the passage in *Dombey and Son*, concerning Florence, which states, "She welcomed back the evening silence as an old friend, but it came now with an altered face, and looked more kindly on her." He wondered if Simon and Garfunkel had lifted that verbiage for their original song, "The Sound of Silence." The belated success of that song (after being remixed) put them back together, launching their stalled career into the ether. He played the album *Wednesday Morning, 3 A.M.* on his stereo; the oddly religious tenor resonated with his mood.

He poured some wine and took up a sketchpad. On a whim he worked on an aerial dogfight, between a Fokker and the Nieuport once flown by his maternal grandfather. That gallant fellow had served in the Lafayette Escadrille. Isaiah descended into the basement, where he had a storage locker, and spent half an hour disturbing the dust under the singular, glaring harshness of a bare bulb. He feared he had discarded the book, and then he found it, the chronicle recording the exploits of his maternal grandfather's combat unit.

Back in his living room he flipped through the pages, hovering over the illustrations that had once fired his boyish imagination. His grandfather had crashed after getting his fifth victory, after making an unauthorized maneuver over his own airfield. He returned to the States badly injured, with medals and ribbons, and seemed to recover gloriously. The family business was the law, however, and in 1922 he entered this field where glory had to be won in paper trials of dubious honor.

His sense of values, and his own purpose among these, had gotten misplaced overseas. The doctors were perplexed by the chronic condition of his unseen wounds. He began suffering relapses while at work, causing embarrassment to clients and his colleagues. The family exerted considerable influence and he became a pitiful man of leisure, receiving disability payments. The wife was none too happy about this turn of events; henceforth, she ruled the household, as he played a more ceremonial role. He was popular in local taverns and came to know everything about the value of local properties, which information he passed on to his wife, who became a local power broker in the real estate game.

When Isaiah first came to know his Grampa, he was pursuing the ghosts of his war in countless history books. He was the epitome of the war hero to his grandson; whom he made breathless with fantastic tales of aerial combat. He never spoke to the boy of those wretches who had perished in the trenches, or tried to explain his own confusion as to why all that carnage had been necessary.

It was the height of chivalry how the grounded pilot shared his books with the boy. And the way he described the combat missions he had flown above the waste lands. Isaiah could still see the man's hands twisting and turning in the air as he enacted scenes of his last proud moments. Martha Cook, his grandmother, would interrupt these outdoor reviews to chastise him for wasting his time with such plain nonsense. He would be chased inside, to do his homework.

She was forever looking askance at anything that kept one from 'bearing up,' and looking to the future. His interest in art was considered to be a sign of emotional weakness, which she blamed on his paternal lineage. In her catechism, the godly strove to do good works, which meant, first of all, achieving high social status, and then, becoming patrons to others. The lesser souls remained comfortably beneath you, and were forever grateful to have a place in the shadows.

To her spouse, and the romantic boy, this woman was a visitation of death upon romantic notions. She became a dragon, a creature not to be trifled with, as she scorched his ideas about having fun, in countless ways. As often as he could, he escaped to the yard where romance made light of reason, building castles from the fleece torn out of the clouds in little handfuls.

He recalled the time she slapped him hard for saying something derogatory about her forbears, who had been local slaveholders. Her people were commemorated in local histories as great, bourgeois pilgrims in the region. She had explained to him that those slaves 'were treated like family.' He still felt that horrible sting. He was aggrieved to find how much he still smarted from that blow. It had caught him completely unawares. But to feel that way now, after so much time, when the real injury had nothing to do with him?

It was difficult to think about his mother. He could not imagine her childhood in that home. She sent word that she was too sick herself to return for her mother's funeral. Isaiah had gone to St. Margaret's for the mass, said to honor the noble dragon. After the service he lingered in the old house, visiting the yard like it was the venue of an ancient battle; feeling estranged from everything. It was then that his uncle introduced him to Molly, who later married Jacob Gates.

He had almost become good friends with Molly and Jacob. And at first, Edith was surprisingly amenable to associating with 'that north county crowd'; probably because she wouldn't encounter anyone she knew up there. He remembered how Marx regarded Edith as a stock figure, drawn out of his Marxist constructs. In like manner, she condescended to him as a rather shabby academic, who had earned no laurels in his field, and lacked all cultural polish. In her eyes he wore the costume of an intellectual jester. It struck Isaiah now that each person used a stereotype to belittle the other one, and that he must have appeared in a like manner as the precious faux *artiste* in the eyes of many.

Feeling restless, he called Timothy to see if he wanted to go out for a hearty meal someplace, with outdoor seating and a hearty batch of beers on tap.

Marx answered his landline in a voice that sounded guarded.

"Want to grab dinner? My treat!" Isaiah exclaimed.

"Well," Timothy sounded uncomfortable. There was music playing in his apartment ("Home Again"); from the album *Tapestry*, by Carole King.

"Is that your album playing?"

"No."

"Is that the radio?"

"No."

He could hear a voice in the background addressing his friend.

"Tim, is somebody there with you?"

"Yes, Patricia. It's her album, we just bought it today."

"Who?"

"My neighbor, Patricia Skuffles."

"Oh." He thought of teasing his friend, posing ironic questions, alluding to past adventures no longer relevant. Nothing seemed appropriate any longer. Isaiah waited a moment, unsure of himself.

"Well, we were just heading out."

"Oh, okay." He thought of trying to insinuate himself into whatever they were setting out to do; and suppressed the urge, as the silence on the other end was answer enough to his untendered plea.

"Well, I'll catch you later, then." Timothy's voice rang out sharply in a cheerful cadence. The inflection carried a subtle merriment that harkened to times *long* past.

"Sure." Isaiah's voice fell flat; the line had gone dead.

IT WAS PERSEPHONE, one of the first drawings I sold, that made me feel I had accomplished something pretty damn good. I was proud of the simple elegance of the piece. I had used as my model the statue by Raffaello Romanelli, which still resides at the Botanical Gardens. A young girl, just coming of age, is to one side of the statue, seen in profile, raptly staring up at this austere lady of the underworld. Can that be right, I no longer have prints of this one, to make available for sale?

At any rate, I had read an interesting work about Henry Shaw, the merchant who retired young, very rich, to embark on a life of pleasure and cultural refinement. The suave bachelor would stroll about his garden, drawing schools of fashionable young women to come forth to see themselves in his shining armor. In time there was a great scandal. He was sued for breach of promise; I think his suit held up pretty well. For some reason, much later, this got me sauntering about these same grounds, attracting no attention whatsoever. I was free to steal images, to compensate for my poverty . . .

After that picture sold I was keen to do another one. In this piece she was taken off her pedestal, and depicted crouching on the ground, on one knee. She has just come back from the Abyss. She is looking upwards, as if to question the empty sky. One hand instinctively plucks at the tender shoots newly risen from the soil; while her other hand reveals a fist unfurling and held out, as if to offer, or to accept, something precious.

All around her the modern day (now past) is progressing as usual. Many people are moving around her in that somnolence born of excessive freedom and leisure. They are passing the time in the expected way, doing the expected things; ridding themselves of even more tedious hours. They are sharing gossip, pushing baby carriages, enjoying this genteel masquerade of rude Nature. Most of the visitors remain oblivious of this goddess squatting in plain sight.

Although, some of the guests have noticed her, and they are concerned. She is not quite right. Most of the visitors instinctively recoil and move further away. A few try offering the poor woman assistance; wanting it to be noticed they are doing so. Several are clearly afraid; the creature is very possibly deranged. Is she homeless? She might be an escapee from the asylum. What kind of costume is she is wearing? She can't possibly work here. Perfect strangers are whispering to one another, questioning the laxity of management. You cannot tolerate this sort of thing; it's a clear betrayal of the public trust . . .

In the background one can see her fountain structure, where she is supposed to be standing as a static fixture, exhibiting herself for the customers. One is supposed to imagine she will soon climb back up and take her usual station. She will hold out her cups to pour water for the stream of visitors who have no use for her symbolism. This work is already dated. There are no cell phones; that device would have determined the postures of most of these bystanders today. I should see about getting prints for the original work . . .

There was a moment, I was lying all alone, on the ground at her feet; next to her little dogs. A good chapter for a portrait of the artist as a young fool, who then wanted to steal the statue! How can I confess that to anyone without losing face? Only Stephen knew of this plot, which he dismissed out of hand, as being just more of my clowning. In the middle of the night he deserted me. Not before we had climbed over the fence, under a full moon, to approach her, pouring our wild spirits at her feet. We sat on the ground and talked of life, society, the future, scoffing at much, knowing nothing . . .

By then, Stephen and Deborah were inseparable; although they were preparing to go their separate ways. I probably burbled about Art as he confessed he was afraid he might be making the biggest mistake of his life. To part from her then, he said, would have consequences neither could possibly foresee. We queried the quiet goddess to reveal our troubles to ourselves. Stephen had smiled at my outlandish schemes.

I'm sure I fully intended to make off with Raffaello's girl. I justified it by saying it was to be a grandiose prank perpetrated against the desecration of art, or something like that; maybe it was a satiric jab at an entire school, possibly. Who was that young man, willing to bring harm to an innocent piece of art, and thereby disgrace to himself?

He absolved himself in advance by intimating that somehow the stolen prize would be left somewhere obvious, so as to be easily found, and safely recovered. That was the challenge of the prank, to find the incongruous, ironic setting where it might be found, at a later date, and promptly turned over to the rightful authorities. One could never be sure the usual Vandals would not claim, and defile, the prize instead. I pondered long on the problem, in theory. There was no practical solution.

In the morning I was escorted off the grounds. Because of his youth that person felt rather splendid; he had avoided something very dire that day. He had succeeded in escaping from something treacherous working inside himself. He had walked home feeling weary beyond his years. Today I have to believe there was no way I would have attempted such a stupid act. And I never could have done it alone, and, as Marx quipped, the best clowns always work alone . . .

While speaking of my statue fetish, I should mention another incident regarding the horseman on Art Hill. It was an adventure we executed quite well. It was one of those narcotic spring nights. The velvety atmosphere was a sable cloak draped over my manic figure. I had planned this exploit with accomplices. Our work was to be visible on Sunday to the local golfers who were making the rounds on the public course. It was the day of the final round of the Masters Tournament. Stephen and Deborah were very much involved.

A week earlier we started our limited partnership, to design a jacket for the exiled king. We measured and cut and sewed a replica of the green sport coat, which is presented to the winner of the prestigious golf tournament. It was my noble task to drape and staple the ingenious garment onto the body of Louis, who obliged us by holding his sword up like a putter. Deborah borrowed the truck, the ladder was taken from Stephen's home, and I scaled the edifice to present and place the gown upon his majesty. It went off just as planned.

That Sunday we took our seats on the hill, waiting for the golfers to come and see our handiwork as they trooped along the fairway, which then passed in front of the monument. Many players noticed, gaped, and then pointed and laughed. We sat at the top of the hill and sipped wine out of paper cups, convulsed in our revelry. I was disappointed that a lot of the people thought it had been done on purpose. Well, it had been, Deborah said, laughing at me. You know what I mean, I replied. Stephen laughed at me too. I took photographs of them with my Leica, in those last days of my being their court jester . . .

It is sorrowful to look at these images now, when I am feeling a certain way about things; well, nearly all things anymore. It is one thing to blame the fates for those times you were blown off course, by some accident, quite another to see plainly you never seemed to have the faculties to make for yourself the life you really wanted. And far worse, to continue in the belief you actually did possess all that was required, in your own way, but didn't have the sense to know what you wanted. It raises questions regarding one's inner fitness. Why must the famously corrupt recorders of memory insist on keeping clean books on just these matters?

9

The summer's foliage was mottled, blotted, smutted, and frayed badly along the edges; all that mass of breathing tissue was under duress. One sensed enormous, inexorable cycles, tending towards distant ends, that required many more aeons of fiery, apocalyptic work had to be done. Our early industrial universe, in all that tenuous forging of time, space, and matter, was just getting started. The clashing of galactic wheels has hardly begun to grind out the last stitch of reality. Thank god, intimations of this savage fertility perturb just a little bit the necessitous, reliable hypnosis of any one particular species of consciousness.

Isaiah was having visions of vast fields of staple crops swaying under a harvest moon. He slumps over his drafting table, staring out at his cloister of oaks, observing a moment of silence. He tries to register the delicate changes wrought by the fading light. He leafs through one of his art books, and starts an idle sketch. It is no good.

He puts on his standard walking outfit and proceeds towards the Loop; persisting despite many minor aches and pains. Arriving at the point where the lions are stationed atop their concrete posts, marking the entrance, he turns back due to his worrisome fatigue.

Once he is at home again he tells himself everything is perfectly fine. He *is* happy. He has his work; something of worth. He need not worry about other deficiencies. So he has gotten old. There is no need to feel despondent. He is satisfied with his residence, which ought to be a place of rest; his only productive life is at the studio. It was no comfort that he had to administer these regular doses of reassurance.

He opens a Norton Critical Edition of *Hard Times*. The stiff pages, first printed in 1966, are discolored, and none are effaced by his own hand. It is a charm from his beginnings; his memory is sealed in the binding of these very pages. The book cost him fifteen cents, when it was purchased at the annual book fair, held under a tent outside Famous-Barr in Clayton. The desiccate little volume was wildly evocative of that vernal day. He could see again all those native blooms growing among the many concrete pillars supporting an overpass. He could almost hear the dull roar of traffic that was irrelevant to his happiness.

There had been a light spatter of rain, the perfumes of local flora, and that wild yeast of young love fermenting inside his taut, eager body. Gabriella was coming to meet him there, and was due any moment. The lusty wind made the loose canvas shudder in lusty responses, and the poles creaked as if to protest the season's inordinate strain. He remembered that precise moment, when he had picked up this volume, and actually shivered in anticipation of being with her again.

He reads the chapter entitled, "Rachael," entering the surreal dream of Stephen, the forlorn weaver shackled to a miserable, drunken wife. In his dream he faces a vast crowd, and "they all abhorred him." Later in the text he is referred to as "the stranger in the land," who meets not a friendly face anywhere. His futile longing is for the sympathetic woman of virtue he has known so long, and cannot have now, because of his ruinous marriage contract.

The portrayal of this character subsumes all that we modern moderns know of existential despair; that dead null space that deforms our conceptions of what we know. One discovers here an antecedent of *The Stranger*, written by Camus; something very old and very new is coiled up in this sticky, fecund mass. The antihero of our day is couched here in utero. You can choose to abort such doubts in healthy living, but they germinate nonetheless, especially when you are not being careful. You suddenly find the universe crouching over you, as a feral mother, expecting more than you can even comprehend.

For our Victorian Teacher God is hardly more than a remote symbol, standing for supreme justice, and thus his parables pertain to the morals of society, as it exists here. And humanity is a slow moving beast. The dream, as given, fixes for the hero his terrible dilemma. To live, he must have hope; to have hope, he must believe in something, even if it is not himself. He must strive against himself to keep from degradation. Isaiah imbibes a fresh draught, experiencing the ineffable charm of a good fable. The voice that intones the sad verities of life. And here, such a voice; so trenchant, so true!

He passes through a range of emotions as he reads; "The dreams of childhood—its airy fables; its graceful, beautiful, humane, impossible adornments of the world beyond: so good to be believed in once, so good to be remembered when outgrown . . ." That time of treasures, which are stored up by some genetic clairvoyance to last for a lifetime, *if* the childhood was not atrophied by insufficient means, nor maimed by poor cultivation.

He reads with commiseration how Sissy whispers, with tremulous breath, the word "clown," when speaking of her father's profession. He has relinquished his hold on her, for her own good. She has come to the house where they teach only hard facts. Isaiah is touched more profoundly than he knows, as he ponders things as they were, and are, fearing what will come.

He reads out loud a part from when the girl is taking leave of her circus folk, the artists, entertainers, all the low traffickers in senseless fun: "Goodbye, Cecilia!" "Goodbye Sissy!" "God bless you dear!" Edith would mutter that line, in wicked glee, to signal her mild contempt for certain friends, who were hard to take, being overly officious, or déclassé, in some fashion. He could hardly tell what the problem was, most of the time, and she never brought him around to see her really close friends, so that he might distinguish such matters for himself.

One string of pearls rose to mind; a gift from her father, the imperious Albert, who brought gifts back from his foreign junkets. A reminder of how things happened among the right people. He thought of how often such things had made him feel estranged from her. And then, how could he forget, that expensive designer purse. He had been shocked by the amount she had paid for it, and the other one, hardly used, which it replaced.

He had painted his response, *The Dumpster Angels*. The view of the dumpster is from the ground level. Perched on the lip are several feral kittens. On the ground, among drifts of refuse, sits the purse. In the background, barely visible, lying to to one side of the scene, rests a prone man, half buried in garbage. The picture achieved some success for him. The kittens got all the attention, as he had imagined they would, although one critic noticed something more. He exclaimed, "Very delightful commentary on the unexpected beauty of wild things found out of the way, transcending their shabby environment." He had met this critic, at a café in the Loop.

"I really felt very good about it, I really did!" Isaiah let himself feed off the critic's lucrative enthusiasm. There was a shrill note, as if he were explaining his support of the capitalistic system, that divine aegis which protects the artist and the securities analyst, quite alike, for their worthy labors. They were two enchained creatures, acting parts in a system of mutual exchange.

"What about the bum?" He had asked, trying to cover up his own complicity.

"What bum?" The critic replied, with a mocking smile; looking around, not sure of meeting there, too far from the safest sections of the Loop.

"The bum life of the abandoned kittens. So bleak, and full of wonders."

"That's what I wrote about!"

"It was a beautiful review, it really was."

"Natalie says she's in my debt." He smiled like a child, overcome by doting adulation.

"I have no doubt." Neither of them had ever braved the New York scene; why bother?

Another critic (a rival at *Muddy Currents*) alleged the piece was a pastiche of shticky, schlocky sentimentality. He claimed the dead, or sleeping bum, was a perfect symbol of incongruous, aesthetic vulgarity. He was a student of the dead Ruskin; redux and newly laid out in an open casket.

Later in the afternoon Theo dropped by to discuss their strategy for getting more prints on the website. Isaiah had to bite his tongue, to avoid expressing a thought that they were not selling labels to paste on cans of soup. He was unable to focus as Theo made his case for creating a new format for the site. Growing tired of being ignored, Theo flung out his arms, tromped around, pausing for breath, demanding to be heard.

"We're selling more prints on line—" The son bore down.

"That's good, that's really good. But we have to be careful with the costs."

"But what I'm telling you is, we could be doing more volume, at higher profit margins. We're paying the Gallery too much in commissions. And you no longer need their imprimatur. I could show you a spreadsheet; we should be making a lot more—"

"What? No, you haven't said anything to Missy about this, have you?"

"No." Theo appeared firm, determined. "I did talk to Mrs. Kinfe, I wanted to show her the—"

"Oh Theo. You didn't bring this matter up with her, did you?" The father's face expressed exquisite horror; it made the son's skin crawl. The mere prospect of the Lady Kinfe being accosted, over something so trifling as the principle of fair economic value, this put fear and trembling into his father.

"I was in the Gallery trying to discuss my ideas with that damned ice queen, Knobler, and then Kinfe came in, and *she* invited me up into that little office of hers."

"You just dropped in? You shouldn't do that; you have to be extremely careful with her." Isaiah was worried; his hands locked together and then began wrestling with one another. "I can't afford to have you antagonizing . . ." Isaiah stopped talking, seeing the mortification on Theo's face.

"Oh, I know all about that, Dad." His voice rang with disgust. The last word reverberated with the ghostly echoes of a child's anger directed at parental tyranny. "She wasn't returning my calls. What was I supposed to do?"

"You should have come to me."

"Always the same answer; not to do anything. To come to you, to have you do it instead of me. I mean . . ." He looked down, and away, and around, and shook his head. His countenance shouted his certitude any further attempts to make the old man see reason, from his perspective, were futile.

"I don't want to discourage you."

"No, of course not." He gave a short, derisive laugh.

"We just have to make sure she knows everything you are doing."

"That's why I'm here, why we're talking."

"I know, I just—"

I know what you just, you just don't trust me."

"It's not that, come on." Isaiah was frustrated, unable to explain the delicate tumblers safeguarding the gallery's prestige. "I'm just trying to help you to understand the risks involved—"

Theo stood up, in preparation to leave.

"We haven't decided on anything. Have we?"

"You want me to bring you the proofs on the last batch we've done, and then you'll decide on a price."

"I want to talk to Natalie once we have all our materials ready. We need to show her what we intend to do."

"Wouldn't we go to Missy first?"

"No, no. I need to see what Natalie is thinking about all of this; make sure she's okay with how things are going with our website."

"Yes, our website. You mean with me getting involved. Like I'm involved in anything that matters."

"Don't say that."

"It doesn't matter."

"I want to hear your input on this."

"No you don't"

"Theo, come on." He made a feeble gesture of reaching out. "Sit down, why don't you."

"I have to go. I have to pick up Anne."

"Is something the matter with her?" It was aggravating to be reminded again that he hardly ever got the chance to see his granddaughters.

"No." Theo spoke brusquely. Isaiah was an exile from his son's personal life, and his resentment was adulterated with his own culpability. Once more, in his mind, he stood accused of paternal malfeasance. They both turned away, in strikingly similar postures.

"Don't let these things get to you, that's all I'm saying."

"Don't worry, I'm not. I can see what you're trying to tell me. Knobler has to be appeased, with great deference, and, when I go before Lady Kinfe, I must kowtow."

"Kowtow?"

"I was just reading about how the English 'opened up China,' leading to the Opium Wars. It's good stuff. Your friend, what do you call him, Marx? He explained to me the exact, groveling ritual they expected the British officer to perform. The Englishman refused, choking on the indignity. And then the gunboats came, demanding another kind of homage. He can be really funny. He suggested some titles for me."

"You were discussing history with O'Rourke? Where have you been talking to him?"

"In the Loop, at the Feral Hog. I've seen him there a couple of times."

"Who all was there with him?"

"I don't know."

"Do you really think I'm *that* subservient to Natalie?"

"I think you do what you believe you have to do, to keep her on your side, and that you're very afraid she might abandon you. It's your living, I get that."

"Well, I do want to keep our partnership going."

"If that's what you want to call it."

Isaiah started to speak but Theo held up his hand and made for the door. The pattern of letting unfinished things go back into the simmering pot of their mutual animus was an all too familiar maneuver. Theo left Isaiah fuming over his son's obstinate nature. He had conceded that he understood why Isaiah had to be very cautious. It *was* his livelihood. What then, was his problem? The miasma of rancor, which constantly whelmed up to choke his paternal pieties, left Isaiah feeling even more solitary than normal. This was not something he used to fret about, not that much, now it was becoming an obsession.

He sat down with *Hard Times* and a glass of wine; fine instrumentalities for his mental infirmity! He reads of the character Sissy catching her mistress in a painful moment of shame. She looks at her mistress with pity on her features. The genteel woman cannot allow her servant to look at her in that way, she immediately becomes resentful, and then disdainful. She was "changed to her altogether."

He reads of the factory owner, who would rather be known as a primitive marvel, that worked his way up from the gutter, than someone who came from a good, but lowly family. He disowns his mother, who regularly tramps from afar just to catch a glimpse of him, as he comes and goes from his mansion. She hides from sight as she does so. Her love is worthy of her father; that is, the fatherly scribe, who never turned his back on the promise of salvation, which is bound up in good acts, and has nothing to do with social class. His zealous pen took especial notice of the squalid sacrifices enforced upon human souls at the altars of social hierarchy.

Isaiah lays the book aside and looks up. He studies the daylight filtering into his space through the skylight. He remembers times when he was embarrassed by his father, unable to understand why that has occurred to him. At the same time he feels again the universal smart of envy, as he once more considers all that has eluded him. The emotion he dreads most is guilt, and it is whelming up everywhere now, tainting every feeling. He sits in quiet stillness for some time, until his mind grows weary of looking into the darkness of his space. He relents, and gravitates towards his normal routines.

10

Isaiah attempted to resurrect a few rusty, malformed ideas from his scrap yard; but it only drove home the fact he had lost his passion. There was more life in his old failures than his current belabored output. And now, to add insult, his one dependable, wanton mistress, lovely Nature herself, had become merely a brutal nurse, sternly indifferent to his progress. He was missing already, ahead of its festive time, that high romance of autumn leaves.

For a long time he was convinced a serviceable portion of happiness was something you procured for yourself. The habit had come to him early, and he had taken this power for granted. Once upon a time, people said that he was lucky; meaning what? That it was not his talent, nor his work, but merely his good fortune, to have met the right people along the way?

Tired of asking himself such questions, he drove to the Loop, where he encountered Timothy and Raphael at The Feral Hog.

"What are you doing, just standing there?" Timothy demanded, noticing him after a moment. "Take a seat!"

"Hey there!" Raphael's voice rang with artificial cheer. The fine weather encouraged one to imbibe intemperately. The umbrella over the table invited one to loll in the shades of autumnal moods.

"Raphe's going to loan me some books." Marx stated significantly.

"Yeah?" Isaiah was confused by their camaraderie. "Be careful, I've known him to steal borrowed books."

"Who doesn't!" Raphe retorted. Marx joined him in a bout of laughter, tapping the table with his palm.

Raphe looked different, for some reason. Isaiah studied his face. He was bald with patches of fine, short hair on the sides of his head. His smooth, bland face was beaming. His pale, hesitant, blue eyes shone out with an unknown fervor that explained why he appeared so different. He was quite happy. His standard look was that of a morose hermit.

"He's a creature of extreme humors." Isaiah concluded.

"We've discovered that I'm woefully ignorant of the history of the fur trade," Marx intoned, "especially, as it was once conducted around these parts."

Isaiah seldom heard him admit to voids in his historical knowledge, and never so blithely. He recalled him saying once that you cannot know the topography of all the narrative streams, but you must understand the underlying factors that govern the life and motion of every stream. He tried to make a joke,

"The Mississippi river is—"

"The Chouteau brothers!" Marx interposed, his bushy face resembling a bear who has just stumbled upon a giant honeycomb. "Their alliance with the Osage tribes.

The avoidance of Spanish law, while courting the local authorities; all done to thrive in that global enterprise. It was all based on the fashions of bourgeois customs—or did the existence of the beaver demand somehow that a custom be invented to exploit same? We've been arguing over that point."

"He knew a little about the global trade in furs, but he didn't know who Madame Chouteau was!" Raphe spoke as if bearing witness at a revivalist camp meeting.

"She's more interesting than I knew." Marx confessed in humble reverence.

"She's truly a marvelous figure." Raphe gloried in his novel role as tutor. "I've just told him, he needs to read of her reaction after someone killed one of her favorite slaves. It's very telling; of her, and those times. Her fury against her townsmen is Shakespearean. I think they were lovers."

"He has several books that I *have to read*." Marx was enjoying himself; accepting his place as gracious student. It was drawing him back to a golden period in his life. "He's made a complete study of these things. I had no idea Laclede was such a glamorous character. He came up the river with a carton of choice books from the Enlightenment. Imagine, he brought Voltaire, Jean-Jacques Rousseau, and Diderot into Spanish Illinois."

"He probably spent time in the West Indies before coming to New Orleans," Raphael took up the narrative, "where he then becomes enamored of another man's wife. Then he treks into the heart of darkness and sets up shop, trading with the natives."

"I sort of knew some of that, but I don't know much about it." Isaiah spoke in a leaden voice.

"I. Thomas! You need to read the letter Laclede wrote to his woman, when he was on the river, trying to get home. He died on the way, the same year Voltaire came out of exile, returned to Paris, and expired in glory." Here Marx gulped more beer, as if to cool his aroused temper. He sighed, wiped his mouth in lusty fervor.

Raphael began again. "He was a brave captain, chasing down rivals, making treaties with Indian tribes, conducting illicit trade with the British traders. He died in debt after establishing for others a great trading house."

"In the fur wars the voyagers were always trying to get other rival traders to change their allegiance, and that was called debauching someone." Marx explained to Isaiah.

"After Laclede's death Marie Chouteau took over and prospered, and became a civic force." Raphe continued, "She was like the queen of Spanish Illinois; her sons being the barons."

Isaiah shook his head, bewildered by the sight of them. He was lamenting the loss of something not so very clear to him, and he wanted to broach the topic of the prospective magazine article, but it did not seem apropos in this giddy moment.

"Now *I'm* the one who has no standing in these Loop revels?" He thought miserably. He ordered a glass of wine and began taking sips; looking anxiously up and down the street, as if expecting new arrivals to come any minute, as they would have done in the old days. They continued the discussion of the founding of the city, as he sat and watched them, not listening to a word.

"Hey, Meriwether," Marx cried, "this guy really knows his Mencken." Marx was originally from Baltimore, and he had gleefully ingested the books of the famous cynic when he was only a tender boy. Some things take more than an age to rinse away, he had once quipped.

"We couldn't get enough of that stuff in our nonage." Raphe said.

"Who's that?" Isaiah questioned.

"Oh, me and Paul."

"Hereford?"

"Yeah."

"You know, Molly was telling me about something that made me think about you." Raphe said to Isaiah.

"Molly?" Isaiah felt encroached upon.

"Molly, the famous earth mother in Ferdinand?" Marx asked.

The other two men looked at him, then at each other, in grave silence, then Raphe proceeded.

"She said you might be interested in giving people an idea of how you go about doing portraits. That should be the focus of the article."

Isaiah now felt certain Molly was the force behind the whole project. He was being patronized. "I don't know. I haven't given it that much thought, lately."

"I meant to call you earlier about the project." Raphe said to mollify him.

"It doesn't matter," Isaiah responded irritably. "That vein's run dry."

"I'm reading *The Life of Johnson*." Marx spoke as if to quash any digressive turns that might ruin his happy mood. "Those old lions put us to shame. The linguistic mastery, the erudition! Boswell cites a Greek quotation from Homer, to explicate an idea put forth by Johnson, and he translates this passage for his readers, into Latin!"

"Didn't Johnson state that the lowest of all human beings are those who write to promote the interests of a party? Now that breed is thriving like rats in large cities!"

"Except that they're broadcast into our living rooms!"

"Johnson was entreated to enter holy orders, but he refused; he couldn't give up the sweet life he lead about town."

"That incorrigible society of impious scribes."

"Hey, Isaiah, you're a dog of an infidel, in that way he speaks of; someone who he says has never really thought upon a subject."

Isaiah stared without responding. He watched as two more bottles of beer were placed on the table by a waitress, who paused for a moment. Isaiah put his hand over his wine glass and she spun about and retired. There was no honor here in serious deliberation; topics were taken up, handled with raucous derision, and quickly exchanged for others. Marx said if the Bête Noir lost his office in the fall election it would do the body politic tremendous good.

Isaiah recalled how Marx had once thought the whole system was so rotten, it badly needed a complete overhaul.

"It will be like taking a good shit." Raphe agreed. "When you know you've voided all your solid waste."

"The body still has the vitals working properly, they just have to be used efficiently." Marx exclaimed.

"Let's hope everyone takes a good shit on election day." Raphe quipped. The other two erupted in spumy laughter, but Isaiah was too sober. He began to think out loud as a way to stay relevant.

"I've been reading *David Copperfield* again, carefully, and I'm struck by the modern tone." Isaiah broke into their revelry. They regarded him with smirks, because any new motion, which could not be turned into a joke, was deemed ipso facto out of order. They laughed in his face to illustrate this principle.

"I read that book so long ago . . ." Raphael managed to utter, after regaining a semblance of his composure.

"I've never read that one, never had the time." Marx asserted.

"You've always used that excuse for that lack in your reading." Isaiah retorted.

"Time *is* the insurmountable obstacle, to almost all the enormous ambitions of our species." Marx was roused. "It washes away everything, even our crimes. Money outlasts morality. Take BMW, Siemens, Ford, IBM, Mitsubishi. You must buy shares in bad times! Time mocks our arrogance—besides, none can know even a few abbreviated chapters of our history. We do not know it, not truly—"

"There! You've read Hemingway, Conrad, Dostoevsky, many others, but not Dickens. Why?" Isaiah was adamant.

"I never aspired to be a literary devotee. I have claimed to be a good historian, just as you have staked your career on being a good portrait painter, no?"

Isaiah stared at him, disconcerted by this last statement.

"Whereas, Raphe here, he has the great distinction of not laying claim to anything in that line, *do you*, my friend?"

Raphael smiled as if this jibe were a grand joke between the two of them.

"There is that one book I put together, using Paul's writing, and some imagined reveries; that was done as well as I was able to do anything. It sort of became its own thing in the making." Raphe paused, his face acknowledging he could not convey what he wished to say. Marx began laughing and so, in consequence, did the crestfallen Raphe.

It was clear that Marx was having a grand time. His fingers kept going up to ruffle his beard as if he wished to verify the existence of his laughing face under the heavy brush.

"I would like to get a copy of that book of yours." Isaiah said, but Raphe did not seem to hear him.

"I took my time on my novel; it was a turgid opus." Raphael launched into an account of the weighty novel he had published himself, after his friend Paul passed away. He had used the money bequeathed to him by Hereford. It was during those flush days when he was straining after a new life, and breaking his relations with everyone close to him.

"Everyone told me it was too long, by many epochs." He laughed pitifully.

"We all have our bundles in our waste baskets." Marx regaled them with stories of the unpublished papers he had written on Marxism, and how the popularity of that figure and his nebulous dogma had waxed and waned over time. The two men took turns offering up wry recitals of their tribulations, while Isaiah decided that he had no desire to try and catch up to these roistering comrades. He muttered something about being low on fuel, meaning mental energy, but of course they assumed he referred to his lack of wine.

"I had better be going."

"He goes into the desert on a spiritual quest. He must find a way to redeem the family name!" Marx exclaimed, slapping the table top as he saw Raphe falling helplessly into a new bout of laughter.

Isaiah felt gratuitously slandered, and as one left out of a game. His mind began recording their physiognomies as caricatures; they were laughing so hard, and he had no idea why, but raw loathing rose into his gorge.

"Where are you going?" Marx roared. "The best time of the day is just now coming upon us. This is still our Loop! Help us to to defend our holy ground against the infidels!"

"I have to work."

"You going to your studio?"

"No, the gallery."

"Oh, he must be about his diplomacy! Time to curtsey for your patroness."

"Fuckers." Isaiah grumbled.

"He's afraid if he stays we'll debauch him, scare away his patroness."

"Don't let them despoil your romantic notions!"

"Don't worry, that's already been done by others."

"Why so downcast? It's not good to go forth among the heathens that way."

"He does look wounded."

"Heal thyself, don't pass away on some painted river."

"Seek not, and ye shall not be disillusioned."

They lobbed such bon mots at his person as he loped off in his somewhat ungainly haste. Once out of range, he began to amble more slowly, very much aware he had no clear destination in mind. It didn't matter, just so long as he was able to get away from what was causing his mind to turn against itself in the pitiless light of others' happiness.

11

The suburb of Clayton once played the role of ingénue, the becoming face of good society, forever embowered in decorous wraps of the most stylish currency. She is now a quite fashionable madam; kept by the most respectable agencies. She serves as surrogate for an older city that must carry the inelegant burdens of history.

This proud upstart has built towers and townhomes on the bedrock of bourgeois values. She affects a cosmopolitan manner; despite the squeaks, peeps, screams, bruxing, and hissing sounds coming out of the ground. Actually, these noises rise from sewers, charnel houses, ghostly basements, and immaculate sepulchers. The point being, this is no place for quixotic craftsmen, magicians, vagrants, seers, or saviors of any stamp.

On these streets you will find no cigarette butts, empty beer cans, nor homeless bodies. Fancy shops are plentiful. One is able to stroll along these streets with no worries, other than one's current bank account, which is completely one's own affair. It is pleasant to sit outside, imbibing cordials, expressing the state of one's fine, blessed nature, which justifies everything you do in life. Such faith is never out of vogue here. It is fashionable to dismiss ideas that might alter how you feel about this orthodoxy.

In this lucrative setting the Kinfe Art Gallery has long flourished, and at the present moment is open to the public, by appointment only. This is due to the *fucking force majeure*, as the manager, Missy Knobler, has often quipped to her friends. She frequents the local pubs, where lawyers come in droves, to be fed, watered, and groomed, after shedding the dry, scented lather of fiercely contested trials.

"I like it this way." She affirms to the gallery owner, Natalie Kinfe. "It makes it more exclusive."

Mrs. Kinfe rebukes her employee for trespassing into her realm of strategic thinking, by looking very sternly at her without actually looking at her, and then putting a finger to her pursed lips, as if to hush the entire world, so that her slightest commands might be heard.

"However, you cannot expect our best customers to abide by such strictures. They must be free to come and go as they choose."

"Well, that is always understood."

"Really, Missy; just be careful how you enforce this ridiculous necessity. I don't like it, not at all. It's just the sort of thing you want for some, but not for all, and nothing is to be enforced at all times, for all people. Oh—" Natalie often broke off her speech this way, when it became impossible to condescend intelligibly to someone who had no sense of her innate impertinence.

"Yes ma'am." The manager mimicked the owner's severity, in a slightly altered intonation, that reflected a wholly different meaning.

Natalie now looked at Missy, struck by her trim figure, sophisticated ensemble, and ghastly imperturbability. One virtue of Ms. Knobler was that she did not require a lot of delicate instructions; nonetheless, Natalie still felt a need to tell her certain things, once in a while. The best customers required a very discreet, tasteful, obsequious dignity, such as their pastors (civic and spiritual) continually dole out in rich, unctuous portions.

"You know what I mean." Natalie said calmly. Missy recognized at once she was not to say anything more on this score, not at the moment.

"Yes, ma'am!" Missy could not help saying, to mark and call attention to the boundaries constraining her natural talents. She was clever, having sharp, intellectual edges. Her most accurate, and never written, resume would reveal that she had been a docent, a curator, a decorator, a waitress, and was, once upon a time, the most stylish of all the Ph. D. candidates tripping along the local groves of academe.

Not long after graduation, she chanced to serve as 'official' mistress of Bernie Quakely, a fearsome mogul, involved in bonds, or coal, or something just as grandiose, and whose capricious liberality opened all doors. She was said to be a distant relation to Mrs. Hokumb, a very dear friend-cum-customer of Natalie, who was not to be put out of favor on any account, god forbid!

Natalie frowned; discountenanced at being referred to as ma'am. It bespoke her frightful age; which this younger woman knew with awful precision. The simple convention of addressing one another had been a point of contention for some time. They had long fretted together in search of a proper system.

Hearing her first name used in a familiar tone by her manager, in front of prominent women, who were almost *her* friends, was too galling. She held her tongue, for a while, but then she needed to set the right tone. At first, it was decided they might try a more fluid system; she was to be spoken to differently when in front of her genuine friends, otherwise they were to be just as they were. That had not worked either; it had not been clear enough. Finally, it had been left up in the air, and Missy had found a novel approach for overstepping and staying within her bounds.

"She spends way too much on her clothing." Natalie thought to herself. It was not always apparent that she *was* the manager, and not one of those holding an equity stake. But then, that was useful, too, sometimes . . .

"So we will just try and make the best of it, I suppose." Natalie said, her hand returning again to her chin. They had quit wearing masks in front of each other, and were never sure that was a prudent course of action. Natalie wanted to tell Missy she ought to start wearing hers again, but was not so sure she wanted to do so herself. It was a trial having to explain such distinctions to a subordinate. "We don't need to make a whole production out of it."

"Oh, I'm sure our friends will know—"

"Now Missy, dear, just make sure you take care of our best customers, in the way in which they are accustomed to being taken care of, that's all I'm saying." She did not understand this use of 'our friends' all of a sudden! For a woman so impossibly svelte, she could be rather cheeky.

Missy discerned it was time to cease taking liberties to assuage her ample pride. She partially closed her eyes, like a feline pet who does not defer to anyone. She smiled, with an enigmatic suggestion of sensual pleasures, abashing her rather long-in-the-tooth mistress.

Natalie felt again the impact of the woman's subtle impudence. She made a fresh appraisal of the woman's attire and makeup: she was a tad garish; somehow just a bit excessive; like a beauty contestant. In fact, Missy had been used as a model to sell lingerie. Her looks were sometimes a liability, in the eyes of some customers; and a doleful reminder of the days that are no more to the substantial figure of Natalie.

They now smiled at one another, very brightly, and fixedly, ending this conversation.

"Mr. Meriwether is due any moment, so let's not get caught up in—" Natalie spoke in a crisp, authoritative voice.

"He has not made an appointment."

Natalie had not been facing her employee, but now flung her face around to glare at the woman. Missy caught her error, she had meant to phrase it another way, wanting to know why the painter was coming, and if anything were expected of her in the upcoming interview. She was made vulnerable due to her feeling of being slighted, too much kept in the dark.

"He has spoken with my assistant."

"Of course, ma'am!" Missy assented. Natalie's personal assistants did not ever last very long in her employ, and so, at some point they had quit referring to them by name.

"I meant to tell you, several things, you'll see in due time. Now, I must attend to some of those things." She strode off and climbed the stairs to get to the offices on the mezzanine floor.

At that moment Isaiah walked into the gallery and saw her from behind, as she ascended the stairs. The picture of her sturdy physique, hauling itself upwards, seized in his mind as a cartoon image. He felt a pang of sympathy. The climb to reach eminence is never entirely dignified, not for anyone. He framed her womanly fortitude in deft lines. By instinct he wanted to call out to her in lively jest, but knew such brazen acts of familiarity were verboten.

He found himself facing Missy, and his heart sank. He had hoped to slip by her to see Natalie about the prospect she had unearthed for him. The assistant had emailed him with explicit instructions. He had always sensed the tension between these two fearsome women, but feared to make any glib reference of this fact. At other times, in other venues, it was a sound tactic, used to curry favor, playing one party off against another with a careful, delicate touch. His father had explained this to him over beers to great laughter on his own part.

Seeing the grim look on Missy's face he was forced to swallow a joke that came to him.

"So how have you been, Isaiah?" She put out her hand, and he clasped the tender offering. They both glanced at one of the hand-soap dispensers placed all around the floor.

"I'm doing very well, thank you."

"How are you managing in this frightful plague?" She kept her eyes on him while moving to a dispenser where she disinfected her hands. He followed suit, again holding his tongue.

"Can't be too careful." She said as they finished up. She began brushing at her blazer as though he'd ushered a host of dust particles into the gallery with him.

"Have things been going well around here?"

"Not so bad, really. I almost sold another one of your large scenes. I do love those." Her voice indicated these might be all she favored, or that it was only these she could pretend to admire. "It looks promising."

"Oh, great. That's good to hear."

Missy reminded him of a woman he had once known, in a crazy, Old Testament fashion, when he first broke through into a little light of his own. She was to him as Circe had been to the ancient, tribal cuckolds. She was curvaceous and confident, playful and seductive; very exquisite in her flirtatious manners. To him she was a cheetah, capable of being very fast, in wild, indiscreet bursts, that might destroy someone's cozy life. From the outset he had known it was hopeless; he was merely her 'artist' for that month. He had not the looks necessary (nor the social manners) to compete for her favors over any length of time. Missy's resemblance to this dead flame only roused his fears and insecurities.

"You may go up." Missy told him, as if his destination were an altar, where some innocent creature had to bleed. Upstairs in Natalie's tiny, cramped office, they sat facing each other across her cluttered desk. Her face bore at times an uncanny resemblance to a large flower, long past its initial bloom, and yet still fraught with a life's intricate mass of enduring, convoluted mysteries. It also suggested a will that exerted a strong opposition to the laws of decay.

"Thank you so much for coming down." She spoke now in her superior and gracious manner.

He nodded, attentive, awaiting his cues.

"I think we will be able to get this one." She pushed a magazine across the desk to him, opened to the spread that had been done on their prospect. "The wife is very keen on having his portrait done."

"Well, let me take a look at this."

"Yes, take that with you." She leaned forward, her bust pressing against the fabric of her blouse in startling relief. "Tell me, you didn't have any trouble with Missy, did you?"

"What? No. Everything is fine."

"She can't help it, but she's prone to stepping out of her place." She leaned back in her chair.

"Yes." He understood his was not a speaking role in these matters.

"Well..." She lit a cigarette, letting him wait courteously. "Let's act promptly on this one, shall we?" She confided that she had more than a passing acquaintance with the couple. She wished to impart certain things, which he ought to know. He listened to her practiced incantation that always conjured the ideas of caste and money; only her normal voice could break the spell again.

"We cannot afford to let this opportunity pass us by."
"No ma'am." He saw her eyes contract harshly.

There ensued a burst of instructions, and then several hasty questions regarding how things were really going with him. Before his terse response was nearly finished she made a joke about a hapless woman who was presently going through a nasty divorce, on the verge of losing the preponderance of her social advantages. She cackled at the prospect. He smiled tepidly and was soon escorted to the door.

Once outside, he looked around like a paroled prisoner. Breathing the fresh atmosphere, he started to walk briskly, while staring up at the glassy towers. He studied a greenish façade, reflecting the blurry, immobile world around him. He wondered what it was like up there where the financial wizards read the leaves of every fertile, legal tender. The glassy visions made him dizzy. He passed several people who were in a great hurry, dressed impeccably, intent on going places. He felt drab by comparison. When he was first appearing in periodicals Natalie gave him valuable tips on the clothes he ought to wear. It seemed absurd, and he laughed, until he had made a serious blunder, and found himself in dire need of her counsel.

He had disparaged the work of another painter, which was being collected by Mrs. Hokumb. Isaiah had stated that no skilled labor was required in that style, just a different manner of throwing paint onto a piece of canvas. His words were printed. He wanted to convey that he had only meant to instigate discourse on the form, not the man himself. Natalie explained that would only aggravate the problem.

"Isaiah, dear, you mustn't, you just mustn't alienate Mrs. Hokumb." Natalie whispered to her foundling, as if sacrilege against all the higher orders were at issue. It was not clear to her that she would be able to carry him as a client any longer.

"What should I do?" He had humbly asked, crushing the laughter that had started to rise inside his shaken mortal coil. She gently lifted him out of his morass. She had a friendly editor sanction a printed correction of his heresy.

He had not even known the painter he had maligned, one Godfrey Tootman, whom he found to be rather friendly afterwards, when they met in the Loop. He acted superior, of course, to the chastised arriviste; being wise to the game. He had his patrons, too. He was benevolent. It was made clear to him that such tiny village feuds, over tiny portions, were prohibitively costly to the disputants. In the years that followed Natalie was glad to shepherd him very nicely through this labyrinth, instilling invaluable knowledge. He had learned he had much to learn of the ways and means that determine how expensive art is sold to roughly 4.21% of the population.

"It *is* wallpaper, darling; very expensive, *fashionable* wallpaper, that everyone is supposed to see when they visit. Think of valuable heirlooms."

"That makes sense." He was genuinely dumbfounded by her teachings.

He recalled weirdly ancient scenes as he walked past Edith's old townhouse; aggrieved to see they had put a For Sale sign in one of the windows. He stared at the vacant upper story where they had shared intimacies. Staying over on Saturday night meant getting up early to walk and buy the *New York Times*. The lyrics of Elton John's song "Levon" wafted through his mind as he saw himself reading the newspaper over coffee, swapping sections, discussing the news, as if it were symbolic of something meaningful they had forgotten, acting as though they were an established couple.

Her face might have been called homely, a trait they shared; but her body (at times) was a model for classic statuary. She clothed herself in elegance and complacency. Being true to her stature was paramount. Her altars had been erected over swamps of money so old generations of lichen obliterated the tablet's original characters and sins. They had walked in the falling snow, sharing the onset of that inner glow of animal heat. She took up his rites of watching the seasons change. On these streets, a mob of singing leaves had chased after them, like a crowd of Romans, celebrating a triumph over distant savages.

Surely, at that time he had been in love. The word was never used by either party, not in this eminently practical arrangement. She once said, apropos of nothing he was able to decipher, that she was not able to imagine losing her freedom in that way for anyone. He could only imagine the depth of her loyalty to something he could not fully grasp. Merely her nebulous social rank? She refused to introduce him to her family, or 'dearest friends.' How he had hated to hear her use that phrase. Why had he persisted in believing in the passion of dead leaves!

He continued walking, somewhat embarrassed to be passing so many professionals, who obviously belonged there; ardently engaged with the invincible spirits natural to that milieu. Such folks held fast to values proven by the standard weights and measures of ordinary existence. They were able to evaluate what was important, and what was not, at least for them and their own. His own pursuit of that which he pretended not to value, now seemed to mark his passage, to actually flutter on his figure like the rags of a mendicant, or even worse, the officious street performer seeking alms! He had not the heart to ask how one might slough such trappings, to seek a higher state of being.

12

A week later Isaiah could be seen marching down a sidewalk in the Loop, entirely sober, although listing somewhat, his eyes rolling over the scenery. His gloomy mind was often turned aside by the random play of light seen on material objects.

Passing by some outdoor tables he noticed the antics of a peculiar man, who had just flung his hand up in the air, responding to a comment made by his female companion. He leaned back in his chair, raised his head, and slapped his knee in sheer delight.

Isaiah came abreast of the table and stared at Timothy O'Rourke. His flushed face shone weirdly. He was now clean-shaven, and also neatly shorn of his signature mass of black, curly hair. His attire was crisp and dapper.

"And there he is!" He proclaimed to his companion, who stared at Isaiah as if his arrival were the result of a conjurer's trick. "I was just talking about you!"

"I hardly recognize you." Isaiah sputtered.

"What brings you to the Loop?" Timothy offered this standard joke from the past.

"I almost walked right by you." Isaiah managed to say after sitting down with them, unconsciously putting a hand up to fondle his own smooth chin.

"I've decided to clean house. No more rotting away in dusty retreats. The sun disinfects the soul, too, did you know that, Meriwether?"

Isaiah laughed. "Well, you look like a new man."

"We've been discussing congenital diseases in the body politic." The woman spoke in a firm, pedagogical diction. It was consonant with the manner used by O'Rourke. Isaiah was introduced to Patricia Skuffles, the neighbor from across the hall. Her disposition was cool, demure, cerebral, and playful; an attractive blend of her own making. She was very trim of frame. Her face was a solemn, narrow cast of delicate features. Isaiah envisioned a falcon roosting on a titled woman's gloved fist. She began to explain how she and 'Timmy' had chanced to meet.

"I was getting bored out of my mind; watching TV all the time." Patricia spoke assuredly. "I really felt like I was going insane." She spoke with confidence. "You really have to wonder, what is the meaning of this endless stream of television?" She feigned a look of utter confusion.

"She was shocked that I did not own one." Timothy offered.

"That's not true, I used to live without one. It was the music that caught my interest. One day, I thought to myself, it's like being in college. I'll take the initiative!" Her head tilted up, her fine teeth flashed at the others.

"That's how she is." Marx was giddy. "Isaiah, you know how Marx called his books his slaves? *She* said to me, that equation can be turned the other way! She doesn't fear to tread." He tapped the table, and began laughing, until a wheezing condition came upon him.

"He needs to take better care of himself." She explained with a frown.

"We've been going mobile!" Marx proclaimed. "So many places we have yet to see."

"I'm making him get out and walk," she added.

Isaiah learned that they were traveling around in her convertible, visiting various places, almost at random.

"Some days we just set off and decide which way to go at every major crossing." Patricia sounded very young at heart.

"We don't really do much of anything, but we come home exhausted." Timothy said proudly. "I've entered a period of rejuvenescence."

Patricia beamed at her beau's wonderment.

"Suffer the children, Meriwether? Better yet, become a child again. That's our motto." He began laughing, slapping his knee for good effect.

"We still watch an inordinate amount TV, mostly in the evening." She cautioned, "I mean, all those addictive series they have now."

"I. Thomas!" Timothy reached out and grabbed his shoulder and shook him. "Life in a convertible. You ought to try it yourself."

"I tell him he should take a hand at driving, but he doesn't want to." She feigned consternation.

"I just want to look at things. Now I see why you were always trekking out to the rivers, my friend. We spent a day visiting the confluence, on both sides! And then, we had a meal up in Alton, that old hump of a town. We stood at the foot of Lovejoy's angel, and raised a glass to commemorate his glorious battles—champion of the sovereign printing press! Where is that old machinery now!" Ha ha ha. "Oh, and there were hawks perched on the monument, and she knew the species!"

"Sounds like good times."

"Next week we're going up the river road, along the rock bluffs, and further; maybe we'll venture out and climb up the Starved Rock!"

Patricia's face made it clear she was sympathetic to his extravagant proposals, but was sure to temper any reckless flouting of frail bodies before the fates. "He wants to narrate for me the story of how the Illinois Indians fled down the river to escape from the Iroquois."

Isaiah asked them where else they had gone, and failed to stay abreast of the rushing narrative, as the two voices chirped together in syncopated bursts. He felt stodgy, as he watched them leaning close, sharing intimacies as though he were not there. They marveled over recent experiences that seemed utterly prosaic to the rest of the world.

"It sounds like you're really covering a lot of ground," Isaiah said at one point; whereupon they both looked at him with blank stares. It was a variant of that aspect used by people holding onto secrets no one else is supposed to know about. It did not take long before Isaiah began preparing to leave, feeling sullen, as they began to reprise the first hours of their courtship.

"I noticed certain magazines he was receiving, and I thought, this must be an educated fellow. So I—"

"She guessed that I had once taught history. I told her I'm no longer reading the current works, as I tried to do in the past." His eyes popped open as he said the last, looking intently at Isaiah, as if making a plea for him to behave himself. Patricia bit her lip and laughed inaudibly.

"Something made me very curious."

"The pot?" Isaiah jested; and was swamped by their mutual chorus of ringing laughter.

"She *was* spying on me."

"I was doing no such thing. He tries to make it sound like I pursued him, with devilish wiles."

"You did!"

"But you were playing your music *so loud*, trying to provoke me. What did you expect me to do, call the police?"

"You don't mind so much now."

"Not if I'm there with you." She turned to Isaiah. "It helps when you also take his medicine." She emitted a little girlish shriek, after which the two infatuated ones stared at each other; having feelings that have no need of words.

Isaiah started to say something, but they erupted in laughter, so he fell silent and listened as they continued the marvelous tale of themselves. Patricia's composure was that of a woman who has known her share of duress, and who does not allow herself to harden over regrets.

She had explained that, among other subjects, such as history and English, she had taught Latin, her entire career, to prep school pupils. It was a laughing matter to the giddy pair that she was now teaching that forever dying tongue to Timothy O'Rourke.

"What was that one line from Catullus?" He asked her.

"About Julius Caesar?"

"The other one, on the evil man." He asked and she provided the phrase, and they fell into a recital of ancient aphorisms.

This talk made Isaiah think of Uriah Heep, whom he had recently begun to study once more, consulting various critical volumes in his Dickens Memorial Library. Uriah had declined Copperfield's offer to teach him Latin. He begged off, groveling; while secretly he was plotting against his patrons. The grotesque figure explained to David that his father taught him that "people like to be above you, best to be umble, keep yourself down." Heep was a troublesome character to digest, for some reason, now that he was being exhumed yet again.

Timothy and Patricia were talking about bird watching; making plans to buy O'Rourke some good binoculars, so he could partake of her favorite pastime.

"Do you know when St. Louis died?" Isaiah queried abruptly.

Marx glared at him for an instant, and then smiled, his happiness washing away his annoyance. There was no way for Isaiah to play the fool and cause a stir, as they were wont to do in the old days. Timothy only found yet more to savor in his stroke of good fortune.

"He died in the middle ages." Patricia spoke in a slow, didactic voice." After gauging Timothy's face for an astute moment, she became jovial. "It was after Caesar conquered Gaul, and later than Charlemagne's time, but before Henry the Great was stabbed by that religious fanatic, who was drawn and quartered for his trouble."

Marx laughed lustily. "He reads Charles Dickens, and hardly anything else. He doesn't know any history."

"That's not true," Isaiah retorted. "I've had to listen to your homilies all these years, haven't I? If you let him, he'll drown you in . . ." He stopped, aware he was not apt to receive a favorable response from this woman, who was of the same guild. "I guess it's true, I've always been sort of obsessed by Dickens."

"I've read some of his books," Patricia offered.

"Oh no; here we go." Marx said, "You must be tested."

"Which ones have you read?" Isaiah wanted to know.

She had read those few, which most everyone has, among those who have bothered to read any; and usually this occurred while attending high school.

"If you want to read another, I'd recommend *David Copperfield*. Isaiah commenced to lecture the infidels on the power of the Teacher's craftsmanship to build worlds. The maturity shown, as a man, a writer, a student of human nature. His supreme mastery of the native tongue. The stealth of his design; putting himself and us back into the skin of the child once more.

"It's almost surreal, this quasi self-portrait . . ."

They murmured uneasily, exchanging looks, as if he were a salesman trying to sell them a timeshare at the desolate ruins of Petra.

"I'll certainly take that under consideration." Patricia replied in her winsome manner, which made Marx chuckle.

"I started it, once." Marx replied politely, in his new manner. "Never did finish it, though."

"I highly recommend *The Old Curiosity Shop*, as well." Isaiah rushed to add. "If only for the character named Uriah Heep. One of his best grotesque figures, who is, in fact, a cunning rival to David, for Heep — no, wait, that's Quilp." Isaiah realized he was confusing Daniel Quilp, the brilliant, outrageous fairy tale monster, with the much more darkly twisted human shape of Uriah Heep, the personification of resentment. Quilp finds joy in misery. He takes immense pleasure in doing evil, is only too happy to wreak vengeance on everyone for despising his grotesque being. One almost comes to admire him, in some odd Miltonic fashion . . .

"Okay, then," Timothy chided his friend, "you are the maven, then."

"An allusion to David and Uriah, from the Bible story?" Patricia responded, seeing that Isaiah was embarrassed.

"Not exactly," Isaiah had not expected to be questioned on such allusions. "Well, maybe in the way he plays with names; but I think he used him as an allegory." Isaiah forgot he wished to leave them to be by himself. "He is bringing forth certain psychic horrors, that a normal person would suppress, and he's overcome — "

"Oh yes, allegory. The precious allegory!" Marx threw up his hands. "What is all human drama, but an allegory of life, that greatest of all mysteries, as seen through human eyes?" Timothy had adopted his late, philosophic tone.

Isaiah leaned back, puzzled, and amused. This was not the O'Rourke of former times. The old fox had a delightful new companion, and she had changed his appearance to match his new manner.

"Tim says you're a very fine artist." Patricia offered, after seeing how subdued the other two had become.

"I have done pretty well. I've always—"

"He doesn't like to talk about it. Do you? No, only with other artists, didn't you tell me that one time?"

"I may have, a long time ago, but that's not really my stance anymore."

"No matter. We should all go to the museum sometime. I was just telling Patricia, about you climbing up on the statue to have an audience with St. Louis. And how it wasn't the first time—"

"That's right! I saw people talking about you on the news!" Patricia cried, her eyes flashing wildly.

"Yes, I was playing the fool on Art Hill, for the sake of the publicity." Isaiah was unable to explain himself.

"Did you use the opportunity to give a speech?" She prodded him.

"I'm afraid I couldn't find my voice in that moment." He vaguely recalled something had been said, but it didn't register. "I had to consider the immortal Mr. Pickwick." Isaiah ducked behind a mask. He regaled them with the parable of the Blues and Buffs, the two parties of an English borough, unalterably opposed to one another, on all matters, at all times

"When Pickwick encountered these two warring mobs in public, he said it was best to shout with the largest one."

"Pretty timid mobs we had there that day, eh?" Marx chided him.

"It was a nascent mob." Isaiah stated firmly.

"The local Catholics are tame enough." Marx asserted. "The others were from that tribe of illiterate nihilists, drawn hence like boys at the prospect of iconoclastic destruction."

"When I came out of the Art Museum I did hear them chanting, really loud, 'Tear it down.' And I saw those others trying to explain the value of the symbol, as part of our heritage, I guess. It was incredible. I felt so out of place . . ."

"Odi et amo." Patricia quoted from a poem by Catullus.

"That's the one!"

"I hate and I love." Timothy translated her quotation. "She really is teaching me some Latin. It's amazing. I tried long ago, but never really took it up in a serious way. Now, I'm making progress. She's a good teacher; she makes me take notes." Timothy directed a modest leer in her direction.

"You're putty in my hands." She replied.

Marx leaned back and slapped his knee.

In the next hour Isaiah imbibed freely. At some point he interjected a political comment. It became apparent his listeners had no interest in the Bête Noire. He was literally beneath their contempt.

"In politics, it's all about patrons and clients, as it was in ancient Rome." Patricia said. "However, it is much more democratic now, there are far more factions contending for power." Isaiah noticed the pride on Timothy's features as he listened to his girlfriend.

"We've been looking at the some of the award-winning political actors." Marx intoned happily.

"Party loyalty is paramount, of course, until it's not; no system is ever stable with humans." Patricia spoke as if in the front of a class. "When Obama crossed the Rubicon, to challenge the forces standing behind Hillary, she instantly lost half her legions."

"There's no veneration for oratory any more." Marx interjected in a plaintive note."

"No, the polemics are stated for the widest possible audience. The strategy is all about attacking ad hominem. If you effectively assassinate the character, you never have to answer the person's argument."

"These attempts by factions to control the narratives are a continual process now; it never stops. This has spawned a new caste." Marx gestured happily with his hands. "We're calling this class the nouveau sophists. You find them everywhere, in government, universities, businesses, all those phony think tanks; they've long infested TV, and now social media even more so. They pretend to be objective voices. It's wonderfully absurd."

"The founding fathers were prescient on this very human evil; knowing how it would sap the strength of a democracy. They were just as guilty themselves."

"There's so much more money now, for advocacy, and the party tentacles reach into everything."

"Here's to being a truly disinterested party." Patricia raised her glass.

"Here, here." Marx tapped his mug against her glass.

"Still, it makes for a pretty nice merry-go-round, if you can climb aboard." Isaiah affirmed wearily. The art world had its own analogue in this dreary business of making, and unmaking, reputations and careers.

"That's good! Marx fairly shouted. "See! He's the man of images. Karl Marx wrote of the bourgeoisie as if they were people infected with some nefarious virus that turned them into amoral social being, whose only devotion was to prosperity and social status."

Isaiah nodded, his face reflecting the tedium of being told again what he'd been told before, many times, by this studious orator.

"He treated them as an invasive species; and his hope? That some system of rabbinical historicism will judge them! Really? History! What *is* history? No, in our era of instant communication, these new sophists recognize the general public has no interest in history, unless partial scripts can be doctored and used to advance certain aims of the present moment."

"There is no limit to human hypocrisy!" Patricia said, before she started writing Latin phrases on napkins for Tim to decipher. He had to ask many questions as he tried to muddle through her tutorials, and there was much laughter stirred up between them.

When Isaiah made motions to depart he found they did not even notice. As he rose they tossed off perfunctory salutations and swung back to continue spooning each other syrupy morsels sweetened by and to their own tastes.

Isaiah wound up at home, slumped over his work table. He began an elaborate sketch, based partially on an image found in the Book of Ezekiel. He wanted to conceptualize an actual merry-go-round being used by those fortunate souls gliding about on the upper echelon of the status quo. He placed the whirling mechanism in a holding pattern, just above the trees, slowly cruising along and trailing diesel fumes. The contraption had an escort of angels, in the shape of runway models adorned with fake gossamer wings.

He toiled to render various details of the machinery beneath the upper carousel. The lower deck resembled an obsolete factory floor, now being tended by horned devils. One could see large wheels, gigantic motors, and a dense array of complicated gearing mechanisms; all of which was needed to drive the platform above which was designed to keep going round and round. It was going at full tilt, as evidenced by the bodies being flung backwards on their lifeless chargers.

Isaiah had to laugh at his curious turn of mind. He felt childish, and vaguely penitent. "Why am I always wasting my time?" He answered himself satirically by drawing a Sopwith Camel, breaking out of the clouds, the pilot's scarf trailing behind, attacking the merry-go-round with his righteous little Lewis popgun. He finally trudged to his bed and stared at the ceiling, his mind racing; and sometime before dawn he lost consciousness.

13

On the feast day of St. Louis Isaiah drove to his favorite park, where prominent features were as landmarks honoring major turning points in his life. This was a sacred place, suffused with stories and the fruits (some bitter) of remembrance. An old excitement came over him upon seeing the colorful, shifting air currents vying for position overhead. He imagined armadas of rival queens closing upon one another; opposing faiths brewed of the very same elements by intransigent covens.

He was sitting in his panel truck, pouring red wine into a clean, unused paper cup he had just taken away from Java Monkey. Soon he was walking across the grassy incline of Art Hill, looking at the equestrian statue. He sat down some distance away, noticing concrete barriers had been arranged around the small courtyard. There were no protesters to be seen on this blustery, storm-portending Tuesday.

"He looks a little nervous." Isaiah quipped. He sipped his wine and wished he had thought to take his sketchpad from the truck with him. He wanted to have another go at the king. In his early days at *Muddy Currents*, this horseman was a stock figure of his craft: often portrayed wearing a fedora, sometimes holding a polo mallet, and one time he wore the skull cap of a church cardinal, while sporting a baseball jersey (Bob Gibson). In one instance he was drawn wearing a hardhat, adorned with a flag sticker; the caption reading, "Pray with us, or stay quiet."

In those days Hruuck let him do whatever he wanted, for the most part, anyway; they had an understanding. The owner enjoyed pissing *some* people off, but others were sacrosanct. One had to distinguish, almost by instinct, the difference between the elect and the reprobates. It was not always clear to him, and the policy set him against his own grain. In the end Isaiah decided to breach the rules, out of disgust, or from the hubris of his success, it is hard to tell. In no time, Hruuck let him go. The summary dismissal had shaken him to his core.

He remembered how his ex-wife delivered sarcastic jabs through the embassy of their son. It was odd that she had never gone to the park with him. She was always too busy. She wanted to work hard and get places, while he had boasted of how restorative it was to set aside all ambitions to replenish other coffers. She deemed this flighty talk to be proof of faulty mettle. She was always bettering herself, climbing upwards, while he struggled in his own muddled quest. Had she only been more honest, and dedicated, in seeking social position? He stopped thinking of her, afraid to dwell on what lay beyond this precinct of self-serving remorse.

It was amusing to think of Timothy and Patricia, acting as love-struck teenagers. Isaiah recalled the corduroy sport coat with elbow patches, worn by Professor O'Rourke; the populist Marxist, wearing Ralph Lauren. He had watched closely as Marx tried to impress Madam Skuffles with his axioms. The importance of reading history, is to learn how things actually happen, with human beings, and how they do not happen, with said, sorry creatures. The danger lies in not knowing what human beings are capable of doing, under certain circumstances. Now young disciples of a new, rather unintelligible, radical, and angry movement, were everywhere roaring like prophets; 'Repent, be like us; do just as we tell you!'

He turned his head upwards to absorb the excitement of the troubled atmosphere. He felt himself to be perfectly anonymous. There was no one to answer to out there in the bare elements. The buffeting wind did not disturb his dense, stubborn hair, which was matted like fur on the skull of an animal. He had never worn long hair, even in the days when that look was de rigueur for young men who listened to rock music, and read Hermann Hesse, and were required to question the wisdom passed down by their elders.

He opened the paperback copy of *Barnaby Rudge* he had carried with him. In his youth he began this habit of reading outdoors, when passing the time. He began leafing through the parable of poor Barnaby, the divine idiot. In his blind innocence, the man believes the propaganda thrust upon him by gallant rogues. A brave young fool, he is cozened into becoming a champion for the cause; that of stopping the repeal of sinister anti-Catholic laws. The cry of the mobs: "No popery!"

Into this fable, couched in a political arena, the Teacher inserts a conservative archetype, the amoral hangman, who believes the revolt will be good for his sacred calling, that of hanging people. Society needs sacrificial lambs to appease the fates; which is why wealth is exalted as a great virtue in itself, to counter the evils of poverty. The hangman shouts, "Down with everybody, down with everything! Hurrah for the Protestant religion!"

Isaiah reads the denouement, and Barnaby's affective reprieve. The fool comes at last to live as a "more rational" being, safely at home with his mother (like Nietzsche, after his gospel had been torn out of his heart, secreted in the world's letters for gestation). Barnaby is quite happy to be reunited with his pet raven, who serves in the story to remind readers of the brute sway of human nature. In a final metamorphosis, Barnaby comes into his own: "being in the elements," loving "all that moved or grew"; becoming a blessed innocent, who truly belongs to the joys of this earth.

Isaiah sighs upon closing the book. A memory alights from the swirl of thoughts, like the gorgeous insect on a single blade of grass seen at his feet. He and Edith had been lounging near this very spot, discoursing happily upon the ways of this world. She had purchased one of his drawings. This had been while he was engaged to Dora.

"I just let myself go." Edith confided to him of her girlish affair conducted while studying Italian in Florence. She had seemed, by her telling, to have reached the heights of sophistication, in his narrow vision.

"You were truly wicked." Isaiah teased. Oh, those days, when the heart was so reckless and naïve! At the time he was suffering from an enlarged, even swollen, sense of his masculine prowess. He was having titillating doubts about his betrothal; but also taking counsel with himself regarding the necessity of becoming truly a man of this world, as a man must, and Edith surely belonged to another world altogether . . .

"I *was* wicked." She purred terrifically. "I knew I would never regret having the experience. As long as I was careful, and prepared to come back, putting all of *that* behind me. I knew I would be done with that once I came back." She had paused, staring up into this same sky. "I was so young! I wanted to *be* young. Don't you see?"

"Of course, who could blame you?"

"Oh well. It already seems so long ago. I just knew. I was sure that life wasn't for me."

"Read to me some more, in the tongue used by Dante's parents, when they were preparing to conceive the maker of that great Comedy." He warbled to her, as if intoxicated by impossibilities.

"You're an incorrigible pagan."

"Yes, tell me about the wicked popes holding tenure in Hades." This scene had occurred hereabouts, too, but later, after his divorce, shortly before she and he became intimate. Ah, the sad glory of that early run. Her tiny gestures and exclamations. Her delicious smile as she read the music of very old verses concerning strange, revealing flights of the human soul. She translated some of the lines for him, which he hardly cared about, as he reclined on the embroidered cushions of her refined tastes.

Coming out of such reveries he glances at the people milling about. He appraises the stoical expatriate on his pedestal. It was surely curious, having a Catholic king as patron of the city. In France, they had finally extirpated, root and branch, the royal strain. In England, they hold tight to the reigns of their storied pomp, keeping the stalls open for the living relics of an ancient breed. We hold these truths to be bloody obvious, all persons are *not* born equal, and to pretend otherwise is bloody dangerous nonsense!

What if Edith had been raised in the Protestant mews? They never would have gotten together. He was sure of it. Her genteel Catholicism was a rare product. She treated the doctrinal absurdities the same as he did, however she doted on the gorgeous costumes, solid gold plate, and was oddly taken with the voodoo rites enacted on the altar. He smiled, reflecting upon the pièce de résistance, the gold roses! She had owned several of these decadent totems, bequeathed to her after passing through generations. He had learned the hard way not to disparage those garish heirlooms. His irreverence would quickly turn her body to pious marble; which change was more bitter to him than the salvageable pillar of table salt had been to foolish Lot.

O Edith, the rare sweet Edith! How she lectured him on the actual dogma, which meant nothing to him, less to her — but the niceties of proper etiquette, these always mattered. The metaphysics inspired no real curiosity for either one. He was intrigued, and appalled, by the atavistic, Byzantine machinations of the highest brotherhood of ranking priests. It was her family's prerogative to enjoy the attendance of such high clerics at weddings and funerals. They were trained to speak on their behalf, in a cooing dialect not unlike that used by those tawdry, demented parrots, our mighty republic's earnest White House press secretaries.

Edith coveted the courtly pomp, unable to restrain her pride when showing him pictures of herself nestled close to a brace of bishops. She loved the sacraments, but not that one prized most by woman. She never married. Isaiah was always puzzled by that fact. He had several times been quite close to proposing, but for some reason he always lost his nerve. Had his relentless solicitation damaged her efforts to find a more suitable partner? That was a ghastly thought, and ludicrous, besides, for she was her own woman.

No, she was one to do what *she* wanted; so why had they dallied for so long, as they had? Why had she been his accessory, prolonging the doomed experiment for so long? Had she been considering it, herself? She was exceedingly cautious, and restrained, and private, in so many ways, which he had never really understood. It was two separate tales of yearning that turned to woe—can souls vastly far apart remain entangled like particles?

"My liege." Isaiah raised his empty cup to the king. "You have no barons to muster, with their knights and their yeomen soldiers, to fight for the state, and the name of the heavenly king. Why do you sit there? What are you thinking now? If you could lead us today, where would you try and take us? You'd probably end up being a prisoner again..."

Rising to his feet, making sure not to leave any debris behind, Isaiah walked to his truck and drove home. On the way he started laughing. He remembered what he had said to the people when he had climbed up onto the pedestal that inglorious day. He had spoken as from a stage, but sotto voce; delivering corrupted scraps prized from the pages of a book (John Donne) given to him by Edith. How fortunate the newspapers never caught wind of his mangled speech.

'Enjoy your summer all. This art is the ruin of me. Study me, who shall nothing be, an ordinary beast . . .' He was tottering then. 'For I am every dead thing.' Then vertigo took over and his jester's tumble was the whole story.

That night he began to compare two characters, Paul Dombey and William Dorrit; both were prisoners of social pressures, which they amplified to a ridiculous degree, out of extreme vanity, and other deficiencies of character. They become like scarecrows, strung up in false gestures and manners, thrust upon them by the distortions of their social perceptions. Dorrit rises, only to lose his sanity. Dombey falls, and his heart fails him, but he is saved by his lovely, courageous daughter Florence.

Isaiah asks drowsily, "Am I falling into a permanent despond?" More importantly, he asked, was he devolving, or evolving? Can one really lose the world, and gain his soul? Well, in metaphysics, it is as the author says in *Little Dorrit*, "Only the wisdom that holds the clue to all hearts and all mysteries, can surely know . . ."

Right before crawling into bed Isaiah went online to check the news, hoping to tax his mind, and thus facilitate a faster submergence into sleep. He came across videos of another riot that had just happened in Wisconsin. A young man, not yet old enough to enlist in the military, had shown up at a protest to keep order, armed with an assault-style rifle. The appearance of this modern Barnaby incensed the protesters, and he was harassed, baited, and then physically attacked. He responded, using deadly force. Such revolting behavior was astonishing to Isaiah. Real life was eclipsing anyone's paltry attempt to reduce these conflicts to sensible causes.

It won't be long now, he thought, before they start using Grace Slick's voice to sell us pharmaceuticals. Take heed when the pawns move backwards, ignoring all the bloody rules. Upon losing that faint hope they might one day go forward to exchange themselves for any piece they desire (except a new king), they seek to turn over the board.

In his sleep he dreams of angry mobs running down his street. They see him in his window and collect outside his apartment building. They are pointing at him. He falls into a panic, frantic to protect his paintings, for his studio and apartment have merged into one facility. Afraid they were about to storm the building, he carries what few articles he can hold and flees out the back way, but finds the stairs are blocked by all the useless boxes of clutter he has kept in storage for such a long time.

YOU CANNOT FEIGN the piety found in the letters of Vincent Van Gogh. His life stands as a testament, advocating for the soul's right to experience a fair portion of this world's natural and moral beauty. However bleak and problematic such a venture might be for creatures who wear the mortal mask. It requires a different sort of valor than most of us possess, or even acknowledge in our private storehouse of more practical values. He stood for something larger than himself; the idea that one must vie against the world's indifference, hostility, and corruption, in all its many seductive forms, to pursue these otherworldly ends.

He was brave and diligent, always painting, as he grubbed for his frugal living. He even tried living with a local Magdalene, grappling with those devils. He was a sick man; not right in the head. He suffered, there is no doubt; his trials were an affliction to those who knew him. The burden was terrible on his brother, who loved and supported him, unstintingly. Once he was buried his works became widely known and prized. He was canonized by the secular clergy; his illness transfigured into a martyr's cross.

Gabriella surprised me one day with a three-volume set of his letters, and I became his apostle. He once expressed his wish to paint as Dickens had written, and therefore, I became an assiduous reader of the Teacher. I was not so industrious as Van Gogh had been in reading other literary works; although, I began keeping my own rather prodigal journal. I never wanted to write criticism, not the way it was being done, and it seemed that my own work meant more than that, at least to me. I could not bring myself to traffic in that trade of reputations.

You never find Van Gogh speaking of art as anything but a quest after honest reflection; the attempt to render what is there, and worth the best of our craftsmanship. His forte was bringing things to life in his own idiom. His love could not be separated from the good, ageless, ever-ripening earth. His enormous pity raised him above the general lot of our kind. It is somehow terribly fitting that he was violently torn from the earth, which he so loved, by an act of his own hand. In his gospel he cried out to her, the mother spirit, as the prophets called out to their tribal god, who crudely insisted on liege loyalty, and wreaked vengeance like a Norse god.

The grand English author of the People; he acquired fame and fortune in his own time. However, he never lost the torment of feeling that something precious was missing. Some select portion was amiss; his just rewards remained painfully overdue. Surely, he was deserving of the highest blessings; for he had raised himself by dint of his extraordinary talent, monumental efforts, and the purest devotion to his artistry. Yet he feared that maybe his true destiny had eluded him.

The Teacher performed many good deeds in his time, but he was never satisfied. He gazed upon the world and writhed under the strain of competing claims upon his heart. Who has answered that awful question? How should one measure out his time, money, and passion? None believe it is possible to give all you have, for instance, but how do you handle that essential moral squalor at the heart of our animal nature?

He trusted no established church to house his faith. He had no use for religious hierarchies; in his works he razed such things for sport. He never tired of sneering at the pious hypocrites, whom Jesus constantly rebuked. What would he make of the spectacle of so many sordid boutique charities, flourishing today, designed to enrich a few favored souls? Our rich politicians and their spouses have mastered this game. Where would Dante situate such people who have sworn to work for the common weal?

I suppose a great many of us file our own highly suspect moral earnings sheet, because we fear to list all our unclaimed liabilities. The critics are supposed to keep us honest, but they are busy at the same game, besides using many false currencies. I have the hardest time conceding the right to others to know anything about my work. How often have I turned snarling, aghast at how they refuse to acknowledge the richness of the human comedy. You might call it the only fairy tale that matters. It is forever putting us to flight, whirling us around, making light of our pretensions.

In his chosen form of melodrama Dickens used many stock figures; his specialty being the human angels he painted like a Raphael to illustrate his gospels. He wishes to demonstrate how it should look in daily practice, how it should feel, how it should work for every person. In effect, as he dotes on his girls, in this fashion, he is enlarging the romantic ethic, to epic proportions. He is using the mighty lever of his pen to lift from the mire that intrinsic, ghostly good, in defiance of the figures of reality printed daily in the ledgers kept to balance our success and failure.

In the early works his villains do not trouble us with serious questions of morality, being incredibly grotesque figures, who entertain us with comic brilliance. However, in the novel, David Copperfield, the author makes his initial attempt at using the first person voice. It is interesting how anxious he becomes over his suave rogue, named Steerforth. A personage surely based on a type he knew (partially, himself). He portrays this man as having an abundance of attractive personal qualities. He is handsome, gallant, and charming, a complete liberal spirit; but his heart is cold to the idea of pursuing moral purpose. He uses people as he charms them. He plays roles, manipulating others, to please himself; and, in a weird way, he serves as Barnaby's bourgeois doppelganger.

Steerforth is amazed at the innocence and goodness of David. He laments the fact not all people are constructed the same way. He bemoans the fact he had not been given a better father, and becomes in his distress quite the modern creation of the good, godless citizen, who does not know the man. The Teacher has divined, in his undaunted explorations, that the only meaningful plot mechanism worth driving forward, with all his power, is that of the individual's interior conflict; the self vying against its own nature. And so, the artist works against his own art . . .

It should be noted, that in time, Charles Dickens incorporated the character of David Copperfield into his own personality, just as Mrs. Gamp conjured the fictional Mrs. Harris to bolster her emotional needs. In wry letters to friends he speaks of himself and David as inseparable stalwarts, belonging to a rare guild, whose business is the proper enjoyment of life. In the novel, Charles, writing as David, describes the scene when Steerforth took David under his wing at school. He affirms that he was overcome by the seductive allure of this older boy's patronage, but adds, "I was moved by no interested or selfish motive."

What nonsense! Once he, himself, got too involved, we find that the calculus of social hierarchies was too damning for even the great Teacher to hold up to the light of his genius. The realities are repugnant to his gospel, and thus he is forced to retreat into the secure confines of the fairy tale, as we all do, far too often, lest we open ourselves to the prospect of giving truth a fair hearing on all matters of the heart.

As he prospered, the Teacher did his part, but worried to himself, was it enough? He truly was like the poor, abandoned waif of the workhouse, Oliver Twist, who pleaded, "Please, sir, I want some more." Oliver is speaking to society, as one of the downtrodden, making a plea for a modicum of human dignity, whereas Dickens yearns for something more elusive, something reserved for the man of superior qualities.

He expelled his wife from his house after she had borne ten children. It became quite the public scandal, which he inflamed by writing a plea to the world, defending his honor, as the great man who has raised himself above such judgment. He resorted to base contumely to blacken her name. His outraged heart fed the public what it still craves from celebrities; periodic sacrifices of their dignity, to prove they are but earthen deities of flesh and blood.

He became a different man; his heart turned to stone against the wife. There was a young actress involved, who was kept by him thereafter. You might say, Sir Charles, he dead, he lost his head, for the sake of that vanity we call freedom. Oh yes, freedom is just another word, for nothing left to lose. That's from my generation. In our youth we believed in our causes, never doubting ourselves. A force moved us along, pushing us on our way, towards the front, where it was evident, soon enough, that we were losing our inertia. At the very moment we knew there would be no actual triumph, we began learning to act as though nothing of our own had been lost.

Which is rich, because we were seduced by the glamor of the personal, as such takes form in a social context. In time, one comes around again, resuming the old quest, to find what *truly matters. As time goes by, wearing away the vital substance, one gets frightened of the footman. No, that's not right, it isn't about time, nor what we were, or what we've become; the lament is more about the fact there just isn't enough of some essential quality, of which, it must be said, we are not even sure of its existence. Maybe it is about time, after all. One thing's for sure, there's always a reason for looking askance at the mere show of grandiose ideals, once you've seen them trodden by the ambitious champions themselves. I raise my glass to you, Vincent, in my dissipation, here's to that murder of crows, painted at the very last. You were taking passage for higher realms for which you had lived. Yes, to those who have risen to find stature among our burning stars!*

14

Isaiah was finding it nearly impossible to get in touch with O'Rourke, who was always out doing something with Patricia. He did not want to call her phone to pry into such affairs. He was yet averse to testing the waters with the old crowd; the pandemic had everyone acting funny about the most usual things.

One day he decided to drive to Ferdinand, to revisit those haunts of his youth. While driving he recalled a dream from the night before. He had been walking in the suburbs, and was startled to encounter Edith, who was sitting in the passenger seat of a black hearse. She was hanging out the window, calling to him. He was amazed to see her acting so blithe, and eager to talk to him.

He tried coaxing her out of the car, but she refused; her driver was a prominent politician. The scene shifted and they were on the sidewalks in Ferdinand, strolling past a line of sycamore trees. She was telling him something about where he ought to stay. He did not understand her and then they were on the school grounds, among a crowd of people collected promiscuously from the script of his barely legible past. These memories of his dream vanished completely as he exited onto Florissant Road.

At St. Margaret's he parked in the upper lot, adjacent to his mother's childhood home. It was now occupied by Jacob and Molly Gates. All that had once been so familiar to him, did not feel that way now. He peered into that yard where he had spent a part of his gypsy childhood. It had never been *his* yard. He turned away and walked into the Grotto area, extending from the parking lot to the school grounds. It had been enlarged to include winding paths and a variety of religious statuary. On the side facing the school property there was a large Madonna statue, a more modern version than the one he had known as a boy. It was much larger.

After ambling through the lush Grotto area he returned to his car, and immediately spied Molly, standing in her yard, hands on her hips, looking directly at him. He put his hand up in the air as she waved.

"Isaiah! I thought that was you. I wasn't sure at first. What brings you up this way?" She spoke as he approached her.

"Just thought I'd take a look at the old school grounds. I haven't been up here in a while." He walked up to the fence.

"I was wondering about you, just the other day. We haven't seen you for so long."

"I know, everything is so crazy."

"Oh, everything *is* crazy. So how are *you*, old man?"

"Ah, you're just about in my same cohort."

"No, no, you and Jacob were in the same class at St. Margaret's, long before me."

"I don't remember him—"

"He dropped out."

"From grade school?"

"I'm kidding. His family had to move. Are you going someplace, in particular?"

He turned to look over his shoulder; his face intent on solving a problem. "I think I've come to see you."

"You think? Is there some way we can make sure?"

He laughed. "I don't know what brings me here, except that I'm sick of my old routines. I've always enjoyed driving around aimlessly, to see where I end up."

"You never get lost that way." She motioned for him to enter her yard. "Let's catch up."

"It's something to see this place again. It's evocative of so many memories."

"I remember you telling me about those times, when you were staying with your grandparents. You spoke very fondly of your grandfather."

"Yes. He would sit in his metal chair, right over there, where you have those bushes—"

"Lilacs."

"I can see him there, surrounded by a great riot of peony bushes."

"Peonies? There weren't any of those here when we moved in."

"It was like a whole patch. He would hold court out there. To me he was like a knight of the round table. He had been a fighter pilot—"

"Yes, you told me all about him. Our son Luke really enjoyed those books you gave me, with all the old airplanes and everything. Oh boy, so long ago it seems." She swept her eyes around the upper reaches of the mature oaks that ringed her backyard. His mind began to whirl on memory's carousel.

"Are you keeping busy these days?" He asked, as they stood and faced each other at a distance.

Her brows arched as if that were a strange question. "Well, just now I was going to take a little break, fuss about in the yard for a bit." She held up the pair of clippers in her gloved hand, and started to move off, glancing back, enjoining him to follow.

He proceeded along, watching as she trimmed shrubs and trees along the fence line. She made her way to the back of the property where they stopped in the corner on the stone flooring in front of an ornamental rock structure. It represented an incomplete corner piece of a crumbled wall, meant to suggest old ruins.

"It took me a while, but I found just the place for Isaac." Molly peered at the junipers planted in the primitive wall structure.

"Oh, his ashes! You buried them there?"

"Yes! Before that, his urn was getting moved all over the place. He did time in the basement, in my workroom, out on the patio, and there, nestled in the Cook Gazebo. His remains were of the moveable variety." She smiled, her gray eyes twinkling, as her lips accentuated her mirth.

"He would have approved."

"Oh yes. It's like he was speaking to me." She replied, as she leaned forward to snip delicately at one particular branch.

"Jacob insisted that we select a final resting place. So anyway, we thought this was the ideal setting."

"I don't think you could have done any better." Isaiah gazed upon the dexterous composition of stones, fashioned as though it had been built before the advent of power tools. He commented on the austere trinity of red cedars." Molly explained how she had collected those, and the stones, from bleak, rustic places.

"He used to tell me so much about his time here, when he was a boy." She seemed on the verge of saying more but fell quiet.

"I was left here, on occasion, when he was visiting. They all thought I was being dumped on them, I guess. The abandoned waif."

"Oh, come now, waif?" She chided him. "You were never abandoned."

"Let me have my own romantic narrative, if you don't mind." He affected an exaggeration of what he only felt in part. He needed to mask how soothing it was having her tamper with his foibles, so deftly, with almost matronly assurance. In the spell of this salutary flush he recalled how pleasant it had always seemed being in her presence.

"Men are usually more romantic than women," she stated flatly, laying down a challenge.

"That doesn't sound right."

"We have always been left to cultivate those things that are needed for the family, while you go off to conquer lands you've never seen before. Others must bend to your will. You seek renown for feats that don't amount to much in the larger scheme of things."

Isaiah was pleased to see she was teasing him; and still, he felt somewhat chastened by an elusive note in her voice. He observed the way she slipped her clippers into a pocket of the heavy vest she was wearing. She reached out to test the resilient spring of the tender branches.

"These trees can live a thousand years." She stated proudly.

"Do you think these will?"

She emitted a restrained laugh. "Maybe not here; but out in remote areas, along rocky cliffs, they will. The species has adapted to harsh conditions, poor soil, severe weather, and the ravages of insects. They are the first ones to colonize a newly opened plot of ground, after some great upheaval."

They strolled about, exchanging personal information. The last time they had seen each other was at Isaac's funeral. Isaiah had flown to California for the service. Molly and Jacob had traveled by car, and on their return trip they had become meandering tourists. They merged into the vast landscapes, soaking up the solemnity of vast, empty places. Molly collected rocks at many sites, causing Jacob to mutter under his breath.

"At the funeral you promised you would stay in touch." Molly reprimanded him.

"Here I am." He replied and they enjoyed a good laugh. It felt really good to be restoring this relation.

"Had you stayed in touch with your uncle"

"We exchanged letters, at his behest. His began to indicate he was drifting off, there at the end. He was unable to recall things." He stopped to reflect. "I called him a few times, at the home."

"He was a great friend." Molly said, having to project her voice because they were being careful to maintain a safe distance.

"He bought me a Leica camera when I was in high school; and that really changed my work. Somehow, it gave me a better method for finding my own primal images . . ."

"I remember you told me how much you liked to take pictures for your work."

"That camera started me on that practice. I had no idea how much he paid for it, until much later."

"He was generous, to a fault."

"He could be many things, to a fault." Isaiah responded instantly.

"He would often blame himself to a fault."

"He was sometimes too much himself, to a fault."

"He could perceive his own faults, to a fault."

They both started laughing. They had raised again, in mutual regard, the man's childlike spirit. He would have approved of this levity, as opposed to another pro forma eulogy.

"Now, tell me; are you and Edith still seeing each other?" She spoke carefully, for she had inferred that the two had been, in some peculiar fashion, rather unorthodox in their relations.

"She passed away. The coronavirus."

"Oh my gosh." Her mouth opened, her head tilted, and her eyes began burning. "Isaiah, I am so sorry." She squared herself, moving closer, reaching out, and then faltering, barely touching his hand.

"We weren't together at the time."

"When was this?"

"A couple months ago." His voice seemed to pose this as a question. His tone affected Molly deeply.

"I'm so sorry. Were you able to see her, at the end?"

"No, I wasn't; no one . . . I went to the burial; but that did not go so well."

"Oh, so many are going through this terrible scourge."

They looked at the ground for a while and up at the deciduous leaves of the towering trees that were gently astir in the soft breeze. They began to saunter in tandem again, making their way towards some lawn chairs in a little niche of river birches. Molly sat down and Isaiah followed her example. The chairs were spaced far apart.

"I almost forgot!" Molly cried, after a few moments. "I purchased your *December Trees*."

"You did?" He was at a loss. "How did you do that?"

"I called the gallery—"

"I meant," he was sheepish, "I could have helped you on the price. I wish you had called me first."

"No, I didn't want to haggle with you!" She let out a girlish laugh. "I didn't even want you to know." She paused, as if puzzled. "We like to splurge, now and then. We're both accountants, we budget, and then we splurge, now and then. We do okay, so . . ."

"Well, I appreciate it, Molly. Thanks." He did not know how to tell her that she had inspired him with her own tree pictures.

"Those delicate, woven patterns, set against the rich colors of dusk. You were very precise in the tracery; you can identify the species."

They began to survey the stirrings of little creatures in the yard. In their silence the ageless composition of the day reasserted itself, and Isaiah turned to look at her. She was perfectly still. He was startled by a fleeting impression of an ageless bust from the classical era. The idea vanished just as quickly as it had come upon him when her eyes glimmered. She caught him looking at her and a dubious smile creased her lips.

"That's terrible, about Edith."

He shook his head. "To be honest, I'm not sure what I feel, considering how we were. I'm pretty confused about a lot of things, anymore." He clasped his hands and looked at the ground.

His pitiful manner caused Molly to stand up and walk towards some tangled shrubs, which she was tempted to tear out altogether. She trimmed some branches and then went back and sat down again. Isaiah had gotten up to follow her and felt sort of foolish when she came back to her former seat. He sat down too, and they remained silent for some time.

He could not help stealing looks at her face, averting his gaze quickly, not wanting to disturb her peaceful repose. She turned her head about slowly, looking around, as if plumbing the depths of all that her senses brought to her sensitive nature. She abruptly began to share a memory, a time when Edith spoke to her of her family.

"It was clear that she was very close to her family."

"Yes." He did not know how to explain that he was a persona non grata to those people.

"That seems so long ago, when I talked with her."

"Was that at the Montmartre café?"

"Yes! You said you loved that place; but after a while you never came back."

"Are you guys keeping that place going?"

"Oh, no." Her face dropped. "It didn't last. Beatrice divorced John, and then she sold the house. I hardly know the people who live there now. The sunken garden belongs to the irrevocable past; as Jacob says, it's gone back to the snakes and the mice."

"That's too bad, I wanted to get another chance to sit in that secluded garden at dusk; maybe for as long as it takes to down a bottle of Cabernet."

"We had some good times up there."

"It was like a place that had no real sense of time. You turned it into a province of Paris."

"We tried to, anyway." Her face had seemed girlish and appealing, and now was somber; her emotions often being as plain as the cast of the day when you first step outside from a gloomy room.

"It would have been a perfect spot for getting the gang together, but then . . ." He was halted by doleful thoughts of the people who were no more.

"And what?" Molly questioned.

"I guess I'm getting nostalgic about that old gang we had, once upon a time."

"Your infamous Gang of '73?"

"Yeah, it went through so many changes over the years, and then dwindled to almost nothing, and then it suddenly was nothing."

"You never did induct Jacob, and I doubt he will ever forget that snub."

Isaiah smiled, enjoying the irony wrought on her features. He remembered how he had bantered with Jacob over such ridiculous things.

In their silence it were as though vaporous figures of that irrevocable past crept closer about them. A pained expression suddenly came upon Molly's features.

"Is anything the matter?"

"Oh, nothing. It's just, with all that's going on, and still—well, I was thinking of something that happened this past weekend. I got into an argument with a young woman, at my book club. It was pretty bad."

"What happened?"

"We come together, to break bread, and discuss serious matters. All wearing masks! Anyway, the idea is to be sincere, to speak the truth to one another. Jacob says that's the problem. Well, we stirred up a lot of bitter feelings."

"That doesn't sound so good."

"I didn't handle things very well." She leaned back. "I didn't understand the anger involved." She became very pensive. "I just don't." She was then very still, and he did not want to disturb her. Then her face lightened. "Do you believe suffering produces character?"

"Not sure about that; I guess it depends on how the suffering comes about, and what comes of it afterwards.

I'm alarmed by all the conflicts breaking out. It seems people are actively going out seeking confrontations." He shook his head in troubled bewilderment.

She began to stare at him, very closely. "Well, let's talk about you, and how you're almost famous, again!" Her droll observation inflated his chest.

"So you caught wind of my visitation with St. Louis?"

Her response was lovely, musical laughter.

"I just wanted to hear his side of things for a change. Who knows? Maybe he is tired of sitting up there all alone. I gave him his chance, but he wouldn't say a word to me."

"Still, that must have been quite a moment you had, standing there, beside his horse, like his groom!"

Isaiah laughed. "I guess he could not deign to address someone like me."

"Why's that?"

"I had no rank, nor position, was not one he could deign to recognize."

"It's a pity you did not think of that beforehand."

"I was very lucky, in my final descent." He assumed a serious manner. "The mob lowered me down. Although one guy yelled for me to jump! I wasn't even high enough—"

"What *were* you doing, if I may ask?" Her voice rose, as her face opened up to him in emphatic inquiry. He was not embarrassed. She had used her sorcery to turn his errant deed into an exercise of redemptive humor.

"I don't know." He shook his head. "Although, in my defense, I was not myself that day."

"Who were you?" Her voice was a sounding device that carried into the heart's farthest recesses.

"I was intent on becoming a character in a Dickens's novel." He decided to perform for her.

"I'd say you made a valiant effort. Do you think you achieved your purpose?"

He had to laugh. "That was the question on everyone's mind. What was the reason? Was I one of those, 'Tear it down,' people, or with those hoping to save the venerable icon."

"Well? Which was it?"

"I don't know. Maybe I wanted to let them know there were other positions to consider." *I had moved beyond reason,* he thought to himself. "Mrs. Harris would have you believe that I was taking care of important personal business, and that I was taken out of context."

"What was the proper context?"

"Not sure. Keeping my feet on the ground would have helped my case."

"*Was it*, a sort of publicity stunt?"

"How could you ask me such a thing?" In her hands his embarrassment was molded into confounding shapes.

"You brought your own ladder with you."

"I had it on the truck, for a painting job, which I ended up not taking, anyway."

"So, Mrs. Harris!" Molly exclaimed, after a moment of silence. "I forgot about her. How is *she* doing?"

"I am keeping her rather busy; more so than she or I like to talk about, at any rate. I hate to bring her up in polite company. But the truth is, the stunt proved to be a boon for my sales."

Molly's infectious laughter bubbled forth. "Maybe it's time to retire from that old trade. You need to settle down, get a nice backyard, set up your own garden café." Her face shone with a mischievous light.

"I've never owned my own home." He mused, as if in disbelief.

"That's what I thought you told me one time." As she spoke her attention was constantly drawn elsewhere as though to monitor something of pressing concern which he could not even perceive. She would suddenly swing back and focus on him, and her intense scrutiny caused him to feel negligent in some indefinable way.

"One good thing came out of my splash in the news. I came up with an idea for my next big project; a portrait of Saint Louis."

"Are you going to be sitting up there with him? It might become a thing, people posting images of themselves sitting up there. You might become a cult leader. You can tell them you stand for the good people, on both sides."

He laughed gently. "I'm pretty sure I would only attract the lunatics."

Molly began sweeping her eyes around, taking stock of everything she had cultivated.

"My son thinks it was nothing but a sales stunt. He's taking night classes, one in psychology; I've become his test subject."

"I've had to undergo some of that treatment from my Sophie—in the past, thankfully! Now, we bond as mothers. It's terribly sweet." They began to discuss the life of Sophie, who was now twenty-seven. Molly offered that this was an age when a strong, confident woman becomes very good at taking command of her life, and pushing worries (and other people) aside, when necessary.

Isaiah spoke to her about his fractious relations with Theo, and his words became rather confusing to her. She had not even noticed when his speech turned into a diatribe against his ex-wife, right before an awkward lull broke off their conversation. Molly got up to go sauntering in her yard. Isaiah toddled after her. They proceeded to the wall fragment in the far corner of the yard.

"How does this latest episode, with the statue, compare with the affair of the green jacket?" She began to chortle even as she posed the question.

"Who told you about that?"

"Stephen! At the Montmartre Café, remember?"

"Yes, yes. That time he invited me. And that's the year we kicked him out of the Gang of '73."

"What?" She inclined her head, waiting for more information."

"It's a long story."

"That never stopped anyone in your old crowd."

"My old crowd?"

"You're all pretty old."

"Well, we weren't the old, old crowd then. It's funny how everything looks when you look back through so much empty space. So little is remembered of the past. It's weird not getting together with people anymore, like we used to—well, if you insist, I'll tell you the tale."

Molly directed him to the gazebo where they sat facing each other; fresh breezes passing between them.

"The reason we had to expel Stephen was that he had violated the cardinal rule of the Gang of '73, which was that you could not move away from St. Louis. We were the ones who stayed! We were going to do something *here*! And to make things worse, not only did he move away, but he was quite successful. We couldn't let that stand!"

"No, I am sure."

"Well, I blame Spinoza. I can't remember the precise argument O'Rourke used; he presented the official case for his expulsion. He was acting too much like Spinoza. I remember Stephen was laughing so hard he had tears." A surge of the old warm humors washed through his heart; his smile was briefly radiant.

"It's ironic; we were trying to make that café one of our favorite places, just when everything was falling apart on us." Molly mused upon things for a moment. "Ah, it just wasn't meant to be."

"I wish I had come up this way to hang with you guys, when you were having those fish fries at St. Margaret's. Jacob told me some good stories of those days.:"

"We have good memories. It's so funny how much you remind me of your Uncle Isaac."

"I remember one time trying to get Edith to go back there with me, because she said she had liked it, but then she suddenly lost all interest in returning."

"In our café? Or you?"

Isaiah had to look away, abashed.

"If you had come around to see your uncle more, you would have gotten to know Raphe's childhood friend, Paul Hereford."

"I remember hearing about his funeral. I didn't go—"
"You didn't know him."
"No." He looked up, catching her narrow scrutiny.
"After the funeral they had another service out on the river, in his boat, touring the 'ruined castles,' and spreading his ashes on the water."
"That must have been a nice ceremony."
"I wasn't there." She spoke just above a whisper.
"Oh?"
"It was just a small group. Raphael, Dilsey, and a few other people."
"Was Isaac there?"
"No. I suspect if he had been invited, then Jacob and I would have been as well."
"Why weren't you?"
She looked at him very intently. "Did you ever see the book Raphael put together after Paul died? *The Vampires of Eden.*"
"No, but he has mentioned it to me."
"He regrets using that title. It's from something in their youth. He says he should have called it, *A Lodging in the Wilderness*; adapted from one of the Psalms. The book is a sort of memoir of their friendship, a chronicle of that year Paul returned to Chouteauville.:
"He got sick after moving back?"
"Yes."
"That last year, that's when you and Isaac were going up to Chouteauville to see him?"
"Yes, it was very sad." Her voice wavered delicately. "I gained a lot of respect for Paul in those days. It can be sort of wondrous to see people change . . . And that's

when we met Dilsey. She was an intrepid girl! She was not afraid of anything." The smile on her face was like a vision of the beatitudes. "They all treated her like a kid sister. We would sit on that hill, watching the river, and she would hover about us, observing us. She was always taking photographs of us, and the birds; Paul got her started on that passion of recording images—"

"Do you think she still has any of those images?"

"I don't know. She hasn't said anything to you, about that time in her life?"

"No, I hardly know her. I see her now and then, but it's awkward. I'm too—"

"What?"

He shook his head and frowned. They returned to the chairs among the river birches on the other side of the yard. One of the squirrels, an equal claimant on this piece of property, scampered close to deliver a vociferous rebuke of their intrusive stinginess.

"I refuse to feed them. I don't want to make pets out of them." She explained, as if speaking directly to the pesky animal. Isaiah heard the whispering of the deciduous leaves all about them. He began to comment on her little paradise when she stood up, and moved about gathering clippings, and putting them into a bag. He sat and watched her, enjoying the scene; one worthy of Millet's superb, finished touch, as realized in *The Gleaners*.

Then Jacob was outside, calling to Molly, and they all converged at the chairs. Isaiah stood up.

"You remember Isaac's nephew?"

"Of course. How's it going, Isaiah?"

"Very good. It's great to have a place like this to enjoy this good weather."

They were both conscious of not being able to shake hands due to the pandemic, and there was a slight pause. Jacob searched Molly's face. He was older than his wife by five years; his visage had duly recorded the extenuating passage of years. He had clung to his sanguine nature. After the end of a long relationship, and a tortuous rebound, he had married Molly, who was a widow at the time. She was just getting over the ordeal of her own unspeakable grief. Jacob's heart had been tempered for good in those times.

"I wish I had time to stay and talk, but I need to see about something. It's pretty urgent. Margaret, are you working today?"

"Yes."

"I wanted to make sure of a few things." He and Molly moved off a ways, as Isaiah strolled down to the wall in the back corner of their lot. Behind their yard the contours of the land fell away sharply to a lower elevation. He peered off to the left at the ballfield below on the school grounds. It was the field where he once enacted boyish parodies of the reckless tournaments of men.

He confronted the paucity of language, considering an eighth grader as merely a boy, or even a young man. In fact such larval specimens are neither boys, nor men, but celestial grubs, briefly thriving in a pupal state. The psyche has yet to emerge to face the real dangers of life. They lay in a second womb, feasting on sacred legends, sustained by heroic songs that resound in the blood. Being so closely attuned to primitive origins they heed one faultless truth; unknown powers are making ecstatic promises. In due course the adult mind breaks out of these exaltations to tend to more pressing, practical concerns.

"Well, I better be going," Isaiah said as Molly came up to where he was loitering.

"You don't have to go just yet." Molly said, inferring he must feel he was overstaying his welcome. "I'm working part time, I have a flexible schedule."

"That's for sure." Jacob snorted. She worked for a large charitable organization, that was quite glad to have her, at the salary they dispensed, and they made allowances for the quirky timelessness of her nature.

Jacob wished Isaiah well, before he took his leave and returned to the house.

"It's been good to see you, Molly."

"Some day you need to tell me more about that new painting, of our prince on the hill. So don't be a stranger, stranger."

From the kitchen window Jacob paused to stare at his wife as her head was being lifted in laughter's cadence. He could see that this peculiar man from the past was already in her confidence. He mused over the incongruous fact Molly had few close friends, but many acquaintances, who mostly thought they were very close to her. They were still showing up all the time, despite the apparent risks.

There was something sphinx-like in her composition. You had to get very close to even come into contact with the mystery itself. He chided her sometimes, by calling her the Terrible Margaret. Her first husband, and only son, had died in an automobile accident, right when she had begun to feel that she knew what her life was going to be about, and was sternly gathering herself to robustly prosecute the duration of her term.

A select few had divined that some fundamental part of her being had gotten torn away as she finally came back to herself, having need of passing beyond her inconsolable sorrow. For a long while her heart remained weakened, and she had acquired a habit of withdrawing. To marshal her strength she needed to protect herself from many lulling, degrading cultural niceties.

Jacob feared she had configured her own, private Gethsemane Park, right there, in the backyard. This was among those things he never mentioned to her. And she had others to speak to, as well; however, he no longer permitted himself to feel wronged for being shut out of certain aspects of her innermost life. He never allowed that to happen, not really, not anymore; almost never, anymore.

Isaiah passed by three woman entering Molly's yard just as he was leaving. They were clearly anxious to see her. It recalled something he had learned in his childhood, regarding the curious mixture of people attracted to the famous Galilean rabbi. There were three women mentioned in particular: the Mary who had collected all the devils, and was first to arrive at the open tomb; and Joanna, who was the wife of Herod's steward; and then Susanna, one of those genteel ladies providing funds for the strange teacher's subversive ministry.

In his car, Isaiah had to laugh at this sudden religious experience, occurring after one visit to the parish! Then he thought of painting a scene, using the face of this woman he knew as a model for one of those ancient, possibly fictional, women. Why leave such eternal woman in the hands of Dante and Petrarch! His mind brought forth images of Saint Louis as a child, and his indomitable mother, Blanche of Castile. The royal charge was completely devoted to his mother, causing later problems with his wife Margaret. Blanche had to fight the barons, when only one stood to defend her; the poets cast them as Tristan and Isolde . . .

"What the Dickens!" he cried out loud. "I would not know how to paint her!" He decided to drive around the neighborhood, to explore this miniature world that had once enclosed the greater part of his waking dreams. He studied the streets he once knew so much better when he had roamed about on foot. Back then an evening jaunt was fraught with tremendous excitement, amid the aspirations of meeting certain fair, teenage ladies. One could experience in such fumy transports some order of high chivalry; it was beating in the breast as the trees overhead chanted medieval songs.

Feeling very restless all of a sudden he turned towards the Loop, vowing to revive in some manner the spirit that had inspired his best work. It was still there for him to find. Certain works had always bolstered his sense of himself as a man of this world, who was getting by, quite nicely, let it be said plainly enough, and without false modesty. He must find a way to return to his work!

15

Isaiah began spending more time working; and sulking, fuming, dawdling, while cloistered in his studio. The St. Louis portrait was resistant to his native charms; and he resigned himself to a new series of watercolors. By using old photographs he created facsimiles of the Delmar Loop, as it had been when he was just starting out in his career.

One afternoon, after a good work spell, he repaired to the comfort of his reading station, settled into his chair, and began reading *Our Mutual Friend*. The book's first line is a masterful stroke that seals the genre. "In these times of ours, though concerning the exact year there is no need to be precise . . ." He informs the reader at once, this is to be a parable. The master is not interested in period pieces, and dressing up wooden dolls, like those made by his youthful crone, Jenny Wren. He was a grand master at drawing mangled children!

Isaiah pages through the story of Bella, the fiercely ambitious heroine, who gradually evolves to become an exemplar of goodness and decency. The idée fixe of the author's moral universe. As a young married couple, Mr. and Mrs. Dickens brought the wife's sister Mary into their household. She was only sixteen. It was an innocent mistake. Charles adored the sweet girl, who soon worshipped him. She died when only seventeen. In his memory she had not a single flaw. His genius could not let her go; he copied out a passage from Sir Walter Scott's diary: "She is sentient and conscious of my emotions *somewhere* . . ."

In his subsequent works the Teacher erected temples to cherish her romantic remains, wishing to remove all chance of taint or decay. Sacralized by death, she became the divine model against which he would measure his future angelic creations. He wore one of her rings for the rest of his life. In this heresy against his marriage the man attempted to bend fate, as if by his will alone he might force life to heed *his* dreams. He too often sought another world than the one in which he actually lived.

Isaiah lays aside the biography he has taken up, and pours himself a glass of wine. He sits musing upon his past, and soon a specter teases him. Deborah Spencer floats into the afternoon gloom pervading his studio. He has just read these words of Jenny Wren; "And such a chain has fallen from you, and such a strange good sorrowful happiness comes upon you!"

He looked up through the skylight and made a survey of the dark, gilded cloud formations. The fading sunlight made water molecules into marvelous structures. He had just moments before read the phrase, "sobbing gaslights," and it caused him to think of his father. It evoked images of Gaslight Square; that nightlife bazaar, where soulful goods were exchanged by souls taking hiatus from conventional norms.

How many times had his father taken him there? He recalled how happy the man had always seemed to be when he was there. It was odd, because he did not normally think of his father as being a happy person, yet he could not think of when he had not been irrepressibly present in his own life. His temperament had been finely balanced; he met life on his own terms. There was no doubt of this, was there?

Isaiah deduced he had formed a poor impression of his father, the salesman of electric motors, after the man had been transferred to Cleveland. This was when he himself was struggling to make his own way in life. They saw less and less of each other, and it was then he conceived that his father led a miserable existence on a business treadmill. In fact, he knew hardly anything about his personal life. And yet he wondered why he did not change his circumstances. Talk about projection!

When he did go to see him, after he moved, there was usually a woman in the picture, and that one in particular—she must have moved to be there with him. That had been serious, but he never brought her with him on his visits back to St. Louis. He could not remember her name. It was troubling to reflect how seldom he made the trip to Cleveland. Why had he not been moved to learn more about his father's life?

"Such nomads we've been!" He spoke into the gloom of his studio. "Here I am, a hermit of the Loop. Even Marx is out there having a more interesting life." The wine made him maudlin and histrionic. He began pacing, gesturing, speaking harshly to himself. He fell upon his musty boxes and pored over albums he had put together of his mother and father. There were far more pictures of his father. He had been a boon companion to the boy; always a loyal friend. One photo showed them in the city; his father was escorting yet another very attractive woman.

"I ought to know who she was," he scolded himself with prideful regret.

There was no date signature, but Isaiah was dressed as the proper student at St. Paul's. He looked comical in his fragile, untested, suave mask. Ha! He was trying to emulate his handsome father's expression. The woman's smile was confident, knowing, graced with an aura of earthy wisdom. She was wearing tight slacks, extending a little below her calves, revealing her sensual figure. She wore a loose floral top that left a fair portion of her taut midriff bare for the world to admire. She wore a yellow, spotted scarf over her head, her bright bangs were falling down to shield her flashing eyes.

Tom Meriwether, quite handsome, wore his creased khakis, button-down shirt, and loafers. His arm is around the woman's waist, the hand clamped on her hip. Isaiah is bewildered. He was there, and he saw nothing! He was having fun at the time, but he was terribly uncertain of himself. It was all so strange to him, then, and now! He had been adrift, in the dazzling current of his father's progress. Many years later it would seem the roles had been reversed.

All of a sudden he was getting a peculiar headache; no, his cell phone was ringing. It was Mrs. Kinfe. He stood as he began speaking to her, moving about in the dark corners of his cluttered quarters. She wanted to get together to discuss a commission for a portrait."

"Should I swing by?"

"They're pretty motivated; I know the wife, she really wants the picture."

"I'll come right over."

Getting off the phone he strode about feeling elated. The chance of doing another portrait gave him a burst of energy. He would lose himself in this labor. He finally sat down again to let his mind wander over his past portraits; a few had garnered considerable acclaim. He surveyed the worst failures, and reviewed the probable causes; he was more sure of himself now. He was returning to what he understood; thinking of the enforced discipline he would practice once more assuaged his uneasy spirits.

16

After meeting with Natalie at the gallery, Isaiah went to see the retired man and his wife at their house. The man still owned a distributorship of industrial automation equipment, and had stepped down as the chief officer.

"I see this as a portrait of the founder," Isaiah suggested to them, while sitting at their kitchen table.

"Our employees are like family." The woman said in a bright manner. "Now our son is running things."

The husband pushed away the album of photos, which he had barely grazed over. The wife eyed him dubiously.

"I had a certain look in mind." As she spoke her face indicated she had not seen her ideal anywhere in Isaiah's portfolio.

"Most of these look like the pictures you see on the wall in a bank." The man said forcibly. His wife smiled as if to excuse this peculiarity of his manners.

"I should take some photographs; to see if we can find the facial expression you want to offer posterity."

"Why don't you do that, dear, you two go in the study for that," the wife instructed. In the man's refuge Isaiah found many photographs of the client standing in pristine rivers and streams, fishing for rainbow trout.

"You don't like those stuffed-shirt, bank pictures, do you?" Isaiah asked, sitting in one of the chairs in front of the huge desk, behind which the man slumped in his huge chair, staring out at not quite anything.

The man laughed lightly. "It's not just banks, you see them everywhere. I've seen them in every headquarters I've ever visited. And now it's my time." His face registered the harsh realties of becoming too conscious of one's own time. "They all look the same, and nobody looks at them. They could just as well be insects tacked to a collector's wall."

"Is this something you want to have in your house?"

"Oh, eventually; at first she wants to put it up at the office." He lightly shook his head, showing a great tolerance for the prerogatives bound to one's woman, who is overseer of the house.

Isaiah suggested he might be shown sitting at his desk, or possibly on a job site, but the man only frowned and ran one hand over his short, thick, iron-grey hair. His face had the texture of something solid, dense, and hard, annealed by long periods of industrious contact with the intractable world of business. His dark eyes were piercing in their intensity whenever he decided to take the measure of someone. He had not really looked that closely at Isaiah, not as of yet.

"Well, let's consider doing the standard bank shot." He spoke while posing, changing his expressions, the camera clicking rapidly as if desperate to capture every mask that was being shown.

Isaiah had often listened to his father talking about his approach to selling his wares to maintenance engineers and supervisors. He had explained the virtue of listening astutely, to discover what was of critical importance to the customer. "Picture his situation, the challenges he faces. Pay attention if he speaks of his work, so you can glimpse into how his mind operates." Isaiah could hear the words now. He began asking the man about the places where had gone fishing, and the man began regaling him with stories, divulging his passion for the sport.

"That was mostly when I was younger. I used to take more trips back then. You would think, once you're retired, it will become more frequent. It hasn't been that way for me. It's different now. The wife says go, but back then — and she understood this — I had to get away from things." He paused, as if he were being recorded against his wishes.

"I can see how one would like getting away to clear the head."

"When he was old enough, I took my son with me. I taught him everything out there. I taught him about the values one must uphold so that relations last. It was right there." He held up the album to show the photo of him and his son, sitting before a camp fire. He turned the page and pointed to another scene at a campfire. "That is where I turned the company over to him." He set the album down on his desk.

"Would you consider a picture done of you in your fishing outfit, getting ready to embark—"

"Why not paint me in the stream, actually fishing? Like you see right here." The man leaned forward, pointing to a picture of a man in a magazine.

Pretty quickly a deal was struck, for two portraits; one would be the standard bank shot, and the other would be of the man fishing. There was a brief, sharp piece of haggling over the price, once the wife got involved.

Later the man quipped to Isaiah; "I have to defer to upper management. My boardroom is now my bedroom, you see. I don't always have voting privileges."

No exact pricing for an individual portrait had ever been stated, and he had come out nicely enough. He had pretended to be constrained by his obligations to the gallery, feeling pretty sure this woman would not want to go up against Natalie for another round of negotiations. For a long time he had been selling his portraits through the auspices of the gallery. Natalie's imprimatur carried weight in these investments.

Upon delivery of the goods they all reconvened in the large family room, and the man produced a bottle of old Scotch. They toasted this enterprise that had brought them together, however briefly, and Isaiah felt bereft as he drove away, all his efforts reduced to a sum written on a piece of stock paper. After the intense, at times exhilarating, work done in his studio, the world at large welcomed him back to its main business of advancing the most prosaic concerns with relentless dedication.

17

Strong winds buffeted the oaks outside his window. They waved their stiff, craggy arms in violent protest against the idea of paying a tithe of even useless, shriveled leaves to this cursed, blustery, malevolent force. Isaiah heard a shrill keening, followed by a painful croak emanating from a lone trunk's inmost marrow. Then a low moaning sound carried through the misty air, just as fierce whispers began passing through his clattering windows. A ferocious volley splattered against the panes, and a deluge soon followed. He watched the rain soaking the ground for some minutes.

He finally repaired to his living room and turned on his TV, where all the mysteries of human nature were diminished to easy, simplistic formulations. He recalled a comment of Ms. Skuffles; that she thought she was going insane from watching too much television.

He was constantly struck by the enduring motif of violence; the hallowed sacrament of drama in this land of the free. The repetitious ceremonies sanctified the repeated trials, that proved the rights belonging to the strongest and most aggressive. The godless heroes themselves defined this matter of heroic fitness. He smiled sardonically as an actress brandished her handgun on a new show's promo. She was a good vigilante, able to beat up tough men, like any other hero, and she carried arms to enforce her version of justice. *Law and order is for pussies . . .*

Isaiah chortled and clicked off his TV. He took from his shelves a copy of *David Copperfield,* and soon chanced upon the hero's fairy godmother, his great-aunt, Miss Betsey. When David was in the womb this paternal aunt expressed her ardent desire to see his mother give birth to a girl, whom she expected to name after herself; and then dote upon ever afterwards. Instead, David came forth to balk her joyful designs; the thwarted aunt proceeded to turn away from the entire family.

Much later, after his mother's death, the tormented boy takes flight from his stepfather's brutal grip, and makes a desperate quest to find a better home. David treks to find his father's aunt, and makes an impassioned plea for her protection. Her rugged heart softens. Living under her auspices he quickly begins to prosper; being nurtured and encouraged to reach for goals of his own making.

Isaiah reads the chapter in which Betsey vanquishes the wicked stepfather, when he comes to retrieve the wayward boy, whom he has mistreated so badly. The aunt rouses herself to repudiate him and his sister, who is a superb portrayal of the common, spinsterish witch. The valiant Betsey chases the oppressors from her home with a lashing tongue.

Sometimes the proud woman cannot help but chastise David for not being more like his sister. That is, the unborn girl, whom the aunt had hoped for, and who still lives in the aunt's impregnable heart, as the supreme model of a good child. This phantom sister is held aloft by the aunt as being superior to any other child who has ever been born. She scolds David to keep that in mind. Isaiah marvels over this curious facility of the Teacher, to bring the illogical passions of his human subjects into a fresh, revealing light.

"I suppose that goes for me too." He muses. "What if a better version of me had been born, instead of this me; or rather, what if I were using my own will to form a better me than what I have been making of myself." There is seldom anything gained after such grandiose questionings; better to fall back into the old necromancer's narcotic gaze!

Later in the afternoon he drove the short distance to the Loop. The storm had cleared, the atmospheric effects were tantalizing. He swept his eyes over the glistening gems adorning all surfaces; many flashed in the late sun as if intending to hold his attention. The cafés were attracting smaller, but lively crowds at their outdoor seating. When passing by Pliny's he recognized Timothy, sitting outside. He drove the length of the Loop, gawking at everything, then he turned around to come back, parking on the street.

He found Timothy sitting with Patricia, and Raphe was there as well. They all looked at him as if his arrival was truly a remarkable thing to occur just then.

"Where have you been? I haven't heard from you in a while." Marx challenged him.

"I was working on a portrait. It went really well."

Marx was eyeing him narrowly. "Why so glum?"

"There's always a letdown after a good commission."

"You should write a book on your career doing that." Raphe broke in, quite animated.

"Are you no longer interested in doing that project with me?" Isaiah instantly regretted making this appeal, out of what must have seemed wounded vanity.

"All I've ever done, besides my one misshapen monster of a novel, is work from other peoples' material, pastiches, which have no commercial value."

Timothy smiled in a peculiar way. Patricia observed them like a teacher who is monitoring students taking an exam. Timothy leaned over to ask her something, very quietly, and she shook her head, a stern expression coming to her face.

"I have to go see my sister." Patricia said, addressing the table politely. After rising, she paused by Timothy, touching his shoulder, then she strolled away in a sprightly gait. Marx watched her with keen delight, taking a sip of cold water after she was gone. He smacked his no longer parched lips.

"We're going to a new place, later on." Timothy spoke fervently, already beginning to savor the experience. "Hey, Meriwether, we went out to Chouteauville yesterday. You should see Raphael's river pad; it's a little fortress, perched on a hill looking out over the river. It's your kind of scene."

"Yeah?" Isaiah felt that he ought to be exerting himself more, to move forward out of his doldrums.

"We went for a cruise on his boat. Dilsey took the helm, for most of the way. She regaled us with stories of Raphe and Paul. What a pair of tricksters. You remember Dilsey?

Isaiah nodded, thinking, "Do I remember her? I met her before you."

"It was nice being out on the water, seeing those ruined castles. She's a photographer. Have you ever thought of painting those structures?"

"What? No." Isaiah was irritated by the fact Dilsey was a photographer, which was strange. He feared too many more changes were occurring, these might do incalculable harm to his last really good friendship. Raphael abruptly stood up and took his leave.

"Skuffles and I," Timothy spoke as if making a solemn announcement, "have decided that the first reading of Marx is full of tragedy; the second is laden with farce; and finally, it acquires a lasting note of pathos. We've been reading a biography, which looks at his family life."

Isaiah bore witness to how felicitous life becomes after one acquires a good, sympathetic mate.

"His private life must have been pretty wretched, I guess?" Isaiah imagined the endless ordeals of the lonesome firebrand

"Not really, not his home life."

"You said they lived in squalor, and he was always begging to keep himself afloat. You made him sound like Henry Miller." Raphe stated gleefully.

"For most of their lives, that's true, but in his own way he was a gentle, loving father. And the loyalty of his wife, Jenny, why, it's the stuff of legend. And his daughters, they were nurtured, in all that chaos, to find themselves. They all endured much tragedy. He became a noble paterfamilias! Your father Dickens would have been sorely tested trying to write accurately of such a life; the noblewoman and the radical philosopher. Apostles of a greater faith yet to come on this earth; one involving all the living!"

"So now you're an expert on Dickens?" Isaiah teased, his voice edged by something not so very innocuous.

"I've probably read more than you think. And now there's time—"

"Where is Raphael going?" He asked for no reason."

"He's got something he has to do," Marx explained. "I think he's meeting with Dilsey. If we ever do get the gang together again, he ought to be let in, don't you think?"

"Sure, why not." Isaiah appeared very reflective. "Tell me," he leaned forward. "what do you think our generation brought new to the table? What has endured?"

"In what way?"

"In any way."

"The Sexual Revolution. We served on the front lines. We helped to demolish those ludicrous taboos. Oh man, remember hot pants? It's standard garb for young women now. Just about from that time, in the early seventies, you see on the statistical charts women beginning their long march to equality, and freedom. To a large degree they have caught up, in politics, academia, the professions . . . Well, let's say the white, bourgeois women, at any rate."

"That didn't do me any good." Isaiah made a wry quip.

Marx erupted in boisterous laughter. "We were there, we watched it happen."

Isaiah began to drift into the past. "The fact is, we were just raw recruits. We didn't know anything about what was going on. I didn't, anyway. I was embroiled in too many of my own farces."

"Patricia calls it casting off the cultural chains. For a while a lot of people are still wearing leg bracelets, dragging around pieces of the broken chain—"

"We were going to change the world, though; we thought so much more would happen." He could see Marx laughing at him. "Remember?"

"I think that was always more you, than me. It seemed to me that time was a critical factor, and we just did not have enough, in one generation, to bring about the momentous changes we crowed about."

"Don't you think, too often, we're satisfied to celebrate ourselves in songs and speeches?"

"You are dealing with human nature. Who knows what that rough beast really wants."

"Now they're saying we were, and are, full of shit."

"Who does?"

"Young people! They are so smug, laying down the final opinion on everything." Isaiah was thinking of recent criticism he had received online.

"Who cares about young people? They are not rational beings; not about anything that matters to old people. How dare they?" Marx laughed. "I. Thomas, they *are* superior! They have youth, that magic perspective, which lets them draw new visions out of the inert, glowing mass of old demolished patterns."

Isaiah turned a wounded look upon his friend.

"Why are you letting such things get you down? Life and work, both are short, you know?"

"I don't know anything."

"You just did a portrait, and I know how you used to revel in that work."

"I still value the work."

"Well then, cheer up! I remember you lecturing me on making one's own happiness."

Isaiah shook his head sheepishly. "Stop remembering things so clearly at inopportune moments."

"I remember having fierce arguments over that idea of yours, actually; how far one should try and extend that; to the bootstrap argument, for instance. Oh my gosh, that was so long ago, wasn't it? I am less sure of everything now. She's taught me to explore things with a better attitude." Marx seemed to search delicately for traces of his vanished beard with his fingers grazing his jawline.

"Well, at least you've gotten yourself into a pretty nice situation. I suppose the Latin lessons are still progressing, rather sweetly?"

"Does my improbable romance strike you as funny?" Timothy's voice floated out from from a deep, solemn place.

"Not at all. I'm envious."

Timothy sipped his water; smiling as if something were very amusing. "I'm on reduced beer rations, but the days are swimming by in a royal parade. I can't remember ever feeling just like this before. She carries the classical world in the palm of her hand. All those great figures are strung like charms on a bracelet she wears on her wrist. She knows so many fascinating stories."

"Stop, already. Marx, the romantic fool. I can't take it!"

"I am a perfect fool now."

"You're having that second act, which few ever see."

"Second? We've both had many, no?"

"I suppose that is true."

"They should never stop, my friend, for everything evolves; personalities, culture, and the gods . . ." Marx could not finish his thought; too many voluptuous experiences of the recent past were drawing upon other occasions from a timeless reservoir to nourish his enriched appreciation of life. Isaiah saw something on Tim's face which he did not recognize. He was suddenly mindful of a look he had seen on Molly's face; a brief radiance revealed on the surface of all that frightful, private devotion. He looked fondly at his friend, and for the first time, since the inception of his new relationship, Isaiah was truly happy for him.

18

Isaiah has been busy, but he does not feel productive. He is poring over the news online. As the election draws nigh the vitriol has reached flood stage. The various tribes were conducting war dances, striking the pole, expressing an overwhelming fervor to resume hostilities. Anger was a viral contagion, best treated by releasing finely directed spurts of hatred from the bloated spleen.

He anxiously muses upon the great wild fires that visit California every year, terrible Biblical scenes that blaze forth on TV screens, where it is reported as if nothing like this has ever happened before. They correctly lay blame on the changing climate, and yet never mention the state's poor husbandry of the forest floors.

He repairs to his reading niche, musing upon the fact there had been a time when he liked to add his two cents to the incessant jangle. It made him feel that he was playing his part in the highly vaunted democratic process. Now he viewed 'the people' as a wild horde, subsisting on measly scraps of intelligence, trained to love senseless circuses, and increasingly drawn to the spectacles of blood sports.

Until recently, he had never questioned that democracy was a viable system, allowing for continual improvement. Now, he was not so sure. He saw too clearly the propensity of people to compete, oppose, contend; as individuals, and as partisan groups, seeking their own betterment, usually at the debasement of others. The relentless urge to rise above others was all he could really see anymore.

He was reminded of how attentive the Teacher was to this pervasive social warfare. Countless times, he pauses the grand melodrama he is prosecuting to present a vignette, which reveals this terrible predilection of human nature. His minor characters are often the ones viciously tearing each other apart, so that his good characters may serve as exemplars, pleading the case for how it ought to be done, among our enlightened race, according to the gospels of Charles the Good.

In fact, he was not unlike Tycho Brahe, who observed and recorded movements of the celestial bodies, using only the naked eye. His recordings proved to be so exacting that Johannes Kepler was able to use this information to derive laws of nature. One of the saving graces of the Teacher, in fact, is that he is never doctrinaire. He does not preach to his flock of grandiose political solutions, but rather focuses on individual behavior. His genius leads him straight into caricature, where his figures romp for our edification.

One of his masterful creations was Sarah Gamp, who fought against the odds, with her own outrageous style.

She administers to people giving birth, and also watches over those who are leaving this vale. She stays in healthy contact with the undertaker. She was battered by her deceased husband. Now she drinks, and lies about it, to herself, and the world. She is forced to be entire unto herself in her lowly station.

True to his office, Dickens cannot resist placing her in a primal struggle with one of her colleagues, the only person who might otherwise have been a good friend. The Teacher pits this other woman against Mrs. Gamp to horrific effect. The antagonist tells Sarah Gamp she knows Mrs. Harris is nothing but a fantasy. She destroys this artful construction by which Sarah pretends to have at least one true and loyal friend, who is always ready to testify to others on her behalf. The other woman's exposure of Sarah's innocent fraud destroys any chance of the two being friends, just as it was designed to do.

Oh, the angry, spiteful Teacher. How he glowers at us. He was kindred with ancient prophets when his blood rose. And yet he shook his staff at Human Nature, not the kings, high priests, or pitiful gods. He scoffed at governments. He had seen these puffed-up little men up close, performing at their work for the people. He had once gained acclaim for his highly accurate reportage of their speeches; but he could not stomach playing a part in a body where selfish deceit and hypocrisy were practical virtues.

His whole life he had been enamored of acting, and he exhibited considerable talent for the stage, but to our good fortune he took up his pen to draft wondrous, earthy tales, à la Chaucer, and other ennobled craftsmen.

He created his own mythology, taking upon himself the holy mantle: to respect the animal, as it was constituted, and to pay homage to that holy architecture. He labored to raise the possibilities borne of our own aspirations.

Isaiah was reading *Martin Chuzzlewit* when his son came by to talk to him. Isaiah was glad to see him, hoping to bring everything onto a more solid footing.

Theo asked him about the portrait he'd recently done, his tone demanding to know why he had not been included in any facet of the transaction.

"I know, I know." Isaiah was disconcerted by Theo's anger. "I said I'd include you on the next one, to let you see the whole process, but, it just came up so quickly, and I—" Looking closely he realized his son was not listening to him. He had steeled himself for his angry remonstrance, not this aloof resignation.

"It doesn't matter."

"No. I said I would, I know I should have—"

"I don't care." Theo almost whispered. "I'm stepping back."

"Stepping back?"

"I'm quitting this, whatever *this*, is; this partnership we have, comprised of one partner, and one nonentity." His voice amplified his disgust.

"Quitting? No, I'm telling you, I will start including you more often. It takes time. If it's about remuneration—"

Theo put up his open hand to forestall more words. He spun about and started to pace, and then wheeling on his father, he spoke with rasping vehemence. "I don't want to work for you anymore. You'll have to get someone else to help you with the website."

"I don't know anyone else who can do that, not like you. You understand everything . . ."

Theo's face held briefly a restrained look of triumph. It expressed, with tortured glee, "That's your problem."

"Well, let's take some time to think about it. I know the money has been an issue—"

"No! I'm done with the Isaiah Meriwether show." His fury had taken possession of him.

Isaiah was stunned. He returned to his reading chair, expecting Theo to stomp out of the studio. Instead his son stood still, as if frozen in place.

"I cheated on your mother." Isaiah spoke gravely, as if in shock.

"What?" Theo came closer, towering over him, raising a hand, and seeing it tremble, drawing it down to his side. "Why are you telling me this now?"

"You asked me." He kept looking down. "The truth is, I did that, to her, to us. Okay?" Isaiah glanced up at his son, expecting more questions, accusations, and denunciations. Theo stood mutely, restrained by his rampant emotions. Something on his face made his father remember him as a boy, in some childish mishap, that had seemed to the boy a great tragedy.

"We weren't really together anymore; living separate lives. You were the loadstone; we were on separate orbits around you. I did my part, when she went back to school to get her MBA, but as soon as that was over, and she got that job with the bank . . . she was working long hours, and I was spending a lot more time at home with you." He shook his head, finally looking up to see that Theo's face was like a death mask. He had not wanted to hear any of this, and now wished he had not dug around in the long neglected, family plot.

"It doesn't matter, Dad." Theo drew back, turned, and stared down at him a moment longer.

Isaiah did not move. The son walked out of the studio, never looking back. Isaiah wondered why he had confessed this sin in such a feeble manner. It had been a stupid thing to do, but there was an enormous sense of relief. It felt like something else was gone now, and he was getting used to adjusting himself to that pathetic comfort found among the flowering ruins.

19

When he was ready to quit trying to find novelty in his work, Isaiah resorted to browsing along in his books, or poring over old images. Enjoying wine and music made even his life picturesque, for a while, anyway. He sojourned in memory as a seasoned traveler, one who happens upon marvelous finds in an old country, every time he strays from the beaten path.

One day he sat down with a volume of *Little Dorrit*, leafing to the chapter entitled, "Nobody's Weakness."

"Hadn't he better let it go?" The hero suggests to his friend, the stalwart inventor, who seeks a patent, but has run afoul of the Circumlocution Office, which exists to make sure nothing new is ever taken up.

The engineer's answer is no, he can't leave it alone. The good man insists, he must strive to act as shepherd for his invention; despite the world's resistance. "The thing is as true as it ever was." The man is sustained by his "calm knowledge that what was true must remain true, in spite of all the Barnacles [corrupt bureaucracy] in the family ocean, and would be just the truth, and neither more nor less, when even that sea had run dry—which had a kind of greatness in it, though not of the official quality."

The staggering reach of his moral vision! The stunning revelation of this existential prescience sown into the fabric of a little story. The loneliness of the first explorers. Putting forth the idea that our moral truths, cast out from the foam of the sea—to trumpet these in fine—as being something that shall always exist, with or without our support, or even us! He bounds past the heretics of the 20th century, before they are born! Using his own brand of sterling English, minting his own currency along the way, he lays down the whole basis of our only workable system of faith. It must rest on what we have been given . . .

"I'm not really a part of society, I don't feel—" Isaiah had once tried to explain his social disaffections to Edith, by pointedly looking askance at her society, while burning to possess the laurels granted by another not so very different.

He recalled being in her Clayton townhouse, lazing over coffee, and the scones he had just gone out to purchase. It was Sunday morning. The nocturnes of Chopin spun very precisely on her deluxe stereo system. The crisp, messy tidings of the *New York Times* were strewn at their feet, on the clean, highly burnished hardwood floors.

She inhabited her space in fussy, spoiled languor. She moved about barefoot, robed, her thick wavy clusters of hair wondrously awry. He watched her going about her girlish, womanly movements, in the unconscious splendor of being perfectly at ease in her own dwelling. Why was he so sure this arrangement would last? They were mature enough; why wasn't this life good enough?

"In some ways, we are all that way." Her voice had a weary inflection; he heard, 'Not this again.'

"I don't think so—"

"I was going to say," her inflection halted his speech. "If you will let me finish." What had she said after that?

Isaiah could not remember; by then he was desperate to avoid the change that was coming. He had refused to admit these facts into evidence. The previous afternoon they had seen Marx at the Library Limited bookstore, and Isaiah promptly invited him over for a drink.

It was a grave mistake; Edith began to simmer at once. He had seen the quiet puckering on the surface of her complacency. She found Marx to be incongruous with her style; his mere presence subverted the couture, décor, her china, and place settings, her esteemed connections, who understood money, and how not to talk about it casually.

That afternoon Timothy was more himself than ever. He was rumpled, but his beard had been trimmed, and his oxford shirt was actually nicely tucked into his corduroy trousers. His work boots were scuffed from shuffling beneath the tables at cafés.

"This is a sumptuous nest you have, Edith." He spoke blithely, as if he were oblivious to her animus. He had expected nothing less; he had long before predicted this reception.

"It's been in the family for some time." She replied, not realizing she was confirming his derisive point.

The small talk died quickly. Marx persisted in bringing up the news, so he might bombard her with examples of his erudition. He could undermine any current position held by piling up historical contradictions; and turn anyone against him.

"This looks like it was a festive event." Marx spoke while holding a framed photograph of Edith with her family members, in attendance at the Indus River Society Ball.

"It was." Edith said with icy reserve. "It always is."

Putting the photo back in its place he turned to Isaiah, as Edith retired to the kitchen, and began to rattle various utensils.

"Every generation that increases the principal brings the whole family closer to divinity." He quipped. "That's caste karma. I can see how that has profited her."

"Stop it, man. Be cool." Isaiah scolded as Marx smiled with elfish delight.

Edith came back and they tried to discuss several topics while her features darkened. She began to focus a pitiless light on the man's impossible manners. She later exclaimed that he was imbecilic! They both watched him spreading crumbs about him, and dousing his beard with a beery froth.

When Marx said he had to go, Isaiah was very pleased. At the door Isaiah had no chance to say a propitious word as Marx rested a hand on his shoulder, commiserating with him. How insulting!

"What's the big deal? I asked him over for one drink?" He had challenged her, afterwards.

"You didn't know if I had other plans, or not, did you?"

"No. How could I? You never tell me about all your other secret doings." He'd said it out loud; they did not commune nor move about as a normal couple, and never had done so.

Edith said not a word, but retreated into her feminine routine. Was that the apogee of their most intimate phase of being together? They struck the unflappable Marx like an iceberg; their wounded ship had groaned, gliding forward in the darkness, starting to list, taking in the fatal wash of cold, unfathomable seas. That was the end of those Sunday morning fantasies.

It occurred to him, with a jolt of irony, that it must have been *that* Saturday afternoon, when she had read to him both endings of *Great Expectations*. She had discovered the alternate version in the new paperback he had purchased that very day.

"More of that treacle?" Marx had said, coming up to him in the store.

"It's not." He retorted. Still quite happy.

As he paged through *Little Dorrit* he found the chapter, "Moving in Society." In reading this he was able to quit rubbing old wounds, as if he were a lesser Achilles. In the novel, one of the rich, maternal women is referred to as "the handsome bosom"; she strikes a crass bargain with the déclassé Dorrit sister, who has caught her son's eye.

The other sister, the good angel of the story, is appalled by everything, and of no use to any of the others in any of their dastardly plots. A parrot, owned by a society lady, steals the show. He shrieks and crawls around the outside of his golden cage. He laughs hysterically. He licks the bars with his black tongue. Isaiah remembers he had read this passage to Edith; she must have known he was thinking of a friend she had just spoken of to him, but whom he would never meet in this lifetime.

They never did break up, not properly. After too long a pause Isaiah began to court her again, except this time he conformed to her wishes, as if losing one's pride were a matter of course. He became submissive, and built a sham rationale around this compromise of himself. Henceforth they were more discreet, inhabiting separate spheres. At his behest they began going away; having more fun in other locales. There was no need to acknowledge the strangeness of the perpetual affair. Intimate travels became the norm, in a sort of naughty, Bohemian reversion, practiced by jaded, bourgeois gypsies.

He must have believed at the time this was all rather exceptional. He was supercilious when confiding to Marx after taking one of these jaunts, perhaps to Kansas City, or Nashville.

"Nashville? Very cosmopolitan," Marx would say. "Kansas City? Were you looking to get back your lost rib?"

"We don't want the usual things." Isaiah would fumble at explanations; under this scrutiny, hopelessly perplexed himself.

"Are you sure she doesn't want more?" Marx posed another exasperating question.

"She's not interested in marriage, I'm pretty sure. She's not waiting for me to change, if that's what you mean . . . I'd know if that were the case. She'd tell me, right?"

"More, with someone else."

"Oh, I see what you mean."

Isaiah always made a show of being proud of his brave experiment in freedom; but Marx, in his perspicacious eye, was exposing a badly flawed solution.

"It's not like you have to do actual work for your upkeep." He spat this out one time, near the end; he had the gall to denigrate her 'charity work,' and it was never the same afterwards. He had flung the torch into the nest to burn it all down.

Isaiah started reading the chapter entitled "Spirit," and was soon wryly amused at the farce of the genteel man wasting away in debtor's prison, who is scandalized by his good daughter's indecorous behavior. She is seen coming onto the grounds walking arm in arm with a man from the workhouse. The self-anointed lord of the debtor prison is only too glad to receive the miserable creature, as recipient of his patronage; however, it insults his dignity for his daughter to accept the man as her social equal, out on the prison grounds.

The Teacher superbly portrays the prisoner's exquisite punctilio; the same mechanisms are used by the lackeys at Windsor Castle. They also enforce ludicrous norms upon the degenerate visitors, instructing each one how to stoop, and bow, and scrape, when presented to a common woman who happens to wear a flimsy ornament on her head.

The masquerade is a matter of state. She believes in her magical powers! And so must you; for it is known that morbid systems, in breaking down, often give birth to horrors. It follows logically, she must never, under any circumstances, meet another person who approaches her as an equal. Maybe Yahweh, if he should deign to join the English peerage, acquire property, servants, dogs, learn the etiquette of fox hunting . . .

Isaiah sat in his chair, staring at the gorgeous afternoon light falling into his studio. He felt like letting go. If he only knew what it was that would alleviate this burden of feeling he had not achieved anything he had really sought in life.

"The past doesn't work for me anymore," he says, venturing to advise himself. "Maybe I should leave that alone from now on; look forward, to move forward." The silence closes down on this crazed sentiment. He continues staring into the gloom, motionless, head bowed. A pencil being ready at hand, he starts to draw a picture taken from memory. It is a childish episode, imprinted when he was much more simply a creature of instinct, in awe of nearly everything.

20

The autumnal weather was elegantly staged for waltzing outdoors, or even strolling along leafy old sidewalks. Isaiah started out thus, feeling rather hale, bound for the Loop, but turned back when his legs began to cramp. Instead he drove himself to the Feral Hog, where he found that a familiar group had pushed two tables together.

He takes a place by O'Rourke. "It's like old times."

"We were discussing names for this group. I suggested the Plague Rats." Marx is clearly pleased about everything.

"That's a little macabre, considering all the people—"

"No doubt. I also suggested the Cabal of 2020."

"That's better." Isaiah said, looking around, noticing Godfrey Toots, the Wall Paper artist he had slighted long ago; but that was all in the past. The man was ever a striking example of waning fashion. He had once been a darling of the local media, consecrated by the usual means as an artist of considerable merit. He had learned to speak soothingly into the camera's eye, promoting his works for the good of the community.

The two painters greeted each other, and there was a genuine gleam of ironic pleasure. Both had tasted success, suffered reverses, and had struggled through stagnation before securing a small redoubt just large enough to plant one's modest flag. They gossiped as two rivals who stand aloof from the mass of yapping unknowns.

Raphael was there with his young friend Dilsey. The confident black woman appraised all these older white folks with complex discernment. She turned often to Raphe with a look of amusement. Isaiah wondered if Theo might be coming to join them, and how awkward that might be for him.

"He really wouldn't be the right person to write about your career." Isaiah was startled to see that Dilsey was addressing him. He glanced at Raphael, who must have heard her, but did not look his way.

"That seems to be what we've decided." Isaiah failed to disguise the bitterness in his voice.

"I've told Molly about it." Dilsey said cryptically.

"Oh yes?" He was confused by this statement. Then Mary Jones appeared to take his order. She turned to Marx, who made a quip about his glass being empty, causing her to smile in a curious way. Mary was wearing a man's oxford shirt, and nothing else, except for white tennis shoes. On her body the shirt brought to mind the attitude of those frenzied devotees who participated in ancient fertility rites.

Patricia returned to the table from inside, and stood before Isaiah, who nodded and moved down to the other end of the two tables. He had been tempted to take his leave, but was afraid to act in such a bizarre fashion. He conversed with others whom he knew, and all seemed to be in perfect accord. They spoke so that others might see they were speaking, and know they had something to say. There was talk of politics, art, even religion. It seemed to Isaiah they were tossing around practiced inanities, like a company of freelance jugglers sharing a public stage, which they have discovered by accident, and which no one else is using.

Someone made reference to the fact certain voices in the political forum thought other voices ought to be silenced. It initiated a debate on the sacred tenet known as free speech. Some advocated that silence itself was a violation of one's public duty, given the nation's present trauma. Isaiah stared in dumb wonder at what was happening; a farcical version of his past.

"Let's talk about something else!" Brayed an exultant Marx.

Isaiah caught his eye and they both acknowledged by their looks how peculiar this was, him attempting to steer the group out of an argument. They both shook their heads, smiling; they used to strive heartily to outdo one another in fomenting debates.

Several people began discussing the 1967 movie, *The Graduate*; from the perspective of imagining the actors as being themselves in the story, noting in particular how old they were at the time.

"So the young graduate, Dustin, he's like thirty. He comes home after getting his bachelor's degree, eight years later than normal, and he wants to lay about in the pool, because he's not sure what he wants to do in life."

"And then he starts an affair with Anne, the older woman, who's thirty-six."

"That's right! The real scandal is that Anne would have been like, maybe ten years old, when she had her daughter, Katharine."

"They all must have known of this; and so they connive like devils."

"It explains her sorry husband, and the booze."

"The daughter is horribly repressed; she just wants to punish her parents for being her parents."

"They make Dustin's father out to be a clown, but he's the only sensible one in the whole bunch. He's partner to the guy who married the woman who gave birth when she was a girl. He knows how degenerate his partner, and his wife, really are, but he is trying to make things work. He's made a life for himself. He's built something for his family."

"Which opportunity his son is squandering."

"Yeah, whatever happened to, 'Get a job!'"

"And he doesn't even come home from college as anything worthwhile, like a true radical. He's just a spoiled, naïve, sullen boy, who misses prep school."

"You have to imagine he's the sort who was sleeping in his mom's bed for an awfully long time."

"She probably thought it was normal. You shudder to think about her demons."

"Dustin graduated from a Los Angeles High School in 1955. I mean, the place was swarming with pimps working for the screen moguls. He's right in the middle of America's riotous, postbellum decadence. No more rules for us!"

"Jack and Marilyn playing house at Sinatra's pad, in New Babylon."

"You're right, the father is the one who ought to be applauded."

"He's done everything that was asked of him; all he was supposed to do, in that society. Yet he's the one made to look ridiculous."

"He buys his son that frogman suit. The subconscious attempt to free the lad from the wasteland. Save yourself. Go back to the source!"

"Yes, they should make a movie about the father. He's gotten fed up. He quits his job, leaves his vacuous wife, and moves to San Francisco."

"It was the summer of love."

"He could become a disciple of Timothy Leary."

"They could show him taking off in a brand new corvette, his hair degreased and starting to grow out. Maybe he has to run some Easy Rider types off the road—"

"And there's a fistfight, and he kicks some ass."

"He picks up a hippie chick, a knockout, completely uninhibited, who's dropped out of Wellesley."

"She's hitchhiking to the Monterey Pop Festival, and she turns him on."

"She could be seen coming off that bus when Dustin and Katharine climb on, at their ending. You can see they both know they're in trouble. Dustin is thinking, 'I'm still going to do it with your mom.' She's thinking, 'I hate this guy more my mother.' Then they cut to Dustin's father—"

"He's breezing along, listening to Jimi Hendrix on the radio, in his new convertible, abandoning the whole freak show."

"The hippie chick is like that babe in *Pretty Woman* ; a sexual Madonna, who transcends class and mores."

"She brings salvation to all those yearning to be free, if they have the right look; a great body — and loads of cash."

"All we know; truth is beauty, beauty attracts money, so being crass is good for you!"

"He passes by Kesey's bus, which is going in the other direction, searching to find Timothy Leary in the east. Our hero doesn't pay any attention to that dayglow circus of clowns; he's going west."

"That *would* be anomalous; the wrong time frame."

"What was the name of that bus, again, the Führer?"

"Kesey was the grand master, holding the perquisites of tribal chieftain, and shaman."

"Trying to make a mystery cult out of adolescence."

"We've been there, done that!"

"The graduate dad is on a completely different trip; one of his own making."

"He braves a new world, on his own terms."

"That's the title. For Who So Braves the World."

"Where Have You Gone, Mr. Robinson?"

Someone started to sing a verse from the movie's theme song.

"You mean Mr. Braddock, right?"

"That doesn't have the same ring, though."

The chorus at the two tables dissolved into shrill cries of laughter, and then helpless sputtering.

Isaiah had not participated in the parody. The collective hilarity washed over him like a wave breaking against a rocky coastal formation. He watched as they turned to the subject of a new TV series, which was then taking up the momentum of the last sensation that had successfully been shown to the masses. There is always a lot of human depravity to be seen, as though it were novel once more to acknowledge and revel in such realities.

Each episode was streamed out weekly to all eligible households, as if a great cultural narcotic was issuing from one central nervous system, in order to inoculate the herd. Such celebrations of power, and ruthless violence, being a principal raison d'être of modern television, this new show was deemed to be exceptionally good. Insensate cruelty and brutality are imbibed by the collective unconscious as individuals savor dreams of holding enormous power.

"Make a movie about Salome and John the Baptist." Isaiah whispered, thinking of a painting by Lovis Corinth. His jest drew only odd glances.

At that instant everyone jumped in their seats, startled by a loud, reverberant clang. Mary Jones had just crashed her tray down onto the skull of a stunned patron. He had boasted to his companions that he would prove, by tactile means, that Mary was wearing nothing underneath her long oxford shirt.

This red-faced businessman was now glaring at her. He stood up, his hands clenched, and found himself staring at the ex-biker, who worked there as a floor manager. This manager came towards the customer, whose ears were still ringing.

"She hit me." The customer pleaded in a sort of yelp. Mary passed by him, elbowing him out of her way. The customer looked sick as Mary stepped over to speak to the floor manager. They exchanged low whispers. The manager nodded to her, and she proceeded inside.

"You touched her?" The manager stepped so close to the offender that he could feel his breath.

The man was incapable of speech, seeing at close range the scars on the manager's enormous beefy face. The steely glitter in his eyes quelled the last glimmer of his animal spirits.

"Maybe I ought to touch you. What do you say to that?" The manager stabbed a finger into the man's chest, and he meekly sat down. His companions posed as disinterested parties, looking at the accused with dismissive scorn. The manager crouched over their table

"All of you, pay up. Now! Come back when you learn some manners."

After that scene, Marx came down to sit by Isaiah. They spoke of Mary's action in tones used by giddy fans at sporting events.

"I should have taken some photographs. Instead I just gawked at her."

"You might want to get her permission first."

Isaiah looked confused, and then smiled weakly.

"Meriwether, you have all your equipment, ready to go, but it looks as though you've lost your way." Marx picked up the copy of *Little Dorrit* that Isaiah had brought with him. He glanced at the compact camera sitting on the table. "This reminds me of the old days. You were always wanting to be prepared to capture something."

"O'Rourke, tell me, why didn't you ever file a lawsuit against the university, for sacking you like that?" Isaiah had been thinking of the resilience of his friend. He had always had that inestimable quality of a child, able to bury things and move on, making each day his new world.

"I talked to lawyers about it. Believe me, I thought long and hard about it. But, I couldn't win. Not without a lot of money. It would take prominent lawyers, a PR campaign, and the thrust of powerful allies to get the story into the public arena. Otherwise, the courts can't be bothered with trying to redress every wrong, suffered by every person, every single time a powerful or prestigious institution perpetrates an injustice against such a person as myself. I really pissed them off." He began to chuckle.

"I just never heard you talk about it."

"That doesn't mean I didn't do some time in my own Gethsemane, beseeching my gods to take this burden off my soul."

"And which gods are those? When did you start talking about the soul!"

Marx raised his mug and sipped his beer. "Patricia has her own faith; and she has always been a saver, like you. It's like I've been trying to tell you, I'm a different person now, having come into the promised land."

"It's a good thing to see."

"She's been a godsend."

They stared at one another; sharing in silence many phantom echoes of former conversations.

"She's brought me to life. You should take note." He tapped his fist into Isaiah's shoulder.

"She's a romantic sort?"

"You don't spend your lifetime studying the language and history of Rome, reading Catullus, Ovid, all those characters, unless you have a passionate nature. Let us say, it is not words alone that please her." Timothy's calm, sober demeanor broke into a giddy expression of sheer happiness.

Someone began speaking of the "kitchen table issues," referring to the upcoming election. An image came to mind for Isaiah, that of a younger Marx, looking much more Marx-like, leaning over a kitchen table, snorting a line of cocaine. Isaiah remembered how he had heaved himself upright, his dark beard flecked with that snowy substance.

"Remember the Belle Coke Epoch?" He said.

Marx laughed; he had coined that phrase for their own revels.

"You were like a demented Santa Claus, remember?"

"You were there too, my friend."

Isaiah laughed, remembering how he had laughed until he was weak, that time, after coming upon that scene in that now lost kitchen.

"The light is getting pretty good now; I should get some shots before its gone."

"Let's not forget about getting together, to do some hiking."

"My legs are not much good for that."

"Well, buy some binoculars, they let you see into the distance." He laughed. Then they were both standing. Timothy rested his hand on Isaiah's shoulder.

Isaiah left soon thereafter, forgetting to take his book with him, preoccupied with a new idea. He was considering a piece to be called *The Northern Architecture*. It would depict landscapes of North St. Louis; a place that, throughout his lifetime, served as a dismal reminder that the American Dream is operated as a semi-exclusive franchise governed by very primitive covenants.

He headed for those blighted precincts, hoping to get some telling photos. He was listening to a mix of his favorite Dylan tunes; those lyrical monologues, which submerged one's mind in a stream of surreal, subjective perceptions. Listening to those poetic dirges launched his psyche into a panoramic flight across his own vast interior.

As Isaiah exited from the main roads, and meandered around, he became anxious, running into many dead ends. He was not surprised by what he found, but he could not face the stark reality. His comfortable liberal positioning of himself was shaken; a vile humor oozed into consciousness. He was glad he had not come in his new car.

He began taking photographs from his window. He noticed a brick scavenger, who owned an old truck. They exchanged suspicious glances. The man's activity would make a good framing shot for what he was starting to envision for the series. He took pictures of numerous (once bourgeois) structures reduced to crumbling shells. These comprised perfect symbols for something he was grasping to illustrate.

A band of small children approached his truck. The faces were hardened, and eager to accost him. He snapped several pictures. In silence they observed him with keen eyes, laden with unbearable intensity. Then they began asking satiric questions from a place he could not fathom. He drove slowly away, hearing their catcalls and laughter.

Isaiah felt preposterous, certain there was nothing he had to offer in the way of novel insight. He had no right to present more evidence of what everyone already knew, as though it were worthy of him to do so. It seemed he was only evading the real issues, like nearly everyone else. He drove south to the downtown area, passing by the crowded baseball stadium.

Yes, of course, let's all meet at the coliseum to have fun cheering our team! Let's spend money frivolously to prove what really matters. He recalled someone telling him, not that long ago, about his recent attendance at a game. The crowd kept chanting *USA! USA! USA!* at the least, incongruous provocation. The tamed, Pavlovian citizens, in their assigned seats . . .

He descended to the river front, where tourists were milling around, and parked his truck by an old power station, dating from the time of the World's Fair. Progress was then measured by horsepower and the plethora of new machines which increased the happiness of a rising middle class. There would be no tumbrils in America! Until such time as these could be mechanized and automated to cull the herd . . .

Isaiah scrolled though the pictures on his camera, looking at the faces of the children he had just seen up north. The gulf between their world and his seemed like some metaphysical quandary. He parked his truck and walked along the river, taking the steps leading up to the Arch, where he sat down to read from a Penguin edition of *David Copperfield*. The book was swollen and pulpy, having lain dormant for a long time in the cab of his truck.

He had acquired a newfound fascination with Uriah Heep, the grotesque mechanical creature, who sprang from the author's psyche, and with more force than was probably intended. Heep is the wicked embodiment of morbid social resentment. His dialogues with David Copperfield conjure other nebulous voices, those of Mr. Dickens, subconsciously holding forth with himself. One hears the furtive persona coveting more from society than is seemly for a man who doth protest so much of his radical convictions.

The author had achieved great eminence, and yet he cannot tolerate the condescension of high society. He once declined to answer the summons of the queen, begging off because he was in his stage costume. She sent word; she did not mind. He sent word back, he did (alas). How he must have crowed to himself, and left gnawing at his savage heart.

To those lodged on that pinnacle of ungodly wealth, unassailable power, and ineffable status, he was a gaudy specimen of the nouveau riche. And a mere artist risen from the low mire of literature (not then a vehicle for achieving eminence). His catechism of social progress was likened to the show of ragged street performers. He was patronized by that class while he worked like a devil to maintain himself in the haute bourgeoisie. He really had no place to call his own in his own society.

The ugly, misshapen Heep was a singular foe to raise up for his readers to observe. The wretch has been a ward of the state, which has inculcated the rudiments required to allow him to become a servile creature, who meekly accepts a low station, supporting the greatness of others. He must bow to those who treat him with contempt. He must hold his tongue when being addressed with humiliating unction. He must bear all stings with dumb servility.

For the first time, Isaiah now senses the exotic fear the Teacher had of this peculiar monster. When David comes finally to strike him, it is with an open hand. Heep is genuinely surprised. Why does *he* think he can treat *him* this way, or that it will do *him* any good. They converse as if they comprise one organism. And this explains why Dickens is obliged to play Frankenstein, turning Heep into an utterly repulsive human monster, who is beyond redemption. He is a cringing, plotting, hideous creature who lives only for his despicable, grasping social designs.

And yet he is close to his mother, much like Grendel; for he is an offspring of the unknown darkness, incapable of honorable behavior. He grasps for what is not his to have. He plots treacherously. He is ignoble, unworthy of having intercourse with decent folks. One wonders why the author needed to present this personification of resentment as only that, and thus a thoroughly offensive thing, that must excite every reader's absolute loathing. Unlike Quilp, you do not laugh at Heep, you only despise him.

He manipulates Heep into seeking after the hand of the angelic maiden, who could never accept him, in any rational narrative. This instance of sexual sacrilege is intended to extract the last pound of a reader's visceral hatred. Being thoroughly familiar with the material of the author's life, Isaiah tries his hand, fumbling with various skeleton keys, to unlock this facet of the Teacher's personality.

At one point the artist must let Uriah explain himself. "They taught us all a deal of umbleness—not much else that I know of, from morning to night. We was to be umble to this person, and umble to that; and to pull off our caps here, and to make bows there; and always to know our place, and abase ourselves before our betters. And we had such a lot of betters!" The wretch relates how his father advised him; "People like to be above you, keep yourself down." The child's response is to become a reptilian climber, who works surreptitiously, befouling his master's household.

Isaiah notices a family trudging up the stairs. A little girl is following her parents, bouncing along on her toes, singing some playful rhyme. She looks at him. Isaiah feels embarrassed to be caught reading in public like an insane vagrant.

Isaiah sat there, watching the broad river, solemn in its massive progress. It was mesmerizing to see this inexorable force as a loyal reader of Dickens, whose favorite metaphor (containing all we know of life) was the river flowing to the sea. He turns back to read the last words regarding the poor prisoner, Uriah Heep, near the end of the tale.

David visits a jail out of curiosity, and just happens to discover that his foe is lodged there. The warden claims Heep is indeed a model prisoner. He has been justly put away for his crimes, and has been profitably rehabilitated. The author delivers his own opinion. He depicts an entirely new kind of wretch. Heep has become a perfect example of the lowest order of human beasts, devoid of any will power of his own.

He is meekness personified. And his inheritance? Utter debasement. It has become his religion. He is glad to be incarcerated. It is the only state any sane person could possibly wish for himself. Sin is everywhere, except there. Franz Kafka could not have improved upon Heep's closing scene. He pines to have his mother living there with him. He believes everyone ought to be there, where it's safe. He forgives Copperfield; tells him it would be better if he also would come into the holy fold, and live free, behind bars. Heep expresses pity for the poor man, who was his mortal foe.

Isaiah drops the book on the steps, looking up into the cloudy sky. How different this scene looks now. Indeed, the great subconscious author faces the enemy of every ego, and stands accused of crimes he has committed against his own humanity! Could it be, has Sir Charles lost his head, again? In his renowned genius, does he regret his shabby treatment of this glorious wretch, out of genuine sympathy?

Isaiah smirks, for no good reason, other than his own mind's loyalty to its sovereign ability to look at the world askance. On a whim he leaves the ruffled book on the steps; wanting to believe someone will pick it up and take heed of its counsel. He descends to the street below and walks along the river going towards his truck. Lately he has struggled to find some inner path back to his earliest major works; but in this instant he knows he has gone beyond that material, somehow, and it would be no good trying to go back.

21

One night, unable to sleep, Isaiah drove about in the city; reverting to a practice once taken up in his youth. This time around the eerie lighting of empty streets made him feel uncomfortable. Too many shadows were reaching out to engulf the staid, inactive monuments. The stolid factors enforcing civilization had taken curious leave of counting-house niceties to kneel before much older spirits. Something out there seemed anxious to annul every social contract ever scripted by man (as dictated by his woman).

He fled to his studio, where he took up a hardbound copy of *Bleak House*, searching for the passage where the author describes a scene at night.

"It was a cold, wild night, and the trees shuddered in the wind." The entire passage is a paean to his love of *seeing*, if not knowing, the innate, mystic nature of the perceived world. He writes of "a pale dead light both beautiful and awful." The stylized people he puppets about are only one part of the phenomenal stories being told in his tales.

Isaiah pulls more books from his shelves, and falls into a studious trance as volumes accumulate around his feet. It is common for scholars to tout *Bleak House* as the capstone of the majestic body of works. Isaiah is aware no single text can lay claim to that superlative honor. That work is, of course, a tour de force, done on a stupendous scale, glowing like a fair city in the light of his beneficent genius.

He was a sprawling giant, who could not help casting widely about in myriad realms. He had his father's business to conduct; a patrimony that extended far beyond a single house. His credentials never derived merely from one source, such as those papers having to do with the prophecy of another kingdom yet to come. His principal legacy came to him from the estate of William Shakespeare, who worked his magic in the same fields. He was faithful, in his own manner, to that king's majesty and vision.

In *Bleak House* he divides the narrative between two voices, that of a woman, who speaks to us in the first person (another almost perfect heroine); and the omniscient third person narrator. This latter addresses us as a trustworthy, eccentric friend. His business is to speak on behalf of the moral essence that ought to bind the People together. He is often chiding them, like St. Paul, or an impossible butler, for he makes no bones about the fact he *is* working for them. In a tight spot, he stoops before them, in honor of their native dignity.

After his eyes began to droop, Isaiah gets up and rouses himself, brewing a pot of coffee. All of a sudden he had the bizarre idea of sketching himself. He had never attempted a self-portrait before, and this amazes him. He pages through several books on Van Gogh, peering at his self-portraits. In one he is wearing a bandage, after being mutilated by his own hand. The gaze is sorrowful, ghastly; searingly honest. See the suffering human! Let us just say, injured patient, day laborer, and *the* believing fool of St. Paul! He has retreated to the temple of his shattered self, shutting the doors; the better to be left to his work.

Isaiah studies his face in a mirror. He sees at once the wary aloofness, the fear of looking beneath the façade of his badly worn idealism. He wonders if he is no different than the decayed gentleman, depicted in *Bleak House*, the moral nihilist, who does not really believe in anything, other than the inertia of the status quo, that has positioned him at the top of the rotten social heap. He adorns himself in proper genteel forms, but is enslaved to the sordid privileges of his caste, which pollutes the wisdom of his mind.

His face, like any other exposed surface, has undergone a gradual deterioration. The aging could be seen as lending its own distinguished air to the structure. He has never lost his romantic spark; it is there, he can feel it, but cannot identify it by any actual features seen in the glass. No one knows what lies underneath all this corruptible flesh, he mutters out loud. The romance is necessary! We all lie for a living. One must go about wearing a proper social mask. You have to be seen as one who believes in the species, don't you? Ha ha ha. The comfort of the clown's face provides solace.

His son was not wrong; he had played the sycophantic fool to advance his career. Gabriella once encouraged him, "Use the people who are willing to use you." What had she meant, exactly? And Edith, she could only look down; any stooping to grain traction was done according to those exquisite manners, such that you hardly noticed what was happening, if you were not of her world. He was always flummoxed by the subtle dynamics of power occurring in the loftier social hierarchies. Who has a say in these matters? Who does not? Who discovers the need to cease following along? How many are capable of finding a way to start over?

Edith had been installed as chairperson to manage the affairs of a charity that held an annual ball. The wife of Bernie Quakely had established this affair, and so they had to turn people away at the doors. The proceeds of that one affair paid her annual salary. It was a cause that purported to help girls in the middle class, who were trying to climb a few rungs higher on the social ladder. The charitable ladies taught the chosen ones the lay of the land; gave them clear notions about who and what really mattered, in dress, manners, and all other mandatory shibboleths. They made it clear what persons one ought to court, and those that were to be shunned. Isaiah had been astounded when he found out this was the 'charitable work' she had boasted of when they first became intimate.

He had lived in two worlds after that revelation. He had sought to be among them, as her worthy consort, even though it was apparent he would never be recognized in any regular position there. Why had he allowed this to go on? As a couple they had existed outside of every social context; by necessity they composed curious ideas of their own, striving to make the real world irrelevant. And that world doesn't play along with such heretical conceits. Both were wracked by different forms of unsanctioned longing, for different kinds of notice, and somehow these strands had gotten horribly snarled, eventually choking them both. Was trying to untangle all that falseness now only a senseless, deleterious task?

"I sacrificed my art for her." He spoke into the mirror. That was how he had justified so much of the mésalliance, to make himself feel better. Ha ha. She believed he was not serious enough about that, or in his attempts to enter her world. He was just another pitiful changeling, roaming too far out of his natural habitat. His own face rebukes him as he smirks; nothing is ever so simple. At one time they enjoyed a genuine bond. Why did they come to struggle so much? Why had they moved past each other? Why had he chased after her again, those last futile and pathetic times? Why had she not shouted, get thee hence! Ha.

He had to laugh, remembering how they adopted the Teacher as their mascot. The irony, how they became, in his mind anyway, poor mimics of his masterful characters. It was her connections that got him into the gallery, which Mrs. Kinfe ended up buying later on. He had secured her patronage using his considerable talent for fawning. Edith never let him forget how she had been a benefactress to his early rise. He peers at himself, moving closer to the glass, wondering, "What constitutes my personality?"

The third person narrator of *Bleak House* refers to the tragic mother of the heroine as 'My Lady Dedlock'; all else in that portion of the text is strictly anonymous, third person verbiage, except for that one slippage. The woman is the mother of an illegitimate child, which she abandons to the care of others, and is later led to believe that abandoned child has died. In fact, she is the one telling her story, as the darling of the book. Her moral tone is that which is taught by her father, the Teacher, who has never mastered it for himself.

Why does he intrude, using his third person voice, to refer to the doomed mother as, 'My Lady'? The device is never explained. In his reticence, one feels the immense potential for growth latent in the man's obsession with our species. His ravenous hunger to know is constrained by his standard dramatic forms; but one feels the vital hunger for greater things. His appetite is larger than one author of titanic gifts can appease; there are too many unanswerable questions to take them all on. And he must feed the peoples' insatiable desire for sugary, fatty delicacies.

Leafing through a copy of *David Copperfield*, Isaiah falls upon the following, "I sought out Nature, never sought in vain; and I admitted to my breast the human interest I had lately shrunk from."

Isaiah goes back to his beginning; he sees again how diligently he had prepared, and then worked, in feverish bouts, on his seminal river vistas. He had placed the viewer on the banks of the river, among the rusty impedimenta of various trades that facilitate the unceasing river traffic. Only partial fragments of the buildings of the city were visible. The Arch was a small scrap of glinting metal, having come down from the clouds, like heavenly debris.

A friendly critic captured some of his feeling; that one was intended to feel this broad, orchestral movement as the sweep of time itself. He had mentioned the "primordial body of fresh water." He missed the cardinal fact of this enormous vein, that it was cut into the earth's surface by ages. The painter's intention was to portray the river as an hour glass. As far as we know, only our species is aware of the fact our planet is destined to become a lifeless boulder, scorched or frozen, or maybe even broken into pieces to become the feedstock for other worlds.

He recalled his passion to imbue the great mother stream with just the right coloring. He had studied Utrillo's numerous Paris skies, receiving inspiration. To the country this was the Father of Waters; deserving of every facet of his craft to invoke the awe of our human race. Nothing could halt this precious flow, except for titanic convulsions in the earth's crust. Humans had no say in such matters, and ought to be made to see and to hear what is before them.

He reads a passage where David looks back on his late wife. "I had considered how the things that never happen, are often as much realities to us, in their effects, as those that are accomplished." Momentous incidents, that occurred in his youth, began to drift into his ken, like ceremonial barges in Venice.

He recalls something he had just read in *Bleak House*; "I had for a moment an undefinable impression of myself as being something different from what I then was.

I know it was then, and there, that I had it. I have ever since connected the feeling with that spot and time . . ."

He was instantly transported to the school carnival at St. Margaret's. It was right after the eighth grade ended. He was sporting about with Stephen and Deborah, feeling quite mature at the school carnival. He was greatly moved for a second, as though feeling the reprise of a premonition, that has not expired nor come to pass.

Now he thought of his mother, who was surely *the* lost personage in his life. After the divorce, she soon met her next husband, while on a solitary vacation, and shortly thereafter she moved to California. By the time Isaiah got around to visiting them, he was an awkward house guest.

A baby had come along to bind the seasoned couple. The man's older children acted very put upon when he was thrust into their midst. He tried to ingratiate himself, and was mocked for his stupid gaucheries. They were athletic, blond, and attractive; children living in the gorgeous shade of studio lots. He had come from the anonymous steppes, where there was no glamour, where only dull things were manufactured.

The husband had inherited an operation that rented out the props needed to film westerns. His company rented stage coaches, wagons, horses, mules, even the non-speaking cowboys and Indians. His mother had taken over as financial manager, and the business was thriving. She had acquired a knack for making sound investments. Isaiah was impressed by all the fine things they owned. He noticed the religious icons, pictures of famous actors, hanging on the walls. They were seen posing with these movie stars. Staring at the pictures he thought of how people once sought the royal touch...

He remembered the exalted afternoon service, the hour when alcohol was served. He could not tell what precisely inaugurated these icy, shivering liturgies. They encouraged him to partake of the ritual as a favored novice in an ecstatic order. One had lovely bourgeois visions after the second martini; all the day's troubles were dissolved. Then there was light, and the light became glimmering faith. The real world had no power to darken one's consciousness.

He strove to be a good initiate. The children smiled archly; they were into the latest drugs. He was consigned to the sphere of uncool adults. His head buzzed and the walls vibrated, but the holy relics never dropped from the walls. The movie stars became too blurry to recognize, but the splendor of their fame shimmered in the light that fell all about them.

Everything of their life was smart, reasonably elegant. The clothing, much of the irony, all the sardonic repartee, a little of the playfulness, in not sparing the feelings of others, or even oneself. In his thrall Isaiah tried to talk to them of his art; but they responded like he was being gauche, offering them counterfeit money in exchange for his daily use of their pool house.

His ideas could not possibly be as rich, strange, and magical as the treasures made in Hollywood; explaining perhaps the allure of those first mysteries contained in a shot glass. They knew actors who purchased art; however, such profligacy was not for lesser mortals. Heavens, they were saving for a second home near Lake Tahoe.

She asked him to come back, and he found excuses, many were real, yet insignificant. He just didn't know how to be there with them. That one trip had been awkward enough. She never came back to St. Louis. He grew resentful about that, even though he was equally at fault for never going back to her.

As the breaking day's light began pouring through his skylight he drove home, and watched a morning show on TV for a while. He was affronted by the bright, cheerful demeanors; the gentle, sardonic playfulness was galling. It seemed the resident hosts were paid to affirm that being a successful television personality equates to being happy, virtuous, and highly esteemed, in all the ways that matter in our culture. In this glaring light they seemed grotesquely unreal. He was exhausted, but he still couldn't sleep, so he sat at his drafting table, staring out at the oak trees for a long time. It seemed as if he'd just moved into this peculiar space, and could not figure out why.

I SAY I attended St. Paul's Academy, when people ask, but it's misleading to say so. I never felt as though I belonged there, even though I was a popular kid, during my short tenure. Maybe too popular; having a car, an honest, reliable pot dealer, and my own apartment in the Loop. I was proud to host epic, teen bacchanals. Trashing my place was a common activity; something I resented later on, when that band of friends scattered to higher ground.

You could say going to the 'right school' turned out to be the wrong move for me. I don't confess this to just anyone, but I was expelled during my sophomore year, and subsequently returned to our great public school system, which adheres to the sound orthodoxy based on Darwin's infallible principles. When it seems necessary I sometimes confess that I was caught selling pot to a 'friend,' and it was his father who made sure no charges were filed, and that I was expelled. My father had some small role to play in these proceedings; I don't remember much, except that we never spoke of the matter afterwards.

It is fair to say, I am still resentful, and I don't know why, or rather, to whom, this anger ought to be directed. I used to blame my mother, and father, for years smoldering with animosity; but now, I am not so sure of anything. I have never understood those days, when I was squandering my abilities trying to grow up too fast. Looking further back now, my mother looms large, for a few precious years she was very helpful in my ultimate quest. She took me to museums, purchased books, nurturing my aptitude; before her marriage was spoiled by irreconcilable differences.

I was an educational orphan. I went to St. Margaret's grade school for the first grade, and then was yanked out and forced to go to a public school for several years. My father had nominal charge of me, after my mother had moved on. It's hard to remember those years. Strange to say, I don't know all the reasons, but I was returned to St. Margaret's for the seventh and eighth grades, and it was then that I became friends with Stephen and Deborah. Once more I found myself living with my grandparents in Ferdinand. I set up my little studio in Uncle Isaac's old room.

After high school I began taking classes at a junior college, and I never understood how it came about, but I was encouraged by my dad to apply at the Chatham Academy of Art. It was a new establishment, the brainchild of a politician and his wife. They were going to use loans guaranteed by donations promised to the politician. And when he lost his next election, the proceeds failed to materialize, and the portly wife, who served as our chancellor, jumped overboard, just in the nick of time, with a fat, inflatable Mae West severance package.

Before the final collapse, though, I had an extraordinary year. There were not many of us there. We were granted access to the libraries at several prestigious universities, and I was able to audit their sumptuous classes. I was moving among swarms of students from all over the country, all obsessed with art. In that milieu one never had to worry about becoming actual friends; our primary ethic involved one's unique perspective. We could not imagine the real world of shows, customers, galleries, critics, patrons, money, and the bloodless business of branding human beings.

We shared our youthful dreams; as delicious and perishable as fresh milk. We knew everything that mattered to us. Those were triumphal days, of being, of becoming, of reaching out for the hand of destiny. There was no doubt the promised land existed. I was very conscious of my good fortune. I knew, by some especial grace (which I sorely miss) how to protect my confidence like a miser would his cache of grimy bills. There was a troubling sense that any happiness that devolved upon me was almost certain to spoil eventually, and so I learned to parade about in the moment, cultivating a poor understanding of things.

I give our doomed chancellor some credit, for she purchased a mansion right across from the park to use as the administration building. It was to be a place for holding fancy soirees. She hoped to lure donors hence, so they might glow under the attention of their clients. Unfortunately, very few parents trusted the upstart institution, for the ugly rumors had spread in small, powerful circles. The academy began life with a negative integer of cachet, which is far worse than having poor credit, which only takes the right politicians to solve.

Politics is about outlandish optimism, after all, and before the banks finally called in their notes the academy installed enormous classrooms in the basement of the mansion to entice the celebrated professors who never did take the bait. Gabriella took the initiative to set up a working studio for us there, expecting to entice at least a few visiting professors. But the word had gone out; none dared risk their comfy tenures. And so, for a brief magical while, it was our romantic lair! I was the only one who studied there, as per her dictates. She became my counselor, instructor, confidante; and finally, sexual agonist.

Gabriella was a generous, demanding paramour, who taught a fledgling how to get off the ground, gain altitude, and soar on thrilling drafts. She taught me the joy of flying into storms for the sake of the strenuous rituals of landing blissfully on soft beds once more. She was proud of her voluptuous figure, which understood the rites of abandonment. I recall smoky shadows playing around her ravenous eyes. Her breasts were plump and shapely fonts dispensing that rare blessed milk of sensual blindness, which is next to godliness. Her passion cracked open my reticent heart.

She had me reading Homer, and I was under a spell, too, as surely as those heroes who were attended by naughty goddesses. In the throes of that ecstasy one assumes he is more than he is ever going to be again, and the desire to drown in carnal fatalism takes hold of the faculties. The besotted novice seeks naturally after an impossible destiny. Her hand, resting on my back — I will never forget certain moments. I was a young Abelard, placed in the care of an older, wiser Heloise, who conducted herself with the touch of a matronly Diana. Her techniques, her confidence in herself, and her greedy, wanton, lovely, moody body — Oh god, it was a time of delirious pedagogy!

"The language of the body." She misspoke one day, ready to start another lecture. I had been working on a street scene, trying to render the diminutive human figures in distinctive poses. She had come up close to see my work; her black lustrous strands of hair snaking about me like wires pulled down onto the wet street by electric storms. From the tremendous, seething clouds a vast potential found its path to ground through the braided limbs of our bodies.

"Body language?" I asked, looking up, innocently. She had laughed, drawing away, her features crimson. Then she was right there, so close to me. Too real, I thought to myself, not having any grounding in such matters. Knowing and not knowing. I could feel her breath, the heat of her body. Her hand clasped my neck, pulling my head over to nestle on her breast; my arms loping around her rump.

Being in such close quarter we found a natural concordance. Living that simple abundance of our secret life became a pagan religion. We strolled about inside museums, talking for hours afterwards. The next day I would not remember a fraction of what we had said to one another. The count of paintings I knew rather intimately grew significantly under her critical tutelage.

One day, I had been copying Vermeer's Girl With a Pearl Earring, and as I was finishing my sketch she came up to have a look. She was obviously distracted.

"This is very good, Isaiah." Her voice was leaden; she had never addressed me in quite this way. I must have beamed at her out of my fatuous contentment.

"I hate to tell you this," she began to explain, while I stared at her troubled features. I feared expulsion on some morality clause. Someone had found out about us (which was true, but no one cared, by then, about such trivial things as that kind of impropriety). I was certain it was over. I was there on a scholarship, which had never really been explained to me. Much later I learned my father had put in a goodly sum.

"What?" She just stared at me; as though she didn't want to tell me.

"The school is failing."

"Failing?" I thought she was trying to let me down easily. I was already feeling insensate anger, needing to blame someone.

"I'm afraid so."

I stared at her, dumbstruck.

"You've no doubt heard the rumors." Not the same ones she was hearing, as she was close to several principals involved in the scam.

"The money's not coming in?"

"No." Fingers on her chin, her head shaking dolefully. "A lot of promises were made, that should never have been."

"So, I should — "

"We still have some time, at least we can finish this semester. I just thought you should know."

"Okay."

"I'll tell you what, let's enjoy what we have left. I say the hell with them. Let it crash down." Her wicked charms gleamed forth. Now it was a delicious conspiracy, even more exciting than before. We didn't have to care about anything else that was laying ahead of us. We had our two idols, Love and Art; and only heeded those treacherous witch muses who openly scorn loss and heartache!

Was I more afraid of losing my educational opportunity, or her? By then, in my stomach, I was already feeling the loss of her, not even knowing yet how entangled she and I had gotten in our emotional arrangements. We counted on each other to stave off the conventional importunities of the damning world. My dreams had never conformed to actual life. I sensed the delusional cement that was being used to hold up our badly constructed playhouse. I had to face the fact it was going to have a messy end.

An old sense of dread returned, regarding the idea of future time. We were quite brave. She was determined to persevere to the end. My studies became more arduous. She was determined to impart all that she knew, while we raced the implacable sun.

"There's no time to waste." This was her mantra. I was fed a constant stream of demanding assignments. She taught me how to work, especially when I did not have the heart for it.

"Work for the sake of working." She seemed to want me to collapse from overwork to prove myself to her. She taught me how to build a regimen that would serve me for years to come. One portrait after another she gave me to copy. It was instilled that I was to master my own repertoire of techniques. She schooled me in how to cultivate my own, singular form, that would always be my own. She dredged through sedimentary layers, even her own bitter disappointments, just to help me build my castles.

I carried by sketchbook with me at all times. I made drawings of all the places we visited; so many café scenes, where she poured out her stories. She brought Paris to life, and it became as a place where I had thrilled and suffered myself. She tried to warn me of inevitable pitfalls. She assumed a maternal air while listening to me prate on about my aspirations that could not possibly include her. She knew how to let me feed off the ripest feelings, while gently correcting my flagrant sins of ignorance. She taught me how to build my craft upon a solid foundation, one 'embracing honesty, grace, and a clear personal sentiment.'

Nice, easy words; try and live by them!

"You must study at the Degas school of draftsmanship," she had counseled.

"There are so many good models," I responded.

"I don't want you to become infatuated with schools." She replied.

"Do you think one should try to be utterly fresh?" Being facetious, and serious.

"No, of course not."

"I don't want to limit myself?" I was trying to impress her.

"It's very difficult to develop your own style, your own mode of expression. That's all I'm saying; just keep this in mind. It takes time." Ah, time. Please don't mention that tortuous flow. The songs of Orpheus are played sardonically by the cottonwoods standing along the shores of my rivers!

It was exciting, to be treated as the coveted artist; but one misses a lot when he plays the role of a young Abelard, who doesn't care about, nor understand, the dialectics of enraptured emotions. I was spending too much time attempting to solve one grave problem; how does a woman's mind and body interlace to find peace in such a tangle of powerful tensions? How does one capture such moments, when you are coming to know that you shall never truly grasp the most beautiful, frightful, unreasonable mysteries of your life?

We frequently went to the Tivoli theater. If I got lost in the esoteric plot she would whisper the sibylline keys into my ear, and I would see things more clearly. Sometimes she pushed her tongue into that socket, sending a racing current throughout my body. The past scenes of my life merged into those of the movie and coursed together with dramatic intensity. I began walking around, observing the world from a great remove, all the while listening to a movie score playing only in my head.

She took us to remote places of rustic beauty, where we might look at the world, in detached, serene wonderment. I was able to experience that appetite, feeling, and love, which are the mother's milk of artistic endeavors. She understood this, knowing what moved me, and her touch — by what infinite degrees she tempered her ministrations. I pledged my confidence because of her. It was rather chaotic, but I had a clean consciousness; eager to register anything that was of value — such is the credulity of a young, artistic fool!

We spent a lot of time at my apartment on Westgate. There was one Christmas season when we played the old carols at all times of the day. They became terribly affecting, for I heard them as love songs, grievous laments of wounded hearts. By then we were waking up as wholly separate persons, when not joined in the flesh. Our love was waning. It was tainted by all the usual doubts. Marx said to me once, "In time, every other person is a rival for power." What innocent soul can know the full power of jealousy? The distinct gravity of separate bodies? The inexorable necessities of individuals seeking status among other people? To take up our roles (mine to work under her tutelage) was our refuge. I learned to fix my concentration on the object at hand. It can be a terrible discipline, for one who must be alone for long stretches.

By the time I was married, I was far too passive. I knew what was good for me, and regarded my wife's emotional welfare as a challenge which she was supposed to take care of for herself. It sounds absurd, I know, but I've only come to this realization the hard way. I was miserly with my affections. I still feel immoveable, in that way. It strikes me at the oddest times, when I am painting a portrait, the utter impossibility of knowing another person. My primary requisite has always been to get a particular expression so true, in resemblance, that the image would resonate with those who know the person. The mask is a perfect metaphor for my trade.

When Gabriella passed away, it brought a rush of storied grief. I had not had any contact with her for many years. Her keepers found my early letters in her effects and reached out to me. There are some souls you must lose twice, and for whom you grieve always. When you find one has passed away, there is an uncanny sense of completion. A sad mortal finality strikes home. A living being you knew, in all that beauty and complexity, has vanished forever, leaving you with abstractions that become like poorly done reproductions in the shabby house of memory.

I'm not making much sense. It is difficult, trying to explain yourself to someone else; as soon as you get down into the murky depths of memory, you become lost. Language is not an adequate instrument for putting labels on that dynamic movement of the clever psyche. Perhaps that explains the convention of seeing the soul in the eyes; we must believe we can know the profound depths of others. It is a sort of deviltry, attempting to paint that precious light, knowing we have only a poor grasp of what we really seek to know.

Well, I haven't much more to say on that score. As you can see, my schooling is not something I am comfortable talking about. You know what St. Paul says about 'The wisdom of this world.' So much has happened that has contributed to a feeling of never belonging. Once the academy closed down, my fortunes led me to Muddy Currents. *By dint of Herculean labors, I found further success with my brushes, and eventually, in finding a patronage that smoothed my path. As honorable emeritus of the Gang of '73, that merry breed who sought to stay put near a provincial river, winding through the vast interior, I feel entitled to form my own manifesto. It shall be based on paying homage to idols that have existed throughout time, for reasons we cannot begin to fathom.*

22

Sitting outside at Pliny's café Isaiah sips from a glass of wine, staring vacantly at the urban scenery where his life has played out. The waiter has taken his plate away, and he looks up and recognizes a woman walking towards him on the sidewalk.

"Isaiah!"

"How are you?" He can't remember her name.

"I'm doing well enough." She spoke slowly, as if each word carried enormous weight. Her smile seemed to freeze on her lips as alarm came into her eyes.

"Strange times." He affirmed.

"Yes, certainly." She began handling her cell phone in a nervous manner.

"A lot has changed." Both were thinking of Edith, and neither wished to disturb her inviolate rest.

"It seems more people are getting out." She turned her gaze in the direction she wished to go.

"Would you like to sit down?" He knew she would decline his bizarre offer.

"Oh no; I couldn't." She looked at her watch.

"Say, do you know how St. Louis died?"
She tilted her head and smiled.
"I was just wondering—"
"I really must be going." She looked once more at her tiny watch, and broke into a canter.

One time Edith had purchased an expensive timepiece for him, being embarrassed by his cheap Timex. Isaiah had recently thought of buying an expensive watch, and now laughed at himself. He left his table and began walking.

He was painfully aware of a time when he might have easily made the long trek to the park. He ambled along as an old person. His eyes flicked over people passing by; ever intrigued by the way people, unaware of being observed, conducted themselves in public. At one time his wife had purchased his clothing for him, but that had not lasted very long. She had once advised him to adopt the look of a successful editor.

"I *should* dress the part *I* esteem, assume the part of crazy codger. A straw hat like Van Gogh in Arles."

He went to his studio, knowing he was not going to do any work. He began reading from an ornate copy of *Dombey and Son*. He searched for a passage; his mind knew where it was located on the page. He found the place telling of Mrs. Skewton, the woman who has "sold" her beautiful daughter twice, in respectable, conjugal bargains. As she sits before the mirror, in her diamonds, frills and finery, she collapses on the vanity; "where she lay like a horrible doll that had tumbled down." The doll metaphor is used repeatedly by the renowned fabulist throughout his works.

Feeling despondent Isaiah left the studio and drove homeward. He passed by his building and headed north. In no time it seemed he was driving along Elizabeth Avenue, admiring the sycamore trees. He pulled into the parking lot between St. Margaret's and Molly's house. He ventured into the Grotto area, where he encountered two women tending the grounds. He spoke to them briefly of the weather, and they spoke reverently of the beauty of the day. He moved on to seat himself on a low wall where he could stare into the middle level of the school grounds.

He began to sketch the layout of the parish buildings. The church was on the highest level, on the corner, and the school was attached, and descended down across two lower tiers of ground. It would be hard to get all of this into one picture. He considered how it might be done. After some painstaking attempts to capture the stone walls of one building, on the middle level, he set his pad aside and began reading *Dombey and Sons*.

He decided that little Paul, in *Dombey and Son*, and little Nell, from *The Old Curiosity Shop*, were paradoxical doubles, situated at opposite poles of society. Both children belonged to that order of sacrificial lambs, who were not destined to succeed in society. The frail, sickly, rich boy inquires why money matters? Papa Dombey sternly declaims his creed; it is necessitous, "to be honoured, feared, respected, courted and admired." It is the material that "made us powerful and glorious in the eyes of all men." It is the mud and straw used to make the bricks for erecting steps to climb upwards on our sturdy, beyond ever toppling, Egyptian hierarchies, so one might petition smiling crocodile divinities for succor, favor, and know all the strenuous, maddening, wholesome animal delights besides.

It is noteworthy that Paul's rich father fears the world's opinion of him. It is, "the haunting demon of his mind." He is in torments when imagining how society views him. He trembles at the thought of what society says about him behind his back. This fear is an oppressive, controlling force in his life. His success has become a life sentence; he lives in dread of people who were born above him. Such personages despise him, and all other such menial actors, who must trade goods or services for a living. Even among those he knows as subordinates, "He feels that the world is looking at him out of their eyes."

Isaiah looks out at the empty playground, where a girl and boy, probably siblings, traipse by, climbing the steps to the upper level. They are still in that diminutive world, of rare, mystic happiness, which the outer world cannot touch. He is struck by an unanswerable pang of regret; suffering the fugitive loss of never having known the companionship of a sibling. He had one half-sibling, who was born to his mother in California, and was now to him only a spectral admonition. He remembers, after graduating from St. Margaret's, that his father took him out to dinner in a quiet restaurant. After the meal he looked at him in a way he had never seen before.

"Now, let's talk about your future." His manner was peculiar in its formality. How would you like staying with your mother, going to high school in California?"

He thought of the new friends he had made, it tore at his heart. "No, I don't think so."

"You'd have the ocean, a whole new life to explore."
"I don't know." To himself; *I don't know her!*
"Well, you should think about it. Your mother is doing well out there, and really, it could be a good move for you."

Looking back, Isaiah realized his father was saying it might be good for both of them, in purely financial terms. His father had remained single after his divorce, and had been more of a Bohemian than any of Isaiah's friends would be later on, in his Loop circle, when that was something they affected to prize above their daily labors.

It was strange to look upstream, across the frozen face of indurate time, at what might have been. By staying in place he grew closer to his father; Thomas Meriwether, the salesman of motors. He had run around with a crowd of not very serious bons vivants, or so Isaiah always imagined. It was a construct he fashioned after he was exiled from his boyhood.

He remembered the places where his dad's friends seemed to lead lives so contrary to what was expected by society. There had seemed to be no affectation of being in a separate category of their own. He detected no smug or superior airs, and concluded they must be embarrassed. It was rather that they were comfortably at ease in these experiences they had sought and enjoyed. The attractive women used to tease him; drawing from deep stores of knowledge that left him in speechless entrancement. He blushed as they laughed and squealed over his embarrassment. And there was that one woman—what was her name? She had taken a serious interest in him, treated him as if he were older. He could still remember how she shielded him from that raillery which made him so nervous, when standing in front of them like a poor foreign exchange student dressed in his barrio mufti. His father had surveyed them both from the balcony seat of his happiness. He wondered what became of that remarkable woman . . .

Isaiah began looking around, feeling that sensation of being observed, and he soon noticed a man just outside the back door of the rectory. It was a priest, sitting peaceably at a small table, staring at him. Isaiah felt obliged to account for his presence, so he walked over to greet the fellow.

"How are you?" The priest stood up and extended his hand. "Care to join me?"

Isaiah was pleased to do so. He explained that he had attended St. Margaret's many years ago, and that he was a painter, and was thinking of doing something with these buildings.

"We have a few painters in the parish."

"This little grove you've made here, that's wonderful." Isaiah spread his hand out towards the lush Grotto area.

"A lot of work has gone into that, mostly before I got here."

They both looked out at the many species of evergreens on the grounds. Isaiah studied the young cleric's congenial face, slightly pocked from childhood diseases. The head was crowned with a full crop of neatly groomed hair. His clear hazel eyes complemented his warm, genuine smile.

"You've set up a nice little vantage here. These are your sacred grounds."

"Yes, sitting here, like this, encourages people to come over and talk with me. I found this out by accident. So now I come out here to make myself available."

"Sounds like a good practice. But now you've gotten ahold of me." Isaiah laughed.

"What do you mean?"

"Oh, being the artist, pagan, all of that, not the best subject for your line of work."

"The Church used to shepherd great artists like flocks of sheep."

"That wasn't so good for either side, was it?"

"No." The priest smiled roguishly. "It was wrong, done that way. Be assured, I never proselytize, as a general rule. But tell me, were you baptized?"

"Yes, I was."

"Well, there you are, you cannot ever rub that out, the Church owns your soul." The priest smiled preciously, and it was now clear he possessed a whimsical sense of humor.

Isaiah smiled affably. "Well, somebody ought to have charge of that troublesome gadget, I suppose."

The man stretched out his legs and clasped his hands over his flat stomach.

"Now, you said as a general rule, what about in a particular case?"

"Can't really know about those until you've gotten to know the particular situation."

"Spoken like a politician."

The man grimaced. "Some people look at this collar, and see superstition. Others see evil. And some see both, placing me in a very sinister light."

Isaiah looked at him, on the verge of responding, but rejecting every comment that came to mind.

"I have to appreciate that much of the world is not in accord with my mission. I seek any useful path that lets me move forward, as I believe one should."

Isaiah cautioned himself to be careful in speaking to this man. He turned his eyes to the chimney swifts flying over the playground in wide circles.

"Father, you may see me out here at times, taking photographs, so I can do some work on these subjects later on, if that's alright?"

"Certainly. And you may call me Charles."

"Okay then, I will count on your forbearance." Isaiah was treating the priest as though he were a prospect for a portrait; hoping thereby to avoid running afoul of Molly's gracious fellowship.

They exchanged parcels of personal information. The priest was proud of his early studies in philosophy, and Isaiah was amazed to hear the man quoting Spinoza. Then Molly's name came up, and the conversation became more animated.

"Are you in one of her book clubs?" The priest asked.

"One of her—no. I met her years ago. And she knew my uncle, Isaac Cook, pretty well. He grew up in that house, where Molly lives."

"Oh, okay. She still talks of him, quite fondly." The priest's manner became more relaxed. "So, are you, one of the Cooks?"

"On my mother's side."

They spoke a little of that family history, neither one wishing to dwell in that region of the past for long.

"I would not have thought Spinoza would play a role in your catechism." His scant knowledge of the great Jewish philosopher had come to him secondhand, mostly through the observations of Marx. "Isn't he considered to be outside the fold?"

"In what way?"

"I don't know, just in the fundamental—"

The priest began to expound upon his long dalliance with the ideas of Spinoza and got carried away. "Anyway, my interest began when I was pretty young; I read that Einstein said he believed in Spinoza's god."

"Isn't that god indifferent to human affairs?" Isaiah asked, trying to retrieve dusty articles from his memory banks. He recalled that Marx used to brandish him rather frequently at one time.

So you've spooned up a little Spinoza, have you? This had been a standard quip, used by Marx to mock anyone who tried to sound more knowledgeable than he on such topics.

"The way I look at it, he was devoted to knowing, and seeking blessedness; using such knowledge to become more and more virtuous. He accepted the facility of using human fictions, which are inevitable due to our limitations, using these as guiding principles to improve the way we go about being human beings."

"I'm not really qualified to dispute anything said in this area. All my knowledge on such matters comes from café chatter."

It was interesting to hear the young man talk of his youth. A prime tenet of the Teacher's gospel was that some imperishable part of one's childhood remains with us as a deposit of goodness, if the child had been fortunate, and afforded a proper childhood, by society and the fates and the larger world.

"Does Molly ever come over here, to visit with you at your table?"

"I see Molly all the time. We consult on a regular basis, regarding parish issues. She's always ready to pay a visit to a person in need. Those who are in distress, and vulnerable, are glad to see someone they can trust." After adjusting his legs the priest added, "Someone who is not seen as passing judgment." His finger brushed across his collar. "She is someone who cares about the welfare of the entire parish." He glanced at Isaiah, as if to assay his understanding of such delicate matters; which strangely enough, he himself was now finding difficult to enunciate.

Isaiah had been nodding his head, feeling humbled by the man's unmistakable conviction.

"I had sort of hoped to see Molly out in her yard, so I could speak with her again."

"She usually comes out in the afternoon to work in the yard. She used to come over here to paint, that was some time ago."

"I remember that now, she paints." Isaiah stood up, hefted up his camera and looked at it. "I think I'll just get a few shots. Good talking with you—"

"Charles."

"Say, do you want this book? I have numerous copies of all his works. He's my favorite author. Van Gogh loved him." He stopped, hearing himself sound foolish.

Charles graciously accepted the old Penguin copy and seemed to weigh it in his hands, with a sage expression. He was intrigued to know more about this fellow's relations with Molly. He had noticed him over in her yard not too long in the past.

"Thank you, I appreciate that very much." To Isaiah his warm gratitude confirmed that his kind nature was innate.

Isaiah was not entirely conscious of his own motive in offering this gift to the priest. He entertained a vague notion that he would enjoy sharing his ideas on Dickens with him, if a friendship should ever develop between them. It was also his desire to become better friends with Molly, and she was clearly on close terms with this minister of her church. As he began strolling away the priest called out to him.

"By the way, Molly doesn't work on Fridays, so she's usually in her yard a lot on those days."

"Oh." Isaiah nodded vigorously, not sure what to say. He strolled about, taking photographs. The breezes washed around him and he was quickly swamped by memories from his childhood. Several times he sat down and let the reveries sweep over him; falling away into vast emotional depths. Time seemed to glimmer as the heat seen above the ground on a hot day. His perceptions were passing through refractions, while partaking of sensory information that is not about knowing, but only sensing one's way deeper into that submerged womb of personality. The best parts are stirred as we uncover salutary traces of past experiences that are too precious to be forgotten.

Sitting on the low wall, close to the ground, he smelled the earth's pleasant odors. He noticed a clutch of last year's sassafras leaves gripping the earth around his feet. The skeletal tissues teased his eye like the strange characters inscribed by those primitive instruments of lost ages. His soul took flight through the medium of time, visiting many joys and sorrows. He felt an odd sense of being more alive in that moment; feeling life's inestimable glory.

In his youth this must have been a common occurrence. The close of one season was the inauguration of something else that invariably proved to be even more stimulating. His blood had always reveled in something that cannot be marred by the abrasive grains of spilling time. That feeling of being on the advent of moving forward and knowing more, that was holy, and he supposed now, unrecoverable ground. It was the height of vanity trying to recapture what was gone. He must try something new!

23

The next Friday Isaiah made his way to Ferdinand early in the morning. He wended through the Grotto maze, overcome by the fragrance of the evergreens. He decided to attempt an excursion around the neighborhood, but just as he was starting out Molly called to him.

"What are you doing here so early?"

He hefted his camera by way of answer. She motioned for him to come into her yard, where they stood apart, keeping a proper distance.

"We're not out of the woods yet," Molly said, referring to the pandemic.

"Not by a long shot."

They spoke of the heralded, forthcoming vaccine; the government had opened its coffers of good faith and credit to expedite the development process.

"Yes, we have to be careful." He said, aware how careless he had been getting in this regard.

"What do you want to photograph?"

"Street scenes—those two sycamores on Darst are like two gentle giants taken out of a fairy tale."

"I've painted those."

"Yes? Well, I just wanted to walk around, see what else I might see."

"I wonder if that is some sort of homing instinct coming to life? Be careful, you might be out of season. If you move in now, you'll have to leave again, this fall, with the swifts."

"I'm not sure what it is, but something is tugging at me."

"Well, you sound like someone who has almost found a purpose in life."

He had to laugh; she made it so easy. "Just a man in search of work."

She tilted her head back to scrutinize him from beneath the brim of her large, floppy hat. To anyone who had known her, for any length of time, her ordinary face was fascinating to behold. One was drawn irresistibly into the appealing depths of her being. Her features were cast in lovely shades, her eyes gleaming forth a merry challenge, to come closer, to learn more. Plumes of graying hair tumbled about her shoulders in a lovely accent of her mystic resourcefulness.

"Did you happen to notice our construction project?" She gestured toward the end of her yard.

"Yes, but I was afraid to interrupt the work crew. What are they doing?" He now recognized Jacob, and another man, who were working briskly.

She beckoned him to follow her to the back wall, where he was introduced to her son Luke, who was there to help his father build what they were calling the Look Out. It was to be an elevated, roofed platform, erected between two venerable ash trees. The platform would provide a vantage of the verdant, rolling landscape and the skies above.

The two workmen were dressed in white overalls. Luke was quiet, reserved; a serious young person with long, tangled brown hair, and a shaggy beard. Something in his dark, sensitive eyes bespoke the lineage of Molly; whereas his features were clearly hewn from the same template that had formed Jacob's boyish lineaments

"A place for enjoying the dusk, and to watch the night come alive." Jacob said.

"A seat for peering into the cosmic elements." Molly's voice sounded as a chime.

"This will be like a pew for her." Jacob responded. "A place for spiritual reflections."

"Let's not shock Isaiah with our pagan ways."

"*Our* pagan ways?" Jacob remonstrated, a broad grin lingering on his face. "He favors Isaac, as you've said, so he might be more attuned to such things than we can possibly know."

Isaiah smiled in an ironic way to suggest he must hold on to his secrets. "I'm afraid you two probably knew him better than I did; I was so young when he was around. It wasn't like . . ."

"Like what?" Molly demanded.

"It wasn't like, with some others."

"With who?" Molly insisted.

Seeing Isaiah's growing consternation, Jacob said, "You can't plead no contest when she puts you on the spot."

"I was going to say, my dad. He used to include me in his world, when I was pretty young—"

"You were good friends with your dad?"

"We were buddies, sort of, when I was a kid. It was pretty unorthodox—"

"Well, there you go!" Jacob exclaimed. "That's what we're after here. You need to tell us more, but not now. There is the task at hand." He turned to Luke and motioned towards something on the ground, and they commenced working.

Molly escorted Isaiah back to the middle of the yard, explaining as she walked that Luke played the mandolin in a bluegrass band. He earned his living at a job he did not care for, and he was hoping to change his situation. In her terse commentary she revealed much, and her countenance supplied further context as she spoke.

"My son Theo, he's going through something similar." Isaiah's face was grave. Her eyes swept over his visage.

"You said you were going for a walk?"

"Yes." He felt he was being dismissed.

"Have a good time." She said, and then stopped and turned towards him. "Wait, would you mind taking some photos of those two, working on their project, before you leave?"

"Oh sure, no problem."

He returned to the construction site in the back of the yard.

"I've been instructed to document your work. Just in case there are shortcuts taken, and the insurance companies get involved. We'd hate to see lawsuits."

The two men barely glanced his way. He began taking photos as they hoisted up ponderous beams, holding them up, affixing stays, and hammering the structure in place. He watched them cutting pieces of wood, enjoying the silence after the terrible screech of the saw, and the pungency of the sawdust.

Later on he studied the images on his camera, taking the measure of this man whom Molly had married. His face bore a frank aspect, suggestive of a very old boy. His soul had weathered trials and he had remained a cautious being of good cheer. His blue eyes could still see the world from the child's perspective. He took innocent nourishment from that source; and jealously guarded his treasures from more predatory natures.

Isaiah felt quite nimble as he walked down Elizabeth in sweeping strides, feeling everything on this tilted planet was in balance. His own gliding motions proved this fact. He stared at the lovely sycamore trees, having that feeling of being on intimate terms with these stately beings. He wondered if Jacob and Molly had evolved an elegant system of taking turns at being the realist of the household. He imagined the glory of having someone cover you as your mind travels along higher paths.

He walked up the hill on Adams, and then proceeded on Clay, past the old Spencer house, where Deborah had grown up. The carriage house had once been called The Joint, by the teenagers in the family. At one time it attracted hordes of teens, who arrived at this rendezvous like ancient tribesmen looking for trade goods and adventures. Most of that happened after Isaiah moved away from the parish, the second time. He had gone to live with his father, for a while, and then later by himself, in his own place in the Loop. *How strange all of that seemed to him now.*

Years later, after he had met Jacob and Molly, through his uncle Isaac, the carriage house, or The Joint, had been transformed into a little cottage, and later was transformed into an art gallery. Behind the building they had fashioned a private restaurant, in the sunken garden, as they called it then. This became known as the Montmartre Café, serving a circle of friends who were fairly active in promoting the local community.

Isaiah tramped up Church Street and descended the slight grade on the other side. As he approached Elizabeth he decided to turn around and go tramping across several yards to reach Spencer's hill. He wanted to see the sunken garden once more. The field kitchen had been located where the stables once were, and now it was a vacant, moldering space where only fat spiders and gaunt memories stirred. Native stalks rose insolently from cracks in the dingy stone flooring of the courtyard out front.

He took a seat at the one wobbly table that remained. He sat a moment to enjoy the secluded feeling; it was akin to visiting ruins. He had heard somewhere how the poet Shelley once liked to seat himself in the evocative rubble of Rome, breathing the rich, desolate gloom of that eternal city. Isaiah had only visited the café a few times, the first being in 1998, after Stephen had called him to suggest they go see what this revival of The Joint was all about. They agreed to meet at the church steps of St. Margaret's.

"It's like an exotic temple, in a distant land; something out of Matthew Arnold; say, our Stanzas from the Grand Subterfuge." Stephen gazed at the church with an abstract air. Years of reporting on the behavior of his species, especially those holding great power, had hardened his temper. "What are *we* doing here?"

"You had some great times here. You and Deborah?"

"Yes, we were like children; reared too soon, or was it too late?" He smiled weakly.

"Before reason had time to sort things out, I suppose."

He had looked at Isaiah as though he were receiving unwarranted praise.

"I always wondered why it didn't work out for you two?" Isaiah was bold enough to inquire. His friend did not respond; a rueful expression passed grudgingly across his face.

They were soon trudging across several yards and climbing Spencer's hill, making their way around the retaining wall to descend into the Café Montmartre. There was a crowd in the courtyard. Another group was up in the big house. This party at the sunken garden café had been the handiwork of Molly and her friends. Isaiah remembered that Stephen lost his melancholy reserve and began to act very cavalier, as if liberated from all his past concerns.

There was another time, he recalled, just before dusk, when he had gone there with Edith; she had unexpectedly agreed to come with him. They had a table of their own, until Stephen arrived and sat with them for a while. Isaiah had not known he was in town that time; and now none of these events were distinct in his memory.

Stephen left the table to visit with Molly, and Isaiah remembered watching him, as he was transported into the chimera of his earlier boyhood.

Stephen had been laughing very naturally. It really was a world where souls appeared to themselves, even as fire flies glowed in the purple suburban gloom. Beyond the café one could only see a mass of vegetable growth along the fringes, and above the crepuscular vault arching over them. In that moment they had risen above the land itself, having found a way of transcending whatever had seemed so real in the past.

Isaiah had been keen to see how Edith would receive Stephen, manipulating her sensitive social filtering devices. In fact, she did not seem to know what to make of him. His suave, casual, brotherly charm fascinated women, whom he wished to impress. He had been out in the world, reporting on the movers and shakers, and he spoke of them with such peculiar indifference, which she could neither condone, nor easily disavow, for she did not understand it.

"She's our earth mother," Stephen said of Molly, when he came back to the table, after gliding around among the crowd. He looked very relaxed. The evening became quite boisterous; there was a continuous burst of laughter rising from various tables. People were moving about, mingling, casting their usual reserve to the wanton suburban breezes. The seductive, eternal melodies of their youth wafted over them.

He recalled that Edith had gone off somewhere, with a group clustering around Molly. They had gone down the Magic Path, as they called it. He recalled this unlikely group of women, moving in a slow procession, almost hearing again the bright laughter, and shrill girlish shrieks. Isaiah and Stephen stood against the wall, watching them go, and then, more intently, as they came strolling back. Much was happening that could no longer be seen from this distance in time.

Later they had watched Molly come back and grab a woman by the arm. Then they went down the leafy trail that ran along the back yards of the houses. He had seen Molly coming back, her face stern and troubled; a stir came into the entire group, and they stood apart from this commotion, and so it seemed as though it could not be that important. Nothing was, not there, under the celestial lights.

He could not remember soliciting Stephen's opinion of Edith, after he saw her that one time. He never stayed in town for very long, so he could not bring them together again. That evening they formed a tacit agreement to watch everything happening, without commentary, relinquishing even the pleasure of sharing mordant wisecracks. It was possibly the most essential moment of their friendship. They were observing the other people like two mesmerized infants, kindred in their curiosity, able to share only their wonderment in silence.

Then it was getting late, when Molly had come up to their table, and teased them in that ironic manner she practiced so artfully. She had gleaned information about them, from others she had just spoken to, and now, she wanted to barge into their castles. "I thought you were over here feeling superior, but really, you're just envious." They had to laugh, just a little. She understood they were good friends, who rarely saw each other. She asked them provocative questions about their youthful forays.

They responded to her questions as though the past were of no moment to them. How could it be to anyone? She knew differently, by reading their faces. They affected to act blasé, for the instant fun of it; and she understood that too. She drew them out until she was able to comprehend a nebulous disaffection they really did not understand. So she accused them of something, to see how that would play out.

"You're both devoted to a nostalgic version of the past, that has never happened!"

They gaped at one another. "That's not true." Each of them said, knowing somehow, that something like this was very near the truth. Neither knew what renovated version of the past they would have opted to have instead.

"Tell me, what would you have changed?"

They looked sheepish.

"I would have been with Deborah!" Isaiah exclaimed.

Stephen had looked at him with the strangest smile.

Neither had any idea what exactly they would have changed. She spoke at some length of Deborah, whom she had gotten to know over the years, and they listened eagerly to hear what she was doing presently. Her ability to secure their slavish attention was rather distressing. They chided her for throwing them into confusion by using witchcraft.

"My only cult has been Romanticism." Isaiah bragged.

"Everybody pretends to be in one, or two cults, and really lives in several others." Stephen offered. "They just can't afford to admit that to themselves." Stephen gazed far off, as if appraising something on a higher plane. "They say God, country, family; meaning social status, personal glory, genetic determinism."

"Not everyone starts with such a bleak premise." Molly retorted quickly, before retreating towards the calls of her people coming from one of the tables.

He recalled being there another time with Edith, as crowds were milling about, enfolding them, making them anonymous amidst their loud company. He remembered the whispered talk suggesting that Molly had met someone at work, and that Jacob was intensely jealous. He had been there earlier with his son Luke, a toddler at the time, and then he had gone home rather early. He recalled hearing storms of laughter. How many times had he gone back there on his own? Maybe twice, but it was never the same.

Someone started a lawnmower. He now felt like he was trespassing and got up to leave. He walked for a while and then made his way to Sistah's Vineyard on Florissant Road. He sat at a table outside to devour a good helping of tangy chicken salad. The street scene was, to his eye, like the quaint frontispiece of an old book, imbued with effects that tease the mind with ideal archetypes that have never been realized.

After his meal he walked north to Wabash Park, and explored the perimeter of the small lake. A lovely black oak at the far end caused him to pause and take photographs. After more explorations of the neighborhood he returned to his car. He could not resist taking another jaunt through the resinous copse of fir trees of the Grotto. He was learning the species; the balsam and blue spruce were his favorites. It was going to be a superb afternoon. The children had been let out of school and were gone. He took a seat on his wall. The Madonna stood at his back as he watched the chimney swifts flying above the buildings.

"Did you have a good walk?" Molly had come up to sit down beside him. She reached for his sketchpad, which he had taken from his car, and examined the contents.

"I made very slow progress, and it was splendid. I ate at that place you told me about."

"I wish I could draw like this."

"It's taken me a lifetime to be at ease with that facility. All I ever cared about, starting in that school," he pointed at the stone building straight before them, "was learning the technical aspects of this art. Now I find that isn't nearly enough."

"You've done good things in the past, I'm sure you will do more. You have a penchant for being dramatic." She turned and smiled. "And its done in a sneaky manner."

He made a mirthful sound of assent, while smarting from that astringent assessment.

"Tell me how do you decide to commit to one image, after you've collected so many?"

"I don't really know. I start a lot of pictures, that I never finish."

"Most never come off?"

"Most are abandoned."

"There, you see? You say abandoned, like they were precious to you. But how could they have been?"

"That's true, I guess." He asked her about the genesis of the Café Montmartre, and she spoke on that matter in a succinct fashion, moving quickly to the topic of how she met his uncle Isaac. She regaled him with stories of when Isaac and Paul would hold court at their picnic table, during the weekly fish fries held on Friday.

"I wish you had a photo of of them sitting there."

"So do I."

"You never knew Jacob, before that time?"

"No, that's when we met, after he came back to Ferdinand. For a while he was living in the Joint! That's where I first met him, after a party. It was late, and he was really out of it; but he was making me laugh."

They were silent as she began turning the pages of his sketchpad. His mind was all over the place, infusing the present with countless fleeting remnants of the past. She began moving her face around as if feeling the world's hidden texture. He told her how he had received the news that Stephen had hanged himself in Haiti, and how furious he was at the time; not believing the official account.

"Why not?"

"He told me he was exposing gross misconduct in the handling of the charitable funds. He said to me, 'It reaches up into the highest circles.' He wasn't, in my mind, he wasn't put together that way. He wasn't one who would take his own life. I thought he was probably going to quit what he was doing, and he told me once, 'I should do something else, get out of this racket of trying to speak the truth about power to those who don't care.' He kept saying nobody cares." Isaiah shook his head, as if to disburden himself from the cumbersome task of attempting to explain his seasoned grief.

"Tell me what happened to you and Edith?" She asked abruptly. He looked at her and wondered if she were really asking, 'How have you come to end up so alone?'

"Well, sure, *that's* a simple topic."

"Oh, everyone says I'm too nosy; but I don't purposely go around with the intention of messing around in other people's lives. I just want to know things."

"I can't figure out why I kept trying to make something happen, after it was over. She made it pretty clear things were not going to change."

"What did you want to happen?"

He paused, drew in a breath, and exhaling forcibly. He could not tell her how it made him feel when he knew she was with other men. "I don't know. I was chasing her right up to the end. It makes me cringe now."

"You two seemed very compatible when I saw you together."

"You are relentless." He looked into her unflinching eyes, now that woven mauve color of the overhead skies at dawn. "Our only happiness was when we were free of the tribe. We had evolved our own ways of being separate, and together. Ha! I'm still trying to create a narrative not based on the known facts!"

"What were you trying to achieve with her?"

"To achieve? Well, it wasn't respectability." He was visibly shaken by this confession. "I think I knew that was a lost cause, from the first."

"You don't like discussing this, do you?"

"It's like touching a nerve."

"You know, it really hurt me when you didn't stay in touch. I thought we had started to become good friends. And new friends are easy, it's the old ones who take all the work. You disappeared before it could even get going long enough to become difficult for us. That's when you learn about each other."

"Taking off, that's my modus operandi, or so I've been told. Do you think we only try to understand our lives when we get old, because a certain distance has been obtained, and so much doesn't matter any more?"

"I'm not as old as you and Jacob, so I can't speak from that lofty perch, the way you two like to do."

"Okay, tell me this; do you know how St. Louis died?"

"Did his wife kill him?"

Isaiah laughed loudly. It was too good.

"That stiff figure on the horse, he almost perished that day you paid him a visit, didn't he?"

"He was clearly in peril."

"Did he seem worried to you?"

"I don't think he fully understood what all the fuss was about. Me neither, so I couldn't advise him. I doubt he ever bothered to learn English; so why listen to the colonial natives?"

"I imagine he never learned a lot of things, dressed in his robes as he was." Molly stood up, gazing around, her calm features relaxing, as they faced a myriad of familiar sights that framed her life.

"He's in permanent exile."

"I'm curious, what's bringing you back here, these days, Isaiah?"

"What?" Isaiah looked at her; she was once more doing that curious motion with her face; sampling the atmosphere with all her senses. He stood up.

"A lot of things started for me here. And, in your yard, where I was a happy child, for a while..."

"Are you, now?"

A happy child? He wondered what she meant. They decided to walk through the Grotto maze, moving slowly through the winding path.

"I wonder what it would be like, if parishes still had graves on the church grounds."

"What makes you think of that?" Molly asked, half turning towards him.

Isaiah began to speak of Little Nell's last sojourn, and Gray's famous poem, *Elegy Written in a Country Churchyard*.

"Oh, I *love* that one!" Molly exclaimed. "Raphael went through a poetry phase, and he kept bringing me his treasures."

Isaiah felt a rivalrous pang in his heart. "That poem was a touchstone for the Teacher, he alludes to it many times."

"The teacher?"

"Oh," Isaiah laughed. "I call Dickens that, because he's always preaching, writing parables. He's always showing us how it ought to be with the good people."

"I have to say, I'm really getting into his work." Molly stated calmly.

Isaiah spoke with feeling of the final passage of Little Nell, the doomed angel of *The Old Curiosity Shop*. "Her last request was to be 'put near something that has loved the light, and had the sky above it always.' I had that feeling earlier, passing through the Grotto."

"Something that has loved the light," Molly repeated, "that reminds me of something we studied in one of my chapters. We made a study of the Gnostic gospels."

"One of your secret chapters?" He teased her.

"I host many chapters. I like to refresh the stream of ideas we keep in circulation." She said no more on this subject as Isaiah waited, eager to hear more.

He watched as something came to life on her face, and then receded back into some remote place in her heart. He was dazzled by her visage as her eyes glittered, almost tauntingly, with the tacit musing she kept so closely in her breast. After returning to her property, at the gate, she gave him a last piercing glance. It touched him. Something had just happened, and he concluded there were no words for such things, and thus no need to thrash about in a cognitive sweat. There was an uncanny sense of having known her for a very long time, and having many understandings with her that needed no reiteration, nor confirmation. He feared even the lightest touch of inquiry would spell death for this hallowed recognition . . .

24

Isaiah stood in front of an easel, staring at his drawing of the dying crusader. The image was lifeless to him. He was visiting as merely a pilgrim, hoping to invest the static form with his own spirit. If only the work would shed a few sooty tears . . .

"Leave me alone!" He took solace in cursing whatever was there gloating over his failure. Fortunately he had other labors to pursue. After emailing Molly the photos he had taken of Jacob and Luke, he began a pencil composition of her two craftsmen. He depicted each man leaning against a separate tree, each wearing the same style of overalls and enigmatic smiles.

"I called it, "The Finished Job," as I worked on it." It was obvious he had been eager to present his gift to Molly.

"Nothing's ever finished around here." She replied, as she accepted the piece of paper. "Let me see what you've done. Oh my, these expressions are perfect. How long did it take you to do this?" She held it out before her.

"I couldn't set it aside, once I had the concept in mind."

"I like the subtle use of colors. So many nice touches." She turned to him. "So, how much do I owe you?"

"Nothing."

"No, really! I know you spent some time on this." Her hand rose in the air, as if making a liturgical motion.

He remained silent. He could not possibly charge her anything; and she knew this, he was sure.

"I'm going to frame this; put it in the kitchen." She disappeared into her house, when she came back outside she asked him to please quote her a price. He shook his head. She tried again, he interrupted her to make a request of his own.

"Molly, would you give me a hand with something?"

"What's that?"

"I brought some books for Father Kemble."

"Oh yes?"

"I thought he might like a collected edition of Charles Dickens. He taught his own children there was nothing better than the New Testament for teaching good morals."

"I think maybe Charles has other works that he refers to, quite often." She chided gently.

"Dostoevsky and Tolstoy both spoke of Dickens as a great Christian writer."

They walked to his car and after he opened the trunk he reached into one of the boxes and pulled out a book to hand to her.

"Remember, I told you about this one." He handed her *The Old Curiosity Shop*. "Do you want this?"

"Oh . . . and break up the set? Before you even give it to him?"

"No, you're right. It's just that I have so many copies of his books. It's been a strange obsession of mine. I'll bring you another copy. Or a complete set—I could give—"

"Hold on. I've downloaded some of the novels. And now I can borrow these."

The priest was not at home and they left the books with a woman who did chores there. Isaiah and Molly returned to her backyard; at her behest they climbed the stairs to take a seat in the Look Out. They sat as far apart as they could, to preclude the possible inhalation of viral particles. The anxiety regarding sharing breaths seemed to wax and wane as people strove to maintain customs. Molly brought a fist up to her mouth and coughed, causing Isaiah to turn away. They turned in unison when a troop of children tromped down the parking lot, making their way towards the lower level.

"What kind of world will they come to live in?" Isaiah questioned.

"How many worlds are still alive in them?" She replied softly. He had to think about that for a moment.

"It troubles me to think of the chances I've missed."

"Yes?"

He looked at her, feeling foolish and emboldened. "Do you ever reminisce about the person you never were?"

"What do you mean?"

"Not sure I can explain it, but I'm troubled by what never happened in my life."

"Like what?"

"Well, not any exact thing, so much; just those paths I might have taken, leading to different outcomes. The idea of what might have happened, if I had not been so negligent with my own life."

"Do you really feel that way, regretting your whole life?"

He hunched his shoulders up like a child.

"Do you feel that way about your art?"

"No, that belongs to me, in a different way. I wonder, though, if that commitment of mine has always separated me from other opportunities."

"I suppose it is natural to feel that *something* must be lacking, when you keep raking over the past obsessively. But it's a pointless exercise. A more salient question has to do with what essential qualities have you preserved." She glanced up into the cloudy skies.

"I wished for more success."

"You've done pretty well, haven't you?"

He had, in fact, and yet he hungered for that acclaim which establishes a reputation for a generation.

"I was envious of others whose work I did not respect."

"It's not good to cultivate those regrets, once they've taken root—"

"No, I agree. And I can't complain."

"But you are."

A little breath of extorted amusement came out of him. "Yes, I am. That's the human condition, isn't it."

They stared out at the textured palette of autumn trees; the brilliantly haphazard design surrounded them.

"One of my pictures received good marks from the critics, and it was done as a joke."

"Which one?"

"It was one I called *Face Paint*." He described the piece. It was a slum scene, showing a brick wall on which someone had painted numerous identical Andy Warhol faces. These pigments were melting, in lurid colors; washing down like runny makeup, mixing with the rain, flowing into the maw of a nearby sewer.

"On the ground I scattered the debris from a Monopoly game, all the cards and pieces littering the ground. I placed the painter, J. M. W. Turner, in the picture, dressed as a hobo, pissing against the wall. He's looking over his shoulder, directly at the viewer. You know, he actually had peepholes in his studio, so he could look out at people who came to view his paintings."

"An interesting collage of images you've just given me."

"I was being serious, and ironic, but rather clownish, too, at the same time. People thought I was trying make some sort of profound statement. I know it was trite."

She did not say anything; her attention seeming to be elsewhere.

"Hey, as a student here, I once did a poster for the school carnival that took first prize."

"Do you still have it?"

"I think I have it packed away somewhere." He became animated. "I was in the eighth grade. It was voted the best poster for the school carnival."

"That must have been fun."

He described the picture, of several Huey helicopters, flying over Ferdinand. One was piloted by a nun, and full of children. She was flying them towards the carnival in the distance. The wheel of one of the rides is visible on the horizon. Another Huey, seen in the background, is banking steeply to follow after the nun's chopper. The caption read: Stop What You're Doing! Meet At St. Margaret's!
"You'll have to show me that sometime."
"I'll have to rummage to find that one."
They were silent for a while.
"When your uncle came home, to look after his mother, he changed a great deal. His relations with her were fraught with a lot of troubling issues. She had been a hard woman to know—"
"To say the least."
"But she changed, there at the end. I truly believe her faith sustained that part of her. I was able to see it happen. He said he loved her after she was gone, more than when she was alive."
Isaiah did not know how to respond to this.
"He became a good philanthropist at the end."
"I know. He left me money, which I didn't need."
"What did you do with it?"
He had not thought of it that much until right now. "I put it in the bank. I've always been a saver."
"For a down payment."
"I guess so." He wasn't sure what she meant.
"Some time ago, everyone seemed to be researching their family roots, and I thought, I'd like to do that with my church."

Isaiah listened intently as she broached this topic.

"So I began a new chapter in the book club; and it got really interesting." She told him how they explored some of the scholarly research and discovered the mystic allure of the primitive church. She was very fond of St. Paul's letters, and quoted these frequently. He was amazed by the flow of information; in her mouth these dry concepts came alive, as if leaping from her beating heart.

"There's so much we don't know, about what's out there." She stretched out her arm, pointing an index finger at the fleecy sky. "Or up here." She tapped the same finger against her right temple.

"It's all Greek to me."

She made a wry face at this allusion to Paul's native tongue. "Jacob refers to St. Paul as the Ray Kroc of the Church."

Her serious, and at times playful, attitude was casting a spell over Isaiah. It was reminiscent of the persuasive airs of superiority he encountered in those persons who might be classified as his social betters. The difference being that Molly was here placing herself outside of those distinctions, being concerned only with human perception as it regards absolute values.

"Van Gogh was a prodigious reader, devoted to the Bible and literature. He wrote often of things he found in the great works, as if he subsisted on these ideas the same as his daily bread and tubes of paint."

She stared at him, waiting to hear more, in vain. So she proceeded to talk of the original cult, spawned in a milieu that supported a rank multiplicity of sects, few of which ever became more than a popular craze.

She believed that Paul had been aware of the teachings of Jesus, and probably knew of his being put to death. She described how Paul initially viewed the radical from Nazareth as a dangerous heretic, a dire threat to the national tribe. He writes of persecuting the followers of the movement with brutal chauvinism. Then he bears witness to the murder of Stephen, and something changes inside of his existential makeup. He turns away from his own society. He sets out to wander alone, and ends up deconstructing his inherited faith.

He sojourns in Arabia for many years, and comes back with his spirit inflamed, like a prophet, who understands the mystery of God! He travels tirelessly to synagogues and private homes to spread the new message. He writes his remarkable letters, working out in true diligence, in his own crazed mind, the mystical formula that will eventually become the basis of the new faith. It rests on the cross, the resurrection, and the incontestable reality of Jesus, as the sole arbiter of God's grace.

Listening to her talk, Isaiah is astounded. Her steady, unaffected voice comes from such a deep place inside of her; and yet he hears countless echoes rising inside himself. Her perspective on this received wisdom was resonating with something of his own, which he could not identify.

"It's interesting that he was wrong, about the messiah coming back soon; and the longer he preached of the return of Jesus, the more problematic it must have been for the followers. The only way his teachings continued to catch hold and spread, over time, has to be the soundness of the moral principles, and the way this bound those people together." She paused, and by her face one would believe she had put herself into a trance.

"I bet the people in your book club did not all agree on these things?"

"Oh yes, it got very interesting." She turned a precious smile his way. "There was controversy. There usually is when I start getting worked up! Some were appalled that we would question anything to do with the sacred dogma, much less deduce our own versions of what might have happened. For so many, it is an absolute, that you cannot tamper with; you must accept what has been handed down. That's not me." He watched her hair dance as she shook her head.

"So you're an instigator?" He chided with irony.

"I have to say, I was a little shaken. It was something to go through, seeing that recalcitrance, a refusal to just think about certain things." She looked at him blankly, as if she knew it would be near to impossible to explicate what she had unearthed in her parish. He began to form a thought that might entice her to continue, but she was staring down at the gate into her yard. An elderly man was standing there, looking up at her. He was wearing a stocking cap, and a woefully tattered old sweater.

"Who's that?"

"Oh, that Geoffrey. He lives in Cody's basement. He's trying to get back on his feet, so he can rent one of the duplexes they own, next door."

Isaiah could see she was making ready to leave him. The man just stood there, staring at Molly with his dogged steadfastness.

"I have to go."

"Well, okay then."

Isaiah followed her down the steps and watched as she walked with her visitor to her car. They drove off, heading for the grocery store.

Geoffrey Mulligan was a product of St. Margaret's, and the local public high school; after which schooling he had acquired a variety of uninteresting jobs. He was a fairly industrious worker, although it became his habit to quit jobs, as he quipped, 'to get more vacation time.' He was not considered a success by any normal standard.

At some point he fell in with a cohort of unscrupulous lawyers. They trained him to screen 'clients' who were told they might be eligible for government funds if they would surrender personal data to his firm. It was a scheme to defraud the government and the operation was shut down eventually. By some happy instinct, Mulligan was inspired to quit that job, quite fortuitously, months before the legal jaws snapped shut on the primary culprits. He had left town months before, following his favorite adage, adapted from something Harry Caray once said; 'You can stay too long in a place.'

The prosecutor found it expedient to not find him as one of the liable parties; and, in fact, he never had been cognizant of the scheme. Although, as he said himself, "I knew from the outset these were not trustworthy people." In time he moved back to Ferdinand, and then away again; and these migrations became a regular cycle of his life. He was always going forth to escape his past, or to find his future. Tiring of that, he always came back to the only place that had ever possessed any semblance of a home for him.

This last time he moved back, there was an element of fatalistic bravado, as if he had lost the demon that had chased him around the states for so long. He secured a job working for the federal government, after being told they would hire anybody, and never fired anyone. He decided to accept his fate, and doom. He settled himself in a ghastly annex of purgatory. After a few years passed the temptation to quit became overwhelming.

And then he had met Molly, and soon fell under her aegis; he hated to disappoint her. He thought it best to stick it out for the long haul, which was something else to dread. The harsh, unfeeling, mechanistic behavior of his cohorts made it easy to spend his working hours feeling as though he were still living in exile. His finances were in a bad state because he loved gambling, nearly as much as Dostoevsky. In the old days it was about football, someone always knew a bookie, and it was a good way to pass the Sabbath. It had seemed a relic of his youth, until the casinos came to town, and his fortunes were cast into a degrading state ever verging on perpetual ruin.

Perhaps it was only a selfish instinct that drove him to mass again; drawing into a closer orbit around Molly. She often spoke to him, and listened, and even invited him home to feed him on occasion. She started to advise him and he became her charge. He would stray into her yard at odd times, and just wait for her ministrations. Eventually she gained legal control of his finances, and took him shopping periodically. Jacob's patience was strained, and sometimes ran out when Geoff appeared, standing ruefully at the gate, looking like someone's lost pet. His silent petitions for help often set Jacob's teeth on edge. He would mutter, "Damn it, Margaret! There he is again!"

In time Jacob accommodated himself to the situation. Sometimes he drank beers with the hapless character, and discovered the old gypsy had a fantastic store of knowledge regarding the people he had known, at the various stages of his existence. He was now a much reduced personage, but he had retained a sort of objective facility for observing people with droll, intriguing candor. Once he got going, his descriptions of the extraordinary quirks of human nature could bring hilarious tears to the eyes.

When properly induced he relished telling tales, as if he had been called upon by a higher power to bear witness on all that's not quite right in the world. He said there weren't a lot of people he could talk to, not like Molly, and you, he would say to Jacob, after an unintended pause. These days, he seldom tried to engage people, for it seemed any laughter his stories evoked was sure to reflect back on his sorry state, in a thousand subtle ways.

It had gotten to the point where he only attempted to speak in confidence to Molly. He had grown dependent on the way she received him with her peculiar reverence for all humanity. It was like his life really mattered to her, in ways even he could not comprehend. No one else bothered to honor his dignity, as if that were no longer intact, and he was the sole cause of the damage, which suggested that he had never possessed these conditional rights in the first place. He preferred not to dispute such findings; it only made them more hostile. It was different with Margaret; he talked to her like a child, who is receiving that attention he always craves in his soul. She could always make him feel good about himself, for a short while.

25

It was dusk, after hours of smoky downpours. A vaporous hush smothers the mournful earth. This occult darkness, for an eerie moment, is suffused by an unearthly glow. The solemn trees stand alone in cool, misty niches, receiving a rare, sanctifying light that has no apparent source.

Isaiah stands on his fire escape, after having worked for a long spell. Once the spell is broken he returns to the dry confines of his studio and pours himself a glass of Merlot. He starts reading a first edition copy, which he seldom picks up any more. It is *The Mystery of Edwin Drood*, and the pages are brittle and even his delicate handling causes flakes to crumble away into his lap. He doesn't care. The volume is among those he will never give away or abandon; having only to last as long as he does.

He reads from the beginning page. The story opens with a peculiar question. "An ancient English Cathedral tower?" In the opening scene the character starts to regain his "scattered consciousness," while yet reeling through a reel of disjointed scenery. His altered mind conjures a Sultan, and ten thousand scimitars, as many dancing girls, even princely white elephants; and the damned Cathedral, where it shouldn't be any longer. He collects himself as the cheery mistress of the opium den prepares a fresh pipe. "Here's another ready for ye, deary."

It occurs to Isaiah that Dickens, had he not died early, at fifty-eight, might have given birth to yet greater marvels. He may have broken his shackles, dragged himself away from the ghetto of melodrama, leaving the morass of his own past. One feels an almost dreadful concentration of his powers in this last, unfinished work. He died at his desk, pen in hand. He was preparing himself to look more deeply into the unknown terrors of psychology. He imagines doing his work without any fear whatsoever; not of his reading public, his peers, nor any other opposing force.

"I think he was on the threshold, I really do." Isaiah held up his glass, and was astonished to see his son.

Theo had tentatively knocked, cautiously entered, and was now standing some distance away, staring at him.

"What are you doing, sneaking up on me like that?" He asked, embarrassed and angry.

"You didn't hear me knocking. How much wine have you had?"

He set his glass down with a guilty frown. "You should make yourself known, instead of lurking."

"Oh, sure; *I'm* sorry for lurking." Theo was wearing his hair cut very short; the prickly scalp was gleaming with the evening's luminous dew. Isaiah was reminded of his son's boyhood, when he wore a crewcut, because at the time few adults were doing so.

"You caught me in an odd moment of reflection."

"Yeah, I could see that; is that what you call working?"

"Do you want a glass of wine?"

"No." He spoke under strain, struggling against his anger.

"What brings you by?" Isaiah did not want to deal with anything unpleasant at the moment.

"Have you gotten someone to maintain the website?"

"I'm still looking into that." They both knew he had not done anything of the sort. Isaiah removed the book from his lap and placed it on a small table nearby. He took the glass and raised it to his lips, smacking ostentatiously.

"You sure? Not even a drop? It's really choice."

Theo rebuffed this offer with a fierce glower and shake of his head. It was evident he had something to say, and was loath to proceed. He dropped into a chair, to settle himself, to better face his father without giving way to his rampant emotions. Isaiah stared into the pool of purple evening light, pouring down from the skylight.

"You can see the invisible hand brushing the canvas of Rothko's Chapel walls." He made this comment in a curious tone, which Theo recognized. He closed his eyes, for he had no patience at the moment for his dad's didactic nonsense.

Isaiah was too far gone to notice the extent of Theo's desperate need to air his grievances. Hadn't they done this before? Besides, his studio was no place for this antagonistic wrangling. He liked to think he had control of things here. He laughed to himself. That wasn't even remotely true.

"I'm still taking care of the site for you."

"Thanks for that." Isaiah had counted on him doing so. He drank with delicacy, avoiding Theo's ominous stare. "I promise to look into that; but I have been busy these days. I am working again—"

"What are these?" Theo had picked up one of his sketchbooks and was turning the pages.

"Those are some of my new things."

"Where is this?"

"St. Margaret's parish, in Ferdinand."

"Who is this?" He held up the page.

"Molly."

"Who's she?"

"An old friend, Lately, I've been going up there to visit."

"Wait, is this Molly Gates?"

"Yes, why do you ask?"

"She lives where grandma grew up?"

"Do you remember that house?"

"Somewhat. You took me there when I was a teenager, to see your uncle Isaac. I was probably not very happy about it, in those days."

"No, you probably weren't. Not like now." He teased, and watched involuntary aversion contort his son's face.

Theo was made uneasy by his father's strange, aloof deportment. His condescending amusement was different than what he knew, and it augmented his unease. He laid down the sketchpad. "These are good." He said flatly.

Buried in that faint intonation of approval Isaiah heard echoes of his father's voice, whose praise had come to him in equally succinct forms. He watched as Theo was vaulted out of his seat and began to pace. He wandered over to the easel where the moribund portrait of St. Louis sulked, and cocked his head to make an appraisal.

"Who's this supposed to be?" He was peering closely at the charcoal features.

"That one's become a problem; but I hate to abandon it. I guess the lesson should be, don't dig up too many buried things." Isaiah lifted his glass, as if giving himself a toast.

Theo was reluctant to discuss any familial matters at present. His resolve to petition for a favor faced the intractability of the man. Theo held out his hands in an awkward motion of an entreaty.

"Look, Dad, I wanted to ask you something. We were wondering if we—"

"We?"

"Dilsey and me." Theo took his former seat, turning and leaning forward. "You know her." It sounded like an accusation.

"Raphael's friend."

"And Molly's."

"So you've met—"

"O'Rourke stopped me in the Loop one day, asked me to sit down, and she was there; and, well, he asked about you. He said you're getting very reclusive these days."

"Was he there with Emma Goldman?"

"Who?" Theo frowned at this esoteric quip, which he had no interest in hearing explicated.

"Madam Skuffles?"

"He was there with Patricia."

"The retired teacher, who has helped to inculcate the minds of many bourgeois brats." Isaiah spoke while looking into the textured darkness devolving into his space through the skylight. Theo was feeling an incongruous pity for the man, for whom he had such mixed feelings. He had made assurances to Dilsey, regarding what he would, and would not do, under these very circumstances. It was impossible to comply, even with the simplest terms, once he was confronted with his father's exasperating tendencies.

"Tim and Patricia were having a pretty good time. They got *me* talking politics."

"Yeah, I thought you had no interest in that topic."

"I just don't like arguing about it, to no end. They discuss things in a different way. They had the whole table laughing."

"She's teaching him Latin." Isaiah's voice matched his distant manner.

"Oh?" Theo was confused by his father's attitude. He watched him take a sacerdotal gulp of wine.

"Dad, I wanted to ask you something. Dilsey has a large portfolio of photographs. She's had some things published, ever since her coverage of the Ferguson riots, and things like that, and she's done some journalism. We were wondering if . . ."

Isaiah did not look away from the column of darkness in front of him, barely cognizant that his distant manner infuriated his son.

"She's a very interesting woman—"

"And she wants to put her material on our web site?"

"That, and possibly some other things. She would pay you a fee, for hosting her work. She has ideas—"

"What kind of things are we talking about?"

"Well, she's done a lot with St. Louis scenes. Really extraordinary landscapes, and the habitants, those wards in the north. And a lot of river pictures. I think you'd really like those—"

"It could get confusing. You're the one who told me the site had to maintain a definite focus, and that it would be easy to lose that by trying to offer too much—"

"I know." Theo stopped himself; inwardly writhing in consternation.

"Maybe we can look at this down the road."

"Never mind." Theo made to leave, afraid of not being able to control his temper.

"Are you going, just like that?" Isaiah sat upright from his slumping posture.

"Yes, I have to get going."

"But don't you want to talk about the website? You're going to continue maintaining it, right?"

"I can't do this right now."

"Theo! Look, I know I haven't been the best father." Isaiah had fallen back in his chair.

"I don't want to talk about that!" He cast a withering look at his father's pitiful, slumping posture.

"Why don't you have one drink with me?"

"No."

"You won't sit with me, for one glass of wine?"

"Sorry, I'll have to wait to see all your stations of the cross, if they ever hang them for a viewing at the gallery."

Isaiah flinched at the rather deft and sardonic rebuke of his maudlin theatrics. He could not help suspecting Marx's hand in such. He was tense, watching Theo going towards the door, finally yelling after him.

"Why don't you ever let me see my granddaughters?" Once he heard his own words he recalled Theo asking him long before why he had never gotten the chance to know his paternal grandfather.

Theo paused in his flight, ever so slightly, and then he passed through the door, and was gone. Isaiah continued to stare at the door. The sound of its closing had resounded in the lowest stratum of his dormant remorse. He sat there a long while, feeling those reverberations of that closing of his own door. He fears these portentous movements of fate, pushing him away from others.

He reaches up to turn off his reading lamp, and sits in the sculptured gloom of his most sacred place. He stares up through the skylight, wondering when it would become again the portal through which a magic cascade of light would descend to billow forth into his brushes. He wonders if it might be possible for people to evolve past themselves, in one lifetime, to become something more.

26

Isaiah was avoiding social media; repelled by the sewage seeping from broken septic systems. Professional sophists were working overtime. There was much packaged rancor being disseminated widely. The effluents were filtering into civil discourse as potable pleas, calling for justice.

He found himself more and more drawn to Ferdinand, where he always seemed to have a better grasp of things. He was glad to walk about on his own, exploring the streets, inspecting the yards, where many gardens flourished. He explored the empty church, searching for trace elements of his youthful ardor.

One afternoon, Isaiah was sitting by himself on the wall outside the Grotto entrance, watching the chimney swifts swirling around in elegant maneuvers. He remembered the perfect days, those early June mornings, waiting in agony for the opening of the carnival. It was unconscionable for those lazy, incompetent adults in charge to waste those hours in their dilatory preparations. Casually inflicting agony upon the idolatrous children!

"What are you doing there, old guy?" Molly was looking over his shoulder at the rudiments of a drawing. "Dreaming of other worlds?"

He looked up into the frank welcome of her genial face. "Molly," he managed to say, as if he had just solved a mystery.

"Jacob has been struggling through *Paradise Lost*." Molly's attempt to elucidate her allusion was lost on Isaiah; his mind was awhirl in reflections of its own.

"I have been thinking about a lost world; that of my childhood. Do you remember the carnivals they used to have, every year after school let out?"

"I do, but not that well." She sat down next to him. "They quit holding those when I got older. I barely remember them, to be honest."

She asked him to clarify how many years he had attended St. Margaret's.

"So you were pulled out after the first grade?"

"Yes, that was difficult."

"I bet it was."

"Then I came back, for the seventh, and eighth grade."

She told him of her husband's early years, in a voice that made Isaiah hesitant to ask too many questions. It was just as easy to sit there in silence. He let his mind lope through his past as she provided him with stories of Jacob's youth.

"I remember going to the race track, after my First Communion." Isaiah announced.

"How did that come about?" She asked eagerly.

He explained how his father was on bad terms with his in-laws, and that after the ceremony at the church, instead of repairing to his grandmother's house for the party, they sped off in his father's '58 convertible Impala.

"My parents were at the end of their marriage." Isaiah exhaled a breath of sardonic humor. "My dad wanted me to get a taste of his world, I guess."

"And that was not the world a child usually sees?"

"My father said something about being 'fed up,' and that was all it took. I was his partner in crime when I was young.

"Did you rob banks?"

Isaiah exhaled derisively. "No, but we hit clubs, later I mean, because that's where the music was!"

He wanted to tell her more about that day at the track, but he couldn't remember anything specific about the event. Other than the malediction his father hurled against his mother-in-law, which had surprised him so. He had taken to calling her the dragon. Isaiah told Molly about this, but she was not amused.

"Like father, like son." Molly chimed.

"What do you mean?"

"Well, that was a prank, wasn't it? Doing something bizarre, wanting to throw it in the face of others."

"He wasn't like that, he was no clown." Isaiah found himself rather miffed, at a loss to explain his father to her. "He had no truck with her society . . . I guess he was rather unusual; he never married again after the divorce."

"Again, like you."

"Okay, stop comparing us like that!" Isaiah laughed gently but uncomfortably.

She queried him in a forensic manner, as if searching for other youthful transgressions. She listened to his tales, prodding him when he flagged in his responses.

"Well, because I had my own pad in high school."

"Was that a good thing to have?"

"Probably not; it was down in the Loop. My dad paid for it, and he gave me that old Impala. He was like my guardian, assigned by the state. He provided for me. He also amply demonstrated how one is to live outside the conventional bounds of society."

"That's how you see what he was doing?"

"I'm not sure how to describe those days. My friends thought it was great that I had my own place, but to me, it felt really weird to be out on my own."

"It was too soon; it *must* have been very difficult for you, at such a young age."

It came back to him, that terrible sense of abandonment; it permeated his memories more than he could know. All his friends of that time returned to their families after every adventure, despite the humorous jibes, as to safe fortresses.

"For a while we shared a place, but he said we would drive each other crazy, if we continued to live in the same apartment."

"He wanted his freedom too."

Isaiah looked at her perceptive face, her piercing eyes, and shrank back. She was peering at him so placidly, and knowingly. He could feel her exquisite sensibility at play on his own soul! She grasped many things by inference. One didn't have to tell her everything, and that made it easier to speak from one's heart. It also made him feel vulnerable. Letting one's guard down in front of a seer might lead him to answers he was not hoping to find.

"I guess it's true; we were both like refugees from the normal family life."

"Oh boy, if we start talking about what's normal, we're sure to get into trouble. You need a picnic table for these dialectical exercises."

"Have you thought about putting one in your yard?"

"No thanks. That motion has already been put forth, and struck down. That's why you need your own back yard, so you can do whatever you want. I could find something just right for you. A yard of your own, in Ferdinand, that would be an ideal spot for a picnic table."

He laughed. "Do you really think I ought to buy a house in Ferdinand?"

"Sure, why not?"

"I'm too old. I'm not that far from retiring."

He changed the subject, asking her if she would like to see some family photo albums he had in his car, which he had taken from the studio. They repaired to the gazebo, and began looking at the pictures. He shared stories with her without any self-consciousness.

"Your father was a handsome man."

"Yes, and he didn't pass that trait on to his son, just money." His face colored as he spoke.

"So, he did pretty well for himself?"

As soon as she posed this question Isaiah felt a shiver of guilt. He nodded, a strange smile contorting his face. He had never mentioned his sizable inheritance to anyone before. There must have been no little amount of sacrifice involved in that legacy. How often had he portrayed his father, to himself, and others, as a sort of vagabond? In fact, he had worked for one company his entire career. He cringed to think of how often, in the past, he had impugned 'the salesman' in front of others to garner a laugh, and to assuage his own envious ego.

Molly studied his averted visage, and then resumed looking at photos. His commentaries became dry, factual statements, barren of humorous asides.

"Wait a minute, who is this, with your father?" Molly grew quite animated.

"That's Charlotte." He was surprised he remembered her name. "I took that one, in Gaslight Square."

"Really? Her name is Charlotte." She stared with great interest at the woman's face.

"I don't know anything else about her. I remember my dad would meet me at places, and she was with him a lot of those times."

"They look like a smart couple. I wouldn't exactly call that living outside of society; it's just a different sort of society."

"No, it's just that he had his own life, he was—"

"You know what? I think she's the mother of Paul Hereford."

"What? Of who, now?" Isaiah tried to remember this woman, whose photo was absorbing Molly's attention so intensely.

"So you knew Charlotte?" Her voice was suggestive of wonderful experiences.

"Why do you say it like that? What am I missing?"

"Well, look at her, she was a bombshell."

"I know, she seemed so glamorous to me at the time. I must have seemed quite the awkward little fool to her."

"So, your father and her, they were—"

"I don't know what kind of relationship they had, to be honest. I only saw them together, maybe a half dozen times."

"So they were pretty close, then."

"They liked hanging out, anyway."

"She doesn't look like a woman who just hangs out casually with anyone." Molly was looking up, and around, as if verifying the coordinates of her yard and its bearing upon her life. "I can't believe this. Isaac never told me your father knew Charlotte."

"Is that something he would have known? I mean, why would he have shared that information with you?"

"Isaiah, you have to come over and tell us all that you know about her."

"Wait now, tell who, all of what, that I know?"

She explained to him that one of her book circles had often discussed the beautiful Charlotte, who had led such an unusual life. She raised her son Paul, as a single mother, in the river village of Chouteauville. She often left him for days with her neighbors, the Gallagher's; Raphael's family.

"Paul and Raphael grew up together, they were like brothers." Molly explained. "She must have gone out to explore a separate life for herself; and she met your father out there!"

"That figures."

"It just seems like a mystic connection, or something; we have to dig into this some more." Molly looked around, greatly excited. She looked at him with her eyes glittering. "She had an affair with Raphael, not that long after Paul had moved away from Chouteauville."

"What?" Isaiah was astonished.

"It was around the time Paul published his first novel."

"Raphael and Charlotte?" Isaiah could not believe it. He could only picture Raphe in the present tense, as an older, gaunt, bald, sorrowful personage. It required an inordinate strain on the imagination to place him with this lovely siren in that amorous context. An enormous shifting of perspectives began to take shape after Molly shared these startling revelations.

"Do you have any other photos of her?" Molly asked eagerly.

"I could look." Isaiah's mind was whirling. "I'm sure I do, actually. I just never thought about her that much. I don't know why —"

"Well, you have to bring us everything you have. We'll conduct a Charlotte séance at my house."

He laughed at her exuberance. The sight of her getting excited over such a different sort of sister, from such an incongruous, exotic sorority, stimulated his insecurities. He felt a twinge of the licentious goads meshed into the fiber of humanity's competitive instincts. They made arrangements for him to come to dinner at her house, where he would reveal more of his artifacts.

He had never really discussed those days with anyone; they reposed in his emotional crypt; only unearthed when he was feeling wantonly lugubrious. So many things were coming back to him, reminding him how little he had understood about his own life, as it was being lived. He was at pains to know what lasting wisdom he had ever garnered for himself. It suddenly seemed ridiculous to query, what was true of those times?

Molly was explaining that she would invite Dilsey, of course, but certainly not Raphael, and she really wasn't sure who else to include. Oh, she would figure it out! Some of her parish friends appeared at the gate and he knew it was time for him to leave.

"I think I'll take some more photos of the chimney swifts." He said to her.

"Later, then. Oh, I almost forgot, I know someone who has a lot of photos of those old school carnivals. Would you like to see them?"

"Yeah, sure."

"I'll see about getting them, for when you come over."

Isaiah strolled through the Grotto area, enjoying the sensuous pathways, stopping to stare at the large Madonna at the entrance. Then he sat on the wall. He looked out at the middle level of the school grounds, recalling a scene from one of the rare times his father had volunteered to work at the parish. He had taken a shift that year of his last school carnival.

They assigned him to the booth holding crawdad races. A large piece of plywood had been lain across several barrels. The crawfish were set down in a painted circle, and as soon as one made it all the way into any numbered sector, the holder of that token won the race. At first the prizes were the usual stuffed animals. However, it did not take long before Tom Meriwether suggested they change things up a little, and provide every winner with a can of beer along with the fluffy prize.

This novelty garnered more customers, mostly grown men; and the more lively races whet the appetite for a more liberal dispensation of prizes. Meriwether was the first to recognize when the stuffed animals lost any semblance of commercial value. He changed the prize to one six pack of Falstaff beer, and ticket prices rose accordingly under these inflationary pressures. The crowd only clamored for more. People swarmed the booth; many bold ladies joined the action. Swarms began to coalesce into factions, establishing an urgent need for cheering sections. The din became an integral part of the magnetic draw; a constant, pulsing excitement drawing one towards the center of this happy madness.

Isaiah could see his father's ecstatic face as he bantered with three or four people at once. His voice boomed out to choreograph the uproarious commotion, as though he were tending his own maniacal trade show. He teased with deft aplomb the surly matrons who had come to scold, wagging their fingers, shaking their heads; and most of whom stayed on as loyal cabalists shrieking at the crawdads. The children were pushed to the outskirts, and could only gawk at this unusual spectacle of moms and dads trespassing on their sacred ground, and making fools of themselves.

The young Isaiah was transfixed as his father held up one of the fearsome crustaceans and brayed at the people to 'come take a chance.' After the conclusion of each race a lusty roar went up from the crowd, and the packet of beer was lifted out of a tub of ice water and floated overhead towards the winner. It was soon customary in that merry shuffle of players to divide the loot indiscriminately among themselves. It was not done by lot. People simply pressed forward in a happy moil, reaching up to tear away a single portion. The actual victors were glad to receive a single can of spoils at the end. Then the roar went up for the next race!

Isaiah tried to remember more about that last day he attended that school carnival. They had been talking about their respective high schools. He had wanted to stay at the Dragon's, and attend the Catholic school, where Deborah was going, or the public school Stephen would be attending. There had been discussions, from which he had been excluded. He always believed afterwards his grandmother put her foot down, demanding he leave her house. But he did not know this for certain . . .

He experienced a curious reprise of a premonition he had later that evening; once more alone, heading down the sidewalk towards his grandparents' house. He feared he had come to the end of childhood too abruptly. It was a poignant sense of loss, rising out of the past, and the looming present, contingent upon the advent of something more exacting yet to come. The challenges beckoned as his mind languished in past mysteries. Could it be, that he had never been ready for what was still to come? The thought made him shudder in his bones.

He had learned rather early to feign having knowledge he feared everyone else already possessed; not knowing the world is never certain of any of the portentous matters that govern life. Every person pretends to know more, while avoiding honest considerations of the unknowable. The pretense ends up molding customs that form what shall be deemed fit and proper, providing that sense of decorum which suits those holding a stake in the extant hierarchical structures.

After high school it had seemed to him that Stephen and Deborah transcended such mysteries as they cavorted in a glorious world of their own making. It took him longer to know a woman for the first time; and it did not seem the same, when he rose from a bed where he had lain once feeling he had been duped somehow. That couldn't be it; over almost before it started, with someone he did not really care about. He had come to everything later than what had seemed normal and his faculties were formulated to expect disappointment, and sharp regrets.

In part, his marriage came apart on the treacherous shoals of his preposterous ideas about maintaining one's freedom. And to what extent, and why, exactly, was freedom the most coveted abstraction for one who feels lost? Now, he had to laugh, bolstered by his newly revealed sense of pride in his father. Savoring the memory gave him fortitude to stand up to such bewildering forces. He rose, feeling rejuvenated in his spirit, ready to get on with things; determined to brave his circumstances, in order to thrive in the only way he knew how.

I WAS STANDING my usual watch on the fire escape, trying to figure out where I really was, in my life, until nothing made sense. Then I heard the music of leaves being swept across the pavement, and came back to myself.
Marx and Patricia left my place moments ago. They came to my studio unannounced. They breezed in on the fresh trade winds of life's irrepressible vitality. They are talking of getting a place of their own. It was almost like old times. He is with someone who makes him happy; that changes everything. All I had to celebrate was how good I felt about my work. Marx could see me through my pretense. We laughed at ourselves in our old manner.
He did not bother to act triumphant, even to honor one of our old routines. They wished to include me in their bounty, sharing the proceeds of their fortuitous estate. I was invited to future events. They may have inadvertently expressed more pity for my despondent state than I would have wished to bear in good spirits.
"I feel like someone who has returned home, from a foreign land, after many years." I said this to O'Rourke.
"That's an odd thing to say, my class of '73 brother. Look, I. Thomas, you're dwelling here as if you're locked up in a musty museum." He had whirled his arm across the dark vista of my studio. "You should see this as the motherland. You must fight for it. Forget St. Louis! He died a sickly relic in his bed! Move on, my boy."
I supposed he was speaking to impress Patricia, but in fact he was giving me good advice. He had always been more adept at lending valuable moral support, than workable criticism for my artwork. In truth, one of my best critics was my dad. He brought no predispositions to his opinions; he had no fear

of looking foolish in his pronouncements. He just commented on what he did or did not like, and had no interest in defending his position. He paid attention to what I was doing. He'd ask me about technical aspects without quite knowing that he was doing so, as he pointed out particular, notable features of a certain work. He understood the critical factor, he was really looking; and he would listen to my imperious glosses, taking note of my devotion.

I would fume a little, inwardly, afraid he was being insincere, overly solicitous, wanting to encourage his son, who wished to earn a living in a perilous field. I threw up defensive works against such cheap applause. He was not a serious critic. He was not in the know. He had never cultivated the necessary tastes. He could not possibly understand. His praise had meant everything to me!

He actually sold quite a few of my paintings, and prints. He was always out there selling things, and he would promote my entire catalogue. He sold paintings to his customers, and people he met at bars and restaurants. I didn't really know the extent of this activity until I spoke to the people who came to his funeral. Many a good laugh we shared over his irrepressible charm.

One woman's remembrance stays close to me; "Your father enjoyed being with all kinds of people. He never played that game of wanting to be in certain cliques, that thrive on keeping other people out. He would turn down enviable invitations, giving scarcely any reason, and then just show up at other affairs, making his way in and then becoming the life of the party. He was fun to be around, because he liked people, real people."

I was in the throes of a new phase; poring over the watercolors of John Singer Sargent, Winslow Homer, Andrew Wyeth, John Constable, a few pieces of Reginald Marsh (the locomotives). I cannot resist the romantic appeal of stark, haunting realism. The next bottle I decanted, after my guests departed, perhaps explains this flowery indulgence of pouring myself out for you, in such glaring colors.

You know, the young Charles Dickens showed up at his first job with a black eye. The innate competition of human beings is a sight to behold when you look too closely at the beast hunting in the streets. The novice teacher's cherubic face, his lofty confidence, and his finery, and foppery, all these roused brutal instincts. One understands playful insults, but there are other trials for proving one's right to a certain station in life. The oldest question remains, what place has the religious aesthetic in these contests?

The artist likes to think he has enlisted in a grand cause; but the ego makes sure we seek commerce in productive hypocrisy. We all trade on goods of some sort, and it's a shame we don't believe in sins anymore. Throwing out the concept of original sin makes sense, but what about the selfish, deceitful, and hypocritical nature inherent in our cultural being? Shouldn't we be more rigorous in noting all too numerous manifestations of these traits? Sure, who among us? Try addressing this to one of the mobs online. "Who among you is without sin?" They would all start throwing figurative stones at you.

During my later boyhood Stephen was a good companion, and implacable rival. He caused me much envy; which can be an impetus for putting forth more effort. He ventured off to report upon the world. How he scoffed at one of his own kind, a much venerated apostle, who was being put out to pasture.

Now afforded the privilege of acting the sage, this elder counseled his successors to comfort the afflicted, and afflict the comfortable. He had gotten very comfortable himself and would not suffer fools.

"It's pandering; sheer nonsense. Where's the logic?" Stephen spat out contemptuously. "What about telling the truth, in all circumstances, let everyone reason for themselves? Provide all the meaningful context; including the actual relations between the people involved. He complained of his editors. He complained of his counterparts in the trade. He complained of the readers. He assured me none of the bright lights in his guild is ever completely honest when reporting on how power operates. There are always people being protected. The news must pass through an alembic built by a dizzying array of courtiers that serve those holding power. He confessed to me that he'd gone rogue. He joked about how he might open his current exposé, using various literary analogues.

Call me a pissed-off, white male, home on leave. I want to start pulling ties off the leading officials in charge of this farce. He asserted there are sacred cows, and untouchable rich assholes. Some sensational facts, widely known, being detrimental to some wealthy souls, are buried in piles of ephemera. Secrets abound, and are faithfully kept. There's so much connivance, you can hear the greedy screams in hell. Like PR flacks they push narratives, to protect the white whale. I've been doing this too long . . .

I don't remember all that he said; it was strange to hear him speak of these things, in that way. It was not entirely clear to me then, but I was bearing witness to the last station of his passion "for telling the real story." It had expired. He was thoroughly disillusioned by that time, the last I ever saw him. He had come into his own, by one standard, and by his own, it was now just a travesty. All his writing for prestigious magazines, the awards, it was all for naught.

"It's like high school," he said calmly. "There are circles that matter, and you have to know the lay of the land, if you are going to stay out of trouble, and keep rising. To keep climbing in your own sphere is the primary objective, even the most talented ones eventually submit to this imperative."

We had been drinking, somewhere in the Loop; Marx and Stephen were arguing about Max Weber, social hierarchies, and power, peasant revolts, and the history of great powers, in present times, restrained by the apocalyptic weapons, forced to enter into proxy wars. Their conversations made my head swim. They were able to tabulate most of the bloody horrors convulsing the species on this planet at any given moment.

"Maybe I should have stayed put. This is a clean, well-lighted place," Stephen said to me when we were the only ones left at the café, braving the emergence of a new day's indifference to our late-night hymns. He was gazing around, a subtle irony present on his lips. "Have you ever read that one?"

"Which one?"

"No matter, you artists are like alchemists. You find your gold in plain colors." My face must have asked, which one, though? "Nothing, just a tiny, glimmering facet of our literature. It's all shit, eventually; like Hemingway, truly."

I probably said something clever then, who knows? However sluggish he was, he had his wits about him; unfortunately, they were as a troop of jesters putting on a show, at everyone's expense, including his own.

"The rich aren't like you and me," he intoned in his droll anguish. We were not even drinking anymore, merely lolling in deepest night, recalling scenes of past days. We had been young together, had felt our dreams flicker and fade, and flutter down as gauds pasted into our cheap scrapbooks.

"So now you're F. Scott Fitzgerald. Are you getting ready to move to Hollywood?"

"It's true, though, not the way he was talking about, in his private romances. No, wealth is our virtue, you see."

I must have laughed as he laid out his grand theorem. I didn't know how far beyond being a journalist he had taken himself.

"The white man's burden has become every rich person's burden. It's very primitive, and so eminently practical. The high hypocrisy of state must follow a punctilious set of liturgies. Take those opulent game shows, the large charitable galas, the winners are the rich people who are seen shining."

"Here we go." I noticed there were dark shadows disfiguring his once austere, but always genuine, countenance.

"I met an ambassador once, she was so smart, and funny. Wildly attractive to me; I fell in love. She laughed beautifully. Her family had purchased the position for her! I knew of these things, but to come up against it, like that, to hear it casually spoken of in that way. Something gave way inside of me. I could see everything more clearly; how hopeless everything was." He shook his head, laughing, in a dry, ghastly manner. "I would have given my heart, and all my rags of honor, to be with her."

I must have thought it was just about the late hour, and the drinks, and that I was a poor witness. I was rather stricken myself.

"The Red Cross had to admit they just didn't know. They said this quite openly, as a good streetwalker might to the cop she is paying off anyway. 'It's difficult to know where all the money went.' Just like that; gone, along with all our other good intentions. Ha ha ha." His horrible laughter still haunts me, when it comes back, in some of my more painful moments.

"His whole life, Dickens was embroiled in a war against the heartless elites."

"I would say, rather, it was just ambivalence. He was making his money, playing the social radical, and moving in high circles, enjoying the spoils."

"Which he achieved through Herculean labors and talent."

"No doubt, but he loved the life, and moved in the circles he cried out against in print, those who were maintaining the callous inequity."

"He never lived the life he might have. In Drood you hear echoes of what might have been, if he'd only had more time. He was questioning how lives are preordained by the cultural forces, that imprison us all."

"He was dreaming of having what famous celebrities have now. I've seen, too . . ."

"Not to sound ridiculous, but I think some semblance of that has changed me." I said. "The wearing away of the soul in that endless chase."

He just smiled at me. I am sure he thought there was no comparison. I asked him what had become of another woman, from another good family, as they say, whom he had considered proposing to at one time, in what now seemed so long ago.

"Never worked out. Different lives. I could see how it would go; she was in the tribal alliance. Once they get married, start having kids, move about as a veritable corporation, it's all over. They obey and respect the prescribed narratives. They commit atrocities against the truth, like good soldiers taking back the trenches they lost the month before . . ."

"You're too cynical." I stated in august tones.

He broke into a cackling bout of laughter. Long before we had seen how that phrase was used by people who wanted to convey, not only are you wrong, in the present instance, but your critical faculties are intrinsically flawed. You cannot be trusted to render any opinions on the operative wisdom of this world.

"You've got me there. My baptism has been revoked. I no longer partake of the liberal sacraments."

"Well, you have to admit, a lot of progress has been made over the years. Dickens wrote many articles in support of clean water, fewer hours in the work day, and for improved safety on the factory floor. He was for abolishing slavery in the colonies. He wrote constantly about providing more services for the poor, and giving them more democratic rights, and such things"

"True, but he also celebrated the rewards of achievement; helping to sanctify the idea there should be no limits on wealth. And that's our fatal flaw. Why a great many people are always left behind; and we feel no compunction in ignoring the structural problem." I remember how he shook his head here, looking down at his empty beer bottle, which he then twirled slowly on the table with one hand. The aspect of his resignation shocked me for a moment. My bleary eyes pictured the bare skull underneath his face.

"Do you believe in continual moral progress for the species?"

"I'm not sure how we'd even measure that; it would be like trying to calculate how much corruption there is in the federal government. How much outright fraud, and theft, and nepotism, and the granting of blatant, needless sinecures. Or, what about the hypocrisy of individual humans? Should there be a way to measure that, as a quotient that you can mark down in a ledger? No one in power is interested in telling the truth about how power controls them in conducting their affairs. People don't know a particle of all the ignominious details. It just doesn't matter."

"What doesn't matter?"

"I don't know. How do you like that?" He said we must have talked ourselves sober, and so we were required to order some sort of fine liqueur to finish things off in a proper manner. We sipped sickly doses of Benedictine, like we were the most elegant roués ever to test the night's compassion for homeless intellectuals.

"I should have married Deborah – "

"What?"

"Settle down – "

"Did you ever discuss that with her?"

"I could have been a happy, harmless drudge, working for the Post-Dispatch. Maybe end up an affable columnist, with wild hair, tethered to my ridiculous ties, who writes about how crazy and charming people really are."

"I'm not so sure she would have wanted that life for herself." I was bound to torment him, as he stole upon my maudlin turf.

"No, she took flight too, didn't she?"

"You sound very old, all of a sudden."

"I feel very old these days."

"Well, you should have learned from Spinoza; we tried to warn you."

"Life is a contest, that can never be won, isn't it?"

His face had a resigned, lost aspect which I had never seen before. It was primal resignation, cast in the shape of knowing terrible things, which it does no one any good to know. What if I had known to say something, by some clairvoyance of our fraternal regard, to pierce into the heart of that despair? Why didn't I know to reach out and take him back from the abyss? It was not long after that ghastly scene when Stephen returned to Haiti, and the next thing I knew we had received word that he was no longer among us.

It made me abhor all the comforting words, and feel I had been a mean, pretentious, social climber myself, jealous and protective of my shabby seat. I too have learned to be oblivious to so much that took place around me, while I took up my own fairy tales, very much the exquisite aesthete who places himself above pedestrian concerns. Even his death, then, became a ceremony about my suffering. How far back must one go, to feel a clear consciousness striving to know true things, when yet unpolluted by worldly affairs?

It is interesting to note the behavior of Dickens, when his first comic story was accepted for publication (without pay). "I walked down to Westminster Hall, and turned into it for half an hour, because my eyes were so dimmed with joy and pride that they could not bear the street, and were not fit to be seen there." This for a trifling piece of no real matter, extraneous to his eventual splendor. But to receive that public recognition!

It was his custom to wander about on foot, drawing strength from the very streets; a veritable London Antaeus he was. He often wrote in his letters, when in foreign places, that he needed to get back to his native streets, so that he could write. He habitually took off on long treks, driven like a madman, plunging through the bowels of his country. But in this victorious moment, possibly his happiest hour (for it was untainted), he could not bear to be seen by anyone else. His tender joy was to be sheltered within, kept like a pilot flame, which the outer world could only extinguish at the slightest breath.

I was told (by Stephen, actually) that when his first novel was accepted, F. Scott Fitzgerald also began to float into another world of rare bliss. He spoke of "the delicious mist" he was passing through, and how "short and precious" he knew this time would be. The transience of this extreme happiness, which promises more of what can never last — why is that always the case?

The sale of my first large river picture caused such joy to rise into my breast. It splashed over into the unreal stock bubbling in the cauldron of my dreams. I felt the stir of phantom powers. I rushed to escape the clarification that was sure to follow, if I were sensible, and let things settle of their own accord. I walked for a long time, tramping along the river, truly believing something was there waiting for me. Something wanting to speak to me. My heart was full of whelming, worldly, empty happiness.

In life we learn numerous ways to plunder, as our individual right, to grasp our share of the riches offered by this world. The quest is to break into those secret stores that are reserved for such rare beings as we ourselves have become. You plunge into life's river, beating upstream, believing you've attained the power to master the relentless current. You are swept back down, hardly cleansed or refreshed, but merely exhausted.

And, finding yourself farther downstream than where you started, you pretend one's place doesn't matter. It's a lonely course, believing in the wrong dreams too long, then coming around, acting like you've found your way once more, when it is evident you are adrift, on a course you know nothing about.

27

Isaiah was surprised to find how many photographs of Charlotte he still possessed. He was eager to share these with Molly, and on the appointed day, he noticed Father Charles was sitting at his table. They nodded to one another. Isaiah decided to go over and pay his respects.

"Many people stop by here, before going to see Molly."

"You have me there."

"I know she's expecting you, she told me about it."

"Yes, apparently I've come across some artifacts she's very keen on seeing."

"She knows a lot of people."

They exchanged pleasantries and Isaiah tried to take his leave. "Well, I wanted to deliver these to her." He hefted up the satchel he was carrying, full of papers, drawings, and photographs.

"Do you have a minute?"

"Sure. I'm early."

"You may find it strange, but I see her as the other half of my ministry."

"How is that?" Isaiah was more than a little intrigued.

"Oh, lots of things, But just consider the reverence she has. You can see that even in how she takes care of her yard. The way she is constantly changing and sculpting her own plot of nature. It's quite a place, done in her own likeness."

"I've begun to think of her as a sorceress. She has this maddening habit of getting me to talk about myself, and later I am more confused than before I opened my mouth."

The prelate laughed in a light, subtle manner. "There is that creative state, which happens before enlightenment, which we call sublime confusion."

"We? The Mother Church?"

"No, no. Margaret said that to me once." He used her full name, conscious it might sound indiscreet. Only Jacob was known to call her Margaret, and sometimes it was done out of extreme frustration. "She said that in one of her book club meetings. I heard about it afterwards."

"Are you in Molly's book club?"

"There are many chapters. I only attend a few, once in a while. She wants me to be at certain orthodox chapters, regarding the faith. Sometimes I go to one of the others. Not too often. I don't want to disrupt the free exchange of ideas, which she values so highly." He smiled, as at some private reflection. "I am too outspoken, for some."

"Molly, too?"

"Lord no! I'm too tame for her taste. My word . . ." He brushed at his hair with a sweep of his hand.

"I understand."

"Most people do not want to spend a lot of time explaining their faith, or having to justify it, to others." Charles looked around, and glanced at his watch, as much as granting Isaiah his leave. He stood up. "By the way, I've just finished *Barnaby Rudge*. I enjoyed it tremendously. That eponymous character is drawn with a very delicate touch. I feel I've known him before; in a less exaggerated form, of course."

"Yes, he captures the spirit in caricature, and it breathes fresh life into what the world's gotten too blasé to notice." Isaiah feared he was on the verge of getting carried away with his unsolicited, and somewhat untoward, evangelism.

"Seeing the life, in each life, I would say. Well, I'm glad you got me started on his works."

"You shall find that Dickens was one of the faithful; in his own way."

"I can see that, and there are many ways to forge one's own faith. Take care now."

As Isaiah walked into Molly's backyard he thought, "This place really is her own suburban temple mount."

Glancing around he noticed a new fixture under the Look Out; a piece of statuary, couched in its own little grotto of neatly arranged stones. Coming closer he was astonished to find a miniature replica of the Saint-Gaudens sculpture at the tomb of Henry Adams' wife. The aggrieved husband had instructed the renowned artist to imagine Michelangelo conversing with the Buddha. As Isaiah crouched before the solemn, hooded visage, he invoked for himself an epigraph, "On becoming one's shrouds."

"What do you think?" Molly had appeared."

He looked up, shaking his head. "Where'd you get this wonderful piece?"

"Someone I've known for a long time brought it to me. He and his wife, they left it on my porch, with a note, on their way through town. You can see Jacob lost no time getting to work, making use of that pile of stones we keep handy."

"He's done that very well. It complements the wall."

"People will think I'm getting morbid."

"There's nothing morbid there. It beckons one to visit the far reaches of conscious thought."

"There is a strange, challenging quality, which I really like; but I wonder if it's getting to be too much. I don't want this place to look like an old pagan churchyard. I've heard someone has called it my backyard retreat!"

"I don't know how I'd describe it."

Jacob and Dilsey were waiting for them. It had been decided to meet outside, since the weather was so pleasant. Most of the fatalities caused by the virus consisted of the most elderly and those suffering from other maladies. There was an eerie feeling, when congregating, that the fates were being sorely tested. Who among the complacent were to be taken out of providential spite?

They arranged themselves in a circle and soon found themselves discussing current events. Jacob took orders and brought out drinks. They began airing strong opinions on political matters. Isaiah feared some creeping insinuating animus might incite contumely. After seeing the tempers starting to rise Molly and Jacob went inside and came back to tell them to file through the kitchen to fill their plates. They ate outside, plates on their laps, and afterwards Isaiah brought forth and passed around his photo albums.

As they spoke, Isaiah learned a lot more about Raphael. There was much conjecture about Charlotte, which led to his father, and more questions ensued.

"Your dad was hot!" Dilsey exclaimed.

"He looks really cool," Molly agreed. "I can see why Charlotte was attracted to him."

"Please, you're making me jealous of my dead father." Isaiah found himself making uneasy quips.

"Look at Charlotte's outfit." Molly and Dilsey began talking of the woman's clothing, and complimenting her style, as if she exemplified a forgotten age.

"What was your dad like?" Dilsey asked. "You said he liked going to jazz clubs? He took you to see Miles Davis?"

"He did. He always seemed to know a lot of people, wherever we went. They all loved music."

"How Bohemian, right?" Molly added.

"Was he one of Charlotte's lovers, do you think?" Jacob asked without looking at anyone.

"What do you mean, *one* of her lovers?" Molly retorted in a tone that quieted everyone. She and Jacob exchanged a look that made the others uncomfortable.

"I thought you might invite Raphe." Isaiah ventured to lob into the silence, intending to break the tension.

"Oh, we would never talk about her around him. That part of his life; he doesn't talk about it with anyone. Does he?" Molly looked over at Dilsey, requesting her input."

"Rarely." Dilsey did not look at anyone as she spoke. "He only talks about her when we are on the river. It's pretty weird; actually, he only talks about a lot of things when we're on his boat."

"I've noticed that, too; when we have gone out there with him. Once he's on the water, he seems to change."

"He says his whole life closes around him out there. It's hard for him to talk about, and sometimes things back up on him. But he says it does him good to be out on the water during those times." Dilsey was revealing that she was close to Raphael, and not willing to speak of him too freely in present company.

"You met him when you were a child, isn't that right?" Isaiah asked. She nodded. He wanted to ask her if she had considered inviting Theo to this affair, but that might have been awkward. He had been studying her face, wishing he had taken his camera from the car, so he could circulate among them, taking pictures, waiting till they were barely conscious of him so he might capture genuine expressions.

"We met after my mom moved us to Chouteauville. Paul was our neighbor. He and Raphe had been the closest of friends, as children; and they got that back, before the end." Her poignant smile engaged all present.

"We've heard a lot of interesting stories." Molly said placidly.

"They adopted me like a kid sister. I began to tag along as they went about their strange business of regressing in time." She looked sweetly at Molly. "I was so young, it was exhilarating to be out on the river in that boat, taking my turn at the wheel! I really got to know him years later, when I went back there, as an adult, after being in the world for a while."

She now seemed to emulate Molly, using that sensitive, roving motion of her face, as if she had just lost track of something out there, and by searching she might bring herself back around. "That's when we became friends." Her soft, clear voice commanded attention. They all looked at her, waiting to hear more, but she looked peacefully beyond them, at the newly installed statue.

"I wish we could have him here, even though I know it wouldn't be right, somehow." Molly spoke as to the entire group, not expecting any response.

"You got that right. Old white men be crazy." Dilsey affected a role, and everyone laughed. Isaiah did not fail to notice she had flung a harsh glance his way when she delivered her shot.

Jacob began to charge his pipe with a fresh wad of tobacco. As the others talked approvingly of the burning tobacco's aroma his eyes twinkled merrily at the sight of Molly's riven brow. In a petulant manner she shook her head. For a while a tranquil silence ensued, as if the smoke were a potent incense investing a holy ritual, and now the rite consisted of grave contemplation.

"Have you told us everything you remember?" Molly said to Isaiah after the spell had passed.

"I'm afraid so. Those memories are so faint; there's no meaningful context to build upon."

Molly and Dilsey exchanged a glance, and then began perusing the photos once more. They exclaimed again over Charlotte's chic wardrobe. Isaiah took note of their lively, elegant hand gestures as they critiqued the woman's sense of fashion. He could almost see Charlotte's gracious smile and natural comportment.

"She was who she was," Molly exclaimed. "She owned her life." Isaiah was startled to hear the women make conjectures about Charlotte's sexual history. The men remained silent. The subject remained a safe, lurid product of their imaginative fascination.

"I'm not so sure about everything I'm telling you about those days. She made a lasting impression on me." Isaiah felt like he had failed to bring much purposeful intelligence to the committee.

Molly began sharing something Isaac told her about Charlotte. "He said he heard this story from your dad."

"Did my dad know Isaac that well?"

"I think they got along, as brothers-in-law, pretty well." Molly began parceling out the story she had been waiting to divulge. "Have you ever heard of that book, *Once Upon a Secret*, by Mimi Alford?"

"No." Isaiah replied, anticipation building in his chest, feeding off the emotion in her voice.

"She was fresh out of Miss Porter's boarding school for girls, wanting an interview with Jacqueline and she was invited to speak with her secretary. She met Jack, and he later on released the hounds; she was summoned to the White House to be an intern. In time, Kennedy forced himself on her!"

Jacob drew heavier on his pipe, struck by an echo, from a phrase of banter heard at a certain picnic table at the Fish Fry at St. Margaret's. It was the night he first met his uncle's friend, Paul Hereford, Charlotte's son.

'O the moon shone bright on Mrs. Porter.' Now a wild series of unraveled annotations danced across his mind.

"Someone chose that book for the book club, and then we had to read several more, and pretty soon we were investigating that whole Camelot scene. We learned a whole bunch about Jack Kennedy, the playboy! It was later on, when I was talking to people at the wake for Isaac, where we met a lot of his friends, and there was this one guy." Molly's face recalled her astonishment. "It still gets to me, he told us quite a tale about Charlotte, and it confirmed what your father told Isaac."

Everyone was staring at her in rapt silence.

"This person said that Charlotte had agreed to meet privately with the president; it was all very surreptitious. So, she was waiting for him, one time, when he was making a swing through St. Louis."

"No way." Isaiah said.

"They were going to meet at this nightclub; somebody knew the owner, and he put up a closed sign, apparently, to facilitate the rendezvous. It was somewhere on the outer fringes of Gaslight Square."

Isaiah's eyes flared open; scenes of his father and her in such a place whirled around in his excited mind.

"Do you think that's a true story?"

"I think so. I remember Isaac telling it to me, but he left out the most important details. Trying to spare me?" She looked around. "What I really want to know, is, what was Charlotte thinking, at the time? You know? What was it like for her, to be the daring woman, going for the gusto, as they say. She wanted to experience these things for *herself!*"

Jacob's pipe began sparking as he listened in his own ruminative fog. Everyone began looking at the photographs of Charlotte once more, as though the ghost of randy Jack might be lurking in the background somewhere.

"I wonder if the tryst ever took place?" Isaiah asked.

"Raphael said no, but he doesn't really know. She was what they would have called fast, in those days." Dilsey responded.

"So true." Molly spoke with a quaver in her voice.

"She served at the front lines of the sexual revolution," Isaiah commented dryly.

"She was acting as she wished, just as powerful men do all the time." Dilsey retorted.

Jacob removed his pipe from his mouth. "From what we've read, I think you can thank Kennedy for the legacy of the Secret Service being on such familiar terms with high-class courtesans."

"Did your dad ever talk to you about any of these things?" Molly quickly asked.

"No, never. He wasn't one to spend a lot of time talking about people; gossiping about other lives. He told me once, 'I talk all day, in a role, and when I leave that behind I enjoy life on my own terms.'"

"What's wrong with gossip?" Molly asked peevishly. "It's how you find out about people. Shouldn't we want to know about ourselves, and others?"

"Well, the fact is," Isaiah was chastened, and suddenly thoughtful, "I only know how he was with me. I never knew that much about his life, when I was older. I hardly ever saw him in those places, with that crowd, later on. Once in a while, when I was an adult I'd see him, and we'd go to a quiet place to have a meal together. There was one time, we went again to an old place, to hear jazz. I took Dora with me; my fiancé at the time. Anyway, she was bored. She said my father seemed like the sort that drifts through life."

He could not explain the effect of that one statement. It became a debilitating force that reverberated through his ensuing years. In that early stage of their courtship her fear that he shared those paternal traits was a prophecy of sorts.

"He wanted to be off the trodden path." Jacob made a cryptic offering, on behalf of the slighted man.

"Isaac told me once that your dad was in love with Charlotte, but he knew she wasn't interested. She wouldn't let herself get serious because she knew it wouldn't last." Molly paused. "I doubt many men, back then, could have accommodated themselves to such a woman."

"I'll say this, I feel like I know both of them a lot better, after this evening." Isaiah's voice contained a whispery note of almost childlike awe.

"She didn't believe in conventional marriage. It was not feasible for her. Her beauty cast her into a role, which she had no way to escape." Molly spoke with a note of grave perception.

"A role cast by others." Dilsey responded.

"Exactly." Molly affirmed emphatically.

Dilsey leaned forward to retrieve her wine glass, taking a delicate swallow; then she placed the glass back on the table. Isaiah observed her movements. His eye assayed her complexion; a clear, smooth, rich, light caramel. The strong, distinctive features made him think of the paintings he had labored over, striving to capture a person's character in one almost searing look. The desperate hope to grasp the soul in one fleeting moment, using only dull artifice. The mask of Dilsey became more dynamic as he pondered the facets he could not presume to understand.

It occurred to him that Dilsey carried herself with great caution. She was very present, and very mindful of her own portrayal of herself. It transcended class or race, and was centered in her core belief in her own being. She turned towards the world a politely guarded wariness; to her friends, an unabashed determination to be about the agency of her own story. Her simple, elegant attire completed the picture he imagined of her life. He sensed that Dilsey and Molly were kindred spirits in more ways than he had ever considered before.

"I see her as being very alone, although not necessarily lonely." Molly asserted in a resonant voice. She and Dilsey exchanged a look; they had discussed all these thing in the past, at more length, plumbing female depths with a more wanton license.

Isaiah excused himself to use the bathroom, and when he returned Dilsey was telling them about moving back to Chouteauville, years after Paul had died. She found that Raphael, now enriched beyond what he had ever imagined, had become a bitter, angry man. He was driving his own people away, alienating his neighbors, and at war with the marina, where he kept his boat.

"He was squandering the money Paul bequeathed him. He was on some kind of power trip, trying to create a new world around himself, and no one was having any of it." She spoke solemnly.

Isaiah began thinking of his 'wicked' grandmother; she had been known as a good parishioner, in many ways. Jacob was talking of the good old days with all of that common lyricism that crept so easily into his music.

"We had the best time, up at the Fish Fry every week. We sat at this picnic table, turning over the world." Jacob had a great smile on his face.

"An awful lot of mindless jabbering went on there." Molly said with a sardonic lilt in her voice.

"You never attempted to close it down. You were our hostess, really." He replied in a dry voice, pointing his stem at her. His bowl had gone cold.

Molly made a dismissive motion, and retreated to her kitchen, beckoning for Dilsey to follow along. They soon brought out a delicious, Italian yellow cake, made from that delectable mixture called 'scratch' by culinary experts. It took a while before anything could be heard besides garbled effusions of praise for the moist, spongy cake.

Once the empty plates were taken back inside, they formed the original circle. The conversation became sparse. Shadows lengthened on the ground. Quiet voices fell to unconscious whispers. A host of flirtatious stars appeared as the crisp air caused shivers, invoking instinctive desires for cozy homes. In the motions made towards departure they shared random personal notes, easing gradually into protracted salutations. Before they finally dispersed, Isaiah approached Dilsey.

"You should have invited Theo," He said in a cheerful, familiar tone.

"He didn't want to come." She replied impassively.

"Why not?"

In the silence, and her averted face, he could hear the unspoken response. 'Because he knew you would be here.'

"It was good seeing you, Dilsey."

"The same to you."

"Take care now." He once more felt he had acted in a clumsy fashion. His touchy sense of being alienated from society was exacerbated. He scolded himself. Judge not? Ha! Judge thyself, or at least stop asking questions you are afraid to hear answered.

28

After Isaiah finished two new watercolors, based on the carnival pictures loaned to him by Molly, he rushed to show them to her.

"Oh my gosh. That was quick." Molly exclaimed as she held one of the pictures out before her. "Let's go over here." He followed her to the gazebo and she sat down and spread the sheets on her lap. She grasped one, holding it up for scrutiny. She put it back down in her lap, and held up the other one. Then leaning back, she said, "The colors just swim together. All the little figures, you have each one telling a little story of its own."

"I'm thinking of doing a series—"

"Of carnival pictures?"

"Of various landscapes of Ferdinand."

"You should consider having someplace local, to use as your base of operations."

"I don't know, I really like my studio."

"You can move your studio."

"I don't know."

"Life is about change. You could get a place where you would be more comfortable. And it might be the ideal place for you to end up."

"End up? What do you mean?" He drawled this out as if she were being utterly insensible to him.

"I'm serious, you should think about getting a house. There's one that will be on the market pretty soon; I could show it to you."

He laughed at her rising excitement. "I'm not thinking of moving."

"Why not?"

He was perplexed by her genuine confusion over his purely rational obduracy. For an instant he glimpsed in her earnest, solemn face a model of classic sculpture; wearing an aspect that beggars our modern penchant for raising eyebrows over every trivial annoyance of the day. She appeared as someone having a certain, problematic hold over people; being one who was bound herself to this secret knowledge. She rose and motioned for him to follow her into the Look Out.

"Let's discuss *The Old Curiosity Shop*." Her intonation suggested an official proceeding. He wondered if he were under trial for induction into one of her chapters. She asked him an incisive question and he replied with a monologue. He stole glances at her face while pontificating. He observed that she was listening in her usual, remote, attentive repose.

"I found it poignant that the old man admits to the girl that he is helpless." She interjected into one of his pauses for breath.

"Why so?"

"Well, because the author is taking on that troubling issue of what is to be done with those who cannot take care of themselves."

"Yes." Isaiah was already seeing the text in a new light. "That troubled him his whole life. He was what we would call a progressive, but he was also driven to succeed, and he frequently proclaimed the need of having a fixed purpose, and using hard work to achieve it. He was torn by the challenges posed by that horrible class system existing then."

"And something like it still exists today."

"But the underclass, at the bottom of all that English greatness, it was sort of naked in its exposure, back then. The conditions of dire poverty were far more crushing for those people. The large government programs were not in place yet."

"And yet, even with our subsistence programs, you may only depress the spirit to the point of leaching out the humanity."

"He couldn't understand why so many were content to let so many others waste away in poverty."

"You said to me once, his stories are like parables."

"To me they read that way."

"He sure makes it clear which characters he likes. His good people have clean households." She laughed. "I think that would leave out most of his characters living in dire poverty. Do you suppose he cleaned his own houses?"

"I have a feeling he made life difficult for his wife in that regard. He was fastidious about everything. He could be a real tyrant. He ruled their household. He could be manic, a frenetic bundle of energy. He had definite ideas of how things should be, and was easily exasperated when others didn't understand that his way was to be followed, for his was self-evidently superior!"

"Yes, the charismatic leader, who rules in a flurry of imperious decrees."

"Yes, quite so. He had that social cushion of popular adoration, like movie stars of today."

"He would make a good Dickensian character!" Molly proclaimed.

This idea had just come to him as he had been speaking to her, and now she, the eager novice, had gotten there first. "That's so true."

"Do you have any biographies I might borrow?"

"Only about a dozen. Do you have a time period in mind. Every biographer has his own biases, which are refracted through his own times."

"You pick one or two for me."

"Okay, be glad to." He felt as though he had passed his initiation.

"We'll have to discuss him some more, later on; but let me say something about *this* book." She patted the cover of *The Old Curiosity Shop* which was nestled in her lap. It had been in one of the storage lockers built into the elevated platform. "After they leave the wicked city, the old man of the cottage meets the old man of the road. Then the cart driver picks them up and takes them to the village, advising that they had better take the path which leads through the churchyard."

"Ah, that's a good point." Isaiah concurred. "But he was not really one who favored all the props of organized religion."

"But he *was* religious. When they were walking, he asserts the churches have been built using superfluous funds. He is saying it would be better to lay out that money to make things better for the people in the present moment."

"That is one of his primary motifs. Why can't people just be better to one another, more caring—"

"And you're saying that's not how he lived his life?"

"Well, today he would be seen as a good, rich liberal. He helped support good causes. He worked for necessary reforms that achieved real results. He donated generously to organizations, and many people he knew. But he also wrote scathingly of charitable organizations, that operate to make sure a small coterie at the top have a sumptuous life, and clearly, the welfare of the intended recipients is hardly ever the foremost priority. And as for the Church, well, he wasn't Voltaire, but—"

"'For I am not ashamed of the gospel.'"

"Oh, I'm not saying that *you*—"

"That's a quotation."

"Oh."

"It's from *Romans*. The historian Michael Grant wrote of St. Paul's brilliant, confused intellect; and Coleridge called it the most profound book ever written."

"I see; well, forgive me, if I sound too critical of the Church. I know it's more complicated than I make out."

"Just the same, if I hear you right, you're saying his stance was that we're all hypocrites, when it comes down to it, aren't we? And you agree, don't you?"

"Well," he was startled, looking at her closely. He had done his best to disguise that belief, but she had pierced his diplomacy. "I am cynical, I suppose; too much so." He was certain she was testing him in some fashion, and it made him uneasy.

He looked out over the landscape. "I need to bring my camera up here."

"Oh, there's Janey." Molly scrambled down the stairs to greet her friend, whom she had known since her grade school days.

"Don't mind me," he said loud enough that she glanced at him over her shoulder, with a lovely, admonitory frown, as if piqued by his impertinence.

He watched as her fellow parishioners closed around her, and noted how she ushered them into her house. The good shepherd, he thought. He was reluctant to depart from the comfortable vantage. Seeing Jacob out in the yard, in his work duds, he decided to make himself scarce.

"Hey, Meriwether! Where are you going?" Jacob called out to him as he started down the stairs. "Hold on. I'm coming up." He climbed the stairs he had built and took a seat on the bench. Jacob moved over to the other end. "How do you like sitting here?"

"Oh, this is a great spot. You can really air out the mind up here."

"A perfect vantage for watching the weather. And it also serves as a fort on a dangerous frontier." Jacob intoned wistfully. "Sophie's children have unassailable rights to occupy this edifice at any time. They guard the honor of childhood up here."

"I shall keep the relative orders in mind when I am on these grounds."

"Do so, and if the powers and principalities deign to grant you an audience, make an effort to listen. For this is now the Watchtower." Jacob spoke solemnly, as he began to work at something loaded on his phone. In short order, Dylan's "All Along the Watchtower" was playing in the air around them.

"Oh wow, that's a nice touch."

"Wireless, outdoor speakers, in the trees. No reason to rough it while standing watch, at the frontier."

Isaiah laughed. "You have the best backyard I've ever seen."

"You should get one. Be lord of your own little realm."

"So Molly keeps telling me."

"She can be relentless."

"I'm thinking of retiring, winding down, not gearing up."

"We're all winding down, all the time. Maybe gearing up, at the same time, is essential."

They sat a moment looking out over the peaceful vista, listening to the birds, and distant cries of children down on the school yard below. Jacob turned off the music.

"Were you going to ask Molly about her paintings?" Jacob posed the question without looking at him.

"Oh, I wasn't sure about that. What did she say?"

"She hasn't said anything to me."

"How do you know I haven't asked her about that, then?"

Jacob turned to look at him, with a challenging mien.

"I didn't want to come across as *the* artist; like I was capable of tossing off glib critiques of her work."

"You don't want to critique her work?"

"It's not that." Isaiah was uncomfortable.

"What is it?"

"I don't know. She hasn't mentioned anything to me." This was not quite true. "I am a little afraid to broach that topic . . . I'm rather touchy about my own work."

"She really likes your work. I know that much. Since you've been coming around, she's been spending more time in her workroom. Have you seen that space she has set up in our basement?"

"No."

"If you want to see her things, then you should ask her about her workroom. By the way, I like your work boots."

Isaiah laughed. "Do you remember those blue work shirts they used to sell at J. C. Penney?"

"I purchased many of those."

"Me too, it was part of our garb in the art department."

"But I worked with construction crews, for a pretty long time. Now I'm a casual-wear accountant."

"Do I have to ask Molly to let me into one of her book club chapters?"

"Why do you ask me that?"

I feel like she's considering me for a slot, but she's not sure if it's such a good idea. I don't know why—"

Here Jacob reared back his head and roared out a burst of gusty laughter. It lasted long enough for Isaiah to know he had touched upon some cardinal point of the woman's personality.

"You want me to explain the idiosyncrasies of my wife? I don't understand half of them myself. These are occult matters you are dealing with here."

"Well then, tell me this. Do you know how St. Louis died?" Isaiah asked, by way of jocular non sequitur.

"Did he fall on his sword, by accident?" Jacob lost not a beat in his riposte, being a decorated veteran of Isaac's legendary picnic table.

Isaiah had to stop and chortle for a spell.

"Well? Am I close?"

"I believe he fell ill, while on another crusade, and died in his sickbed."

"Was that a genuine crusade?"

"No, I don't think it was, but then; of course, what is the definition of a genuine crusade?"

Both men began laughing.

"I can't remember what Marx told me about that second crusade—"

"Marx? You mean O'Rourke?"

"Yeah. You know O'Rourke?"

"We've met him; through Raphe."

"You know, that reminds me, I've been wanting to confess something to Molly, and maybe I should tell you, instead."

"Tread lightly there, boy. This isn't a confessional, only a watchtower."

"One time I stole a baby Jesus from a crèche, down on Florissant Road." Isaiah was amazed at himself, as he proceeded to reveal the particulars of how he had attended a riotous teen party, where beer, wine, and pot were the prescribed social relaxants. Upon leaving that locale, he wandered crookedly into the snowy world. He was amazed at the enormous scale of the crèche, sitting on the raised ground of the church lawn. He decided to climb the little hill, falling several times, and scrambling up to take a good long look at the nativity scene. It was outrageously funny to him in that moment.

"I thought, here they are, still abandoned by society. Left out in the cold, during the Christmas season! The next thing I knew, I was trundling down the street cradling my hostage to my breast."

"What did you do with it?"

"I still have it! It's in my studio. I ran across it not too long ago. I had totally forgotten about it."

"Why are you telling me this; making me an accessory after the fatuous act?"

"I have no idea what to do with it. That church is no longer there; a different denomination has moved in. I just wanted to hear what Molly would say to me. What do you think she would tell me to do?"

"That's quite a predicament for an honorable member of the Loop gang." The men looked at each other. "What would that dead English writer bloke of yours say?"

"Oh man, hell if I know." Isaiah looked upwards, as if listening. "You know, he did use the doll metaphor an awful lot. Is that apropos in this instance?"

"Are you asking me to adopt this metaphysical doll into my household?"

"Yes, let's say I am. It must represent something more than we know, and you have already established a regular preserve for sacred symbols, no?"

"This yard is not my house." He reared back and signed. "We need a picnic table for this discussion."

"The child is still swaddled, but he has no place to lay his head."

"Send me the specifications, I can build a manger."

"I can deliver him to you."

"Sure, just drop him off; I'll build a tabernacle down there, against the wall. I'll scavenge some materials from around my place here. We'll install him there during our Midnight Mass festival. My apologies in advance to Father Charles."

"What festival is that?"

"We have people over after the mass lets out. We gather out here for a short time. Feeling the cold, seeing our warm breath, being aware of the universe above. I build a bonfire. Although, I'm not sure they're going to hold Midnight Mass this year." Jacob clapped Isaiah on the knee. "Well, I'm afraid I've got some things to do, my friend."

"I promise to vacate the premises, sir."

"Take your time, you old trickster."

"I guess it can be bothersome, having to deal with all the people that are always coming around here, imposing on your hospitality."

Jacob paused at the top of the stairs, turning around. "I never begrudge her disciples." Their eyes met, and

Jacob descended to the ground and walked towards the house.

Isaiah exited the property and moved into the Grotto area. He took some photographs. He talked with Father Charles and learned that he had relinquished the donated Dickens collection to Molly's custody. He was borrowing volumes from her now. The priest mentioned in passing something about a proposed Dickens chapter, which he was tempted to join.

Isaiah sat on his wall for a long time watching the chimney swifts. Before leaving he visited with Jacob again, who was out in his yard burning leaves. He looked like a Druid; too profoundly absorbed in his esoteric rites to be disturbed for long by any random layman, who hath not true understanding of such matters.

"Hard to beat the smell of burning leaves for stirring up memories." Isaiah spoke as he stared at the multicolored flames, halfway lost in a fragrant trance.

"All the natural smells of the earth are irresistible to me."

"Say, tell me, do you think Molly would let me paint her portrait?"

"Let you?"

"Yeah."

"Meriwether?" He cocked his head. "I would like for you to do just that, and we've already discussed this. She's adamant that you must receive your usual fee."

"I don't even have a usual fee. Besides, I wouldn't be able to charge her. I just couldn't."

"That's what she said you'd say."

"I could tell her it would be good practice—"

"Come on." Jacob appeared mildly ruffled.
"You can never practice enough, according to some."
"Tell me how much it would cost."
"I wouldn't feel right, charging you guys."
"Why not?"
"I don't know."
Jacob sighed heavily. "See if you can get a look at her workroom."

Before their conversation could proceed any further Molly was among them, wanting to know what they were talking about. They were evasive and her eyes narrowed.

"I enjoyed our discussion on Dickens; we should hold some more of those." Isaiah said.

"My book club is getting ready to do *The Old Curiosity Shop*."

"There you go."

"What?"

"Now you're just taunting me."

"Why do you say that?"

At that point more people came out of the house and hailed Molly, needing her attention. Isaiah soon departed and drove home in a giddy state. He had a strange sensation of floating along in his vehicle, and this left him feeling rather perplexed. He was enjoying a new kind of happiness that was somewhat maddening, for it seemed to lack any apparent meaning, and was hardly to be trusted. He was more certain of one thing, his work provided that essential part of his life that he could not bear the thought of ever losing.

29

One evening Timothy invited Isaiah to join Patricia and him for dinner. Since the inception of the pandemic a lot of people were fiercely adamant they must be allowed to continue dining out at their favorite restaurants. Isaiah had hardly any qualms himself, as the power of one's largely self-ascribed social status adroitly modifies incipient fears into practical strains of fatalism.

In a dim, spacious corner, seated at a large table, they enjoyed being treated with genteel deference, fawned over with decorous tact, and served haute cuisine, as if it were their natural due, and happy wont. At the outset Timothy made it clear that Isaiah was their guest. Isaiah understood how important this was for him to be in that position once more. At first, they were all exquisitely gracious with one another, in a way that made him feel uncomfortable.

Isaiah tried talking about something he had recently read in a novel by Dickens; Marx frowned in response.

"I just found it interesting, because he strikes me as one of those very gregarious solitaires. He liked putting on a big show, and then he wanted to get away from things."

"You have some of that, you always have." Timothy interjected.

"You think I do?"

Timothy and Patricia looked at each other, and quickly away.

"What are you working on now?" Patricia asked him.

"We're working on several things presently. In fact, more drawings of the Loop, using old photographs."

"Why do you use the royal we?" Patricia queried with an emboldened tone. Isaiah looked at her beaming face; it was evident that these two had been serving him up in private conversations.

"No." Timothy rushed to explain, having to suppress his signature cackle. "That's entirely his own device. It's the psychiatric we; he is speaking for the whole merry crew; Messieurs Ego, Id, and Superego. Just like, Gallia est omnis divisa in partes tres; so is the artistry of our I. Thomas!

"That's not it—"

"You've always been that way! And another thing, you're phlegmatic."

"What! What does that even mean?" Isaiah turned to Patricia, as if to enlist her support.

"One of stolid temperament." Patricia explains.

Isaiah held out his hands, as if pleading to a jury. "Look, when I said we—"

Fortunately, the waiter appeared, quashing his motion to drag his son into his plight. Their attention was drawn to the special entrées of the house; after this interlude the conversation took on a more pleasant flavor.

"So, you've been going up there to Ferdinand pretty often?" Timothy asked at one point, as if he knew the answer.

Isaiah confirmed that he was, in fact. "So many years later, it's intriguing to look around, as if seeing things for the first time."

"Lately, we've been going to the Botanical Garden quite a lot." Timothy affirmed this as if laying down a superior hand in a game of cards.

Isaiah asked questions to hear them talk more about their activities. He saw the color flow into his friend's face, while subtle, sympathetic waves passed across the visage of Patricia. She had dusted herself demurely with the cosmetic brush. Her attire presented a look of simple elegance. Her hair was straight and glossy. Timothy's hair was a luxurious modern sculpture, having in the front a fine, uplifted scarp, which feature Isaiah could not help but envy. He knew how much women were drawn to a fine thatch of hair. He suddenly had to swat away damnable thoughts of women he had chased to no avail, except that of his own misery.

"We went on that owl watch in the park." Timothy said to Isaiah's blank look.

"That was a lot of fun." Patricia chimed. "You should have seen Tim." She turned to her swain with a naughty smile. "He was asking all these questions about the history of the park. The changes made over time. The poor guy was flustered, he just wanted to tell us about his precious owls. You really were out of control, Timothy."

"I'm not into owls, and churchyards, and such." He explained sheepishly.

"You weren't that bad." She leaned closer to him and shook her head in lovely admonition. Patricia now regaled Isaiah with information they had gleaned regarding great horned owls. Her voice contained irony, amusement, and delight, all swirled into a nice blend.

Isaiah listened and watched as the two parried with each other over things that had happened, or had not, in the course of that prior evening. They spoke of other incidents from the past; each now a pearly object strung on their fine Riviera of sun-washed, fulsome days. Rather abruptly they began discussing politics, from a vast, haughty remove, as if it were ancient, stodgy Rome in question, instead of our republic, that horribly gauche, stylish, badly aging, forever lovely, innocent debutante, and gross, ruthless matron, America.

In time their meals were set before them and consumed with delicate relish. Before digestion had fairly begun these most recent dishes were compared to others eaten at other places at other times. When that inane topic was exhausted the lively pair resumed talking about their local travels.

"Molly said to me, loneliness is a small province, and that everywhere, on the frontiers of loneliness, you find a vast kingdom of rich solitude." Timothy's voice suggested an air of knowing things that lay beyond the scope of this polite conversation.

"Molly Gates?" Isaiah's voice rose higher.

"Yes."

"She *is* something." Patricia confirmed with ardor.

"When did you meet Molly?" Isaiah asked in a petulant manner.

"We were visiting Raphe, at his redoubt up in the river lands, as he calls it—was that a week ago?" He glanced at Patricia, who nodded. "And we dropped by to see her on the way up."

"You dropped by?"

"We were with Raphe at the time. We had been in the Loop and—why are you so concerned about the logistics of our journeys?"

"I'm not, I just—"

"What I want to know is, why you never told me about her?" Timothy's face, in his new glasses, put Isaiah in mind of an old insurance salesman, who has gone senile, and is forever trying to close nonexistent policies.

"I've been busy working."

"I mean back in the day, when Stephen and you were going there, you never mentioned her to me. I had no idea about the Café Montmartre, or any of that business."

"It didn't last very long." He thought of how terribly he then strove to keep things going when he was performing his minstrel shows for Edith.

"Long enough, apparently. Were you smitten with her, back then?"

"Smitten?"

Timothy smiled in a wry fashion, his eyes glittered incredibly behind his refractive lenses.

"I must have told you about her, I'm sure I did; she knew my uncle. Besides, you had no interest in going out into the suburbs back then, remember?" He was unsure why he had not shared his knowledge of Molly with his friend, then, or more recently. "I'll tell you what, though, she wants me to move to Ferdinand."

"Why?" Marx expressed his amazement in a booming voice.

"I lived there as a child, for a while; my mother was a native there..."

"But *you* in a house, with a dining room, a dining set? The standard suburban yard! Are you going to buy a lawn mower?" Marx leaned back, chuckling. "I can't see it."

"You know Marx, all cleaned up like this, you don't look like your patron saint anymore."

"I've told him that!" Patricia exclaimed. She was taking full credit for his transformation. She excused herself to go to the rest room.

"Listen," Timothy leaned forward, raising a didactic finger, "Marx actually cut off his beard, and trimmed his hair, after his Jenny died. He had passed through a lot of sorrow. People change, you know. His devoted daughters took up his quest for justice and knowledge." He appeared deeply affected.

"It looks to me like you have your own Jenny now."

"Ah." Timothy looked at his friend's face, and fell back in his chair. His hands came to rest on his modest paunch. "That's well said."

"After all this time." Isaiah said. Timothy laughed in a deep, resonant release of emotion. He then began to talk of the venerable Baroness von Westphalen, the phenomenal partner of that most elusive radical, whose cults were based on history, and family.

"What are you two talking about? Who was Jenny?" Patricia had come back, and was eager to take up whatever they were discussing. "Tell me."

"I'll explain later," Timothy spoke softly.

For a while they dawdled, feeling no pressure to make way for other diners; none were waiting. Sipping cognac, laughing at the world, as they perceived it to be at the present time. It was easy to find agreement on what was out there, in the real world; easy to fall prey to that human propensity to avow, in a genial mood, whatever sentiments let people feel good about themselves.

Isaiah and Timothy made observations of the sort that are possible only after a very long friendship. They mocked each other in ritual form, taking prideful issue with their good fortunes. The teasing subsided. They lingered in their glowing satiation, that soon devolved into a primal craving for restorative slumbers. A chorus of faint groans finally set in motion final preparations for departure.

Outside Isaiah paused a moment to watch the happy pair wending away, holding hands in a youthful manner. He was feeling proud of them, and this seemed strange, like everything else that was happening these days. He had really enjoyed this ceremony of their friendship, though it burned a little in his heart afterwards. He did not know what he felt, after a while, and he had again that sensation of floating as he traipsed towards his car. He looked up and smiled at the jittery stars; wonderment touched his soul. He shivered keenly, as if struck inwardly and responding, like a mute tuning fork, emitting one pure, silent frequency.

30

Two more statues had been installed in the Grotto, placed in a sort of ancient cave dwelling built in the small center court. These were the brothers, John and James, sons of Zebedee, whom their teacher named sons of thunder.

Isaiah stood there taking pictures. In another moment he was nearly overcome by the poignant redolence of so many fir trees. It was the balsams especially that possessed evocative, regenerative properties impossible to ignore. His being was suddenly inclined towards rare peacefulness as the trees quivered in response to cold bracing winds. He began hearing the faint whispers of deathless carols.

He found his own shelter in the reverence for what has been, and always remains, as proof of something lasting, that has come of us, and is thus forever becoming to our very being's every struggle. He recalled the choir up in the gymnasium, singing carols on the last school day of every year. A perfect keynote; a feeling of being at one with something else that truly mattered. No music had ever sounded so perfect; that joy had seeped into his marrow, and he now trembled in response.

That child he once was, he *had* possessed faith. It was grounded in something hardly known to him, and was at present but an unsorted mass of fugitive sensations. He was suddenly passing in spirit through the fires of youth once more. His persona was now a wavering shadow, still partly composed of the juvenile, a credulous, growing, yearning, Dionysian creature, forever caught in his own heroic fairy tale. He could feel the magic of Christmas resounding in his choiring emotions.

He began to move to clear his head, taking his usual place on the wall. He recalled that at one time he had been accused of trying to paint pictures that were too derivative of an extraordinary piece done by Norman Rockwell. This was treated as artistic malpractice! He was more than a little puzzled by the vengeance taken against him for his simple act of homage. For him, Rockwell had represented many things, but his picture of Ruby Bridges, entitled *The Problem We All Live With*, had moved him tremendously.

Long before, that picture had caused him to get into an argument with his grandmother, and he was slapped as a consequence. On another occasion, when he was older, he had spoken very calmly, pressing her to explain why her church was a segregated space. He was an actor, speaking as the moral spokesman for his generation. He was naïve, arrogant, insulting; however, his moral observation was founded on the treacherous rock upon which we strive to erect a higher purpose. His selfish fervor waned, over time, becoming largely another posture.

He sat upright, sketching the school building. He was not growing tired of this subject. He had arranged to see Molly's basement workroom, and was now waiting for the appointed hour to arrive. He quickly lost track of time, and then found himself in her shadow. She was standing behind him.

"I saw your car; thought you might be over here. You're becoming a fixture yourself."

"There's so much to see."

She laughed. "Not everyone would agree with you there, old man."

"Well, I have my Sumerian memories to dust off when I am here. I'm not really just another tourist."

"Sometimes you remind me of your uncle, so much." She looked down, smiling and shaking her head. "He said to me once, how glad he was that he had learned he could tune out those areas of the world he cared about the most."

"That sounds about right"

Her head bobbed as she chortled. She was swaddled in layers of old comfortable loose clothing and her wondrous hair tumbled about her glowing face. "So? Are you ready to visit my studio?"

He gathered up his things and tramped after her. Her work space was suspended in a state of productive disarray.

"I didn't straighten up." She confessed. "I decided to let you see how it looks most of the time."

Her studio was not really separate from the household warehouse. The washer and dryer commanded a portion of the back wall nearby. There were fresh bundles of clothing on the floor. Many dormant items of home furnishing were strewn about the periphery.

He inspected what she had done recently, viewing her handiwork in various sketchpads. She explained her ideas to him as he studied the pictures. Her primary interest at the moment was in the local housing stock; each one viewed from different perspectives, and always couched in its own, distinctive landscaping design. He remarked on her careful attention to the natural features.

"They are meant to be records of a place, at a certain time."

"They make a definite statement about your feelings for this parish."

"Well, all those houses are owned by people I know, really well." She spoke proudly. "I've had some role in how all of them came to live here. Jacob says its like making a catalogue of my vanity."

"Well, according to Degas," Isaiah's diction intimated he was citing from his own scripture, "one works for two or three friends, who are alive, and for others who are dead, and many others who are unknown to you."

"So, who do you work for?"

"That's not a fair question."

"Why's that?" She exclaimed.

"I don't know."

They both laughed.

Jacob began inspecting various images she had pasted onto her walls. He studied the eclectic mélange of prints and photos and personal mementos. Looking up near the bare rafters he was startled to to see a large print stretched out like a tablature over all the other images. It was Holbein's *The Body of the Dead Christ in the Tomb*.

"Wow." He let his eyes marvel over the whole figure, from the ashen face to the blackened feet. The man's inert manhood arched quietly over the center of the long picture. "This was quite something, especially for its time."

"Behold the man." She said.

He looked at her face, struck by the intensity in her eyes. He was much taken by her practice of being witty and dead serious at the same time.

He gazed fondly at Raphael's, *The Three Graces*. "I once copied this one."

"Yes?"

He murmured, glancing at several photos of funerary portraits, dating from antiquity. One was of a stately, finely-adorned Egyptian woman, looking very severe and proper; done up in her finery and jewels. He felt peculiar because the face seemed to have a somber relevance for him. Molly drew his attention away to a photograph of Jacob's late twin sister, Johanna.

"I was going to try a portrait of her."

"Why don't you?"

She made an excruciating face of reluctance under her mask. She directed him to one of her easels holding a canvas with a vague charcoal face. She said it was going to be her first real attempt at a portrait. She beseeched his opinion on what he could see, so far, with an affecting plea to be mindful of her delicate feelings. They were both wearing masks, but her trepidation shone through her eyes nonetheless. Her keen interest in his opinion moved him and made him hesitate.

"Well, I like the structure you have started, there, and there." He pointed to several features on her drawing, from which she was beginning to work on the canvas.

"That took me forever, and I don't really like the facial expression."

"The alchemy of getting the expression you want is a mysterious business."

She made a sibilant sound which he could not decipher.

"Molly, if you'd like, I'd be glad to do your portrait."

She shook her head. "I don't want to talk about that, but tell me, what do you have there?" She pointed at his large satchel resting on a table.

"I wanted to show you something."

It was a watercolor, which he now laid flat on her large table. She leaned over to examine the picture.

"Oh my, it's Charlotte!" Her delight was thrilling to him.

"It will be a signature piece of my watercolor period." He spoke as if in jest, but his pride was beyond measure.

"Oh, I like it. The feel of it."

"You like it?"

"I love this." She placed it on her easel, covering her sketch. "She has perfect composure, inside all that beauty. She's a creature of mystery. It's like she's aware of the world's stare, and she's gone beyond its coercive influence. She's very quietly reveling in her own moment."

"That's good. I thought of her as being in control of her life, but you've penetrated to the nature of her strength. The way you were talking about her gave me the inspiration to take a stab at her heart."

They looked at one another. Molly was astonished by his verbiage. Isaiah blushed unseen.

"You've brought her to life. I think it's splendid."

"At first I wanted to use some memories of those times when I was there, in her presence, but none of that was very clear to me. It was so nebulous. So, I just went for a certain feeling—"

"Her look, it's almost haunting. Did you have a huge crush on her?"

"Well," he laughed, "I don't think so, not consciously. It was more like adoration. She was beyond mere mortals like me!"

"But not your father?"

"No, not my father." He became diffident, having this topic raised in this way. "I let my imagination run a little wild with her hair."

"You made her very blond, no surprise there."

"I couldn't decide on her pose, until I settled on that scene, and her standing out in front of Gaslight Square. She is the only subject, in front of an abstract background."

"Now, is this supposed to be an exact place?"

"It's some corner where they were standing in one of the photos. I moved her up closer, to get her out of that clutter of riotous scenery."

"You suggest the scene pretty well; all that commotion of lights and movement in the night. Her coloring reflects those background atmospherics."

"Yes." He nodded. "She's just come forth, out of all that glaring nightlife, to meet someone for a private moment."

"Like she's coming into her own."

"Yes, that's right."

"She's of the past, in her clothing, but not so much her face, or hair. You've made her ageless."

"That's how she is in my memory!"

"Are you going to show this to Raphael?"

"Raphael?" He was caught off guard.

"I think he'd really like this."

"I don't know. Do *you* want it?"

"Do I?" Her eyes flared at him, almost wildly. "I want to see what he thinks of it first."

"From what you've said, he wouldn't want to think of her, as she was in these times, would he?"

"I doubt he cares about anything else than the fact he sees *her*, the woman he used to love."

Isaiah stared at his painting; miserable all of a sudden.

"He'll want to buy it from you."

She could see Isaiah was uncomfortable, but wanted to press him so he would understand.

"This is the first serious watercolor portrait I've done."

"You want to keep it for yourself?"

"It's just that," he wasn't sure why he was so adamant that the picture not be sold to Raphael, "this marks the beginning of my early posthumous period." He attempted to make light of his real sentiment, which was not clear to himself

"Okay, I don't want to be accused of forcing you to do something against your will." Her voice rang with delicate echoes of past charges made against her.

"Maybe I'll mention it to him; see how he reacts, the next time I see him."

"Do you see him very often?"

"No, not really."

"Have you two done anything more, on that article?"

"I believe that project is dead." Isaiah shuffled his feet as if he were trying to position himself to heft a precarious burden.

"Let's go outside. I hate wearing these masks." Molly said, leading him into the back yard, where she could not resist walking around as if every feature of the yard was under review for possible renovations. She strolled about a short while before inviting him into the Watchtower, where they settled down, after expressing thoughts on the beauty of the day.

"You know, I think Raphael stole a picture of mine."

"Stole a picture? Of what?"

"Of Charlotte! Back when I had him over, to talk about the article, I showed him some photo albums. I left the room a few times, and then recently, when I was collecting photos of Charlotte, I went back to those albums, and there was one photo missing."

"See!"

"What?"

"Well, if he was willing to steal that picture, there's no doubt he'll want to have your watercolor. You've captured something there; it will be priceless to him."

Isaiah was quite perturbed. He had considered giving the picture to Molly, hoping she would prize it for herself. Now she advocated turning the prize over to Raphael!

He concluded that he must keep it; the value of the piece had soared in his eyes, as it had shone in hers. The woman's image spoke to him of his father, and preserved a lovely vestige of his now fabled adventures. He was taking fright at the prospect of losing the last souvenirs taken from all those times he had never understood. His confusion hardened his heart further against generous motions.

"You know, I'm curious; were you tempted to paint Charlotte with your dad, in that picture?"

"What?" He reacted strongly, for he had thought of this, for a long time; and it still aggrieved him. "I wouldn't have known how to picture them together." He looked up into the sky, musing, and then he had to laugh, as he noticed he was emulating her way of ranging her vision around to encompass her realm.

"Have you ever done a portrait of your mother?"

"No." The question shook him. "I made sketches of her, or tried to, but I was never very successful." He wanted to say something to reconcile turbulent emotions now clashing within his mind. "The distance made me feel that it was hopeless."

"What was hopeless?"

The blood came into his face. Her eyes beseeched him, and he began speaking of his mother as he never had before. He poured out his sorrows, his pain, and his regrets. His hands appeared to twist and defile the fabric of a precious invisible shroud he had found and could not bear to drop. He shared portions of his chronicle as succinctly as possible, but it was overwhelming, and he could not control his voice. When he stopped talking there was a prolonged silence.

"My mother was always a great, silent force."

Isaiah expected her to say more, but she again had her face up to sniff the ether of the universe.

"She was reticent, hard to talk to?"

"Oh no, I don't mean in that way. In her deepest faith, she was quiet, that's all. And yet, I perceived things, *through* her vision, as I somehow knew it to be." She looked over, as if to acknowledge she did not expect him to understand what she was saying.

After her mother died, Molly had a strange experience; feeling she finally understood this woman for the first time in her life. But that wasn't true, either; it was only that she felt closer to the woman than she ever had before. She was overcome by a strange craving, or desire, to journey deeper into herself; to get closer still to that maternal devotion.

"For some reason, after we lost her, my faith came apart on me. I had to face things . . . do you know what I mean?" She looked steadily at him, and knew he could not possibly comprehend all she meant, as she did not herself.

Isaiah was transfixed by the honesty composing her countenance.

"You couldn't believe, anymore?"

"I tried to imagine what lay behind the rituals."

"You had outgrown all that priestly architecture."

She gently shook her head, a slight grimace on her features. "Boy, sometimes I really wish you had served as apprentice at Isaac's picnic table. You might have learned how to listen when someone tries to break herself down."

"Break yourself down, what?" This phrase had clanged against his protective armor, inciting fears of making a spectacle of himself.

"Have you ever read F. Scott Fitzgerald's essays called 'The Crack-Up?'"

"No."

"Raphael brought that to our club one time. Back then he was into all things having to do with Fitzgerald. But it's never done that way, only in private..." She said no more, in her maddening custom of eliciting interest and retreating into reticence.

"So, what is it about?"

The sound of people laughing flocked about their ears. Molly mumbled something and climbed down to greet the newcomers.

Isaiah descended to the ground and departed. Later that afternoon he was imbibing wine at Pliny's, talking to Marx, showing him the book Molly had loaned him while they were in her workroom; *The Writings of St. Paul*, the Norton Critical Edition.

"She gave you a homework assignment?"

"It looks like it. She's read a lot more than this, I'm afraid, and I don't have the heart to tell her I don't want to learn about theology."

"Can I borrow this?" Marx asked, as he paged through the volume. "Here you go, right here, this idea that the desires of the flesh are against the Spirit; where does she stand on that bizarre element of the creed?"

"What do you mean?"

"He speaks of gathering in all people, including slaves and freemen, which meant then ex-slaves. He penetrates to the heart of our bondage, to our own unconscious wiring."

Isaiah watched his friend rifling through the book; his eyes were romping over the copious footnotes. His interest was excited even more by the essays included in the back, written by such powerful lights as Baur, Nietzsche, Shaw, Kierkegaard, and Schweitzer.

"Well, I only just got it from her." Isaiah reached out to regain possession. "She gave it to me to read."

Marx relinquished the prize, with a frown. "Okay, but it's really not your standard fare."

"It's something I need to look at; she's considering me for one of her book club chapters."

"I'm already in one, and being considered for another."

"No you're not." Isaiah was stupefied.

"She doesn't read all the books herself, you know. She has an interest in many subjects, and apparently she really likes to listen to what others, who are more knowledgeable, have to say. That's how Raphael got in; his knowledge of so many novels. So, she hasn't brought you in yet, eh?"

"She's considering me for one of her secret chapters."

"Secret chapters?"

"Hey! Where is Patricia, anyway?" Isaiah was chary of exploring his relative standing with Molly in front of Marx.

"Out of town, visiting relatives."

"You know, you're the worst kind of atheist."

"What?" Marx smiled, in his benign perplexity. "What are you talking about?"

"You don't even think about issues of faith. A lot of people really care about such things."

"You think, because I never discuss such things with you, that I never think of these imponderables?"

"Do you?"

"I'm agnostic. I've discussed my faith with Molly. She has this incredibly fertile imagination. She's very curious to know—"

"Tell me, do you know much about this stuff?" Isaiah shifted instantly from censure to entreaty. "He patted the cover of the book."

"I've read a fair amount, regarding the formation of that cult."

"Teach me the basics. I need to catch up."

Marx pulled the book to himself; his fingers drummed on the cover. "Tell me what you know about this crazed genius we know as Paul."

"He liked to travel."

"Read this," Marx slid the book over to him, "front to back; and then we can talk about it. By the way, Patricia and I are reading Dickens now; we've formed our own club. Maybe we should have you over as a guest speaker."

Isaiah scratched at his temple; irritated by his friend's irrepressible nature. "Just teach me what I need to know." He patted the book.

"How would I know that?"

Isaiah shook his head, exhaling heavily. "Marx?"

"Yeah?"

"It's official, the gang is defunct."

"It had to happen, at some point. Maybe that particular structure has disintegrated, but the energy remains, and we will have other opportunities to build other formulations."

That sounded to Isaiah like something he might have said to curry favor with Molly. He now clutched the book to his breast and broke away, headed for his studio, leaving Marx looking after him, shaking his head. The old professor sat alone a little while; majestic in the savor of this fortuitous moment. You did not need a lot to be happy, only enough of the best of what was inherent to life's self-possession in the face of time. It might well be time to tackle St. Paul again. He was amused at the curious turns life will take, if one only has the grace to allow things to happen according to the laws that are apparently not entirely of this world, while striving valiantly to be happy in this one.

31

One morning Isaiah woke earlier than usual. He watched the oaks out front holding morning prayers. They were wrapped in ephemeral swirls of gorgeous veils. He resolved he ought to go, and had to hurry, and forgo his breakfast, to make the early mass. Molly was going every day.

"I like to be alone in that space." She had explained. "Just being there, in the crux of all that spiritual symbolism, it helps me center myself."

He did not want to impose, so he sat far in the back, as he had done in his youth; letting his imagination run wild. After the service he swung down to the Grotto and Molly came by and invited him over to her house for coffee. They ended up in her living room. Her house was very cluttered, every room appointed with many decorative objects. She kept many totems recording the family's passage through the years.

While they were chatting, Jacob stomped down the stairs from the second floor, and Molly rose to join him in the kitchen. They came into the living room together, and Jacob explained gruffly to Isaiah that some people actually had to go in to work these days.

"I'm practicing for when I retire." Isaiah jested. Jacob nodded, a begrudging smile flitting across his lips. He left the house.

"Well, how are the watercolors coming along?" Molly asked.

"I only have a few sketches; the inspiration is flagging on me."

"What about the suburban scenes?"

"That's what I'm working on, but it's going slow. I am intrigued by the idea of backyards, all of a sudden. That blessed little plot of one's own. To have a sacred piece of the outdoors to cultivate just as you wish."

"You're just trying to get me going, aren't you?"

"What?"

"Going on like that about yards." She shook her head, a look of rueful disgust on her face. "Why don't you get your own, then?"

"It's too late for me." He sounded a plaintive note.

"I don't see why you feel that way."

"I've decided I don't want to be relevant anymore." He stated, as if he'd been struck by a revelation.

"What do you mean?"

"To that world of critical appraisal. I've achieved all I ever will, in that arena. I'm tired of seeking their approval. I'm able to sell my things; that needs to be enough for me now."

"You don't really feel that way." Her voice sounded rather harsh.

"Well, sometimes..."

"You ought to be proud of your success."

"I am."

"You can be honest about wanting acclaim for the work you're doing now."

He stood up and went over to inspect her bookshelves. He gazed fondly at his old Dickens collection. There were all sorts of other books; novels, biographies, memoirs, and quite a few volumes on the subject of Christianity.

"It just seems different now. Like something is over."

"You feel like you were never given your proper due."

He looked at her. "If you mean, do I harbor resentment, I'd say plenty; on many scores. It's like I'm just finding out I was traveling on a road that doesn't end up anywhere." He laughed inaudibly. "I never thought Jackson Pollock, the wallpaper king, was a serious artist."

"And that put you at odds with many others in that world?"

He looked down and snorted derisively; thinking to himself, It was never wise going against Peggy's glamour boy. "It just wasn't for me; all that incoherent, technical complexity, often times brilliant, but devoid of meaningful narrative. To me, anyway; but then, maybe if it were something I wanted to follow, but it just wasn't. I mean, the way they torture the means, to find meanings?" He shook his head. "I don't know." Seeing her face he had to laugh at his confused speech.

"You have to follow what speaks to you."

"That's true enough. And sometimes it profits the man. What do his paintings sell for, hundreds of millions of dollars."

"Because they're traded as precious commodities. That obscene pricing has nothing to do with the intrinsic worth of the painting." Molly spoke with conviction.

He smiled. "Yeah, fortunately the filthy rich we'll have always. Money often chooses what's in vogue. Let us now praise the lords of the dripping, pouring, splashing and smearing schools. Let us all piss into the wind."

Molly's laughter at his peevish complaint was pleasant to his ear.

"It's funny, because one of my best-selling prints is of a human brain, that I found in a medical journal somewhere. A blob of grey matter that had been sliced into thin sections. I called it, *A Slice of Life*, and no one understood what it was supposed to be."

"A spoof of that whole school?"

"Well, maybe, but I spent three months working on it. I was proud of the pencil work. I embedded tiny monsters in the folds of the tissue; modern variations on medieval folklore subjects."

"Why?"

"Not sure. It was Theo who convinced me to offer the prints in various colors, and to arrange them side by side in one setting. It became a cool thing, for college dorm rooms."

"Smart boy, to entrap the young." Her voice carried subtle nuances. "Does Theo help you run your business?"

"Well, it is a business, but not like others. You have to have a feel for the nature of the whole process."

"And you don't think he does?"

"I don't know." He looked away, as if to remove the pained expression from his face. "I guess he and Dilsey are getting along pretty well. He hasn't by any chance said anything to you?"

"That I'm comfortable sharing with you, right now?"

"Yeah."

"No, not really. Dilsey has a lot of great photographs. Did you even look at her work?"

"We never actually got to that point." He felt he had been judged unfairly. That 'even' in her voice pricked his conscience. She must have heard about Theo's request to use his website. "To change the subject, I wouldn't mind joining your book club."

"Oh?" She rose and began fussing with some items on a small table, then she straightened a picture frame. She finally took hold of a small gargoyle figurine and returned to her former seat. "I would have to see what the others say."

"If you're going to start covering the works of Dickens, I know I could help you out. Let me suggest that you should start with *Martin Chuzzlewit*."

"Why should we start with that one?"

"Because, no one will have read it, and it contains a lot of his best humor, in that early, extravagant manner, which he moved away from later on. It makes for a great frolic."

"I have finished *The Old Curiosity Shop* and *Dombey and Son*. Now I'm reading *Great Expectations* again; I read it in high school."

"Oh, that's great. You should read *David Copperfield* first, because that and *Great Expectations* are companions. The two constitute a sort of personal manifesto."

"I've been reading again certain passages dealing with Little Nell."

"She is a good litmus test for people; if they gag on the bathos of that journey, then it's going to be a tough class."

"She reminds me of *The Little Match Girl*; something from my childhood. He fleshed her out for me in a brilliant fashion. Did you ever read that book, by Hans Christian Andersen?"

"Never even heard of it, to be honest."

She told him to wait one minute and rushed upstairs and came back with an old copy of that very book. Isaiah found the illustrations winsome. He slowly turned over the thick pages.

"Go ahead, read it." She left the room and he settled back to do as he was bid.

"I see what you mean." He said when she resumed her seat. "A moving tale."

"I like that it's about visions; what we are capable of bringing to life in our minds. That is what allows us to keep alive a greater sense of what life might be; if only, right?"

"Yes. It's provocative." It occurred to him this might be another interview for his possible admission into the club, which was now being guarded like Kafka's castle. He began to tell her how Andersen had visited the Dickens's family, intending to stay for two weeks, and extended his trip to five weeks. Charles had quipped that it had seemed ages to the family.

"His daughters called the Dane a 'bony bore.' I think he was too maudlin for Dickens! If you can image that!"

Molly smiled at his eagerness to enlighten her.

"This story actually reminds me of a parable in his last complete novel, *Our Mutual Friend*; which includes the vignette of Old Betty Higden. She's homeless, and yet she refuses to take charity; rather she goes on the road to earn her keep, as a seamstress, I think it was. She refuses to be returned to her parish, as a pauper, to be put on the dole. She accepts the hard road, and suffers greatly, refusing help that is offered. And then, at the end she comes together with one of the good angels, and passes away, her awful dignity intact. I suppose, that's what we're to believe. It's not quite clear. The chapter is titled, "The End of a Long Journey.""

"I've noticed he likes to lecture his audience." Molly stated impassively. Before she could say anything more, Isaiah launched into a story about the Teacher's late love, for a young actress.

"She was the precipitating cause of his break with his wife."

"You blame that on the young woman?"

"No, but their marital situation became unbearable under that added stress."

"I've read that he had ten children with his wife."

"Yes, and seemed always to regret it. Of course, in that time, they didn't have a very good means for being more careful about . . ."

"About what?"

"You know."

"Yes, but I was thinking of all the huge families I knew at St. Margaret's, when I was a little child. It was a colony of huge Catholic households."

"Dickens acted like a manic depressive. He experienced wild bursts of elation, pitching himself into huge projects, and then later, he would crash. He had to keep to a frenetic pace of writing, for monthly, and even weekly, publication. At times he was driven to wander through the streets. He told a close companion once, 'I want to escape from myself.' Sometimes I wonder about his torments, his devils, and such."

"It's not always so easy to avoid being at the mercy of wild emotional swings. Life is always going to have intense joys and sorrows. It's a trial to keep things in balance."

"Yes." He came out of his didactic posture, noticing the depth of her contemplation.

"Have you ever read that book by Henry Adams, on the Gothic cathedrals, and the Virgin?" She posed this, as if it were a product of great deliberation.

"No. I remember Marx talking about it, long ago."

"Marx?"

"O'Rourke."

"Oh yes, yes. He's read so much!"

"Well, other than Dickens. I've always kept my nose in the art books, for the most part. I like to know about the struggles of their lives; what lays behind the works." His manner changed. "Being myself, a lesser, but true apostle of the creed."

"You think of yourself as an apostle?"

He was surprised she had taken his joke seriously. "It's just that so many people treat the craft as a religious cult. In the beginning, I looked upon Van Gogh as a sort of Christ figure!" He laughed, rather loudly, in his embarrassment.

"What's so funny?"

"It just sounds silly to me, now, for some reason. There's a place in *Our Mutual Friend*, in which the Teacher speaks of the sublime message of the New Testament."

"That's clear in all his writing."

He was preparing to launch into a dissertation on the Teacher's overarching metaphor of the sea, so often woven into his works. It represented life and death, and all that lay between; the movements of providence, and the fates, and the question of free will, and all that encompasses morality, and the struggles against brute instincts. His treatment begs many questions regarding the destiny of humankind.

The sound of footsteps came to them from the front porch, and the entire room suddenly reverberated with the sound of knocking. In the next moment more knocking was heard at the back door.

"Time for me to go," he announced, standing up; aware he was trying too hard to impress her, and probably doing the opposite.

He wended politely through the people on the back porch, nodding as they stared doubtfully at him. He drove to his favorite art supply store, and took his time loading up for a good regimen of work. He returned to Ferdinand and ate lunch at Sistah's Vineyard; afterwards taking a lazy stroll around Ferdinand.

He ended up at the Grotto again, where he was soon accosted by Father Charles. They walked leisurely about the grounds. The priest clasped his hands behind his back as he began to offer his précis of his latest reading of Dickens.

"Your gift was fortuitous. I'm determined to read all his novels, in no particular order. I'm taking my time."

"I take it you already covered a lot of ground, before you even came upon his works."

"It appears we are going to put together a preliminary chapter, for people who want to read Dickens, in a serious way."

"You don't say?"

"Yes, it appears so." The cleric avoided looking at Isaiah.

Isaiah studied the man's face, gauging what he might be thinking about his own place in Molly's world. "Do people vote on letting people in to these new chapters?"

"What?" He began laughing.

"What's so funny?"

"That you're so anxious to gain entry, and you have no idea how."

"She does like to toy with me, which shows there must be some interest."

"Ah, it feels like a good time for a nip of amaretto. Care for a snifter, Mr. Meriwether? It's good for dissolving those slight, metaphysical injuries that graze the ego."

"Sure enough." They sat at the little table, cozy in their jackets, sipping the rich contents of their tiny glasses, as if imbibing residual doses of the beautiful weather.

"I guess you fancy yourself the Dickens expert, and thus, deserving of special consideration?"

"I wouldn't say expert, but yeah."

"There's no vote, my friend. Molly decides all of that business. Did you ask her directly?"

"Yes."

"And she said no?"

"She said she'd have to ask the others."

Charles tipped his head back and laughed. "Perhaps the world of Dickens is too much with you."

"Not sure what that means. I don't even know why I care so much."

They enjoyed the silence, savoring the intense, cobalt sky, the movement of leaves, and the pungent smell of fresh, moldering decay. More intoxicating than the sugary, biting fluid in their glasses was the neat draft of pure mythos coursing musically through the changing season.

"Well, let me tell you something about Margaret that you may not know. She's very serious about some of her chapters." He paused after a sip; frowning, as if not certain how to proceed. A strange thought occurred to him, that she unwittingly mimics her accounting principles when trying to balance her books of grace and suffering. Isaiah stared at his pensive face.

"What can you tell me?"

"She gets herself into trouble—"

"How so?"

"For instance, there was a crowd from the old Saints John & James parish, which was folded into ours, that began to circle around her." His mouth made a nasty moue. "Those Charismatics, boy; they can be a handful. Well, that sort of thing is not for Molly. Anyway, there was a rivalry, and one of those people joined her religious chapter, in which they were researching the history of the early church. This spy—that's what she was—she comes to me, to let me know that Molly is teaching others to believe in heresies. They were reading about the ancient Gnostics. This one woman, she comes to *me*, to complain about Margaret, for whom I have the utmost respect." He shook his head in wonderment.

Isaiah looked at the priest, anxious to hear more. "What did you do?"

"Nothing! I told them I would talk to her. And I did, that part was true enough. We talked for hours in her yard, about numerous topics, including the history of Ferdinand. We ended up having a really good laugh." The priest tilted his glass and looked to verify it was empty.

"You see, they are both dear to me; there was just no question of any concerns." He chortled gently. "Besides, they both tithe. Jacob through the usual methods; and Molly hands me a check every month. She tells me, every time, 'None of this is to go to Rome.' It's just like her." He shook his head. "She gives me the money, but she wants some say in how it is spent. She forces me to get involved in things, with certain people, which I may not have, otherwise."

"She's no ordinary woman."

"Ha! I tell you, she is just like one of those ancient women in Acts; the ones who took the early believers into their homes. They were the nursemaids of the faith. Those households were like the first Christian synagogues, really; that was clearly the analogue they were using to establish, and promote, their own beliefs. Molly is the one who made *that* clear to me, also."

"She's not one to dance to someone's else's tune."

"Not on your life, brother. She gathers people to her quite easily, and yet, not many get close enough to really know her. She moves in many circles, but she's always moving from one to another, and she has a way of keeping her distance. I cannot explain it to you."

"I think I understand what you're saying." Isaiah spoke as if they were sealing a pact.

Charles looked at him, as if to ask, 'Do you really?' Then he straightened himself, turned over his glass to drain the last few drops onto the earth, and spoke with finality. "I suppose it's time." Charles reached out and Isaiah handed his empty glass over and stood up also. He thanked him for his good company

"My discretion is impeccable when it has to be." He said.

"That's good to hear." The priest nodded to him as he turned to his door.

Isaiah had been surprised to hear the priest talk about Molly in that fashion, but he understood it was out of great respect, and for the first time he had a sense of her struggles with her own faith. He ambled to his car, having no desire to go home, and noticed Jacob was sitting in his tower, watching him. He raised his hand and was beckoned to come over with a hearty shout. Once settled on the bench they looked out over the magic quilt of rolling countryside in silence.

"You have a good chat with our young medicine man?"

"I heard about the John & James cabal, with a nice little nip of pagan spirits."

"The flesh and soul must voyage out on one craft, seeking knowledge while bound together."

"That sounds like material for a sermon."

"Sometimes he likes to test some things on my ear. God knows why. It's usually Margaret who serves him in that role. Did you happen to notice that small, inner grotto Cody and I built for their old statues?"

"Yes, I like it."

"Say, would you like to taste a new stout Cody discovered?"

Isaiah indicated he was feeling spiritually inclined, and the bottled variety was sure to be friendly just now. Jacob climbed down, moving in his lanky gait towards the house. He soon emerged with two mugs containing dark beer. Settling back they took gulps of the malty brew.

"It's like chocolate milk for adults." Jacob exclaimed, after smacking his lips.

"A decadent drink for decadent times."

"An autumn drink, to inspire autumn songs."

Before long Jacob returned to his house to get a fresh bottle, and his guitar. Molly watched him from the kitchen window. She knew he was truly comfortable with someone when he brought out his guitar in this fashion.

"Give me a hand!" Jacob handed the bottle to Isaiah, and clambered up the stairs holding his guitar in front of him. After a few more gulps, and some tuning of the instrument, Jacob began to play a song.

"That's a lovely tune. I can't place it."

"It's 'Für Elise,' Beethoven."

"Oh yes, a song for a woman named Elise?"

"Or maybe Therese, a woman Ludwig proposed to; poor bastard, to no avail. That's Margaret's middle name, Therese."

Isaiah looked carefully at Jacob's somber face.

"He was going deaf, at the time; can you imagine?"

"Maybe we are lucky he didn't get the girl. You get the music distilled out of the sorrow."

"That's often true."

"The piece was meant to be a bagatelle, a trifle as they say; but it has endured, because it moves people."

"Isn't it strange, how much we are drawn to music that evokes sorrow? Why is that, do you suppose?"

"It makes us feel something; maybe that part of us we're always a little afraid of losing. I may be quoting Molly there, that's her province more than mine." After this they drank in silence. Then Isaiah thought of a song from the past.

"Do you remember that Dylan tune? I think it's just called, 'George Jackson.' I heard it on KSHE, a long time ago."

Jacob began playing the song, and both men started singing the lyrics in subdued voices.

"In his lyrics he's able to transcend the topical issue he is singing about." Jacob says with reverence.

"I remember that one really got to me." Isaiah could feel something of his youthful idealism, as though sifting rich, ancient grains through his fingers. "The idea of seeing the world as a prison yard, and the ruling powers fearing moral power."

"That's the point he makes there."

"When I first heard that song on the radio, I was in your house there. I remember it so vividly. I was with my friends; the windows were open, the trees were singing, we smoked a joint. The wicked grandmother was downstairs, listening to us, no doubt fuming. I wasn't living there at the time, but I had begged her to let us in, to get out of the rain. We had been hanging out on the church steps. I'm sure she could smell the pot. She must have thought I was betraying her trust." He smiled apologetically. "And I was..."

Jacob said nothing. Isaiah began to bring forth more hidden treasure from that brief, flowering summer after the eighth grade. Soon Jacob opened up a small locker, which he had built into the Watchtower, and removed a pipe and accouterments he had secreted there. He cleaned the pipe, charged the bowl with fresh tobacco, tamping delicately with a little tool, and then fired up the batch. The flame danced wildly before he achieved a mild, steady burn. He began puffing as if he'd been instantly transported, and was in a spell of noble repose.

"That's a pretty nice ritual you have there." Isaiah said, after watching the ceremony. He pictured a portrait that might capture that strange, troubled contentment on the man's face.

"Margaret hates it when I smoke this thing. I took this up rather late in life." He held the smoldering pipe out in front of him, as if the intrinsic nature of the device puzzled him too, somehow. "This one belonged to my dad. I indulge myself sparingly."

They had both graduated from high school in 1973, and Jacob made a joke about being a naturalized member of Isaiah's old Gang of '73.

"Had you ever managed to get officially inducted you might have risen high in the ranks."

"I would never belong to a club that defiled members into ranks. And I used to get high enough."

"What if the ranks are metaphysical?"

"Even more so. Don't get me started on those circles. I'm never going to take flight to the third heaven."

They began laughing in a show of fraternal irreverence.

"We came of age in the same crazy time," Jacob said after a rather murmurous dialogue with his recharged pipe.

"We inherited a lot of cumbersome baggage left over from the sixties. We didn't do much but play with it, for a short while, and then we put it out for the trash collectors."

"How's that?" Jacob swung to look at the author of this glum philosophy. "I'm not in agreement with you there, comrade."

"All that idealism? Our generation never lived up to that vision. Remember how they started making fun of us in the eighties? All those articles, calling it the decade of greed."

"People who write articles like that, how often are those voices relevant to anything in real life? Making *that* decade out to be *the* decade of greed." He had lowered his pipe to one knee.

"But we really believed in all of that, for a while, and we were wrong, about things, in general, don't you think?"

"Still not sure I'm following you, but then, I never was in your club, the Loopy Knights of Delmar."

"Does Molly . . . ?"

"What?"

"Where did she get—I mean, was that a part of her upbringing, did she come of age in that afterglow of all those social movements?"

"It was in the air, for a long time; to some extent, it's always been there."

"Doesn't it seem like we're in a time of disillusionment? All those great songs, we knew as genuine offerings, they've been sold to the advertising pirates. Everything is for sale, and there's no such thing as selling out, only selling one's brand too cheaply."

Jacob looked over, rather amused by his guest's foray into the crowded field of cynicism. He took counsel with his pipe briefly, before responding.

"I'll tell you what, those complaints have been around for an awfully long time. I was permitted to sit in for one of Molly's sessions with the crones. That's what Cody and I call them. That's the inner sanctum. There was talk of letting men join, but that didn't ever happen, at least not yet." He turned and stabbed his pipe stem at Isaiah. "If you ever rat me out on calling them the crones, you lose your rights to come up here. You got that, Meriwether?"

They exchanged a look and Isaiah almost laughed, but he was actually touched at the same time. "My lips are sealed."

"Anyway, they were reading all these texts, and going back into the Bible, and searching for, like, secret things. But she read something from the Gospel of Truth, that spoke of the joy of receiving, and *knowing* what grace is. At some point she was talking about the suffering of St. Paul, and his tenet which states, as you share in the suffering, so shall you share in the final comfort. I saw something on her face, that I recognized, but I realized I had never fully understood what I had been seeing before."

Jacob began smoking quite studiously. Isaiah waited for him to continue. When he thought there was nothing else forthcoming, he began to speak of his teacher, but Jacob began to speak again and Isaiah fell silent.

"She doesn't always feel like she deserves to feel the pleasures, the joys, of life. Not about certain things. My problem, of course, is just the opposite."

They stared at the prospect of rolling suburban hills in silence. The trees were uncommonly beautiful. Many roads were partially obscured, or completely hidden, and Isaiah thought of all the roads he had taken, and those he had not, and considered all that he had hoped for, which had never come to pass. He felt the passage of years as one hears very faint music in the background of other, more pressing activities. Jacob's voice broke into his reverie, like an echo heard inside a vault.

"She wounded me, once."

Isaiah did not look over at him, but listened and heard the rustling of leaves on the ground, as Jacob continued smoking his pipe in profound concentration.

"When I healed, we were stronger, somehow. I wanted to leave, at first. 'You can't leave,' was all she said to me. She wasn't forbidding me. She was explaining the situation, and myself, to me. She was saying that I, that *I*, acting for myself, could not do it." He shook his head, as Isaiah stole a glance at his visage. Then Jacob stood up and moved up against the railing to look out as if he were on the bridge of a great vessel, returning from a long voyage.

"After my sister died, I stared at our First Communion picture, of her and me, outside that church there." He lifted his arm to point. "Alone in my room, I just kept staring, crying, beseeching her to make some kind of sign for me. I wanted to know she was still out there." He turned and looked at Jacob. "Molly showed me a passage in *Dombey and Son*, in which that desire is expressed very well.

"Oh yes, *Dombey and Son*. I had forgotten where that was." Isaiah replied, instantly recalling it was the angelic Florence who devotes herself to loving her father, despite all his senseless cruelty and indifference. In her epiphany she resolves to save him; to lead him "to a better knowledge of his only child."

"We all end up with our own private faith, you know." Jacob's voice was somber. "We have to."

Isaiah could find nothing to say. Later on he could not remember how long they sat there in deepest silence, until they heard Jacob's friend Cody calling to him from the yard. And right behind him a separate cohort of people were spilling into the yard as well. Molly was soon among them. Her face turned towards her husband, and she hesitated, for a moment, and then she swung back to be with her guests.

"Jacob, when I see you again, I'll be sure to bring some of that stout along. I want to contribute to the loyal guard that keeps watch on the tower."

Jacob smiled equably. "I won't try and stop you from bringing tributes, my friend."

He passed Cody on the steps and drove to his studio, wanting to face his doomed portrait. It was hard, rejecting a project he had once deemed so promising. After his rueful audience he returned to his reading chair, sitting there like Lincoln, who is forever glowering at us from the gloom of his immovable, classic chair. He thought of all the people who were now dying of the plague, condemned to join the anonymous multitudes lost in the spectral burial heap of time.

He stood on his fire escape as the sun painted lovely patterns on the earth's protective atmosphere. He imagined the lurid scenes of the infamous Black Country, wrought by the angry hand of the Right Reverend Dickens. All those ghastly portraits depicting that fiery hearth, forge, and seedbed of material progress. The vile stacks coughing clouds of pollution over the countryside; the forest of chimneys, unrepentant, unrelenting symbols, in a world powered by fires of ruthless competition. What has built these pitiless mills, and consecrated the cruel hierarchies? What beasts are bemoaned, and staunchly fed and cared for in every age?

He stares at the changing effects evolving before his eyes. He is touched by everything that is out there; feeling the same murky tissues in his depths. He knows, at the heart of the Black Country, and our own moral uncertainty, was that unfeeling red glow, the lustful eye of all his kind. What opposing power moves sentient life to take notice of these things? What enforces us to bank our hopes on the future? What does life know about itself, that we have not yet learned to see, much less heed for ourselves?

32

The sun had barely risen, and the light filters through a landscape of hills, trees, and houses. It barely touches directly upon the objects Isaiah sees at eye level as he drives along Elizabeth Avenue. He imagines colossal, ragged brushes applying a very disorderly coat of mystic varnish to the sycamore trees. The stunning clarity seen only in parts is tantalizing. He considers what a brilliant finish this would be, were everything seen in this soft, clear, even light at once. He stops his car for a moment, just to appreciate his sense of vision, and to absorb the stark immediacy of this unearthly effect of the light dressing these stately trees in provocative dishabille.

Soon after parking his car he finds Molly is already making her way towards the church. She turns and waves to him. He follows at a distance, and sits by himself in the middle of the mostly empty pews. Long ago, his strategy was to sit several pews behind a girl on whom his dreams had come to rest in frantic adoration. She did not know this, but she was there to bear witness to his heroic, imaginary deeds. How many valorous fantasies were scripted and played and replayed for Deborah's unknowing heart!

When the sermon began he was astonished to hear Father Charles alluding to the heroic simpleton of *Barnaby Rudge*. He used that story for his exegesis, along with a reading from First Corinthians. He directed one's attention to the civil unrest stalking the land, focusing on the behavior of various nameless actors. He abhorred the inhumanity of those deplorable choices being made that resulted in harm being done to innocent people.

He spoke of Barnaby, the duped idiot, with tenderness. He crafted a cautionary tale, reproaching those who were fostering such depraved acts of patriotism in the present time. He admonished all partisans, of every stripe, who fomented unconscionable wrongs against the Holy Spirit. He quoted scripture to remind the people they were like unto temples where the spirit dwells. His voice rose above the noise of politics.

After mass Molly approached him to ask if he would mind driving to a bakery for her. She was in need of pastries to serve some people who were coming over to see her later that morning. He was glad to be of assistance. When he returned she took the goods inside, and came back out, and they sat in the gazebo.

It was pleasant being outdoors, and Molly was wearing one of her long heavy sweaters. The thick woven strands were of various gray and blue colors; the mixture put him in mind of that fabled ocean cited so often by Dickens. As he stared the texture seemed to become more visibly fluid than mere dry cloth. He studied her physiognomy while she looked about in her wonted aloofness.

"What are you looking at?" She demanded sharply.

He looked up sheepishly. "Your cross."

"Oh, I see." She turned away. He caught the force of her scowl, as if a rebuke had been flung by her injured soul.

"What's the matter?"

"Why are you going to church? To observe *us*, as artistic subjects? You're not a believer, are you?"

"Not in the dogma, no—"

"You shouldn't try to insinuate yourself into the lives of people you don't understand."

He was speechless. She had stuck him with a trenchant pin, and he could only writhe upon its grasp.

"Don't presume that you understand my faith."

"No." He shook his head. "I would never do that, Molly."

"Yes? I get nervous when people tell me what they will never do." She exhaled a gust of emotion. "It's just, I never hear you saying anything on the topic. I don't care what you believe, I don't; but I'm not going to let you make light of my faith."

"I might make conjectures, and never tell you what those are; maybe I'd share them with Marx, sometime, just to see what would come spilling out of that brain of his." He was scrambling to find the right conciliatory note.

"Okay, go ahead, tell me what you really think."

"No, I was actually kidding, I don't really have any idea—"

"You're wondering how I can believe in this medieval institution."

"Not at all."

"What made you look so intently at this, then?" She held up her cross.

He laughed breathlessly. "I was trying to imagine how I would paint that little article." He pointed with his finger. "It has such a wondrous, molten, sort of glow. And the way it changes in every light, like human eyes."

Molly looked down to inspect the unadorned symbol. "It is solid gold." Her voice had modulated in a manner pleasant to his ear. "For a long time I wore one from my childhood, but I found out it was only plated. So, vanity struck, and I decided to get this one. Two hundred bucks."

"Very extravagant."

She narrowed her eyes, deflecting his humor.

"Believe me, I have no interest in trying to question the faith of anyone. I'm not one of your philosophers. I have no theories to advance, on that precious symbol, or anything else, for that matter."

"I just don't know what you want from me."

"I don't want anything, Molly."

She made a harsh grating sound in her throat. Then a subtle smile broke across her visage, allowing Isaiah to feel he had recovered from his inadvertent faux pas. Then she smiled even more broadly, and he was not so certain of his forgiveness. Her countenance only served to confirm that a woman is a creature of profound mysteries. She observed his face a long time with those bewitching eyes, now a delicate shade of smoldering violet.

"And what do you believe in?" She questioned at last.

"I don't know. I'm just a painter. I make images of the world, and it ignores me."

"Oh." Her voice was lush in its mock pity. "Poor man, with his brand new car, and, as he's revealed to me, how closely he keeps tabs on his strong sales figures."

He smiled weakly as she derided his plight of failing to achieve the critical acclaim he had always desired. Her eyes ranged around her property, and he could not help but direct his gaze once more to the cross she was wearing.

"In this outdoor lighting it has a beautiful luster. I like the simplicity of the form."

She stared at him, as a mother at her incorrigible boy, caught in a flagrant act of recidivism.

"Come." She brought him to the decorative cornerstone piece of a wall planted in the back of her yard. She had left a pair of clippers there and she picked them up and studied her red cedars. She seemed more relaxed as she reached out and touched the boughs, putting the clippers back on the wall.

"The truth is, I don't know what I believe, not really. Not in any concrete way you can put into words. Charles knows this about me. We've discussed these things. I can't let him sit in with my religious chapter; it wouldn't be right. Those people don't need to hear him wrestling with his doubts!"

Isaiah took a seat in one of the chairs placed nearby. She paced on the little court before him.

"You know, in the Gospel of Philip, it says that Jesus loved Mary Magdalene more than the other apostles. He would kiss her on the mouth." She looked at him to measure his response.

"I've heard of such things, over the years, of course, I'm no authority—"

"You don't trust authorities, generally, do you?"

"It depends on what the subject matter is, and who is claiming to have the requisite expertise necessary to critique others—"

"Okay, okay. But talking of expertise, that's of little use in these texts. According to the ancient scripture, there is one God, a kind of tribal chieftain, who demands a lord's fealty. He commands his people to wage war, to gain more land, to glorify his name. He is jealous of other gods. He's a red-blooded male, and yet he has no woman. But then he comes to have a son, who is not exactly of his own kind. The mother was visited by one of the favored angels."

Isaiah caught her eye, ever so briefly, and was astounded by her piercing, bantering play, engaging her own faith, and also making note of, and critiquing, his uncritical fascination with same.

"The mother, of course, is human. She has become *like* a goddess—but you cannot pray to her! *That's* too pagan. There is a Holy Spirit needed, because the papa God has been rendered impotent in his rage, and wasn't up to the task. There had to be a single source, a state of being, utterly pure, without human attributes. If you listen to some of the Gnostic heretics, our God is a demiurge, formed by the great silent source of all; which explains his confusion about so many things. Some want to see the great invisible source as a female power. The mother of wisdom."

Isaiah was agog; astonished by her fusion of irony and fervor. She was treading on her sacred ground, keeping abreast of her own faith, while entertaining mortal doubts. She was thinking out loud, possibly for his benefit. He was not unlike the pagans Paul encountered in Ephesus.

"I'm listening." This was all he could manage, fearful of her silence, more than her enmity.

"I speak this way merely to show *my* problem, with all of this inadequacy of words. They speak of grace frequently, without offering any clear definition of what that is. To me, this term simply refers to life; the great blessing, or gift, we have been given. And life, as it has been entrusted to us, has evolved a moral sense; and this makes demands upon us. At our very best, I believe we come into our true grace, but then, we never want to stay there!"

"I like being in the church, I feel my youth coming back to me. I feel that I still have so much left in my bones; whether belief or unbelief, I don't know. Maybe it's all one thing—"

"What do you believe in, besides yourself?"

"Well, I—"

"That's the question you must ask yourself."

Molly sat down on the flagging and crossed her legs, her arms resting on her knees, her hands meshed. Her blue jeans and boots made her look younger. Her hair was a strange, tangled mass of hues.

"For me, it's fitting that Saint Margaret, of Antioch, is the patron saint of expectant mothers. Said to be especially so for those suffering a difficult labor. That's the condition of our Church, as it stands today. For there's no doubt, it's definitely groaning."

Isaiah watched her as if she were on some spartan stage. He could not help thinking of Dickens, who loved acting in comedic plays; but this was actually Molly's only singular role that defined both her inner and outer lives. To him she was magnificent in this enactment of her unbound passion.

"It's about keeping the hope alive, not just in a formal sense, but in that active resolve to fashion better lives. I believe that the Church, in order to survive, will have to undergo a renaissance. She will have to return to seeking more directly after spirit and truth, as we know it, and as we shall find it." She looked at Isaiah intently. He made an awkward, propitious smile.

"This is my house." She slapped her hand on the cold flagging, while looking off at the Grotto.

"Come." She rose from the ground. They walked across the parking lot to the Grotto, and meandered through that space and came to stand by her black cherry tree, looking out over the field below.

"You don't do plein air painting, do you?" She asked.

"I've never tried to, other than for dabbing at colors, for my preliminary work."

"That's how I started painting. I enjoyed being outside. I learned to really concentrate on one subject; usually a tree. It became a way to lose myself, for a while, and afterwards I did not have to think of things so much."

She looked at him closely. "But now I am trying new things. And it's maddening!"

"Why?"

"I think I expect too much, and after too little effort. I want it to come quickly; and that's not how it happens. I have to learn to be happy with less — is it the same with you?"

"Yes, of course. Coming to terms with your work is endless. What you've done well, in the past, you cannot always recapture that medley of technique and form, in another piece."

"And you change, yourself."

"And you change. You have to try something new."

"But it doesn't always work out so well, does it?"

"No." He laughed. "My large portrait of St. Louis, I'm afraid that's officially defunct now."

"Really? At least now you can tell us how he died."

He laughed loudly. "Yes, I was right there, staring at my drawing when the last breath left the body. I could see my concept was completely wrong."

"How so?"

"I have no idea. It didn't do anything for me anymore; at first it really took hold of me. His face—"

"His face? Do they actually know what he looked like?"

"No, I don't think so. I had no reliable portraits to go on."

"Whose face did you use, then?"

He looked at her, floored by her simple question. It had never occurred to him to evaluate that aspect of what he had wrought, in that initial burst of confidence.

"Oh my gosh." He stood up.

"What?"

He had meant to paint his father's face!

"Tell me, what's the matter?"

"My lady, I must remove myself to the security of the Watchtower."

She looked after him as he trundled off, intrigued by the fact something had touched him so deeply. She joined him in the aerie and noticed by his face that he did not want to discuss whatever it was that had just happened. She began looking about, in her abstract manner.

By some instinct she knew when and how to withdraw, at critical moments of emotional intensity. It brought one closer to her, and later bore fruit in the easeful sharing of intimate feelings. Revelations came in honesty's open mien, borne of humility. Her implicit trust in a person's humanity was one of the arts she had mastered and used to enrich the lives of those around her.

"I've been looking at the landscapes of Sisley again." He had to break this spell of the sorceress to regain control of his faculties.

"I've always liked his work."

"His love of the land comes through with such palpable force. You feel the air, the smells of the season. All those river pictures, they have such life in them."

"The Chimney Swifts of St. Margaret's."

"What?"

"You ought to do an oil painting of the chimney swifts. You've said how much you like watching them circle the school grounds. Those beautiful, graceful, living forms; so free, and yet, not really so much. What did you call it?"

"The pageantry honoring one's place."

"And just think, if you lived nearby, you would always know exactly when they left each year, and when they came back again."

"That's very true." He laughed. "You're striking close to home now."

They returned to her yard, discussing various painters, and paintings. They ended up talking of her neighbors, and how peculiar it is that people choose to live such different lives. They spoke to one another with unconscious freedom. In this solemn mood the earth's movement was known to them as shadows moving across her face with inexorable resolve.

Molly expressed her admiration for Jules Breton, and Isaiah marveled over the severe aesthetics of Edgar Degas. They reminisced about the Café Montmartre and shared a fondness for Maurice Utrillo.

"Earlier I was leafing through *Dombey and Son*." Molly interjected. "Reading the passages I had marked."

"That novel is a precursor to Copperfield. He's starting to refine his prose, as a master craftsman. His problem was he could write in any style he wanted, but he had been married off early in life to that messy old country dame, the melodrama. One thing is certain, he never lost his love of the people. He never came to terms with that resident evil of society, seen in the collective instinct for survival and competition, which strangles moral progress in the crib."

He saw Molly's eyes open wide at this affirmation. "Do you remember the place where Paul, as an infant, is being baptized, and the author says that the priest is afraid of the baby? I found that to be a deft touch. The baby cries the whole while, 'with an irrepressible sense of his wrongs.' Again, so perfectly put, don't you think?"

"Yes. I don't remember that part myself."

"Father Charles pointed it out to me. I had to go back and read it again."

"I enjoyed his sermon today. He's quoting Dickens from the pulpit! I thought that was the neatest thing."

"He's very good at making things relatable. His best sermons are consoling, *and* food for thought."

Isaiah began to propound further upon the habits of the Teacher, relapsing into an old role, that of café orator intent on commanding all present at the table. He could not relent; he wanted to build his case for induction into her book club. When he stopped to catch his breath, she was surveying the bounds of her more expansive world.

He watched her retreat into the house, not knowing if she was coming back or not. He was about to leave when she came back with a book in her hand. She handed him a volume by Henry Adams.

"Tell me what you think of this one. He talks eloquently of Mary, and he was by no means an orthodox believer."

"Well, I'd be glad to take a look. I'm afraid I haven't gotten that far in my other assignment. I'm trying to get Marx to help me out."

"You want to cheat on those things you ought to be doing for your own good?"

"Well, I'm not . . ."

"I'm teasing! Stop taking everything I say so seriously. It's not fair to me! Well, time." She said this in a way that sounded like a question, but which he knew by now was a cryptic method of informing one she had other obligations, other responsibilities, other people, calling for her attention.

"Time." He repeated, nodding happily.

"It was good to see you again, Isaiah."

"It's been so lovely seeing you, Margaret." He felt quite bold using her full name.

It was easy because, in his reverence, there was no way for him to become foolishly romantic about her, not in that mundane fashion. She had merely rekindled his life's sworn devotion to his own school of Romanticism. Throughout his career he had scavenged his materials from art, nature, his studies of people, and his own idyllic visions, not to mention the rather submerged and endless quest to visit again the lost glory of childhood.

While musing upon many such things Isaiah discovers that he must paint her portrait. He would have to be careful not to try and force the issue. It would have to be handled delicately. It was good though, he was beyond worrying that he could not do her justice. Just making the attempt would enliven him considerably. It had to be done (she had brought him back to the beginning of his earliest and most pristine love of life).

He was pulling out of his parking space when he glanced into her yard and saw that she was turning her little cross in her fingers. It glinted at him. He imagined a tiny control feature, in contact with some ponderous spiritual apparatus situated somewhere in the universe. It required that fine, periodic adjustments were made by unfaltering hands. Once he was proceeding southward on Florissant Road he turned up the volume as "Visions of Johanna" started playing on his sound system. He began to sing. He started speeding, and then quickly caught himself, and slowed down once more. His floating sensation had become for a moment one of soaring.

33

The little bistro called Sistah's Vineyard was opened by the late Frances Ambers. The ex-nun had been an active parishioner of St. Margaret's; her relentless passion earned her a curious standing in the congregation. She had meant so much, to so many, and was too much, for so many others. She left the business to her friends, Cody and Sally, after Molly confirmed there was no better way to preserve the good will of the establishment.

Isaiah was sitting there, under one of the ash trees placed along the curb, taking his time, making a study of the interwoven branches. There were no leaves. Each tree was preparing for the long, breathless sojourn of winter. He had been over at Molly's earlier that day, to present to her his watercolor portrait of Charlotte.

"I want you to have it. You can do with it whatever you like."

"Are you sure?" She tried to give him money. She tried to convince him he ought to show it to Raphael, to see if he wished to buy it. He listened placidly till she paused.

"It's my gift to you; for opening your home to me. But no strings, do with it as you wish. It should have a good home; that's all that matters. I know you understand." He was hoping to spend more time with her right then, but she could not oblige him.

"I'm sorry, there's too much I have to do."

"What time is it?" He was thinking of going to Sistah's to have a glass of wine, and had wanted to treat her if she were free.

"You know, now is the moment for you to wake from sleep."

"What?" He was fond of her playful allusions. Her face remained ironically impassive. "That's good to know," he answered, aware she would offer no elucidation. It was her custom to leave people with such hard, crusty nuts for later cogitation, and possible cracking.

"Accept me as a fool, so I may boast a little." He sought to charm her, by using words from his recent studies.

Her eyes narrowed, and glittered, as she smiled in an odd way; showing her appreciation for his attempt to quote to her from the letters of St. Paul.

"I don't really see you that way at all, but then, you must come to your right mind." She had ignored his reference, and drove straight to the issue of his actual insecurities. He could not respond, and so had wandered off, nearly in a trance.

He landed at Sistah's, nursing a glass of wine, staring down the street. He began moving his glass to manipulate the visible spectrum of the sunlight captured by the wine. He thought of being a child in these mystic hours, in that delicious freedom after school, when Nature extended her maternal greeting to the imp holding residence inside every unbound child.

"You ever think of painting this place?" Cody stood at his table, blocking the sun, before taking a seat for himself. They were now friends, by virtue of his being on such good terms with the Gates.

"I would like to do some watercolors of these scenes."

"That's what Jacob said, so I'm thinking, why not one of Sistah's?"

Isaiah looked at him. "Not a bad idea."

"As you see, this is a great spot for watching everything out there. Nothing ever seems to be happening, so you can really pay attention."

Isaiah laughed, almost silently. Most of the time Cody was innately reserved, even rudely impassive. It was often difficult to find a clear intent in his laconic speech. His face bore an inscrutable aspect, conveying an uncanny distrust of what often lies behind polite manners.

Looking at Cody's face Isaiah recalled that someone close had once described his own as being nondescript. He had resorted to his dictionary; and now reflected that one meaning was quite apropos. *Belonging or appearing to belong to no class or kind.* Just precisely that complex representation a portrait painter strives to capture. The distinctive imprint of one unique personality.

"Are you in Molly's book club?" Isaiah asked, as they both sipped wine under the naked ash tree.

"Well, sort of, but I hardly ever attend the discussion groups anymore. I can't read all those books. Sally likes to sit in, to hear the gossip, but she only goes if she has read the book. I tell her, 'Don't worry about that, Molly doesn't care.' Jacob tells me the good stuff later, if he goes, which is seldom."

"Jacob doesn't attend, on a regular basis?"

"No. There are so many chapters. A lot of the time Jacob will call me to see if I can hang with him out in the yard. We have our own Druid rituals to keep us busy. There's always some new yard project. For instance, now we're going to extend that wall across the back of his yard. We like to make fires, down a few cold ones, listen to our medicine songs."

It looked like Cody was about to take his leave, when he suddenly hunched his head down and began speaking in a confidential tone.

"Molly enjoys debating all those grand issues, whereas Jacob doesn't take to it in the same way. Molly can't help it, but she stirs up trouble. Now, I'm not saying she encourages it, or anything, but she can be stubborn. She tries to gather disparate groups of people, and prompts them to voice their opinions, and that can be a volatile mixture."

"Especially these days."

"Amen." Cody looked suddenly uncertain of himself. "It wasn't so long ago when Molly got really angry at one of her meetings. That's not like her." He paused, as if unable to remember something.

"What book were they discussing?"

"I have no idea. It probably had nothing to do with any book. There was an argument between a woman's daughter and Molly. Do you know Cicely Morgan? No. Well, Molly wanted her in her religious chapter, the one with the crones. And she's a Baptist. So, anyway, I guess Cicely's daughter came as well, and at some point she starts lecturing Molly, telling her she just doesn't understand."

Cody attempted to describe this scene which he had not witnessed; how the young woman became irate at the older white people there, who could not possibly comprehend her perspective. She and her mother were the only black people present, and the daughter, at one point, told Molly she had no right to speak to them on these matters.

"That had to be a tense moment."

"Well, Molly got up, and they were facing each other, pointing fingers, all of that, and the younger woman says, 'You just need to listen.' And then Molly is like; 'I will not be silenced in my own home. It doesn't work like that, it can't work that way.' Something like that—has Jacob ever told you any of this?"

"No."

"I probably shouldn't have brought this up. It's just that Molly is passionate about making a difference."

"I can see that."

"Well, that little fracas really shook her. She's hard on herself. I mean, if you don't know her, sometimes . . ."

"No, I understand. Say no more, Cody."

Cody said he had better get back to work and went inside. Isaiah paid his bill and departed.

He then drove to his studio, where he collapsed into his reading chair, browsing through the Henry Adams book. He decided to invite Marx and Patricia to dinner, insisting they simply had to explain Henry Adams to him. Thus, he learned how Adams, the dispossessed American nobleman, became a wandering soul after his beloved wife (a professed atheist) committed suicide. His genteel spirit poured a pure casting of his enduring love into that curious paean to Gothic cathedrals, and mourned for his own conception of love by investigating what had once been the Virgin's very real and tangible power to move people.

He was later at his studio again staring at photographs of his father. Now he knew why he had been struggling with his St. Louis portrait. He had never made a credible drawing of his father before, because he had never really *seen* him before in his reflections. He started sketching the man from various angles, using old photographs. There was no ultimate design that came to him; and none mattered at the present. The thing was to master the distinctive features, to work up to the eventual choice, of just one of those telling expressions, in an attempt to reveal the man's private joy.

He fell into reveries contemplating scenes under the street lamps of Gaslight Square. His father always brought him there with such rare fellowship; the sort that lays bare what obtains beyond social relationships. He was baring his soul to the boy; letting him see that he did not care if he were hopelessly out of step with the conventional lives others were leading. He had no desire to float on that stream, congested with family cars, those docile beasts moving in droves with 'savage servility,' and bound for what they wished to ensure for tomorrow by making the manifold efforts today. Yes, one must lay up stores, but there is such a multiplicity of goods out there . . .

He tried to remember the time he was taken to see Miles Davis perform, but it was a shadowy, smoky remembrance, devoid of living substance. He possessed instead a deposit of knowledge regarding how that boy had experienced possibly his first seminal, adult wonderment. He was being baptized again under the neon frenzy, sanctioned to accept a greater portion of the world's rich offering. He had been transfixed, trying to listen as he saw his father nodding, so dreamily, in his appreciation. He had witnessed how the music brought an uncommon peace into his spirit. In his own tacit way the man had instilled this sensibility of keeping a revered personal space of one's own.

Isaiah fell asleep while drifting through the pages of *The Virgin of Chartres*. One of the last lines he read was that she "exacted prompt and willing obedience from King and Archbishops as well as from beggars and drunken priests. She protected her friends and punished her enemies." In the last glimmers of consciousness, without inordinate, selfish aforethought, he reprised a childhood practice of praying to the Madonna. It was in the last throes of this ancient practice that he whispered himself to sleep. In his dreams he was in the Watchtower, with his dad, and he addressed himself to the glowing, quilted land. "Maybe it's time for a pilgrimage of my own."

34

Isaiah almost tripped as he hurried through Molly's gate. He greeted Jacob, who was raking leaves, appraising him with an ironic smile.

"You're back?" Jacob challenged him.

"I almost dropped it." Isaiah looked at the wall relief sculpture he was holding with both hands. "Molly said this would be a good time to drop by."

"She's not here."

"Oh."

"That for us?" Jacob came closer. Isaiah held up the stone to let him see its face.

"Yes, I found it buried under a pile of old things. I've been getting rid of a lot of old clutter. Don't worry, it's not contraband. Maybe something for the yard?"

"Sure. Now, who is it supposed to be?"

"Asherah. She may have been the wife of Yahweh, for a minute."

"Yeah? How did that arranged marriage fall apart."

"I was thinking you could put it someplace, like over by that hooded character who's all by himself over there."

Jacob made an equivocal murmuring sound, as he was looking around the yard. "Best to wait and see what she wants to do with it. She ought to be back before too long. You can't depend on her to keep to her schedules."

"I'm sure."

They ambled towards the back of the yard and stopped at the ornamental wall. They looked out over the field below just as a troop of boys passed by on the parking lot. They shambled towards the field below in a juvenile swagger, uttering awkward profanities. They were very conscious of the two adults; very intent on ignoring them even as they made their presence known to them. The men monitored their progress with sardonic smiles.

"Looks like the fifth grade?" Isaiah postulated.

"I remember that attitude; the young galoots. Some say I still have too much of that myself. Say, let's get a better vantage of the outer world." Jacob climbed into the tower. "I'm tired of raking, anyway." They settled down in the lofty perch.

"I remember, one time, my grandmother washed my mouth out with soap." Isaiah stated this as if he were proud of the fact. "She was trying to purge certain words from my vocabulary."

"Did it work?"

"Around her; not when I was in other company The words came back when I was talking about her! I guess she deserves some credit, though, for trying to tame a first grader. Imagine, trapping a wild animal like that in one's bathroom."

Jacob rummaged in his locker, and quickly fired up one of his pipes. The burning tobacco was richly gripping, like a friendly incense the senses have long known. They spoke of the current political discourse, and how an old Germanic word (*usu obscene*) was now very much in vogue.

Jacob began reciting from a text; 'As the elms bent to one another, like giants who were whispering secrets.' Do you recognize that?" Jacob asked with a smirk.

"Do I know what, now?"

"Where that quote comes from."

"Oh." He smacked his lips and turned his head. "Yes, it sounds like something . . ." He smiled, "Is that from Dickens?"

"Which book?."

"I don't know." He shook his head, vexed. "Wait, let me say it properly, so that you know I'm being sincere. I don't fucking know."

"That's a shame, because it's from your *David Fucking Copperfield*."

"Ah, I couldn't place it. He's very good at drawing little nature sketches that evoke emotions like a musical score."

"When we were children, there were two huge elms, over there at Darst and Elizabeth, on diagonal corners. I can still remember them whispering to each other."

"Are you now a student of the Teacher's catechism?"

"Well, Molly is, that's for sure. You told her she should read *Great Expectations* and *David Copperfield*, as two parts of one whole. 'Two vital chambers of the Teacher's heart.' I think that was how it was put to me."

"Yes, that's true." He shook his head in wonder; his evangelism was bearing the most promising fruit.

"What about this one: 'Such a fresh, blooming, modest little bud.' Huh?"

Isaiah considered that perhaps Jacob and Molly had worked together compiling these test questions. It would be just their sort of deviltry; setting out to prove he did not know his Dickens quite so well as he professed. "Wait! Don't say it." The word leering came into his mind, and then he exclaimed, "That's Quilp. He once stated, 'I don't eat babies; I don't like 'em.' He provides the force of evil tension in *The Old Curiosity Shop*."

"Raphael said that personage reminded him of *Lolita*. He said it possessed a vibrant, subversive prurience."

"You've brought Raphe into your cabal?"

"I don't know about any cabals, but have you read *Lolita*?"

"No, but if Dickens had lived, he would have written something better."

"Better than something you know nothing about."

"That's my fucking position. I'm a member in good standing of the Coodle party; we're always right."

"Right. Well, Raphe said he really doubts that you had read much of anything, other than the fucking Teacher."

"Okay, no more of that stuff. Is he in your book club?"

"Oh sure, he participates in several chapters. He's been a member—well, maybe not in good standing, necessarily—but for quite some time. Anyway, now that he's caught wind of Molly's new Dickens chapter, he wants in."

"So you're telling me she has started recruiting for the Dickens chapter?"

"Didn't she tell you that?" His face was funny to see, and maddening; he enjoyed needling people. After his pipe was out he made ready to leave the perch.

"I'm going to do some more raking."

"I better let you get back to it then."

"I have an extra rake, if you know how to use one of those, and if you have any fucking interest in earning your beer rations."

They took up stations at opposite ends of the yard, and strove to bring most of the leaves together in the middle. The physical exertion was good for a body. The pungent smell of decaying leaves, mixed into the aroma of the newly scraped earth, released floods of inarticulate remembrance.

"I hope you didn't ruin your work boots." Jacob said after they had completed a productive shift. They retired to the Watchtower with mugs full of malted brew; feeling no need to justify their ways to any local god just then. Isaiah shared a line from *The Old Curiosity Shop*, where Nell, in her pensive, closing scenes, ascends into an old tower, and marvels over 'the freshness of the fields and woods.'

"It's nice to have a way to climb out of the morass of the day; leave behind that world of screaming headlines."

"Why won't Molly consider me for her book club?"

Jacob appraised the demeanor of his officious guest.

"I mean, come on, she's doing Dickens, and she doesn't think I might have something to contribute? I've read all his works, numerous times. He's more than just another author to me, as I've told her more than once, trying to make my case, as best I can." Isaiah realized he was making a spectacle of himself, but he didn't care. "I think his corpus constitutes a testament that she would appreciate, and I—"

"Like I said, she does!" Jacob was starting up his pipe again.

"He was writing more than just fairy tales." Isaiah's fervor was waning, as it was clear Jacob was unmoved by his entreaty.

"I suppose you could say the gospels are fairy tales, too, couldn't you?" Jacob replied with enormous equanimity. "I'm not able to plead your case, you must know that." Jacob smoked his pipe in peace.

"I know."

"You have to realize, she trusts you. The stakes go way up, once that happens. She has a way of making demands, without actually doing so explicitly."

"I think I know what you mean."

"If you actually move somewhere, nearby, there will be more of that to contend with, I assure you." He resumed tending his pipe, in pure Jacobean mysticism.

When the mugs were empty and the vista beginning to wear a semblance of the prosaic, the men climbed down to greet Molly, who had come outside. Isaiah excused himself to use the bathroom in the basement, and when he returned he found Molly alone in the gazebo.

"Isaiah, you know, I have considered you for the club." She assured him.

"Sorry for being such a baby about it. But, I guess, I don't understand the problem. Why don't you want me to participate? Just tell me, if there's some other consideration, just tell me. I can take it."

"Well, I wanted to have people catch up, read more of the books, before we get into it the way you would like to do. As far as participation—"

"So I still have a chance?"

"You are persistent, I will say that for you."

"I can be."

"On some things?"

"Yes, isn't that true with everyone?"

"I suppose." She smiled in her most sardonic manner.

They heard childish noises entering the yard; Molly's daughter Sophie had stopped by with her daughter, who was calling out to her grandmother. Molly moved quickly up to the child, holding out her arms; the girl took hold of both of her wrists and began pulling her and imploring her to come quickly with her to the fortress.

Isaiah watched as Molly stepped slowly up the stairs behind the plodding little girl. He smiled graciously at Sophie in passing, as she too made her way towards the Watchtower. Isaiah crossed the parking lot, and entered the Grotto's sheltered paradise of evergreens. He was glad to see Father Charles at his table, reading *Bleak House*. He explained that he was gathering material for a sermon.

"I'm finding the people are very receptive to this author." He explained.

"He was beloved in his day, and he was extremely loyal to his readers."

"People respond to his voice. He's like a wonderful, mischievous host, accepting you into his magic kingdom. He gathers you in and makes you happy for his people, and glad to be one of these yourself. He's brought a new richness to my voice. He's made me more popular. I fear it's gone to my head!"

"Well, I enjoy your sermons."

"At the moment, I'm working on the idea that there are really two bleak houses. At first, there is the old, traditional, great house, a moral rubbish pile of decaying norms; and then, at the end, there is the little, renovated cottage. A place fashioned by the good people, where they can live their simple, profound lives, according to cherished ideals."

Isaiah suggested that the character of Jo provides rich material for a homily, and Charles responded ardently.

"At his death, the author's voice, it's not just society, or even History, but Spinoza's entire universe, that is looking down, appalled."

Isaiah was moved by the man's fervor. "What do you make of the motif of the dead child?" Isaiah asked.

"Tell me what you mean there."

Isaiah offered his exegesis of the Teacher's obsessional concern for the archetypal child, who preserves the grace of an ideal childhood throughout its life. It was naïve, it was sublime; it pierces into the core of the author's heart. It is all about redemption; the restoration of life, and the costs, the painful penalties, when we do not abide by the laws of the good heart. Isaiah told of the way this theme of childhood becomes an allegorical banner ever hanging from the rafters of the author's fabulous dream factory.

Esther buries a doll when she is a child. When she finally comes, near the end, to find her own mother lying dead, in the climactic scene, at first she believes it is another woman, who is known to be the mother of a dead child. And Esther herself was thought to be dead, by her mother, who gave her up after giving birth to her. Esther eventually becomes the heroine, who is offered the old Bleak House, but ends up in the more modest idyllic one at the end of the tale.

He thought he must be boring the priest, until Charles began scribbling notes in his college notebook. Isaiah asked him if he would like to go to Sistah's for lunch, his treat, and Charles assented. It was a pleasant meal and they listened as other diners spoke vehemently of politics. Isaiah made a study of the prelate's face, remembering Molly's suggestion that he ought to consider painting the man's portrait. She had not been clear how he was to approach him regarding such a project. Was the priest expected to pay? Or was he to offer his services gratuitously?

When they later parted ways in the parking lot, by the Grotto, Isaiah hesitated at his car, hearing the sound of Molly's voice. She waved for him to come over.

"Sorry I had to break away earlier. I saw that piece of sculpture you brought us. That was so nice of you." She cocked her head, and looked at him with her beautiful eyes. "I hope you don't intend to set up your own encampment in my yard, like your grandfather. You must make your own place somewhere."

He was very tickled by the idea. They ended up in the tower. He asked her directly what she thought of him doing a portrait for Charles, and she said he would really like that; he would undoubtedly send it to his mother.

"You could portray him celebrating the Easter Mass, in those vestments."

"I'd be glad to." He still wasn't sure how he was to proceed with this endeavor. She acted as if it were all too obvious for her to explain.

"Here's one. 'Don't know yah, don't know yah, pon my soul don't know yah!'" Molly was voicing (in character) the part of Trabb's boy, a nemesis from *Great Expectations*, who had mocked Pip when he returned triumphant to his town wearing a gorgeous costume.

Isaiah chuckled. "That would be Trabb's boy."

"And for you, all your worst critics, no?"

Isaiah shook his head in wry exasperation. In that scene Trabb's boy was pretending to be Pip, in his new hauteur. "You have me there." He observed her broadly smiling face, and noticed her bundle of greyish hair in the sun's flashing backlight had become an aura.

"Have you brought me up here to offer me all of this." He swept his arm out to indicate a broad vista of the rolling hills, strewn with modest dwellings.

"What are you saying?"

"You want me to stake my lot in this realm."

"Is that so unimaginable?"

"It makes me feel so worn out, considering the work involved. Trying to . . . I wish . . ."

"What?"

"I wish I wanted to move to a better place."

"You don't like where you're at now?"

"That's the thing, I don't feel like I am there, anymore; not the way I was in the past. I've moved on, in my mind, and I don't know what would be best for me."

"Well, you're coming over here all the time. Jacob says we should have you sign a timeshare agreement."

He looked over at her and laughed lightly. "I'm not restless when I'm here, or at my studio; otherwise I keep thinking about what's coming next."

"What keeps drawing you up here?"

"I'm like a stray cat, and you keep feeding me."

"Do you think you'd like having your studio in your own house?"

He had never given that idea serious consideration, until now. Stepping away from an easel and walking directly into one's own garden, it was almost too fantastic to imagine.

"I could follow in Monet's footsteps."

"That's what I've been trying to tell you!" She folded her arms, a pouty moue formed on her mouth. "I suppose you are familiar with Quilp's boy, how he would go off and stand on his head, after being treated badly by others?"

Isaiah chortled happily. "That's a superb example of his bizarre, wonderful sense of humor."

"Well, that's your foolishness too; you need to land on your feet, and stay there. Find your own ground."

"That's absolutely true." He looked at her closely. "And now I know how you became Margaret the Terrible."

"That's terrible of you to say that to me." She raised and swung her shoulders, as she held herself in a pose of being aghast at his shameless effrontery. "You will need to say it the right way; it's *that* terrible Margaret."

They quietly shared the rich, silly moment, looking at the stirring cloud formations. The colors offered a prophecy of snowfalls certain to come when the season was more ripe.

"I've never been able to host a barbecue in my own yard, and I've attended so many. I would always pretend that I was visiting the provincial natives in the suburbs."

"Well, you have always been a native. Wasn't that the whole thing, about being in that gang, of whatever?"

"Yes, that's true. I refused to move away; it was like an article of faith. Ha! Don't ask me which faith was involved."

"Okay, how about this. 'I sold all I had.' Do you know that one?"

"Too easy; that's Philip, the immortal Pip. That's the Teacher's darling boy, coming at last to an understanding of his destiny."

"Too easy, you say." She peered at him with her clear, twinkling, violet-gray eyes.

"Or say, too simplistic, maybe. It's unfortunate that in selling all you have, one is then unable to purchase a house, say, in a sleepy, leafy, gossipy old suburb."

"Are you always so literal?"

"I'm just stating where things stand, from a practical standpoint."

"I've found, there are times when it becomes necessary to sell stable assets, to move into other instruments of more lasting value, and more suitable for one's larger goals."

"My portfolio is doing quite well."

"Which one?"

"You're hard to keep up with here."

"Maybe you're hard of hearing."

He laughed. "Maybe so."

"In my field we are tasked with making sure all true costs are accounted for, before declaring our profits. It's the same way when you consider grace."

Isaiah noticed how she was rubbing her cross between two fingers as she spoke; one of her involuntary gestures. He was unable to utter what he was thinking.

"You say that your former café life no longer appeals to you, is that right?"

"Yeah, as a way of life; that whole scene feels like it's gone stale on me. That's the problem, it scares me to have more things dropping away."

"On reading *Great Expectations* again, I was taken by how guilt-ridden the main character is."

"Yes, that theme is brought to saturation."

"It's a very intimate portrait, as you've said, and I can really feel the author's anxiety in those pages."

"No doubt. He's opening himself up on the page, you can see him developing himself, like a film negative. By the time of that work he had come so far from the blacking factory. He had lost a great deal of his romanticism along the way. And he never did settle down. He was always one to throw himself headlong into the chase after adventures. He was driven to perform, possessed by some deep craving to be out there in front of people, being greatly loved."

"He needed adulation more than true human contact?"

"He just always wanted more."

"Do you remember, right before that line about selling everything, Pip is talking about going up to see his old room, to rest there a few minutes by myself?"

"Sort of, yeah. So, are you saying I ought to go inside, visit my old room up there, and meditate?"

"I think you ought to go somewhere inside yourself, and think it over; decide whether a move here, or someplace else, would be good for you. Someplace where you have a plot of land to cultivate, and neighbors you will have to get to know. It is others who challenge us to do a better job of watching over ourselves. In community we do that for one another." She raised a finger to wag at him. "You could have a really nice place where your granddaughters enjoyed visiting."

"Ah." He sighed, thinking it might be too late for that; nonetheless, she had moved him with her inimitable touch. "It would be good to have such a place. But the amount of work to be done, it scares me."

"You will have to turn to people, ask for help."

"It's not about my abode, why Theo refuses to include me in the lives of his daughters."

"Well, I don't know about that, but I can't imagine a scenario in which I would not be seeing my grandchildren. I hate to think how that would go, if Sophie and I—I just, I just can't imagine."

"I haven't been a model father. He has good reason to be resentful. I never spent the time . . ." He paused, looking down. "I cheated on his mother, but she was cheating on me, first, that's the thing. At the time we were both—"

"Isaiah, don't tell me about this."

"Okay." He could see anguish rising in her moist eyes. "It's important to me, though, that I didn't ever cheat on her, until it no longer seemed to matter, that is . . ."

"Some things belong to you, and you alone, in such matters. You have to deal with it on your own terms."

Isaiah fell silent, feeling penitent and embarrassed.

"The thing is, what do you want now? You need to start moving forward, going in a certain direction. Do you want to stay an outsider forever?"

"An outsider?"

"I hope you don't mind if I try breaking you down here, a little bit."

"No, go on."

"In the past, when you would pull your pranks, it was like you wanted to gain attention, but remain anonymous, at the same time." As she spoke he listened intently. "But you climbed up on the statue that day in front of a crowd. You wanted everyone to see you."

"But why?"

"You were grieving, for her, and yourself, more than you were able to comprehend. You wanted it to be known you were suffering a great loss."

"I never knew who she was to me."

"Did you love her?"

"Yes."

"That's who she was to you; someone you loved. You cannot grieve the loss if you've never come to terms with what the two of you meant to each other. That's always with you, resolved or not."

"I climbed up there for everyone to see." He was really going back into things now. "I thought I was renouncing my old life, but maybe, I just wanted to testify . . ."

The spirit was upon you." She laughed in her high delightful ironic tones. "I don't know what more I can say to you."

"I wanted to bare my soul." He spoke as if questioning himself. There was a period of ruminative silence, and then a beatific smile began spreading on her face.

"Jacob," she emitted a rasp of mirth, "he's been quoting Milton to me at night. Recently there was something about 'those thousand decencies that daily flow'; and I thought yes, of course, this is our work, to be done with those we love. And that can be many." She looked at him demurely, as if to lighten the weight of her guidance.

Isaiah stared back, struck by how casually she was able to create a sense of awe about her person.

"By owning a house, keeping it in good order, and in time, turning it over to others, you are leaving something valuable behind. Helping to keep the larger community as a livable place, that's no small thing."

"No, not at all."

He could only smile at his own transformation. Months ago he would have thought she was interested in the actual housing stock, actively fostering the welfare of her beloved village. Now he knew this appeal regarding the houses was about the life inside those houses; what of value endured and was passed on. Her concern for others was inextricably bound into the flowing richness of her pulse. Her love of the green, cradling earth sheltering these suburban domiciles derived from a profound set of convictions.

"I would never find better neighbors anywhere else, I know that much."

"Just give it some thought." She smiled at him very gently, as if relieved to have given her best effort. She stood up, preparatory to descending. "I promise, I won't bother you on this subject anymore."

She climbed down and he followed her. It was getting late, but he didn't want to leave. Noticing this she strolled with him into the Grotto. They moved to the edge of the hill that looked over the field below. They stood on either side of her black cherry tree, which she had planted there long before. He knew that she had painted this tree dozens of times.

"Molly, do you want to hear something weird?"

She looked at him.

"I was praying to the Virgin Mary before I fell asleep last night."

"Really?" She began to lean closer to him. "Interesting."

"Why do you say it like that?"

"Oh, I was praying for you last night."

"You pray for me?"

"I pray for lots of people. It keeps my mind tuned to frequencies of sorrow other than my own. Everyone is out there struggling, in some way or other; I want to keep that in mind."

"I started praying to her, for toys, when I was a kid. Somehow I figured out that Mary had to be more influential than the bureaucrats who worked for Santa Claus. I started sending my petitions directly to her."

"Did that work?"

"It seemed to, that's how it became a ritual, I guess. My mother must have been aware of my petitions. She played a critical role in that supply chain."

"Sounds like you had a good system going." Molly's voice phrased ambivalence in delicate shades. She added in her most confident voice, "You have things to consider, I am sure, and have issues that I cannot pretend to understand." She placed her hand on his arm.

"I promise to give it some thought."

She spoke dramatically; 'I don't know how it is, unless it's on account of being stupid, but my head never can pick and choose its people. They come and they go, and they don't come and they don't go, just as they like.'

Isaiah started to laugh, a gust of restrained emotions bursting out of him. For a moment he was breathless, and could not speak. Finally he said, "That's Peggotty! I only know, because, I just read that passage again myself."

"She's a terrific example of that enduring life force that the Teacher holds up with such devotion."

"One of the best of those good simple souls he likes to parade before us." He almost added, "Just like you." But he restrained himself; expressing that sentiment would have been terribly out of key just then. There was really nothing simple about Margaret Gates.

35

The river sweeps past, just as it has since the glaciers retreated, the last mastodons battled swarms of armed men, a studious, agrarian people, on great mounds of dirt, worshipped the sun, the Illinois nation declined, waging war against the Iroquois and other tribes, and Pierre Laclede drove a stake into the ground and told Marie's boy, here is where we build our house.

The congestive river blithely skirts all signs of neglect, blight, and ruin; even licking at putrefaction as it nourishes life everywhere. Isaiah is close to the shoreline, kicking at the scattered refuse he finds at his feet. He stops walking to study the rugged, stained and weathered features of the Eads Bridge. He once read that Walt Whitman stood on this putrid bank, to stare at this remarkable structure in the moonlight. He was no doubt savoring, at the same time, the magnificence of his own constitution.

Isaiah's mind is crowded with shadowy images. He begins to worry that he has parked his vehicle in a place that might tempt thieves to break a window to search for his useless valuables. He thinks he must go back, but he cannot turn around. He has conjured a vestige of the resourceful means he had used so effectively in the past. For a fleeting moment he reprises a sensation of having gotten away from his besetting fears, and is coming upon the source of his best work.

Isaiah stops to watch a small tug ferrying supplies up and down the mighty course. He had once painted a series of these handsome little boats. The prints sold very well at one time. It occurs to him he has come to the Arch grounds by way of the city's back alley as he climbs the monumental steps. He stands under the peculiar stainless ribbon to view the buildings downtown.

He turns away to face the river again; after sitting down he opens the copy of *David Copperfield* he has carried with him. It is a strange, battered totem. He leafs through the volume without much interest, until he comes to the glorious chapter entitled, "Martha." How many authors ascend to the heights of these majestic pages? Isaiah knows every detail of this chapter, and he closes the book and places it beside him on the steps.

The 'fallen woman' makes her pilgrimage to the river, for there is no hell she has to fear, other than people. She is ready to embrace the stream of life, to surrender her body to the endless flow, feeling utterly forsaken. The author has other ideas, and his godchildren have followed her. They come upon her depleted, prostrate figure. They take her up, assuage her pains, and bring her back to life. They enlist her in the cause of helping them to find another lost soul, and in this endeavor she is thereby saved herself.

Isaiah decides to leave his book on the steps and heads back to his car; he wants to get back to his studio. While unlocking his car door he notices a great blue heron beating upriver on strong, ponderous wings. The feathered creature makes his progress in a way ordained by nature. It was mesmerizing to the human eye. Once at the studio he began taking an inventory of all the projects he had left laying around. He stares at these foreign images in a sort of trance; continually glancing beyond everything he's done.

For a long while he sat before the portrait of his father. He understood this project now; the scene was clear to him. His father, standing on a street corner, in all that commotion that once comprised Gaslight Square. He would have to be careful to render several landmarks to establish the venue. He wanted to paint Thomas Meriwether fully situated in his natural habitat; pursuing music, companionship, and other psychic enrichments.

Isaiah seldom played music when working, but now he put on an old Stones' album. He was in a soulful mood as he began adding touches to various sketches of his father's face. He began singing accompaniment to the song, "I'm Free," in a loud, strident voice. He had no way of hearing Theo and Dilsey entering his quarters, coming near and staring at him in amazement.

When he noticed them he turned down the music and waved them over to the reading area.

"I forgot you were coming." He said, as he watched his son's expression become instantly downcast. Theo had told him of this visit earlier in the week.

"Dad?" Theo's face, for a second, mirrored his father's. "Hope we're not bothering you, we just wanted to look around a little bit."

"That's fine. I was down on the riverfront."

"Were you taking pictures?" Dilsey asked him eagerly. She was holding a compact camera in one hand.

"No, I just walked for a spell. Just looking. It was very satisfactory."

"It's a great place for walking." She replied.

"When I was young, I went down there all the time. I'd go roaming, exploring. Now, I guess I'm more tentative."

"More afraid?" She said with a sharp inflection.

"Yes, that too. I have those fears. When I was young, I was more confident than I should have been, in myself, and now, I am probably more frightened of others, than I ought to be."

She stared at him with a prolonged, level gaze; in her eyes a steely discernment made him feel more comfortable with her. Something keen and honest was percolating there in her mind, which she had chosen to keep to herself, in that moment, at any rate. She glanced over at Theo, who had been watching them, very intently, and her smile prompted him to speak.

"We are thinking of getting a work place—well," he looked at Dilsey and laughed. "Dilsey is thinking of getting a place, something like this one. I am but her escort." He blushed. Isaiah looked more closely at him, and then at Dilsey, who looked down as soon as he did so.

"That's very good!" He exclaimed, after a long pause.

"What?" Theo wasn't sure what he was referring to, and was instantly suspicious of his father's attitude. Isaiah laid down his pencil and ushered them to his bookshelves.

"If you will direct your party this way, I will show you my library." He spoke in lilting tones, as if playing an idle fool expostulating on the stage between the main acts.

Dilsey began to examine his art books. Theo pulled out a volume of Dickens.

"He's a huge fan of Dickens." He said to Dilsey, who looked at him with a bemused smile, for this was something he had made very clear to her already.

"Mr. — "

"Isaiah."

"You said this *is* a library?"

"That's how I — yes!" He divined her intention "Do you want to borrow anything?"

"I would like to take a look at some of these art books. You have so many."

"Help yourself, by all means. I'll charge Theo for any late fees." He noticed a wry look on his son's face at the mention, even ironic, of money transactions taking place between them.

"Which of these do you suggest I should read first?" Theo asked, running his hand across the spines of several novels."

"Let me see." Isaiah was intrigued. "*Dombey and Son*." He said this authoritatively, as if in a role. He watched as Theo searched and found a copy of that title among the Penguin 'black bricks.'

"Wait a minute." He squared himself in front of Theo. "Please tell me you're not in Molly's book club."

"I've been asked to join one chapter."

"I brought him in." Dilsey said.

"Can you get me in?"

Dilsey looked at Theo, and began laughing. She then made a worried face, not sure how to handle this imbroglio with this largely unknown ego. Isaiah began to plead with her in mock of the standard pathetic supplicant. He made her laugh genuinely and his simmering spirits rose higher.

"Oh, I don't think we're supposed to talk to you about that." She bent forward. She thrust out her arm and grabbed Theo's shoulder.

"What are you saying, now?" Theo asked her.

"It is starting to get a little insulting." Isaiah spoke in a voice that was laden with conflicting tones.

"Well, it's a pretty exclusive club." Theo said, hoping to join the waning mischief of the other two.

"Well, I say it's time for a drink." Isaiah said this as a pronouncement of serious moment.

Theo looked at his watch and mumbled something about not having a lot of time. They were conferring with one another with facial expressions and Isaiah could see he was about to lose them.

"Come on now, be a good son. Have one drink with me. I keep good spirits for such occasions. That's something you have to keep in mind for a good studio, you must have the proper accouterments; those for the craft, and those for the craftsman!"

"What occasion is this?" Theo asked dubiously. His father's incongruous mania was troubling to him.

He selected a bottle he had been saving; after opening it he poured a glass for each of them. Dilsey accepted hers graciously.

"Let's pretend this is the last bottle of the old Madeira." Isaiah held up his glass.

Theo's smile was strained, as he indulged his father, who was embarrassing him by his dramatic airs. Dilsey made an admonitory face, as she read his shifting moods. In response he complimented his father on his good taste after taking a hearty sip of the wine.

"I will give you the deluxe tour."

They walked about his cavernous space, where light and shadows roomed together as Isaiah spoke to them with obvious pride about his favorite projects of the past. Dilsey asked technical questions, which gave Isaiah a keen delight in answering. He complimented her on her perceptive eye. Theo knew how happy the man was when he picked up random brushes and waved them like batons. He was acting rather childish, and he was not inebriated. It was all very strange.

"This is a wonderful space. It exudes something that makes you want to start working." Dilsey exclaimed.

"It's always been a good space for me." Isaiah stated in a grave tone. "I hope I don't miss it too much."

"Why would you miss it?" Theo demanded, suddenly concerned.

"Over the years, I made sacrifices, to make sure I could keep this place for myself." He watched for Theo's reaction, and felt hurt when he saw it, even though he had prepared himself.

Theo stared at him, as if he owed him an immediate explanation. Dilsey met his gaze. Her eyes were very clear, and looked at him with an unshakable resolve to know him better. She was younger than Theo, but she acted more mature in some exotic shading that defied explanation. She had experienced harsh aspects of life, which neither of the Meriwether men had been required to go through, as a mater of course. Her response to these rigors had been to strengthen herself, and it was moving to bear witness to her strength.

She had a voluptuous body and moved with lissome grace. Theo loved to watch her swaying along when she was aloft in her reveries. She had gone off to look at something again, and to let the father and son speak in confidence of some matter that was clearly bubbling up between them.

"Dad, what's going on?"

"Hold on. First, an order of business." Isaiah raised his voice, and his glass, summoning the attention of Dilsey. Theo was sure his father had something important to say; his heart shuddered faintly.

"I have an announcement to make."

"Dad, what's wrong?"

"I'm moving."

"Your studio?"

"No, myself."

"Where are you going?"

"Ferdinand."

"What?" Theo was astonished.

"Did you buy a house?" Dilsey had rushed up.
"No, I still have to do that."
"You've been looking?" Theo asked.
"No, I've just now decided to do it."
"Just now?" Theo asked, looking at Dilsey.
She laughed in a loud, natural effusion.
They congratulated him with wild, genuine effusions. They clinked their glasses together, and spoke for some time about Ferdinand, and what it would be like for him living there.

"I'm really happy for you, Isaiah, but we really do have another thing; we're expected—" Dilsey tried to explain.

"But you can't go just yet." Isaiah held up his hand and beseeched them to stay one moment longer.

"We can't drink any more." Theo spoke brusquely; his face changing to soften the imputation that his father was a little profligate in that regard. "I just mean—"

"No, that's fine, but Theo, listen, won't you have a seat. Both of you, please. I want to talk to you."

"We should probably do that later."

"I have some more news, and it concerns you."

"Me?"

They brought chairs together.

"You sit there." Isaiah directed Dilsey to take the good chair. Isaiah looked intently at Theo. "I'm going to give you power of attorney, so you can run the business for me. I want to keep painting, without all those worries."

"You want me to run the business?" Theo stood up. He shook his head like he was not certain of what was being proposed. "Dad, we should probably discuss this some more, at a later date. Just you and me."

"We'll have plenty of time to do that, but I wanted you to know. My mind's made up."

"I don't understand, though, how this could work."

"You will take a percentage of all sales."

"Okay, but like I've said before, it would take at least ten percent, and then we would have to see—"

Isaiah put up his hand, in one of his worst paternal mannerisms, to indicate the child must stop speaking. Theo grimaced and turned his head.

"I've gone over everything with my accountant, very thoroughly, and we're going to set your commission at twenty-five percent, to start. I think that's fair. If you and Dilsey want to put other things on the website, to make it more appealing, and to sell your own things, that's fine. You will run the website as your own franchise." He got up to pour himself more wine.

"What about Mrs. Kinfe?"

"This is none of her concern. This is the house of Meriwether and Son. Oh yes, didn't you say Gretchen is now taking a keen interest in doing illustrations? Well, we should commission her for a sign. I can put it up in my new place."

"I'm not sure what to say." Theo was having trouble assimilating this welter of transformative information.

"Tell me that you want to be in business with your old man. That you are looking forward to embarking on this journey!" Isaiah's head reared back, laughter poured out of him.

"Well, yes, I do, of course." Theo spoke slowly, his voice barely audible. He was overcome. He was moving in a new direction and it was thrilling. He glanced all around the studio, as if he had never been there before.

"Once I have the house, I will move my studio there. This place will be available for you. You could both work here. I own the place outright; so that means one day it will be yours. Just like the house I buy; so don't be a stranger there." He looked around his studio. "Make any changes you want. I'm going to start fresh."

Dilsey appeared in front of Theo, her face awash in exuberant feelings. Isaiah watched them embrace, unable to control their emotions. He left them alone, moving over to face the portrait of his father. He was beyond feelings of regret, holding fast to certainties he had always held in his possession. He thought of leaves tumbling over the earth—he would have a place with his own trees!

"Do you know who this is?"

"Saint Louis, right? On his last crusade, or something."

"No, it's your grandfather. That's Gaslight Square, in those charcoal markings. I've barely begun, you can't tell yet, but there it is. I can see it." He stated proudly.

"Dad . . . ?" Theo murmured.

"Yeah."

"Nothing."

"Dad, I think this is going to work out pretty well, but are you sure this is what you want to do?"

"There's no doubt in my mind. I'm going to have sunflowers on my property. I might wear a straw hat."

"So, you're going to buy a house in Ferdinand?" Theo was still having trouble reasoning while in this flood of happiness. "That sounds like a really good idea."

"Molly's going to help me find something."

"Well, that means there's no turning back for you." Dilsey said emphatically. "It took you long enough to fall in line."

"I don't think she's done working on you, young lady."

"Oh, I know that, don't worry, I know." Dilsey started laughing, as did Isaiah. Theo watched them. He was unable to utter a single one of the questions now whirling through his mind.

"I don't know about you Theo, but I would like another drink." Dilsey spoke with soothing conviction. "We can change our plans for later. Let's toast this change in our lives."

"Why don't we remove this celebration to Pliny's. My treat."

Isaiah took upon himself the role of grand seigneur.

"Having a work space in the Loop." Dilsey said in a low, thrilling voice, looking into his eyes.

"That will be so cool." Theo agreed.

"Dilsey, I'm afraid I don't really know that much about you." Isaiah said, "I want to take this opportunity to get to know you better."

Theo looked at his father, as if he'd said something rather awkward and foolish. At the restaurant Dilsey put her hand on his arm every time he was getting uncomfortable about her outpourings. She told Isaiah her life story in concise phrases that revealed much about her very being. He heard everything a parent might wish to know at this time. Theo interrupted her quite often, when he heard new information, and incited her laughter at his consternation.

At one point Dilsey said that was enough about her. Then she told them of an incident which occurred at Sistah's, where she had been dining with several of her friends, some time in the past. Molly's name was brought up by a person new to their group. She started acting funny, and then intimated she believed Molly was encouraging white people to move to Ferdinand.

"So, I'm like, what? 'What are you saying?' She had heard someone say that Molly was always getting involved in other people's affairs, trying to ensure the 'right kind of people' settled in Ferdinand. The inference being, Molly was a bigot!"

Here Dilsey was looking down, shaking her head back and forth. "So, for a minute nobody says anything. Then we're all looking at each other; we all know each other really well. We're all black women! We're going to tell you what we think. But we just sat there. And then, someone pipes up and says, 'It was Molly who convinced me to move here.' Another explains, 'She let me know my house was going to be available soon, and wouldn't last long.' Then yet another woman shared a similar experience. And, as it turns out, all of us—except for me—at that table, had been encouraged by Molly to move to Ferdinand!" She turned a meaningful look at each of the men. "I said to them, 'She's been trying to get me to move here ever since I can remember.' And then we all started laughing. Everyone in the place was staring at us."

Dilsey paused, seeming to relish the memory, and not being ready to pass on, she narrated the voices from that episode at Sistah's.

'She's one of my best white friends, but she will get all up in your business.'

'Oh, she'll get in your business.'

'You know that's true.'

'I had to tell her one time, You don't know me as well as you think you know me.'

"Oh, we made quite a scene that time."

Dilsey bit her lip and shook her head as her laughter subsided. "Molly." She said simply.

The two men appeared slightly out of sorts, not able to appreciate altogether the tenor of this archly serious and complicated mirth.

Theo brought up new ideas to be considered for the website. Isaiah and Dilsey talked about cameras, and this led to stories of events she had covered as a photojournalist. She had placed her work with various news outlets. Isaiah spoke of the strange diminutive glory of being a creature who exists on the printed page of local magazines. Dilsey pointed out there were precious few printed pages left to pore over. They talked of art and life; comparing fact and image. They expressed their ideas freely. Theo watched as something went back and forth between these two loved ones; each was garnering confidence from the other, and using this empowerment to facilitate the thoughts they did not always choose to express, or at least not so exuberantly, without inhibitions.

He marveled at how everything seemed different, and better, now, and it left him feeling a little anxious; he was unable to concentrate. He must slow things down, to catch up to these changes and be ready to act in a way that befitted all that was happening. His father glanced at him, seeking assurance he had caught some witticism he had just put forth. All his son perceived was his father's most natural, shining happiness.

36

Theo went to see his father on Thanksgiving, taking along his daughters. Making this change to their schedules had been difficult to arrange with their mother, but well worth the effort. The early visit had to be a brief one. Isaiah was enormously pleased to have them over.

He quizzed the girls about their lives and savored their predictably terse replies. He took many pictures and they acted as great martyrs, who are being pressed by the world to conform to ridiculous norms. He was amused to hear himself addressed in a strange, formal diction. He inferred they wished to make it clear to him they were not children anymore. They were very busy in high school, rounding out 'really crazy' curricula vitae.

In his mind they were notable for practicing alchemy; having the power to transmute ages of cynicism he had laid away in his dusty storeroom. The most dingy articles were brought back to new life by their impeccable vision. Right before their arrival he had been reading the Pauline letters. He boasted silently, Never flag, be aglow. He swore to himself that he must stay keenly aware of their passions, so that he might help ensure they would continue to bloom.

Theo became anxious as time grew short. He sat in the living room with his dad, who was already drinking amaretto, having no place else to go. He seemed like an old child to his son. The girls were in his work room, and the men could hear them talking.

"Some of Grampa's work is pretty cool."

"That one is his dad."

"Oh wow. Who's that woman he's with?"

"Somebody he knew, I guess."

"Look at this."

"That's us when we were little."

"How'd you figure that out, genius."

"Shut up." The younger whispered.

Theo exchanged a look with his father and they both chuckled in the same exact manner. When it was time for them to go, the grandfather pressed a large envelope upon each of the girls, containing a pencil sketch of the girl (at a much younger age), and a personal check.

The days fluttered by and Isaiah's quest to find a house had fairly commenced. He wound up in the Watchtower quite often, taking a moment with Jacob, before exploring the neighborhood with Molly. She took him around to see houses that were not yet listed, and enjoyed visiting with the current occupants.

"It's uncanny." He said to Theo one day, who was trying to explain the challenges of keeping the site in order. "I keep meeting people who are interested in portraits."

"Did you hear what I said, though?"

"Yes, you have carte blanche with those changes. Don't worry about those other expenses."

"Okay, but I also wanted to tell you about Molly's portrait."

"I'm working on some preliminary ideas. Dilsey took some photographs I can use. I'm falling under the spell of Rembrandt . . ." He looked up as if he'd just remembered something. "But my search for just the right look is proving to be a problem. I'm enjoying the search too much!"

"Everyone is sure you'll do something really good."

Isaiah was feeling more than a little daunted by this weighty task.

"I want to keep Jacob aware of what I'm doing. And he wants it to be a surprise; that alone makes it a challenge."

"You want Jacob to approve of the final design?"

"Well, I'm not sure. You let me know."

"Now, are you sure you don't care what we charge them?"

"I don't want to have anything to do with that, you can figure that out with Jacob. Okay?"

"Well, I tried to do just that, but he wants to barter. He's suggesting a trade of his future labor, at your new house, whenever that happens, for the portrait you're working on now."

"That's good. And there's not going to be any deadline. Tell him he has to supply the stout."

Theo smiled. "He said you would have to provide all liquid refreshments."

"You have to negotiate, uphold the family honor."

"Should we draw up a document?"

"For fun, we ought to do that. I bet Gretchen could be hired to make something really grand—"

"Oh, that reminds me, Dad; Natalie wants you to do her portrait."

"What? When did she tell you that?"

"About a week ago. We had just finished our meeting, on a whole list of topics she had drawn up, and then she started asking me a lot of questions about you. Then right before I left she brought that up. She wanted me to tell you that she would pay the customary fee."

Isaiah laughed. "That was a code we used with new customers, when we could not tell how much the market would bear."

"She said something about how you never come to the gallery anymore."

"That's true. I've got to make up for lost time."

"I think she misses you. She kept asking me about what you're doing, and everything."

"She's not giving you a hard time about anything, is she?"

"No, just the opposite. She just told me today, on the phone, that she wants to have dinner with you sometime."

"That means I'm supposed to call her." He shook his head smiling. "Time's gotten away from me. I have a feeling this will be some dinner!"

His work sessions galloped by; he had mounted that noble steed called Purpose. He no longer dawdled at the studio scratching at his ego. He kept strange hours. His car could be seen in the lot near the Grotto so often that people were asking Molly if 'that man' was now homeless, fearing he might pose an additional burden for her generous heart.

One day he wheeled into the parking lot, late in the afternoon, and was met by Jacob, who ran up to him as if anxious to receive something he had come expressly there to deliver. Jacob was in a state, glaring around, then waving for Isaiah to follow him into the yard. He turned around, standing still, not able to look at anything.

"Margaret has Covid." Jacob heaved this out in his anguished breath.

"Oh my gosh. Is she—"

"She's at the hospital. She was having a hard time breathing. She's fine, though, she's okay, right now, she's fine." His face appeared more tortured at each word. Isaiah felt a grave, foreboding impulse strike into his heart.

"Are you able to see her?"

Jacob shook his head.

Isaiah thought of Edith's travail, and was overcome by a silent, wracking dread.

"She'll pull through." Jacob blurted out, seeing Isaiah's pale, blanched face. His voice quavered. They moved apart, both staring at the ground.

"I need you to watch the house for me. I'm bringing some things to the hospital, and Janey is coming over here in a little while. But when people come, tell them everything is fine, and there are no visitors allowed. There's going to be a lot of food delivered; do what you can, put it away in the kitchen."

Somewhat dazed, Isaiah watched him drive off, and then began wandering around the yard. He lingered by the ornamental wall that now looked like a frightful shambles of what it once had been. He climbed into the tower, but felt queasy and hollow in his stomach and had to go back down. The world's beauty had blurred senselessly before his eyes. Soon the deputations began to arrive, everyone demanding information. He tried to console them, wishing he had more to say, and tending to exaggerate what he did know in a positive manner. But this only increased his own misery. He feared that he was already making a fine mess of things, as the horrified faces passed before him in a ghastly review.

Janey finally arrived and took charge of the house. In times of sorrow the people they knew brought food to the home of the afflicted family. They left food on the front porch. They brought it into the kitchen upon finding the back door was unlocked. Some remained to do cleaning chores that were unnecessary. They began preparing food for each other, while keeping vigil, eventually moving about sharing household chores they had made necessary, and shared, very quietly, their anguish. Isaiah decided it was time for him to leave, being sure there was nothing more he could do for anyone there.

I WILL START by addressing the Teacher's place in the world. Forget the literary scribes, for a moment, and consider what the world has done with his imperishable remains. Enter the shrine at Westminster Abbey, see the company he keeps there; but also, visit his local temples, the homes, where his texts are still being used. Go to places (like this one) where his works are devoured because they fortify something (hard to even take into account); the health and welfare of our civic sensibilities.

Every generation has witnessed a fresh swarm of hungry scholars, who circle on the heated, topical currents, dropping to the ground, waddling over to batten on that prolific carrion. He was never a man of letters, but more like a brilliant churchyard custodian, who tended to the practical needs of his flock, even to the extent of seeing after the charnel house. He was a mighty, prophetic scold, warning people, be good, useful, and purposeful; to reach for higher ends. This may be the wrong approach to take right at first. I may be too close to other concerns just now . . .

In fact, the world easily tires of moral crusaders. That flinty, hard-headed Carlyle claimed Dickens "had not written anything which would be found of much use in solving the problems of life." Margaret quipped once, "Tell me who has?" I would deign to say, poor Carlyle, if those were his only feelings on the matter, but he also eulogized the great man's spirit. "The good, the gentle, ever friendly, noble Dickens — every inch of him an Honest Man." How do we masters of deception ever come to enter such a plea? A capital idea, being totally honest, what human being has ever come close?

Well then, let us say he was one of us; a flawed specimen, marred by hypocrisy, deceit, and selfishness. He tore his work from his savage heart for us. He was loyal to that which is so often scorned in real life; he celebrates the 'simple annals of the poor,' as being as worthy and respectable as any other chronicle. His eternal blacksmith, our dear, unimpeachable Joe, beautifully illustrates this central article of his faith. In him we are told everything in plainest terms. Pip was able to change his wobbly, straying orbit because of Joe's unerring moral gravity.

In Pip's final, poignant grappling to distinguish between what's natural, and unnatural, he reflects on his history with Miss Havisham. He comes into the grace of trying to really understand the suffering of another human soul. Somehow the Teacher was able to subsume our best qualities and still give voice to the ineffable doubts we too easily come to ignore out of practical necessity. The very stuff of our higher learning, which should be as play, too, and never cease, as it is for children . . .

Someday, we may not need the poetry; now we apparently need a charm to stay tuned to higher things. Listen to his rival, William M. Thackeray, how he responded to one chapter in Dombey and Son. "There is no writing against such power as this — one has no chance! Read that chapter describing young Paul's death: it is unsurpassed — it is stupendous!" These two writers were friends, their children played together, and as things go, they eventually had a falling out. And they made up right before the end, but what rewards of fellowship had they missed in the interim? If only we could do these things sooner, not later. Mock the terrible fates — I shouldn't speak this way, not now.

The world is always too much with us, even in the congested ghostly pews of our own private inner sphere. In Copperfield there is an interesting exchange between David and his faithless, worldly companion, who seems to hold such promise, and is so morally problematic:

"This is a wild kind of place, Steerforth, is it not?"

"Dismal enough in the dark,' he said; 'and the sea roars as if it were hungry for us."

Yes, he knew of the distant roaring of the inscrutable fates. It hardly makes any sound, none that we actually hear, not as we ought to hear, and heed, if we have the heart, and time enough. You move past the portents, the actual pain, ourselves, to know the life, and how we must believe, once we know. Humans easily learn to take precautions before braving the elements; so it seems to be in our handling of the truth. We construct narratives to soften, mitigate, block out, and assuage the terrible effect of truth, when it impinges too harshly upon our precious sense of honor. Do you know Emperor Hadrian's last poem?

In time the Teacher put away the comic villains; knowing the true monsters come to us out of our own nature; he feared to tread too far down that path, just like us. He was the grand master of mustering companies of mechanical puppets. One should treat all of his caricatures as primitive facets of the great human psyche. Alas, life is a fairy tale. We were bred to be liars and hypocrites, we know this in our marrow, and must refute any notion that it shall remain so for the sake of our souls.

We have many reasons for wearing masks. That witty chap, George Bernard Shaw, wrote "Thackeray could see Chesney wold [the nobleman's estate, and the unbending, unfeeling, decadent society holding it up]; but Dickens could see through it." In his stories, housed together in a great inspiring tenement, he becomes our loyal Prospero. He puts us under his spell, and calls forth outlandish, intriguing shapes, forming beauty out of the stubborn human clay. His hands were ever at the task of molding his own reverence.

WILLIAM M. O'BRIEN

Some time back I was talking to Jacob about Paul Dombey, and how the fey, sickly child would have them pull his carriage down to the sea, so he could sit there and listen. "I want to know what it says." He wanted to see further into things. Your mother said this sort of seeking was too dreamy, detrimental to dealing with the real concerns of life. Ha! Nothing to be gained by ignoring what is real in life. Forgive me, I am wandering all over the place in these notes. I can't seem to steady myself . . .

Now, Henry Adams, in his Education, writes that "Dickens never felt at home, and seldom appeared, in society." Adams was in all likelihood just the sort of fellow the Teacher wanted to avoid. The man of entitled blood and flush with sheaves of dusty paper to feather his bed. His ancestry had purchased Henry's entry into society. Dickens wrote in a letter, "I declare I never go into what is called Society." He recorded that he despised it, hated it, and rejected it. The more of it he witnessed the more taken he was by the "extraordinary conceit, and its stupendous ignorance of what is passing out of doors." Well, in the end, our Father Charles found his own letters patent engraved on the hearts of all aspiring members of humankind.

I must make note of a tribute offered by Leo Tolstoy. "If you sift the world's prose literature, Dickens will remain; sift Dickens, David Copperfield will remain; sift Copperfield, the description of the storm at sea will remain." Here, the noble Russian alludes to that chapter entitled, "The Tempest," wherein the story takes a wild, climactic turn, and the fates claim their bounty. The writing is strong, moving, pure, fluent, and natural; a great animating force of its own. That voice springs unfiltered out of the Teacher's most sacred font; in that moment of artistic testimony he was at peace with all the turmoil and mire of his own veins. His heart's control of his peerless craft raised him up to see far across the waters, to glimpse undiscovered realms.

I do believe that all his gospels rest on this thematic bedrock of change; he sought the potential that lies (maybe spoiling) inside of us. His portrayal of Riah, in Our Mutual Friend, is a triumph of his tremendous growth pangs. He appeals to those of his own time, and to posterity, laying out the case for universal dignity to be recognized among us. In his treatment of this sublime character he exposed the horrendous anti-Semitism that then permeated all classes of his society. We witness a remarkable power turning the intricate, watchlike mechanisms of his mind, keeping time for our ever faltering steps towards progress. He strove to raise his pen like a staff . . .

We often laugh at such grandiose pretensions. It's easy to do, knowing ourselves as we unfortunately do. Near the end of his life he barely survived a horrendous train wreck, and it caused a lasting trauma. It becomes a perfect metaphor for the trajectory of his moral life as well. His grand hopes had gotten thrown off track, despite his wild success, and that changed him at his core. The wife left behind, the young woman he turned to in love, but could not bring himself to acknowledge as such. His business was the layman's study of Life's Torah, explicating the naked human heart, that has no religion, class, or incorruptible master to compel obedience by rights. None, that is, other than nature Herself. That's why his books are rife with questions regarding what is natural, and what is not; for his life became that of the penitent, torn by bitter flails, fearful of unseen demons. He was not unlike St. Paul, who hoped finally to visit Spain, as he envisioned, the last virgin territory open for conversion . . .

Some look askance at what is deemed the Teacher's primitive psychology. Well, many celebrated Hollywood productions are also founded on laughably simplistic equations. None come close to working out the primal intricacy of human psychology. They have too many accountants keeping records, and so, time and again, they resort to shopworn formulae, which are soothing to weary souls, and profitable for the executive producers. Why, even that curious modern maestro of Vienna worked his magic in his own variant of melodrama. His cast of caricatures were stolen from antiquity! Ah, she would probably scold me for wandering off this way, like Tolstoy did at the end of his epic war book, and then in the final act of his actual life!

Well, well, Raphe just came over a short while ago. I opened one of my best bottles of Cabernet. We spoke of the past, afraid to bring up what the future might bring. He told me Dilsey would be doing the article. I chided him for abandoning me. We talked of being so old and out of touch. We enjoyed some gallows humor. The laughter flushed the foul dregs of our stagnating emotions. He really has become a fine, reputable, '73 fellow; he understands things. His wit seldom fails to hit the right tone. He quipped that Sir Charles, the Only, 'He do the Psyche in different voices.' We talked a long while about the galaxy of characters he created, and the allegorical splendor of his universe. We agreed, that if one is ready for the pilgrimage, his world draws a reader deep into the elusive mystery of our beings.

"Art is the temple of the imagination," I pronounced at one point. "Trying to flush it from there only makes it more wild."

"Yes, we can imagine what has never been, and somehow come to believe in this more than what we actually know."

"Much of that does come to pass." I affirmed.
"And some seem destined to show us the way?"
"Yes, yes. God help us."
"Here, fill my glass again, please."
"Why does it take such terrible circumstances to bring us around to facing things?"
"Life is a curious gift. How many know what to do with it?" I was actually regurgitating something she had told me.
"How much time do we waste on banal inanities?"
"Like us, now?" Healing laughter.
"Well, we know one thing for sure; the old curiosity shop of the Teacher's great manuscript is an ideal place to go shopping for life's most valuable commodities."
"Here, here, till the future dares to bring us to a better place."

The book Raphael compiled about Hereford's last year, The Vampires of Eden, calls attention to how susceptible we are to the ego's cruel, competitive devices. We nourish ourselves in our friendships, using each other in beneficial ways. Sometimes it becomes like a grisly feeding, taking of someone's vital substance, and not offering anything of equal value in return. In any scenario these exchanges tend to get rather ghastly, if society is too much with us . . .

One thinks of Thackeray, who lamented the power of his rival, "I can't touch him – I can't get near him." What had they squandered, out of pride? Which achieves in the end, what? Try and move beyond such things. But here, in my inaugural attempt, I should not shirk my duty of bringing him to life. There's so much to say, and time is short; what hope is there?

One thing to remember, we all must take heed and not end up like Vholes, described as a Vampire, having "not a human *passion or emotion in his nature." When people inspire us, and we transcend ourselves, and choose to share the best of our humanity, this is the highest Art of life. All else is some form of vanity; which pays the bills, and lets the mask smile at itself in the mirror, once in a while. The mask likes to see other reliable masks, as the soul peers outward from another place. It seems the sacred obligation is to learn all we can about the work, and the workings, before we worry ourselves to death over the mask of the spirit that lays behind such incomprehensible realities.*

I'm no philosopher, but I fondly dream. I have to wonder, do we choose our subjects, or do these come to us out of the elements? You know how easily I grow maudlin, and I confess it is now a habit to refresh that weepy mash with a splash of amaretto. I'm tired of trying to paint the moral aspect writ provocatively large for others to see. The truth is, humans don't know what the truth is, most of the time, when they argue over the great questions. We glimpse but faint shadows and become entranced by contrived visions distorted by our own desires. She said once that barely anything is perceptible, so we must hold on to what is happening in our hearts.

Maybe a dark night of the soul is a time when you are able to see past the merely human, in the truest light that ever shines, to see glimmers of the most valuable parts of yourself. True feelings, not symbols. It's easy to become debauched by shibboleths, Nobel speeches, the orderly tolling of ancient words, using bells cast in the forging of totems, the ringing of strength, courage, honor, hope, pride, compassion, pity, sacrifice, and endurance. We never break these notions down to find true Justice. We are left with one conflict that matters; that is when the heart challenges itself. We hardly even bother to explore the many mansions of love. Yes, I've left the field now – I was just outside preaching to the trees from my balcony.

I was stirred by something Janey told me, about the grace in holding fast to what we must believe, so that we might come together, to combine our strengths. Her face as she spoke was so perfect; it shone outward to great effect, as those unknown models used by the masters to create the great visions of our religious instincts.

Margaret said to me once that we are just starting to learn how to use consciousness. Most run from it like savages afraid of storms. They take refuge in all the conventional bomb shelters. For a long time it was an aesthetic of mine to see life and art as noble partners; the latter being primus inter pares, because it was more lasting. The shadow more lasting than life itself? The beauty of which we have barely touched in our own lives; no, I've come to find that art is really only a servant of life, not the other way around.

So much remains a contrived sham of the psyche's cry for attention, or its ignorant response to our sadly common lot of suffering. The ego's work of propping up social (or antisocial) constructs, in the most primitive mode, believed to be current. The tribe's shaman scratching the latest symbols onto cave walls for public acclaim. It doesn't feel like I'm making much progress here. I keep going astray. The keynote was supposed to be one of humility. The Sun King would have blushed through his rouge at such lavish self-promotion! It's worse than a PBS fund drive.

The honorable Citizen Dickens was tireless in his quest to record his explorations. Up to the very end he was putting himself at risk, in defiance of doctors orders, trooping back onto the stage to act out scenes taken from his books. He could not resist *those voracious audiences. He gloried in being the sole player of every part. I believe he added the death scene of Nancy to his repertoire near the end. He was determined to depict the angels and the monsters. His beginning was sure to be his end. He longed to bare himself to his public. Who is not sorely tempted to follow in his footsteps?*

I cannot do this any longer, not now. My quiet hours are raising too many ghosts. I'm almost afraid to let anyone find me here. There's no peace for me here. It won't ever be the same. I must keep busy, as best I can, there will be a time to work. I must be ready for whatever happens. She said that too. I keep thinking of a line from the Teacher's last epistle, wherein the crone offers her lost customer, 'Here's another ready for ye, deary.' How to choose from the cups that are passed our way, as everything is shifting about so strangely, unaccountably, and threatening such terrible ends!

37

There were strings of lights everywhere, multiplying like glowing tapeworms, excreted profusely from damnable (or damned able), industrial alimentary canals, tended by devils serving infernal overlords. One could see these lurid bulbs draped in bushes, wound in trees, strung between gaunt, swaying telephone poles, flung garishly upon the smallest, confused houses, and looped fatuously across the blushing facades of commercial buildings.

These trappings of good cheer stirred only melancholy inside of Isaiah as he was driving north. He had to report to Janey who was watching the house while Jacob roved about on his awful rounds. After arriving she told him of a curious incident involving Molly, who was still on a breathalyzer. Somehow she had retained limited access to her cell phone, by virtue of the kind offices of a nurse on her floor. This woman knew someone, who happened to know Molly from St. Margaret's. This nurse took it upon herself to tend to her private needs during her breaks, and then again when she was off duty.

Molly entreated this woman to help her send an email to Janey. She had promised to get Geoffrey a good winter coat this season, and now she wanted to enlist Janey's help in making this happen. She intended to contact only Janey, but the harried nurse inadvertently sent the message to a master list tagged with a similar name. Shortly thereafter, seven new overcoats, and twelve baskets of neatly folded clothing, were delivered to Molly's home. People assumed there was another charity drive underway. When Molly heard of this imbroglio she requested help in finding persons to whom they might distribute the surplus clothing.

A flurry of calls and texts and further emails quickly followed, and a firm purpose soon took shape. Her friends never could agree on the scope, or the exact nature, of the mission. Molly tried to direct traffic from her hospital bed, but was dissuaded by all of her caretakers, who assured her they would keep her appraised of how things were going.

The Gates's house became a shipping depot. A steering committee was formed, and these people congregated in an atmosphere of ever increasing urgency. They drank a lot of coffee, and wine, expounding to one another. They became engrossed in endless deliberations over details as dozens of volunteers came forth to offer support.

A few close friends started referring to the movement as the first annual DAM Drive; derived somehow from the phrase, 'Damn it, Margaret!.' Tears of laughter washed through their strained anguish. Seeing so many cars in the parking lot caused more people to investigate what was going on, and the ranks continued to swell.

One day Isaiah was stacking boxes in the living room when a gang of teens from the John & James contingent arrived at the front door.

"I think you have a pickup for us?" One said, as if it were obvious who they were. The puzzle was solved and they proceeded to load their two cars with various clothing and household goods. Molly had suggested they provide such essentials along with toys.

"Are you hungry?" Isaiah asked them. "Come in to the kitchen and take some food. We have too much. Take it with you." They trooped out laden with boxes of baked goods. People stopped bringing food, until the word went out that more food was needed for the staff workers, and that too soon got out of hand once more.

Arguments erupted in the kitchen as people not in the high council voiced their opinions on how best to manage the operation. Everyone spoke loudly at once. What gifts were to be purchased? Which names on which list were to take precedence? Who was to oversee distribution? Was cash a superior gift to use, in some situations? After all Jacob's stout was gone Isaiah sipped black coffee, watching them in utter amazement.

They got excited, speaking roughly to one another, but they did not hold grudges, apparently, even though they squabbled fiercely. In the end they closed ranks, as a sort of elite force, able to steel themselves for the battle at hand. It was decided they should begin making deliveries to the smaller homes at random. This was done at Molly's behest. She wanted them to make it known these gifts were from the people of St. Margaret's. They were to say they wanted to enlist their help in distributing these gifts more widely. Some began to combine this work with random caroling.

Janey was doing the lion's share of the administrative functions. She was keeping her personnel focused on the matters at hand. A few words from her about Molly and everyone fell into line at once. Jacob came and went, often with hardly any notice by anyone else. They said he was handling things very well, but he was not really doing well at all. Isaiah was making runs like a bootlegger of olden times. He often had someone riding shotgun who gave him directions as they were received on the phone.

The time came to start drawing the operation to a close, and there was no good news on Molly's progress. Janey gave out the latest information to the people who came to the house just to be near others who cared for her in the same way they did. Janey spoke frequently with the nurse they knew. She was able to get messages to Molly, and in return she received suggestions on how to wind up the operation.

Late one afternoon Isaiah was lingering in the yard; for the first time there was nothing to do. He was about to go home, when he noticed Charles was sitting alone in the Watchtower. He was staring upwards. Isaiah went back to the wall and looked up and caught his attention. The priest held up a bottle of amaretto as way of invitation.

"It doesn't feel like Christmas is so near, does it?" Isaiah was looking at the lights strung in the trees at the Grotto."

"That was Molly's idea, to use those lights. I said it was not really proper for that setting; but she insisted, saying the children would enjoy it."

"May I?" Isaiah reached for the glass.

"I'm not sure . . ." The priest's face seemed to be wracked by some arcane question.

"You're right." Isaiah leaned back. "I don't know what I was thinking." He looked upwards.

"Oh, I don't care. Here."

"I don't care either," Isaiah whispered, after taking a sip of the sweet fiery liquid. Both men looked upwards, into the firmament; that unknown totality that looks down on so much mortal ache, and so much more.

"Here's to the return of that fellowship of Isaac's lost picnic table." Charles spoke with strange accent; taking the glass back and quaffing the contents and then pouring more from the bottle. Isaiah's chest rumbled with a painful sort of humor. They were both wearing heavy coats and stocking caps. There was no need to speak of Molly's condition; they knew she was stable and there had been no more recent updates. They watched the heavenly lights, and how their warm breaths and hopes were dispersing as ghostly vapors into the cold atmosphere.

"We used to talk at great length about the letters of St. Paul; she was utterly taken with the mysticism. That line about elemental spirits of the universe, which she interprets for herself to mean the vast inherent meaning that evades our comprehension." He looked up as if straining to see something.

"Be warned, Father, I'm not of Paul, nor Apollos, rather I am one of Margaret's pupils."

Charles turned to look at his friend, startled to hear this reference to one of the Pauline letters. He knew it was due to Molly's influence. "I could say me, too. To be sure, she is hardly one of mine.

"I've learned she ponders things more deeply than one would imagine." Isaiah was almost numb in his ravaged emotions.

"I can't tell you how many times she has thrown the dogma in my face." Charles sat upright; he was excited. "She composes her own midrashim, like a brilliant child at play. She nurtures heretical ideas, with no compunction whatsoever. She believes Jesus was merely mortal. She has inspired her own cult in those secret chapters of hers."

"If you don't mind me asking, why do you think she stays in the Church?"

"Because, 'It's just so human'; as she says. She's let me know, this is her parish as much as mine. She has detractors, who believe I'm harboring Gnostics in my congregation." He looked over at Isaiah, as if to make sure that idea had sunk in.

"Gnosis means knowledge." Isaiah said in such a quiet voice it could not be distinguished as statement or question. He glanced at the cleric; there was no visible torment. He could divine only a sort of trembling light, as the flame of honest passions bathed his features.

They looked up to peer at the wheeling universe, which appeared to earthly eyes as a mechanism that has long been frozen in place. The sky was partially clear, studded with stars, and there was a mix of heavy clouds laden with snowy materials. In the quiet sweep of the night one sensed vast movements were taking place. Little flakes appeared, touching them with a sense of wonder. In a twinkling the men were glancing around eagerly, wanting to know how much of this sacred material might fall on their ground.

"She's my better half too, you know."

"What?" Isaiah was surprised by this expression, most often used by married folk, to tout the quality of a spouse, and thereby draw attention to the genteel sensibility of the speaker, who recognizes and has come into holding a share of such virtue.

"She *is*," the priest insisted, as Isaiah stared at him, rather at a loss.

"I imagine I could say something similar."

"St. Paul teaches that nothing good dwells in the flesh. Molly doesn't believe any such debasement of life can be true. I don't either. She has a profound gift for finding the humanity in every formulation. In every soul, I might say."

"Yes." Isaiah breathed out lightly, staring out into empty space.

"She's never read Spinoza, not very seriously, but I fear she understands his noble heart better than I do. She strives against herself, sometimes; she understands all the intricate powers of love . . ." He lost his voice.

"When I first heard she was sick, I had the terrible thought that not all losses are equal, and I know I shouldn't think like that, but I just—"

"Thoughts are not actions."

"That's true."

"Margaret said that to me once. Casting aside another piece of scripture." He chuckled lightly to himself. "This morning I was having Irish coffee, taking comfort with Lucretius and Ecclesiastes, feeling rather sorry for myself. Thinking of her brought me out of it."

"Do you know Latin pretty well?"

"I used to, at one time. I was a very diligent student."

"I have to bring my friend Timothy up here; he's seeing a woman who taught Latin her whole life. I think you two would have a lot to talk about."

"Yes, you should do that, certainly." The priest gazed upwards and thought of an old Gnostic idea, "She who is before all things."

"Hey! What are you guys doing?" Cody yelled up to them. Isaiah held up the glass he was now holding. Cody stomped slowly up the stairs, his breath puffing out like steam from a trusty old engine. He stood at the top of the flight, looking outward.

"Does anybody need anything?" Isaiah asked him.

"Don't think so." Cody looked around at the house. "Check with Janey." His head was bare and the cold breeze tousled his hair. His cheeks were burning red.

"I did. She said she's good."

"How are you doing?" Charles asked.

"I'm chauffeuring Jacob around, keeping him moving. He's pretty good at Sophie's, able to relax, somewhat. At Luke's they don't say anything, they play music. It's the most incredible fusion of genres you've ever heard."

"How is Jacob doing?" Charles asked.

Cody grimaced, looking at each of them in turn. "He's a mess. He's been talking about going to Spain.

It sounds awful. She was planning a trip, for next year. Something about the mother of St. Louis being from Spain? I don't know, but he starts talking about doing that with her, and then he's whispering to himself, in this weird voice." He inhaled deeply, and expelled a small, warm cloud into the frigid, ravenous atmosphere. "I've seen him suffer before, but I've never seen him afraid of anything. He's terrified."

Cody stared at the sky. No one said anything, until someone called from the house. It was time to go back to the hospital, where Jacob would once more be imploring the nurses to make allowances for him and let him see his wife; always to no avail.

At this time Isaiah was hearing from more of his old circle; he was acceding to invitations to gather as in the old days. Now that his work was having this late resurgence, he himself was also in more demand. According to Theo the website was 'going gangbusters.' Which wasn't proof of anything, but it was fun to be associated with the hubbub.

They all wanted to know about his decision to move to Ferdinand. Many asked him why. He did not know what to tell them. The issue touched sorely upon other matters he was not willing to discuss with them. It would have seemed like a profanation to attempt an explanation of Margaret to any who did not know her. Timothy never raised her name in front of these others, understanding his friend's sorrow.

"Should I grow a beard?" Isaiah asked. "To improve my artistic value?"

"You should!" Marx slapped his knee. "I'll grow mine back."

"No, no, that's not happening." Patricia asserted.

"Did you buy binoculars?" Timothy demanded. Isaiah had not; he promised to do so. They decided to make a trip to Chouteauville, to watch eagles. They promised he would have a good time. He was able to let everything happen now without effort, or so it seemed. It was a simple matter of going on with things, even though nothing was quite right, and you couldn't talk about the reasons why that was so with anyone else.

Theo cared for his father in a way he never imagined he would have to, or want to, hefting the onus of the business onto his shoulders. Once in a while he wanted to make sure about something in particular.

"Dad, I'm not sure on some of the pricing."

"Do what you think is best."

Theo stared at him. "We should discuss some things."

"I know, but can we do it later?"

"Sure. Have you heard anything?"

"Nothing new. She's still on the breathalyzer."

"Dad. About Christmas, is it alright to come over early for a few hours, like we said, with the girls, and Dilsey."

"Yes." He turned to face him. "Yes, of course."

"They like Dilsey."

"Yes, of course, I would miss all of you very much if you did not come over."

Then his world was jolted back into balance once more. He drove to Ferdinand and walked across the back porch and into the kitchen, only to be accosted by a madwoman. She was right in his face, grapping both his shoulders. It was Janey, her fingers sinking to his bones.

"She coming home!" Janey exclaimed. Isaiah asked her a question, but she repeated what she had just said, and said it again. She released him and began whirling in a small circle, as if chanting an inaudible refrain to herself. It meant she would *be* home, she would *be* herself again, she would *be* with them again.

For a while Isaiah stayed away from Ferdinand. He called Jacob periodically to verify Molly's convalescence was going well. Jacob told him at last that he should feel free to call Molly. When he finally did so, she immediately asked him if he was ready to look at some houses. "Because there's one on Darst that's perfect for you. It had a workshop, in the back, letting out on the common area. You have to see it." Her voice had not regained the old vigor, but the subtle timbre was unmistakable, and it was wondrous to hear.

He began to haunt the Botanical Gardens, taking many photographs of the Persephone statue. By some stroke of good fortune, Gretchen asked to accompany him, and she had to strike a bargain, letting Anne tag along too. They trooped about the grounds for hours; the girls speaking to him politely and often chattering to each other as though he were not even present. His head was swimming; they were revealing their personalities to him.

He started a drawing of Persephone, to be presented to Molly as a belated birthday gift. She had been in the hospital on December seventh, and the family would gather belatedly to celebrate the event. The day before that he brought his picture to Jacob, whom he found stacking firewood in the yard.

"No, you give it to her." He said. "She will come to the door."

"No. I have other errands. I'm quite busy these days. I may have to buy new work boots."

Jacob looked at the picture. "Ah, she's really going to like this. Your granddaughters, standing on either side of the statue? Ah, good job, I. Thomas."

Jacob motioned for him to come back to the wall. They stood in silence, staring at the red cedars. He found if one remained very quiet he might hear these junipers whispering ever so faintly in the cold air.

"Don't forget, Christmas Eve, right here. Come anytime after ten or so." Jacob spoke at last.

"I thought it was supposed to be after Midnight Mass."

"There's not going to be a mass this year; so we're moving things up a little."

"Should I bring anything?"

"Well, as I told you, for the Sorrow Club, you might have a few words prepared for someone."

"Sure."

"People think we pray to the dead."

"Well, why not?" Isaiah laughed.

"We'll see you then, neighbor. It's supposed to be cold, so dress accordingly."

Isaiah found himself feeling more cheerful than he had in a very long time. He purchased more presents than he ever had before. Paying the least for the most was his great challenge. The gifts had to mean something to the person. He purchased a Christmas tree for the first time in years and Gretchen helped him decorate it. Everything he was doing meant more to him. All was happening as though he'd fallen into a strange harmony with an elusive mysticism, which he did not understand, nor feel the need to unravel. He could not explain himself to anyone, except for Molly; and it wasn't time for that yet. In his work he was roiling these confusing emotions into new things. He was doing a series he called abstract homes.

Then it was Christmas Eve, and the sun rose and arced over the day; as the light waned the houses began to glow in anticipation of the hallowed hours of sacred ritual. Isaiah travelled north and found a fire roaring and crackling near the ruined wall. He was the only person present who was not of the family circle.

"Molly said we had to include you." Jacob explained. "For this is the year we place the eternal child in his booth at our memorial wall."

Isaiah laughed, looking up towards the house.

Jacob handed Isaiah a bottle. "This has become my traditional drink for this occasion, at least for this year." They sat in the Watchtower quaffing Guinness stout from bottles. Isaiah admired the elegant label with the harp and the moment was printed on his memory.

"This won't take long, this year. It's so cold."

A traditional rendition of "Silent Night" was playing in the naked trees.

Molly came out of the house with her children and grandchildren. She was draped in a long hooded coat, her face was partially obscured. It was thought that she had probably acquired an increased resistance to the virus, but the doctors were hesitant in their predictions.

She carried the stolen crèche baby to the wall and set him down in a curious structure Jacob had fashioned. Some years back they had inaugurated the rite of having each person in attendance speak briefly of a person he or she had lost, however recently, or long ago. Sometimes they spoke of other people they never got a chance to properly know, and how they liked to think of that person at certain times, in certain ways.

When he was prompted to speak, Isaiah eulogized Stephen. "He went out to try and tell the fatal truth about the flaws in our nature. He faced all that plagues our world; wanting to know if we might find vaccines for corruption and violence. He found it necessary to battle dragons, and he lost his life." Isaiah choked up. He had intended to say more, but knew it was not meet."

Molly caught his eye and smiled very delicately. "He's still able to move your spirit?"

"Yes, he definitely is." He raised his bottle, exclaiming, "To Stephen, a good man who sought the truth!" Everyone amplified his cheer and imbibed a cordial.

The others began to take turns, speaking of persons they had lost. They told amusing anecdotes, applying a blend of pathos and humor. It seemed the very stuff of life's own wisdom; rich in the pith of sentiments we like to voice, but have a hard time heeding.

Isaiah began to think of his father; he had known not to speak of him in this setting, for he would have completely lost his composure. It was good to recite a benediction in his mind. "In childhood I saw him one way, and then, as a grown man, all that changed, and now that I am even older, my perspective has shifted even more dramatically. Each soul deserves the privacy of its own temple. I believe he chose to live as he did, for reasons known only to him. He was a good man, and he never bemoaned his choices. His was a generous spirit that I was fortunate to know."

At one point Father Charles, upon seeing them outside, turned on the 'Christmas' lights in the Grotto. Molly turned to him, and said, "Come." They strolled into the copse of fragrant evergreens, cast in the veils of diaphanous lights.

"Here." She had removed from her coat a little gargoyle figurine and presented it to him. "Frances gave me her collection before she passed . . ."

He thanked her and held it as a prize he had won.

"For your new studio." She began speaking to him in a soft, trembly voice, that he strained to hear at first, and then his mind adjusted and there was no other sound in the universe. She spoke of the 'heretical' Gospel of Truth, which some scholars believe was a product of that unorthodox mind of Valentinus. He had believed that people who come to know themselves truly, as God's children, are able to enter a higher realm of consciousness.

They listened to the chilly breezes moving the fir trees.

"In Philippians there's a passage, "'Finally, brethren'—always with the brethren—'whatever is pure, whatever is lovely, whatever is gracious, if there is any excellence, if there is anything worthy of praise, think about these things.' I need to do this more, and spend less time trying to arrange things to my own liking."

They moved over to stand by her black cherry tree, and stood on opposite sides looking up into the brilliant sky. She put one gloved hand onto the trunk of the tree, the other rested on her breast.

"I no longer want to search for reasons in my faith. I want to be more open to life. I am prolife, and pro-choice; just as life is, I suppose. It's easy to find the right words to direct us, not so easy to live up to them."

"No doubt."

"I ask too much of people. I'm not always reasonable."

"You're better than that, you're true, you're—"

"Once you get your house—

"If I ever manage to find one."

"Once you move into your house on Darst—I have them holding it for you—if it ever seems like I'm asking too much of you, please be patient with me, don't hold it against me that I have this compulsion—"

"Molly! There's no question of any of that coming between us. Treat me as you will, the honor is mine. Being your friend . . ."

"Our friendship is very strong, don't you think?"

"I do." His heart was too full to speak further; but his mind blurted out like a child that needs to verify something that he has just inferred. "It's unbreakable."

"When I was leaving, I saw other people waiting to hear the fate of their loved ones." She shook her head, almost imperceptibly. "Something has changed in me. I no longer believed in suffering as a means of proving one's character. We should be striving to learn the causes of suffering, so as to alleviate as much as we can. Oh, I don't know; suffering is a part of life." Her voice was hardly more than a whisper, but her heart's throbbing passed through Isaiah's being. They looked upwards in silence.

"Say, I ran into Mulligan down at Sistah's. He was wearing his new coat. He wanted to show it to me. He made me feel the fabric. He told me, 'Margaret gave this to me.' He was very happy about it."

"Others bought it. I didn't do hardly anything."

"Besides starting a charity drive from a hospital bed."

She shook her head gently. "I have grown tired of wallowing in mysticism. In the Gospel of Thomas Jesus is said to have referred to his divine mother, the Holy Spirit. Irenaeus, one of the principal builders of the canon, which he used to establish unity and control, noted that women were especially drawn to heretical groups. So maybe the Holy Spirit needs our guidance!" She laughed in a light, childish manner.

"I've been going through Paul's letters, but so much of it seems to be going in circles. The moral advice is superb, but the doctrine is all connected to the new god, the Christ, the cross, the suffering, and how that has to be accepted for any chance at salvation, and immortality."

"I know. It's the mark of a human cult; the elevation of one personality over all others. I cannot believe in anything that requires one single person to hold it all up. Look up there. I would imagine there are millions of other sentient, moral species out there. I often wonder how we would measure up against them."

"I'd hate to even guess at that." He said, feeling very calm and happy, just to be there in the cold, staring at the stars, with her.

She quoted a phrase from *The Old Curiosity Shop*, 'And still the game went on, and still the anxious child was quite forgotten.' She turned to smile broadly at him. He could only smile back.

"We better get back with the others. I'm so glad you brought us your Ferdinand baby."

"I'm glad I could find him a good home."

It was not long before Jacob was walking Isaiah to his car, looking pointedly at the gargoyle. "You can come any year you want now. As you've seen, it's become a pretty small circle now. It will start to increase, in time; but no more stolen items. They will not be accepted. That will be our official position anyway." With that he gave him a little shove as way of saying goodbye, and over his shoulder Isaiah could hear him say, "We'll see you, brother."

Isaiah always remembered driving home that night. He was able to secure a nice setting for his gargoyle on his dash, so they could keep an eye on each other. He drove slowly along Hanley Road, which was nearly deserted; peering at the wet stars through a warm mist while listening very intently to his favorite carols. His mind entered the stream of his entire life, as if submerged in some strange, timeless atmosphere. Some ineffable part of his being was roused by the simple fact he was at peace and looking forward to the days to come.

The holiday season marched along in a garish flurry, and then abruptly vanished, after everyone had stopped paying attention. Many forlorn trees were lain at the curb, bare except for a few strands of ironic tinsel, stirred by derisive, or indifferent airs. The new year brought vaccines, a resurgence of hope; a certitude the species had endured (at great cost), and this trial of the flesh was now recorded as that which belongs to our past. Such prophesies are not always reliable; nonetheless, a strenuous exercise of faith strengthens the living force, which has sanctified but one eternal song that we know of for the time being, "Life goes on."

38

When daffodils again came early to flower, dance, and pollinate, Isaiah was living one block over from Molly and Jacob. To his way of thinking this nicely settled plot lay in the verdant landscape like something rendered by those half-crazed masters of past ages.

His new dwelling was folded snugly into a corner of what had once been an outflung woodland suburb. It was now just another puzzle piece forming the inner ring, recording another layer of natural growth. Out in back of his house the land fell away and merged into a broad piece of mostly level terrain that reached out across the fringes of many properties. There was a small, trickling stream that, on rare occasions, inundated that lower tract of ground. This minute tributary wended under Darst to join another small artery, which itself flowed more freely, and further on met up with the great Moline creek. That proud stream has long been renowned among children of this region.

During high school Stephen had lived in a house at the other end of this rustic expanse, which many treated as common ground. Isaiah recalled how they once made a campfire inside a stand of cottonwood trees, and told ghost stories. They were smoking pot, and were swayed towards the occult, by that inducement, and the whispering of the shifting, fire-lambent trees. They became quite emotional, and were laughing way too hard at the prospect of being afraid of whatever might be out there. This innocent party had been comprised of Stephen, Deborah, himself, and some girl whose name he could no longer remember.

Standing at his kitchen window he had to smile at this return to his own tiny part of the world. His coffee being cold, he dashed the dregs of his cup into the sink. It occurred to him that Gretchen would be arriving any minute to help him set up for his big day. She was running late, and this made him even more happy. He started to move around the house fussing with his arrangement; but the weather was so perfect, he had to go outside to feel the breath of the day on his face.

He had been reading Tolkien again; and sometimes he pictured himself climbing the Lonely Mountain. Jacob had jested he might have some Hobbit blood moving through his unsettled bloodlines. At times he referred to him as Meriwether Baggins; or just Merry; which Raphael construed as more of a gloss on the influence of one of the heretics he had introduced more recently, that of Henry Miller.

Since the first days of his resettlement it was his custom to take walks along the drowsy streets. He liked to usher in and enjoy the dusk; watching as the sunlight dissolved into his own brooding consciousness of life's precious depths. He passed like a ghost before the yellow windows of quiet homes. He enjoyed the sharp little sounds as he sauntered around his block. He always wound up back at his house leading a procession of unearthly sensations that belonged to him alone.

When Easter came he walked up to Molly's place late in the afternoon, as she had directed him to do. It was soon apparent, this was her feast day. As soon as he entered the yard he heard rushes of her musical laughter. It was one of those rare days when she let herself become tipsy. He was greeted warmly by many very satiated guests who were just starting to leave. At that late hour everyone had fallen into a state of mellow torpor. The day was cool, but sunny, with just a wisp of a breeze; the radiance of the season entered everyone's sluggish blood to excite the simmering of all tender mercies.

Molly sat with him for a short while. She spoke of people and their usual affairs while he lazed in the luxury of being one of her confidants. She abruptly rose and bid him follow. There was a tiny lilac sprouting in the wall, and she told him he must come later and remove it for transplanting into his yard. He had much to tell her, but she had said goodbye, for now. He smiled and twirled about to meander homeward.

There was no beginning, nor end, to such conversations anymore. The periods in between were laden with so much shared knowledge, and perennial whorls of sympathy, he often could hear her words in his mind, as though they were inextricable from those parts of himself that formulated his own speech. He was too embarrassed to tell even her how much her sentiments enriched his solitude.

By June another school year was over, and the chimney swifts were active in their work, and professions of faith in same. The suburb's wild plethora of fresh, vibrant leafage fashioned a fabric of spotless tissue for playing healthy airs for higher aspirations of this life-moldy earth. Isaiah was glad to experience, close at hand, the myriad changes in the natural growth of all living things. Watching the starlings sing, as he sat in his yard, was better than sitting restless among a rigid crowd, arranged in tiers, setting aside life's mystery to enjoy a human composer's work.

Molly would often drop by when she was out walking, taking time to inspect his grounds, making brief comments. She had subtle ways of intimating what else might be done to improve things. The way her face twisted might cause some of his ideas to be quashed at the outset. At the same time she had become rather tactful these days. She didn't insist on much of anything, although she usually left him with a feeling there was a lot more he had better consider.

By autumn he was taking on airs like a native. She had enlisted him in many of her causes and he was kept quite busy. His calendar was a mess of active notes speaking to him of his stated obligations. And today he was to speak to his first chapter meeting; and he was taking a break, sitting in his side yard, which formed a level shelf of ground. On three sides this plot of earth fell gently away. On the lower level of his backyard there was a very old maple tree. It had weathered storms, and bore the scars, and every year hosted a brood of starlings.

On this verdant shelf of ground, under the branches of the maple, he had placed two sturdy iron chairs, where he could look out over the common area. Each chair had its own peony bush stationed at its side. Isaiah was sitting here, enjoying the pristine October day, when Gretchen arrived. She had agreed to help him get everything in order in exchange for access to his computer, the one in his studio.

She needed his help in learning the software which he used for editing images. She was a quick study and hardly needed his assistance these days. More satisfying was how she sought his opinions of her work. He was enthralled to be watching her put her novel visions onto the screen, as he provided suggestions on various techniques she might consider using. She had begun to share her ideas with him as a fellow guild member. The strange dialect of her young exited voice, burgeoning so rapidly with so many interests, made him chortle to himself for hours.

Leaving her alone he began perusing his notes. He had to prepare himself to address the 'select' Charles Dickens chapter. She had inducted him into her club while laid up in the hospital; informing him he ought to get ready to attend the first meeting. Then after she was released she rescinded her decree and told him he should wait until the master class was ready to begin holding meetings. She was changing things around, however; some months earlier she had decided to let other people start hosting some of her chapters.

Isaiah had been rehearsing in his mind what he was going to say to the people who had read a preponderance of the Teacher's teeming oeuvre. He was eager to give them information about the author's life, hoping to instigate a lively discussion. He had written some notes, but in fact, lately he found those to be rather tedious, and probably incoherent besides, so he laid them aside and strolled about the grounds.

Timothy and Patricia suddenly appeared in his yard, looking jaunty in their vests and other regalia. They wanted to see if he would like to join them for some birdwatching.

"I have my first book club meeting today."

"Why weren't we invited?" Timothy demanded.

"You were." Isaiah replied impassively.

"Oh yes, I forgot. Well, we were just over here, and you didn't say anything. I thought maybe—well, what time does that start?"

"Hey, was that a pileated woodpecker? Can we go out there?" Patricia pointed to the mature trees out in the middle of the great common field, and they both lunged forward in step.

"Sure, why not?" Isaiah said softly once they had gone too far to hear him.

He chuckled as he watched them tramping across the field. He decided he better make sure there was not more to be done in the house. He straightened up some more. He kept getting up to verify he had finished certain tasks. He had no idea how many people were coming. He felt a tinge of irritation at Molly, and then himself, for not having clarified these issues beforehand. Timothy and Patricia came back and said they were going for a walk around the neighborhood.

It was not long before the people (many he had not expected) began arriving. They said they had heard from Molly about this 'thing' and thought they might drop by, and see what was happening. More stragglers appeared, ready to make themselves at home. None of these people had ever been to his house before; so apparently it was only natural for them to explore his quarters as freely as pest inspectors.

Many wanted to visit his studio on the bottom level. He showed them the way to the basement, and then pausing in the kitchen he listened to them talking about the works he had in progress. He had left these out for their viewing. He had hidden his portrait of Molly in his bedroom, because he didn't want people to see that at this time.

He feared he did not have enough food and drinks for his guests, as they continued to arrive in droves. He moved among the people who were congregating outside, and then he found himself standing at the foot of his driveway, greeting people and ushering them part way into the yard like a grand marshal. At one point he saw Theo walking down the street alone.

"Where's Dilsey?"

"She's at Molly's. She wanted to talk to her . . . about something."

"Some thing?" Isaiah could see his son was distraught.

Theo looked at him, and then began walking across the yard. Isaiah followed across the the small side yard, down a small flight of stone steps, and out into the field.

"What is it, Theo?"

"She's pregnant."

"What? Oh, that's . . ." He stopped himself, seeing his son's face. "There's nothing wrong with her? Is there a problem—"

"She's not sure what she wants to do."

"Oh."

"I'm not sure what to say to her."

Someone up at the house started calling for Isaiah's attention.

"Go on." Theo said.

"I wouldn't worry, I mean—"

"No, I know. Dad, it's alright. Go on, do what you have to do, go on now."

He put his hand on Theo's shoulder, and stared at his downcast face. "You have to wait and see—"

"I know." Theo looked at his father with a peculiar expression, reflective of a certain disgust at having to deal with all the usual words. "Go on! See about your people."

"You mean Molly's mob!" Isaiah nearly shouted as he jaunted towards his house.

In the studio a little group was huddled around several pieces of a series he was calling Celestial Nocturnes. Upon completion he assigned each one a sequential number. At first it was just for fun, but then Molly's daughter Sophie had been extravagant in her praise of the first one. He sold it to her, after he tried to give it to her. She had gone to Theo, who had spoken with Molly, and they struck a bargain.

After that he sold every piece when it was finished, as word spread among the congregation. He was including exact star formations that fixed the perspective as seen from Ferdinand, at certain points in the festive calendar. For the first time he felt like a journeyman; one who has learned his trade. He often wore white overalls when he worked, striking off pieces that made no exquisite demands upon his psyche. He was free to pursue private visions, enjoying the process as a devout novice, rather shy of the world's glare. He often whistled as he succumbed to unconscious reveries.

"Have you sold this one yet?" A woman asked him, as he entered his studio.

"I don't really know. I've just finished it. You would have to talk to Theo."

"What is this, though? Is that like a cross, just forming up?"

"It might become that, each one is supposed to evoke a sacred theme as we see it from here. How lasting is it, you know?"

He explained to them how he saw the unerring galactic furnaces as our proving grounds. He was using images produced by the Hubble Space Telescope to create his own unique formations. He gladly expounded upon the idea of gold being a perfect metaphor.

"The Aztecs believed gold was the sweat of the sun." He held in his fingers a delicate cross hanging from a nail above his drafting table. "All these atoms may have been formed in the collision of two neutron stars."

Molly had given him this cross as a Christmas present.

"For all that you have to bear." She had whispered to him.

Exiting his studio into the backyard, and climbing up into the side yard, he immediately saw that a small circle had formed around someone who was causing a stir.

"Is our sister Margaret here?" Geoffrey was addressing several women, mistaking them for the crones.

"Now, whose sister are you looking for?" One of the woman asked politely, just as Isaiah came over.

"She's not here, Geoff. I expect her any time, but then you know how that goes. Are you hungry? Do you want something to drink?"

Geoffrey just stood there, gazing around at the swarm of people.

"Come with me." Isaiah said and Geoff followed him to the picnic table. "Wait here. I'll let Molly know you're here, okay?" Geoff nodded and began staring out over the field, as if he were taking up his assigned station, and was resolved to remain vigilant for the rest of the afternoon.

Isaiah spent some time outside talking to people and then decided to see if any were in the living room waiting to start the official meeting. There was a lively conversation going on, having nothing to do with books, and he decided to bring Geoff a beer and a plate of food. He chatted with him about the club and invited him to come into the house later to join them there.

"I'll wait for Margaret."

"When she gets here, she will be in the club meeting, I expect."

Geoff looked at him warily, as though he suspected Isaiah was trying to fool him because he was considered a simpleton.

"Well, you just wait here then." Isaiah told him. "I'm sure Molly will be coming soon. He watched the man revert to his dogged surveillance of his surroundings.

Isaiah returned to the end of his driveway to welcome more people arriving at his soiree. Looking up Darst he saw Molly and Dilsey gliding down the sidewalk; both women were attired in full-length dresses. Dilsey's had no collar and wide sleeves, and was decorated with a modern pattern of meshed squares. Molly's dress was a solid maroon color, with a demure collar, slender sleeves, the front was overlaid with a brocade of intricate floral stitching.

"I wish I had a camera," Isaiah said to himself; and then caught himself. Just relishing this moment was the thing to do. It took his breath away, seeing Molly approaching in her sure, stately manner, the heavy folds of her dress unable to mask the gracefulness of her carriage. Her measured steps were contrasted by the wild tossing of her long, flowing mane. She had grown her hair longer, and the silvery mass shone beautifully in the sun.

He began to laugh, seeing that Molly's little neighbor friend was leading her down the hill. He was a standard black poodle, always neatly groomed. He now fell back and pranced at her side with the discipline of a palace guard. He belonged to a retired doctor who lived in the house down on the lower level behind Molly's backyard. This clever dog was adept at escaping from confined spaces, and was now a frequent visitor to her yard.

Apparently the haughty creature enjoyed being around her, observing her as she tended her gardens; for he seldom came up to be petted, and she never fed him.

This was the first time Isaiah had ever seen him escorting her in this outlandish manner. He watched them stop across the street, Molly leaning over to rap him on the snout as she commanded him to go home. She pointed with her arm and stamped her foot, exclaiming,

"You go, now!"

The pooch looked up, as if moved by great sorrow, and then proceeded to trot down a driveway, scale a fence, lope across the yard, and then climb the fence on the other side to return to his property. His master was a retired doctor, who had lately become fascinated by the life of Sir Isaac Newton. He was making a study of that great mind's explorations of religion and alchemy. Molly had recently convinced him to host his own ad hoc book club to share his knowledge of that genius.

"Are you going to be able to feed everyone?" Molly asked Isaiah.

"Not sure, I wasn't expecting so many. These people aren't all here for the book club, are they?"

"What now?" She was already taking a survey of who was there, and peering off at his neighbor, Cicely Morgan, who was out in her yard, taking note of all the commotion. Once she noticed Molly their eyes locked and they nodded gravely to one another.

"I think I'll have a word with Cicely."

Isaiah turned to ask her something, but she was already gone, so he ambled over to his chairs under the maple tree. He stood there, observing those at the picnic table down below, which was more like a large outdoor booth. His picnic table was a custom job, constructed under the influence of many bottled spirits. Geoffrey sat there with Jacob, Cody, and Timothy and Patricia, all under the large umbrella.

Isaiah listened as Jacob expounded upon his fondness for the song, "After the Gold Rush." "It starts with Neil on his upright piano, those frail notes, the trembling keys, that choirboy's strained voice."

"The sadness and wonder of lost idealism that won't die."

"Sad, fresh, wild regret over days that are no more." Raphe piped up.

"The single flugelhorn provides a more fully resolved note to the disillusioned voice—"

"Which a critic called 'pre-adolescent whining,' right?" Marx interjected.

Isaiah could see Jacob restraining himself, knowing it would be impossible to say all he wanted in this present company. Everyone was eager to have a say in all matters.

While Isaiah listened to them speaking of music he was cognizant of something Molly had told him. He was hearing the winsome exchange of playful souls. Patricia also lauded Young's song, comparing it to "that mortal longing that wafts from the Byzantium poems of Yeats."

"It has a tone that sweeps across time."

"That scene of being in the basement."

"At least you were never burned out when you lived on Allen Place; not altogether." Cody challenged, with a peculiar note of satisfaction.

Isaiah began reflecting fondly on days that were, and were no more, when Gretchen came up, seeking his advice on something. She sat down on the arm of the other chair; coming to rest as neatly as a cat landing on a windowsill. She asked a question, and as soon as she received an answer she vanished. No time to waste! He marveled over the apparition of that young, excited face; it had been composed with the concerted intensity of the highest purpose. Her eyes had glistened with the bright, virtuous expectation the world would gladly conspire to promote her pursuit of happiness.

He ranged his vision around as old paintings rose to mind; the gorgeous portrayals of saints and martyrs, their assisting crowds of angels. Looking upwards he was much taken by the yellow leaves that fluttered above him. They were as airborne relics of some ruined choir. This made him think of stained glass windows; here all the raw pieces were yet to be assembled, having been lain out as on a shop floor. All was in perfect readiness for hands to take up impossible designs.

He noticed that Molly had gone back to his neighbor's, and was talking to Cicely. Her husband worked at chores in his yard. Isaiah walked over to talk to Mr. Morgan.

"You got quite a crowd going over there." Mr. Morgan said.

"You should come over for drinks."

"Maybe so. We'll see." Mr. Morgan was a stout man with broad, smooth features. His hair was dense, gray and curly. His visage exuded vast contentment. He was a retired policeman; his two children were grown, married, and raising children. Isaiah was still learning the names of all the little ones. In their first encounters Morgan had been confused by Isaiah; he was a difficult one to figure.

In short order he pieced together a new type in his official registry. The man hardly cared what anyone thought of him. It was clear in the way he wandered around when outside; he didn't care about appeasing the larger world for any reason. He could not know of the man's journey before he had come nicely to the end of all that business.

Morgan appreciated especially his neighbor's obvious respect for property; his own and that of others. Morgan had started some years earlier cultivating roses and Isaiah was eager to learn about such things. He had taken many photographs, while crawling around on the ground. He had meant to paint a watercolor of his neighbor's house; the roses would have to be very prominent in the foreground. He had not yet done the painting, and he chided himself for being overconfident in his ability to produce; but that felt right, too, now. Morgan had grown to appreciate Isaiah's eccentric ways. His wife remained leery of his suspicious hesitancy in stating opinions on important issues.

"Is there any way we can borrow your grill?" Isaiah asked.

"What do you have to cook?"

"I'll have to get something."

Mr. Morgan laughed, emitting a shrill whistling sound. "When you going to build that pit you keep talking about? You need to quit making plans, and start finishing some of them. So, you didn't expect so many people?"

"No."

"Did Molly help you set it up?"

"Yes, that's why—" He could not finish. They both laughed freely.

"Well, why don't you see about getting something to grill and I can do that right here. I was going to anyway, for us."

Cicely had gone inside and Molly came over to where the men were standing. They began making arrangements to enlist someone to procure viands to barbecue.

"It's hard to sit inside talking about books on a day like this," she said to them.

"Molly, we're going to turn over some of the common ground, plant a large garden." Mr. Morgan explained.

"We may learn who owns it then!" She said quickly.

"Have to wait and see."

Molly had hoped to convince Cicely to host a book club event. It had not gone so well. She wondered if she was being overly insensitive in her persistence. She would have to try again later on, when it seemed more fortuitous. She looked around musingly, as from an outpost recently planted in virgin territory. She was not dismayed when thwarted, not as she had been in the not so distant past. She knew real progress moved according to forces that were more mystic than those pushing the tides.

For some time now she was feeling more at ease, about everything. There was no place she could not go in her parish, there was no trepidation in her breast. She had not any fears of being rebuffed. Indeed every mischance was an opportunity to learn something; about herself, for instance, when her perceptions or intuition had proven faulty.

Molly began walking towards Isaiah's house as both men watched her with keen appreciation.

"She's something." Mr. Morgan said, his head nodding ever so slightly.

"Yes she is." Isaiah said softly, thinking of her strange, majestic serenity.

"I believe Cicely's coming around, she said something about taking on a chapter. On her own, mind you!"

Isaiah exchanged a glance with Morgan's wry visage, before returning to his own party. He jogged upstairs to use the bathroom; on his way back downstairs he heard voices coming from his bedroom. He pushed open the door, rather warily, and found Natalie Kinfe, and a few other people, who were unknown to him. All were discussing his portrait of Molly. Natalie had propped the picture up against his headboard. She was critiquing his colors, and touching upon certain of his signature techniques, in a way he had never heard before.

"And what is this?" He said to his trespassers. None paid any attention to his vexation. He was glad he had made his bed; it was quite presentable thanks to Molly's housewarming gifts.

"This is a departure." Natalie nodded as she explained. "Subtle, but yes, I can see . . ."

"I wasn't going to show this one yet."

The other people quietly departed as Natalie squared herself in front of Isaiah and adopted a proprietary attitude. Once they were alone she moved around the room, looking at everything, stopping before two old photographs placed above a large dresser.

"Who are these two, now?"

"My parents."

"Oh." She turned back to the portrait.

"Let me say, you've done something with this one. Isaiah, really, this one has, oh, the obvious change in idiom, but you've done something else." She was leaning over, staring at the piece."

"Don't say it's rather pretty."

"Oh stop! You've turned to Rembrandt, *and* Sargent, I can tell about these things. I sense the pencil beneath the paint. When did you start doing things like this? And who is this?"

"Very recently. You probably haven't met her; Molly Gates?"

"No, is she here?"

"She's wearing a long burgundy dress, she has—"

"She's the one with all that striking white hair!" She read the answer on his face. "Oh, yes, I *saw her* with a man outside." She looked again at the painting. "She has a way about her."

"She does."

"Oh, now I see what you've done here." She was leaning over, looking at the cross. "I *have* to talk to her."

"Natalie, how did you come to be here?" His eyes assayed her person; the elegant outfit, the finely sculptured coiffure, her smoothly-textured, wondrously cosmetic face, and the harsh, flashing jargon of jewelry. The ornamental richness weighed on her as though she had been prepared for a tomb. He had to smile; she rather stood out among this crowd he was hosting.

"The front door was left wide open, and no one there to greet me. I followed someone downstairs—the place was just being overrun—no one knew where you were, and then some person spoke of having just discovered *the* portrait upstairs."

"And naturally it was assumed everyone had the right to ransack my quarters—"

"These are your guests, aren't they? I just followed along. And now I've found you!" She noticed he was having fun with her. "You've really changed, now I see."

"I have?"

"You used to want to know what *I* was hearing, out there, in my world."

"I still do."

"Oh stop. *Please*. When have you contacted me? You're incorrigible. You always have been, in your own way."

Jacob appeared in the doorway, wanting to ask Isaiah about the beer shortage causing a panic with the crew at the picnic table.

"I don't want to say they're getting ugly, but the honor of our table is at stake, Merry."

Isaiah said he would defray someone's trip to Paul's Market to replenish their stores. In the meantime, Isaiah introduced Jacob to Natalie, who sized him up in a second.

"This is your wife?" She asked, indicating the portrait with her hand.

Jacob now noticed it and moved closer to the portrait. He stared with an open mouth at the subtle expression he knew so well.

"He's made a medieval saint of her." Natalie exclaimed with quiet dignity.

"What do you think?" Isaiah asked him. "Do you like it?" He was very anxious.

"Yes." He replied, in breathless tones. His wife was positioned against the garden wall, bathed in the light of a fire, the cosmos formed an aureole around her white hair. Isaiah had meant to suggest one of those original followers of the way.

"The look in those eyes." Jacob tried to articulate his appreciation, "and that expression of hers. The light on her face, and the cross there, how that glows in the darkness." His voice failed him again. Natalie looked at Isaiah, smiling in a peculiar, almost gloating, and proud manner. And she was feeling intense, sorrowful pride; bearing witness to the completion of her role as patroness.

"When is this going to be ready?" Jacob asked.

Isaiah made a smacking sound with his lips. "Not quite sure. I probably have to come back and finish it, just a little more—"

"No!" Natalie spoke dramatically. "It *is* finished. Look at it, now. You cannot touch this again. You can't start your infernal fussing around with this one. It's on its own now. "It's alive, more captivating than you can see yet."

"It breathes with her mystery." Jacob whispered.

"I know what this would bring at my gallery. I am sure you've gotten your money's worth, Mr. Gates."

"Well, no money has actually changed hands." Jacob said somewhat feebly.

"Oh, well that *is* perfect." Natalie said, a confused look coming onto her heavily painted features.

"When can we pick it up?"

"Whenever you want to, I guess."

"Is something the matter?" Jacob asked. "Is it about—"

"No, no." Isaiah divined he was going to ask him about remuneration. "Please, nothing like that . . ."

"He labored over this one." Natalie laid a finger on her chin, as she addressed Jacob. "He gets peevish, just like a child, when he has to part with one that has tested him. After he prevails, he comes back to us in his grand, penitent fashion." Natalie became silent, a triumphant smile lighting up her face, as Isaiah became very pensive.

Jacob noticed how these two people were appraising one another in a very intimate manner, and he broke away, wanting to know if he would be the first to tell Molly about her painting. He abruptly turned back and rushed up to grab Isaiah's hand, shaking it vigorously. He looked at him a moment, and then he sprang away once more.

"Molly is the one who convinced you to move here?"

"I suppose she was the prime mover. She can be rather insistent when she sets her mind on something."

"You." She was shaking her head, staring at him.

"What?"

"You've always been able to get women to mother you. You old," she paused, selecting her words, "roguish boy!"

"Why do you say that? It's not even remotely true."

"It is, you know it is."

He shook his head, smiling as if mystified; his eyes whelming with his fondest humors. His present happiness left him speechless.

"We like doing it."

"Were you wanting to stay a while?"

"I can't. Not enough notice. I shouldn't be here now. Oh, you are shameless. Now tell me, when's a good time for you to come and start taking photographs of me? It will take a while, different outfits to consider. And I will want to see all the early sketches. The whole process. I'm an insufferable widow now; you know that, don't you?"

"Yes." He did not know what else to say.

"I'll pay the full price. Come on, then, walk me out. I suppose I ought to leave you to your guests. Do you *really* know all of these people? Yes? Oh stop; I'm chiding you. Look at it, though. My goodness. People were saying you were getting too exclusive to be seen. Should I go and say goodbye to Molly? Who is that she's talking to? Oh, I'll let you go about your affairs, at your own home! My, my; now do you have anything else, you're starting, right now? You have to keep me informed, you know. So, we'll begin next week? It's all settled." At her Mercedes she turned to him.

"Now you must call me."

"I will, I promise."

She fell into him, wrapping him in a tremendous hug, which was unprecedented for them.

Isaiah fell back, rather giddy. All these moments had become like a succession of movie scenes, shown in a trailer depicting a surreal Mardi Gras atmosphere; except the most marvelous aspects here were the quiet sensations passing through his mind. He walked over to speak with Molly, who was once more engaged in a conversation with Cicely Morgan.

"They might be a while." Mr. Morgan said to him.

"What's it about this time?"

"Mr. Meriwether, do you want me to answer that?"

"No, Mr. Morgan, that is not necessary." The two men often addressed each other in a formal diction. The practice began in a palliating moment of humor, continued as ironic playfulness, and took final shape as an exclusive rite. It was also found to be useful in that old art of engendering annoyance among those unknowing others who poke about too freely in what they don't yet understand.

They talked genuinely of steps that had to be taken before commencing with their garden in the spring. They also made reference to numerous yard chores of a more pressing nature, as if each were reciting the articles of a local confederation. They lodged complaints against authority figures not present, with obvious pride, before turning back each to his own fief.

Isaiah mingled for a while. He asked questions to elicit opinions and practiced listening equably to views different from his own. He eventually took a seat in his side yard under the maple tree. At the picnic table below Jacob was in command; the audience had grown quite large. He declared it was time that he inaugurate a book chapter of his own. He explained how he had recently gone back to his Dostoevsky collection.

"This will be called the picnic table chapter, which shall meet at irregular and unscheduled times."

"How would that work?" Raphe asked.

"The directors will convene to establish a schedule, if you insist."

"How will the directors be chosen?" Marx wanted to know.

"That has already been decided. It will be Cody and myself. He will preside in absentia. You can be a minor partner on an interim basis—"

"We should form a central committee."

"And why Dostoevsky?"

"We need to vote."

"No voting; that leads to factions. We start with Dostoevsky, simply because he considered the wisdom of this world, and found it wanting. He peered long into the inner workings of the human psyche, and became a little deranged himself. And so we are to be advised."

"Please explain to us his notion of fantastic realism?" Raphael posed the question as a sort of challenge.

"He explored the heights and the depths of spiritual agonies."

"Yeah, there's certainly a lot of existential banter, that just goes on and on."

"He knew he was verbose."

Cody began to punctuate his friend's speech with sarcastic jibes relating to the days when Jacob had been his neighbor, living in the basement of a house owned by Frances Ambers. Geoff seemed rather glum, watching as though from a great remove; but on occasion he uttered his own commentary, not apropos of anything being discussed at the table.

"I don't even remember which books I've read by the Russian madman." Raphael confessed.

Isaiah wanted to stay and listen, but his duties as host mandated that he keep engaging unfamiliar faces.

Everyone became friendly when encouraged to speak of their own place in this world. He attempted on several occasions to get Molly alone, always to no avail, until it just happened, as though foreordained. They were both in the kitchen. She was looking out the window at the field, as if she'd just seen something that moved her greatly.

"Mrs. Gates, I have something I want to give you." He said to her.

She turned to look at him; she seemed utterly at peace.

"Even though the book chapter has been neglected somewhat, I still think it's been a success, don't you?"

"You make a good host. You know how to drift around, letting others do most of the work."

He smiled at her little gibe, that was also something of a compliment. He held out his present.

"Now what is this?" She lifted the dense, heavy gold rose from his hand. "How extraordinary. How old is this thing?"

"The atoms, or this form they've taken here?"

"How did *you* get this? Wait, please tell me it's not, back in the day, you didn't—"

"No." He shook his head, laughing. "There was no theft involved—*you* tree thief! It was bequeathed to me."

"Oh." Her moist eyes flared. "It's from Edith!" She leaned forward, looking into his eyes.

"I guess it took a while to settle all the legal wrangling. That must have gone on for quite some time. It was about a month ago, I got a call from a lawyer. She told me that Edith once owned two of these, which I knew, and I was left this one."

"No telling who got the other one?" Molly teased him.

"No telling."

"Well, it shows you."

"What?"

"How much she cared for you."

"I'm coming to know her better, actually, looking back, without my tetchy ego being so badly involved. She had a sense of keeping one's freedom, that was all her own. That was separate from me in ways I never understood."

"Not all women want to be married."

"I think we helped each other, at certain times; when the world was too much with us, you know?"

"I'm sure."

"I think, under different circumstances, you and she would have become very good friends."

"I think so too."

"She was the master of such small, and yet not so small, gestures. Molly, I want you to have it."

Margaret was silent. These days she was often reticent precisely when she would have been quite vocal in the past. She knew there was a lot she didn't know, and would never know, especially about other people. Her attention was too easily drawn away to an awareness of sanctities, that were too exacting, and for which the usual lofty words only lost their meanings.

She had also come to understand that she had never shared all of herself with anyone. She had tried to do so with Jacob; but she had gotten too close to him, and found she was unwilling to burden his heart with certain tribulations that belonged to her alone. She had only tarnished what she had come to cherish when floundering in these experiences; sharing too grievously (the abridged portions with others) could only hamper her own growth. To share the very best demanded the withholding of that uncertainly which lies beneath all our self-evident verities.

Isaiah was then able to peer into one such sacred niche, enfolding her ageless blooms of wondrous passions. There was a sympathetic light wavering between their eyes as they stared in silence. It was a rich, timeless, catholic rite, and the instant elapsed quickly.

"I don't know." Molly said, after turning away. "What am I supposed to do with something like this?"

"What am I supposed to do with it? You have to admit, it makes for a great ornament, if nothing else. You could put it out at the wall for special occasions."

"Use it as a ceremonial piece?" Molly once more held his gaze. Her tranquility came apart and she laughed. "Did you really tell Jacob you want to be interred in our wall?" Her eyes glimmered in curious delight. "Were you joking?"

"No." He spoke hardly above a whisper, nodding his head. "Now, you don't have to tell anyone about it, of course."

"Now you've got him going. Oh, that's just like you. It's getting a little—"

"Macabre?"

"Can that be true of such a thing? Maybe, emotionally, a little unhygienic?"

"If my dust is not worthy . . ."

"You know what I mean."

"A critic said recently that I'm all over the place now. Perhaps my remains ought to be dumped in that little creek over there."

"That's what you always do, fretting over the world's opinion. Be glad you have critics."

He was moved to laughter by the saving grace of her mirthful nature, and the fact he was far advanced in that good cause. She now looked very serious.

"We have put the contents of another urn in there. It's getting out of hand."

"So it's true. I had heard that was happening."

"Yes." She looked down, gently shaking her head. "It seems pretty weird when I think about it."

"We should raise the topic with our crew at the table."

"That's okay. He almost has the wall in back finished. I guess there's plenty of room. A lot of it will run off into the doctor's yard." Her resonant laughter burbled forth for a few delicate measures.

"It's all good ground."

She looked at the rose. "Here, I don't want to carry this around with me."

He took it from her and told her he would bring it to her later on. Then the kitchen was full of people, and she was engulfed in their officious chatter. They exchanged a parting look and Isaiah ducked into the living room where a political debate was underway. The noise drove him downstairs to his studio, where he found Gretchen. Her hands were flying over the keyboard of his computer.

"I'm going to stay; help you clean up, grandpa." She barely interrupted her work to look his way.

"You don't have to do that, Gretchen." He was the only person who called her by that sobriquet (She was Greta to her friends) and she always told him to stop, until lately when she only shook her head and smiled preciously.

"I told Dad I would."

"I have plenty of time to do that; you go have fun."

She turned a wry smile his way and her shoulders came up, expressing her reluctance to go back on her word.

"Well, as you wish."

"And also, Molly wants to talk to me about helping her babysit."

"Well, that sounds promising."

Isaiah went out into the back and circulated around his property for a while. He was hardly drinking, but when he did so the wine put his humors into a more lovely balance. He enjoyed watching everything that was happening, as if he might be called upon later to bear witness to every minute detail of the occasion. He observed people very closely, making note of the shifting emotions passing across their faces. By the time he returned to the living room he found O'Rourke leading the book club attendees on a lively romp.

"Jenny once wrote that they were sailing with all sails into bourgeois life." He was regaling them with anecdotes, fleshing out the lives of Charles Dickens and Karl

Marx, providing a deft, beginner's course in the historical context. Everyone listened raptly to the old professor. Isaiah settled in to listen.

"Ah, this is classic Marx," Isaiah thought, as the old pedagogue reveled in dispensing glinting gold pieces of his erudition. He described London as historian, cartographer, radical scholar, and the eternal romantic soul that finds breathing life in the long record of human affairs. He inducted each person there to join him on a pilgrimage into a past that still, from a proper attitude, resonates so clearly with the present.

"Karl regarded Jenny as an equal. They enjoyed many joys and heartaches." He constructed an ingenious fancy of letting several Ghosts of Christmas alternately visit the households of Charles Dickens and Karl Marx at various periods. It would be impossible to say which family was more happy, more to be admired. There was plenty of pity and sorrow to go around for both celebrated houses.

Isaiah was astounded by his friend's performance. He looked like a retired executive, who had dropped weight, was smartly dressed in casual attire, and possessed gentle, polite manners. His quiet fervor recalled a certain rabbi who once taught his disciples in closed sessions, imparting the arcane knowledge only after the mobs at the camp meetings had dispersed.

"This must be how he taught his college classes," Isaiah marveled. "He knows a lot more about those days when Dickens lived than I do."

Timothy told them how Marx and Engels used to work together upstairs in the Marx household, and Jenny would become alarmed at the outbursts of raucous laughter that often spilled down the stairs into the family quarters. His listeners began asking questions.

"Now wait, wait. Here is the man of the hour." Timothy flung an arm out to indicate Isaiah. "He is the one to tell us about the many parables." All the heads in the room turned towards him. He could see their alarm that he was going to ruin their dialogue with this beguiling speaker.

"Would you mind continuing, Tim? I have a few things I need to tend to, it will only take a short while."

"That's what he says when he's taking off on one of his jaunts. He's a peripatetic soul, and so was Dickens! Now, let me speak of that house that inspired wonder in the boy, and which the celebrated author later purchased for himself."

Outside Isaiah noticed Jacob was having a word with Molly, before returning to the party at the picnic table. He was now a royal consort to his wife; following her, in all things, and having the grace to know when he must intercede, and when he needed to hold back, and let her make her way alone. He was always ready to move forward to try and make things right, if need be, or to be there at her side, in whatever role was necessary.

He had finally emptied himself in his love for her. In those hollow depths, being flung into weakness, he had found his strength; losing the need of mastery, in any sense, for he was in awe of her spirit. He had gone through storms and come out to find his own paradise, and he possessed the only key to her garden.

The sun had passed over to start its solemn descent. Isaiah pictured his guests as docile, somewhat confused marauders, who had been debauched, much like the ancient lotus-eaters. He drifted about in slow motion, visiting with different crowds. The book club had disbanded, the people merging imperceptibly into a general drift of things. In the living room Patricia was talking about her surprise at the pricing of several houses she had visited.

Outside a golden aura had been gathered from the plangent radiance shining down from the oddly drifting sun. Isaiah and Molly were sitting under the limbs of the maple tree; in chairs between the flanking peony bushes. The picnic table down below was booked solid; extra chairs had been carried down and occupied, and still others were standing on the periphery.

"I never imagined you'd ever get so many at that silly picnic table." Molly exclaimed quietly, glancing at Isaiah.

"Let's bring the meeting to order." Jacob demanded with a loud voice that trembled to suppress his humor.

"It's been brought forward that we haven't properly addressed membership issues."

Mr. Morgan responded with an affable chuckle that was rather hard to decipher; it could be taken as a sardonic rebuff, or congenial assent. He was using this serviceable device without any restraint whatsoever.

"The members are those who show up; like right now. This is our quorum for this assembly."

"We're not going to get involved in any of that now." Cicely whispered to her husband as she leaned over his shoulder. He glanced around and caught one of her most ambivalent little smiles. It was known only to him, and was used when she was intrigued, slightly confused, and wanting to see more. She was beseeching him to not forget that she was there too. His laughter suddenly became much louder, and much more resonant.

"Which book are we starting with?"

"As I've said earlier, something from Dostoevsky."

There were long, affected groans.

"No, this is my table—"

"Already it's his table!

"It's not his table, it belongs to Baggins."

Isaiah looked at Molly and they began to giggle.

"Do you approve of this expropriation of your table?"

"I don't have much choice, do I?"

"Let's do *The Eternal Husband*."

"No, not that one."

"It's an exquisite piece of craftsmanship."

"Those puppets are unnatural, though, I mean, really, the dance of the two men, it's not real. It's too fantastic. Who can abide such conduct? It is pure Dostoevsky; a must read, but for another time."

"He wrote to someone that he had hated that story from its inception. And his young second wife recorded in her diary that he said to her once that a wife was the natural enemy of her husband."

"Okay, okay. How about another short one, *Notes from Underground*?"

"The scarecrow, missing Dorothy, once they're back in Kansas. She's gotten famous, married a director, has no time for him anymore." Raphael's voice sounded like he was speaking to himself, halfway gone into a trance.

"Yes," Jacob agreed hesitantly, "that story is a mash of satiric parody that will be difficult for our young club to digest, at first that is. The problem is, he never addresses the most salient issue, concerning the enchanted mice one finds nibbling at the bottom of things."

"A man deciding, of his own free will, there is no such thing as free will."

"Too much worship of these profound thoughts brings paralysis to cogitation; the wheels turn, but no work is done; no forward motion is imparted to any purposeful idea, not in any meaningful way."

"Okay professor. But this author deals in myth more than history, trying to tease out the real truths from the artistic rendering of human life."

"How about *Crime and Punishment*?"

"It's so trite anymore; every night on TV this material is ground into a worthless powder."

"The Brothers—"

"No!"

"We would have to work ourselves up to *Karamazov*, don't you think, Jacob?"

There was a staged pause, and then he quoted from the Constance Garnett translation. 'You must know that there is nothing higher and stronger and more wholesome and good for life in the future than some good memory, especially a memory of childhood, of home.'

Molly whispered a refrain, 'Some sacred memory that makes us safe till the end of days.'

"I propose that we start with *The Devils*."

"I know it well. That's where Hereford got the title for his first novel; from the Stavrogin character. In his notes the author describes him as gentle, quiet, infinitely proud and bestially cruel."

"Yes, he had to incorporate the usual Gothic horrors."

"I know that work. He makes fools out of the political radicals, and he skewers the godless liberals of his prime."

"That's the stuff we want. Down with the Nihilists, young and old, who have no respect for the work people have done, and are doing, to improve what we have."

"Do you think I ought to build one of those outdoor fireplaces down there?"

"Oh, you know Jacob and Cody would be all over that project. You'd hardly have to do any of the work."

"There are so many things I can envision, that will take me beyond my own time. It's getting sort of confusing."

She could only smile, a covetous twinkle in her eye.

"He's always trying to demonstrate the irreconcilable differences between the ideal of Christian love, and the intractable faults of human beings."

"At our best, there's much falseness. At our worst, the good is still latent, but what does it all mean? He doesn't know, except we must turn to Russian orthodoxy, if there is to be any hope."

"Yes, that's the thing! He believes Russia is the one incomparably great and wonderful nation, because of the common Russians, who retain the spirit of true orthodoxy."

"And once a man loses his roots, becomes deracinated, he loses that contact with the truth—"

"Now that we have so much of the wall completed, would you be interested in helping me get some more red cedars?"

"Sure. Do you buy them at a nursery?" He was teasing.

She smiled girlishly. "You know I take them from rocky bluffs, overlooking the rivers, or the highways, or wherever I can find them."

"You desecrate our public lands."

"I spend a lot of time selecting the right ones. Some are already quite old, even though they are not that large."

"Could we involve Tim and Patricia? Make a day of it. One truck, for you and Jacob, and one car, for us. We would make an adventurous party. Oh yes, they've learned how to search for arrow points, and we may have to do that too."

"It sounds like something Jacob would enjoy. We could stop for lunch someplace . . ."

She was watching her husband give an oration down at the table. His ringing words conjured a ghostly chorus of voices from the past. Sitting there, Isaiah never felt so close to this man and his wife; hearing in his mind what it must have been like at the old picnic table up at St. Margaret's.

"Yeah, he believed in the Russian Church. And he also loved the Tsar. He believed the Russian people were more noble, more honest, more worthy than those of the western powers. He believed the Russian people were destined to one day restore the one true faith for the entire world."

"He was delusional, chauvinistic, wed to his strange, messianic solutions."

"History shows pretty clearly how the exaltation of one people, over all others, leads to genocide, and fascism."

"All those diseased variants of human ideals, taken up by mobs, parties, governments—"

"Picnic table pagans!"

"Let us praise the earth's orthodoxy."

"Yes, and what is that?"

"Why not just say, follow life, the rudiments of which we have hardly begun to unravel for ourselves."

"Down with orthodoxy!" An eruption of laughter rose from the tablelands.

"You should read *Moby-Dick* as a primer."

"No prerequisites! No rules whatsoever!"

"One of the old, superannuated liberals takes off at the end, like Tolstoy actually did, in fact, he's given a pastoral requiem to close out his story."

"We must not forsake beauty!"

"Are you glad you moved here?" Molly asked.

"Do you have to ask?"

"Look at you." Her smile was wickedly delicious. She was now holding up her glass of wine, which she had hardly touched, as if assaying the effect of the fading light on the pale golden fluid. Her eyes glimmered seductively. He was fascinated by the dusky color; suddenly reminiscent of vernal storms breaking apart after washing the land for a proper gloaming. The maple leaves overhead moved and he raised his eyes; feeling a coalescence of all that touched upon his core being.

The guests were drawn to her. Isaiah watched them individually coming up to engage her in lively banter. He studied the happy masks; seeing far into their desires to be a part of something that she curated so exquisitely within herself.

"Why not do *The Idiot*, then?"

"The knight with no lance, nor shield; only his feverish dreams of another world, if not here, then hereafter."

"No, no; that one is sacred to me. I'm not going to start out having to break that one down with you heathens."

"It expresses his personal vision. He compares Quixote with Christ, to further confuse matters."

"The love triangle. The noble fool having two women fighting over him; which calls to mind that Dostoevsky once proposed to three women in a row, with no luck."

"The text poses the question, how can one love two at once."

"With different kinds of love, of course, why not?"

"He speaks of creatures possessing boundless idealism, and boundless sensuality; asking how can both exist in one breast?"

"Are you going to paint my house?" Isaiah asked Molly.

"I guess now I'll have to; but I could never capture all this." She swept a hand out to encompass the crowd at the picnic table and the bucolic vista beyond them.

It seemed like no time at all had gone by when the din below at the table became a crescendo, and then began to subside, as reluctant waves are drawn back to the sea.

"That's safe to say."

"Anything is safe to say!"

"I'm not saying that it's not."

"What are you saying, then?"

"I was only saying Dostoevsky became incensed at the atheists who dismissed God, believing we cannot depend on ourselves. He thought all such rational, godless roads lead to the bloodbath of the Paris Commune."

"He raised suffering to an idol, serving the secular and the religious impulses; making Nietzsche cry out in pain."

"He believed that old nostrum that war was necessary to a nation—and maybe it is, as they now exist—but his idea that one needs to suffer, to understand happiness, that's absurd, to my way of thinking."

"You don't believe ideals must pass through suffering in the same way the ancients put gold into the furnace?"

"He was exploring the sources of hypocrisy, like one of those intrepid Englishman, free of all taboos, not having to do with temporal power, wanting to find the headwaters of the Nile, except he could not bother ascending the river."

"He gets lost in his explorations of human nature."

"As he was writing *The Devils* he relapsed and started gambling again. He left his pregnant wife and went back to the tables. He returned to her as a penitent, on his knees, wallowing in his self-loathing. The great hope, that such behavior absolves one of his guilt."

"He takes great pains to make it clear pure Christian love is impossible on earth."

"And that's where I take issue. I don't see the point of endlessly circling that paradox. Imagine the earth was not created for that vision, said to be created by one sublime being, who might not even be a genuine part of history, not as it was put down in scripture."

"Dostoevsky couldn't see beyond human ignorance, or the fact we are evolving. His concept of the soul is trapped in the characters drawn on our worn, fading parchments. His heroes suffer as penitents engaged in ritual flagellation, which disguises the fact they can find no ultimate truths in old folk tales."

"Yes, but Tim, he plumbed the depths of the human psyche, in so much of what he accomplished."

"That is what we don't understand. Our notion of love is surely but a vestige of something much more expansive. The original power is something we do not know how to comprehend. I say, before we renounce the things of the flesh, we ought to come to understand what makes it work. Let's figure out how jealousy might be conquered, just for starters!"

"He said love, not conquest, should be the foundation of the state."

"Molly, the hour has come." A cry from below. "We need more wine."

"No, *you* don't!"

"Ah, the best wine has been reserved for last." Isaiah mused over his glass.

"It's the very same stuff." Molly replied.

"No, I hardly drank any before. Now I taste all the richness afresh. I saved my palate."

"We don't know who owns all this property, and we don't want to find out." Mr. Morgan was talking to them about the community garden that was to be established in the spring.

They heard a strange whirring sound and Mulligan wheeled up in Cody's golf cart.

"Hey there." Isaiah said to the man, who just stared at them. Molly and Isaiah exchanged a look, afraid Geoff had taken the cart without permission.

"He said I could borrow it; but only to come here."

"That's fine."

"Can I take some food home with me?"

"Take all you want."

They sat and listened to the fluttering leaves for a while.

"Here's one for you. 'For my own part, my occupation in my solitary pilgrimages was to recall every yard of the old road as I went along it, and to haunt the old spots, of which I never tired.' Any idea?"

Isaiah leaned back. "I can only guess. I don't know. The old spots, that is so good, and it has to be, yes, *Copperfield*."

"Yes, it is. I've been sauntering through that again."

"This is my last *old* spot now."

"Dickens used the word old constantly, in the sense of former, didn't he?

"Yes."

"This is where your spirit shall linger in the trees."

"It's lovely to think that will be allowed."

"Isaiah?"

"Yes?" He remained looking out over the field, as did she.

"Remember when I talked to you about doing a portrait of Jacob's sister, Johanna?"

"Yes, have your started it?" He was eager to hear what she had done.

"No, I want you to do it instead. And we mustn't let Jacob know. It would be for his birthday."

"That's not far off."

"I know, would it be possible?"

"I've actually been working on something."

"Really? But how?"

"I stole some pictures from one of your albums."

"I didn't notice."

"I have her holding a book down on her lap, my oldest copy of *The Old Curiosity Shop*, and she's looking outward at the viewer. She's dressed in a timeless garment, a slip, I guess, suggesting an almost classical figure. It's meant to represent the storybook of life, as seen through innocent eyes."

"I can't wait to see it. I've already talked to Theo, so we'll handle all of that haggling business without you, Old Baggins!"

"When Fyodor and Anna were struggling in poverty they referred to themselves as Mr. and Mrs. Micawber." Jacob explained to the table.

"Dickens had his parents in mind when he created those two mourning doves."

"He could not have carved a more lovely memorial on the headstone of literature."

"Dostoevsky believed suffering was the fire that proves the temper of the soul."

"The idea being that man is not born for happiness."

"One must conquer oneself."

"Okay, who knows this one? 'But do you think that among these many papers, there is much truth and justice, Richard?' Anyone?" Jacob looked up and caught the eye of Isaiah, who nodded and smiled, not bothering to divulge the source of his quote.

It was from *Bleak House*; Richard being the man who is ruined by placing all his hopes on the outcome of the vast, interminable lawsuit. The wheels of justice finally grind to a halt when the legal system, feeding off the funds at issue, beggars the estate, leaving the deluded Richard in a state of fatal desolation. Isaiah knows his evangelism has also come to its natural conclusion. The disciples had taken over the mission, and he was now free to move onward.

"They say I've abandoned any pretense of holding on to my old artistic principles."

"You used to have such things, stapled together and filed away?"

He laughed at her refusal to take this matter seriously. It was not a problem any longer to worry his sentient hours.

"Yes, I think I'm going to turn over all my chapters to other people."

"Really?"

"I don't want to spend my time trying to make things happen anymore. I want to enjoy people more. Have dinner parties, go to parks, just go strolling about. Listening to others tell their stories to me as they are evolving. I want to help young people discover who they want to be; nurturing, not inculcating, well, not as much, anyway! Is that terrible of me?"

"Yes, it's an abdication. You don't mean to say you are done with me?"

"I hardly ever began with you. You're a natural child, and will remain one. That's why I wanted you here. I never tire of your playfulness."

"Well, then; I hope I never grow up."

"That reminds me, I'm trying to get someone to take up the diaries of Anaïs Nin."

Isaiah looked at her.

"Don't worry, that's not you."

"Having no luck?"

"Not yet, although, you ought to think about doing something on Van Gogh, since this one didn't really come out the right way for you, did it?"

"Better than I had hoped, actually, and that's not a bad idea about a series on painters." His mind was set awhirl.

"So next week Gretchen is coming over to help me babysit. I'm going to suggest that we call you to see if you want to have lunch with us. So be ready to invite us over."

"She loves my homemade spinach pizza."

The land glimmered around them. A genuine pastoral took shape in the mind of every individual who remained to partake of the last light. Vast glowing brush strokes had decorated the skies that seemed to brood over the darkened landscape. The apparent stillness grew loud in suggesting a vast, stored energy; begetting a vision that everything the world needed for peace was there in plain sight.

"It's a perfect time to sit still." Isaiah said to Molly, who only murmured. She was intent on listening to Jacob, who was playing his guitar for the last few guests who lingered. They had started a fire in an old wheelbarrow, which Sam Morgan had wheeled over. The fire brought the small circle closer together. Stars crouched over their company. Only those few who would be walking home were left to look upwards in drowsy wonderment.

Then there was little talk left in them at this late hour. Solemn thoughts came forth, from deep seas of tranquility, but there was hardly any mortal breaths to be spared for such wasteful inanities. In this mood the people understood the paltriness of speech, accepting on faith the restorative properties of shared silence. They absorbed the goodness of accepting ancient mysteries; felt as intimately as the gentle breezes of night.

Isaiah would be the last one to slip out from under the brilliant, molten batter of our constantly mixing galaxy. He had the shortest distance of any to go before he lay down in his nesting shrouds. Once his head molded itself into the pillow his audience with the Virgin commenced right where he had left off that morning. His mind began wandering, as though taking flight on a journey into unseen realms. He traveled as Ulysses, with his own personal goddess; except that his holy, maternal ghost never lost her temper, and she understood everything. Her silence contained all things; only strengthening one's purpose to be a better man.

Printed in the USA
CPSIA information can be obtained
at www.ICGtesting.com
LVHW091407280224
773024LV00059B/1575